Rhea Hawke: Galactic Enforcer

Inner Diverse

Book 2: Splintered Universe Trilogy

By

Nina Munteanu

Starfire World Syndicate

Inner Diverse

Cover Design and Typography: Costi Gurgu
Interior Design: Nina Munteanu

Published in United States by:

Starfire World Syndicate
2132 Cherokee Pkwy
Suite 2
Louisville, 40204, KY, United States
www.thepassionatewriter.com

ISBN 978-0-9823783-5-9 Trade paperback (alk. paper)
ISBN 978-0-9823783-6-6 Digital

Library of Congress Control Number: 2012955817

Printed in the United States of America on acid-free paper

Still For Kevin

Acknowledgements

I consulted the wisdom and science of many authorities in the areas of space exploration and habitable zones, AI, biotechnology, sleep biology, neurobiology, and ecology. The most notable source was NASA. Any mistakes are mine, not theirs. Thank you, Costi and Vali, for creating an impeccable cover. Karen, as always, you have my heartfelt thanks for all matters relating to making dreams come true. I'm honored and so grateful.

Praise for *Outer Diverse*:

"Nina Munteanu is … a master of metaphor … a creator of fantastic worlds and cultures. She combines her biological background with the infinite possibilities of the cosmos and turns an adventure story into a wonderland of alien rabbit holes. When the action starts it goes into hyper-drive … Rhea Hawke, is a fresh and multi-faceted heroine."
> — **Craig H. Bowlsby**, author of *Horth in Killing Reach* and creator of *Commander's Log*

"… A rollicking science fiction plot with all the trappings … Hawke is a maverick in the Wild West tradition, up against the world … a genetic mystery with lethal powers."
> — **Lynda Williams**, author of the *Okal Rel Series*

Praise for Munteanu's previous works:

"*Angel of Chaos* is a gripping blend of big scientific ideas, cutthroat politics and complex yet sympathetic characters that will engage readers from its thrilling opening to its surprising and satisfying conclusion."
> — **Hayden Trenholm**, Aurora-winning author of *The Steele Chronicles*

Darwin's Paradox is "a thill ride that makes us think and tugs the heart."
> — **Robert J. Sawyer**, Hugo-Award authot of *Wake*

Angel's Promises is "a stunning example of good storytelling with an excellent setting and cast of characters."
> — **Tangent Online**

Collision with Paradise is" a very intelligent story, with fantastic world-building."
> — **Romantic Times**

"Munteanu asserts her mastery of the sensual SF romantic thriller. [*Collision with Paradise* is] an unforgettable read that's immensely alluring, surprising, and heart-throbbing."
> — **Yet Another Book Review**

"These dark sounds are the mystery, the roots thrusting into the fertile loam known to all of us, ignored by all of us, but from which we get what is real…"

Federico Garcia Lorca

ONE

I pulled out a second wad of soyka gum and chewed nervously then resumed paddling, eyes sharp for any boiling masses of water snakes. With each stroke of the paddle I disturbed the surface scum and left a wake of swirling colour. It released a foul stench of rotting compost. The brown mist hovered like a cobweb over the oily film. I searched for any sign of agitation and listened over the gentle chortling of the water between each paddle stroke.

I was in the Boiling Sea of Horus, after all; the sea that had once ensnared me with its numbing narcotic and whose nasty inhabitants had almost consumed me. It was here that I'd first heard that strangely familiar woman's voice in my head. I thought initially that it had been the drug of the mist and sea. But the voice had followed me off planet, stayed in my brain along with some additional amino acids I'd acquired from those horrible snakes that had briefly invaded my body. Somehow compelled to return here, I was in search of...I wasn't certain, except for the remote chance of finding my lost grandmother. She was, according to Ka, the answer to my past and my future.

I swept the hair back from my face and squinted, trying to see beyond the ten meters of visibility the dank mist allowed. Following my internal compass, I negotiated the towering islands with unease. The only warning that I was approaching one of their vertical cliffs came in the sudden slap, slosh and gurgle of the waves against the sheer rock face. Then within a heartbeat the slimy dark rock would thrust up like an apparition through the oily mist and I'd steer clear with a sharp intake of air. I must have passed at least a dozen islands as I continued toward my destination, a place in my mind, perhaps planted there by those beasts that had taken brief residence inside me. Ever watchful for the apophus, the giant snake that had previously batted my ship out of the sky then set its babies to consume me, I was acutely aware of my vulnerability in this small canoe. If the apophus was hungry it could easily overturn my boat and spill me into the churning water to either consume me directly or feed me in slow agonizing ecstasy to those nasty babies of hers.

A thin oily residue settled over everything and made me feel wet and clammy. It came from the vapour of suspended stench. I felt it already affecting me as my thoughts began to wander. They drifted as if in a dream, dangerously on the edge of being beyond my control. I tried to reign in feverish thoughts of the past few months. They swirled through my head like a hurricane, circling on *him*. Always on him...*the bastard*. The pirate who'd stolen more from me than I cared to admit.

I steered my mind from Serge and let it settle briefly on what had brought me here. It started with my dismal failure to warn Ka about the unknown traitor in his midst. Ka was, of course, still in seclusion on Uma 1 and blithely unaware that I was accused of assassinating his mentor Rashamon. His acolytes, knowing who and what I was, swiftly reported me to the authorities who'd given immediate chase. To elude them I had to abandon Ka's *scimitar* that we'd been towing. And when Eclipse's shadow trackers found us, I had to also ditch its precious cargo and my prize: the pirate Serge, who I'd finally captured. Now I was here, chasing yet another elusive thing: my truant grandmother and an answer to why she had done the unthinkable....

My head began to spin and I felt slightly nauseous...the cloying smell was overpowering. Was I going the right way? Some compass in my head had compelled me to bear toward a northern point on the convoluted shoreline. I'd been paddling for hours, but I could make out nothing in the thick fog. I shook my head to clear my mind and pulled out another soyka gum wad then joined it to the mass already in my mouth. My gaze settled on the iridescent swirling patterns of the whirlpools left in the wake of the draw of my paddle. An eerie quiet pervaded as if the mist veiled any sound except for the gurgle and trickle of my paddle dips. What had I been thinking? I had no idea and leaned back in the canoe, languidly chewing and wondering what I was doing here. I shut my eyes, paddle poised in my hands, and stopped chewing. I listened to the gentle lapping of the water and the lyrical sigh of the wind caressing distant trees and mountains. There were no other sounds. No birds, no animals. The quiet was almost oppressive.

...Why did all the women in my family do atrocious things? If Shlsh was telling the truth, my grandmother had been the worst. She'd betrayed all of humanity by letting the Vos into my world. It was absurd, really. Why did I believe Ka and that old Ngu—or Serge, for that matter—about soul-drifting? To enter someone's dream and change the reality of an entire world?...

According to the fantastical journal of Genevieve Dubois, the first—and only—human to land on the planet Eos: Azaes, the leader of the Eosians, had kept all the previous human missions from landing on Eos by soul-drifting into their dreams and driving them literally mad. Only Genevieve, who had hidden powers of her own, had entered her own dream and manipulated it and Azaes; in turn driving *him* mad. When I had first read that, I'd laughed out loud, except now it was too close to home: Azaes, Earth's first alien contact, was presumably my great-grandfather.

My grandmother had apparently entered the dreams of a hundred spiritual leaders and compelled them to create a gate— some kind of dimensional worm-hole, I supposed—in this real world. It was inconceivable. How could someone, a single person, have that kind of power?

>*I didn't...It wasn't just me...I had help, Vos help...*

"What—" I inhaled my gum and my hand slipped on the

paddle. It fell into the oily water and drifted away from the canoe. I flung out my arms to retrieve it, throwing the boat into a violent rock. Warm water flooded into the boat with a burst of rank fumes and I jerked back, pitching the boat into a counter rock and nearly fell out. I threw myself onto my stomach and groped for the slippery handle floating in the iridescent scum. Hands scrabbling, I found purchase, bringing more water in. As I pulled the oil-covered paddle into the boat and kneeled to wipe the slime off my arms with shaky hands, the voice returned:

>*I was in love and I fell. Love tricks you. Love blinds you. I think you know about that, Rhea...*

"Shut up!" I shouted, clamping slime-covered hands over my ears. But the voice was inside my head. I raked back the hair off my face in a brisk sweep and in a more subdued tone I asked, "Who are you?"

>*Come this way. You will have your answers soon enough. Are you brave enough to handle them? You are almost there...*

I followed my intuition and paddled warily, anticipating and dreading what I would discover on shore. Would I find my missing grandmother? Diana Wood had been missing for over twenty standard galactic years. Was she the voice in my head? Or was it the giant apophus, whose babies had left a remnant of something inside me, seducing me with dreams and luring me into its lair?

A russet shore rose out of the fog like a ghost. The land immediate to shore was a fairly flat shelf of about a hundred meters before steeply rising into an almost vertical incline like the rest of the towering islands around me. The shelf was barren of vegetation, although the rust-coloured rocks were covered in that same iridescent film of putrid shallik oil and microbes that seeped from the mountains and islands of the Boiling Sea.

I made it to the shore and thanked God I hadn't encountered any 'boils' in the water. This was one of the few places where the land was flat enough to beach a boat and get ashore, I considered as I scrambled out of the canoe onto the slimy rocks. I slipped off balance a few times but managed to get a stable footing and pulled the boat farther in. At dawn I'd left

Benny at the southern end of this large body of water with instructions to remain there until I contacted him within fifteen hours—sunset. If I didn't he was to go for help. That was seven hours ago. It was now midday. Bas wasn't too far away, doing a reconnaissance with Raekwon in the outer 47 Ursae Majoris system, thanks to Ennos's invisible hand of help. Under no circumstance was Benny to fly into the Boiling Sea mist, looking for me. The giant apophus was sure to bat him out of the air and then we'd both be jagged.

I straightened, wiping my hands on my self-cleaning Great Coat, and cast my gaze around, taking in the looming mountains ahead whose tops faded in a cloud of mist. I spotted the opening of a dark cave about a hundred metres away in one of the vertical cliffs and struck toward it, hand resting on my holstered MEC.

As I approached the cave, the wind appeared to increase. Then I realized with a chill on the back of my neck that the sighing came from within the cave. Pulling out my MEC, I crept to the entrance and, keeping to a sidewall, peered inside. I saw nothing except more rock, glistening with oily water. The sighing grew louder and I could now hear another sound as I moved toward the dark interior: the sound of shuffling. I let my eyes grow accustomed to the darkness before inching forward with a two-handed grip on my MEC. Something hissed lightly above me and I looked up. Just as I made out two glowing eyes, something large swept out from the darkness ahead and startled me into jerking back with a sharp inhale—

I gaped at the giant serpent-like creature towering above me. It had a woman's wrinkled face, hoary wispy hair and multiple tentacle-like arms that protruded from its upper trunk. The wizened face hissed and its iridescent trunk coiled toward me with ominous purpose.

I stood my ground and swung my MEC up to the creature's head. Before I could shoot the serpent knocked the weapon from my hand, and within a heartbeat another 'arm' lashed out and tried to pierce my left shoulder with its sharp talon. It thankfully failed to penetrate the Great Coat's Kevlar-strength thixtropic material. Before I had a chance to react, it lashed out again, this time catching my exposed thigh. The claw pierced through my flight trouser material and sank deep into my flesh. Did I cry out? I wasn't sure but the smarting pain grew instantly numb and I felt it spread through me. I scrambled to retrieve my MEC on the ground. Before I got very far I lost feeling in both legs and collapsed, unable to move.

The serpent bent its human-like face low until liquid green eyes peered directly at me. I drew in a sharp breath of alarm. The face resembled an ancient version of me! Then, fear slipped away as I contemplated a hideous thought: was this my grandmother?

The snake took my limp body up onto its scaly trunk and, supporting me with two of its 'arms', slithered down the shore toward the boiling sea. Panicking, my breaths grew shallow and I felt my heart thunder madly. This demon-thing was taking me to my doom. To feed her babies! Despite my horror I felt the pulsing rush of longing at the memory of her baby snakes dancing between my thighs. I remembered the shameless desire I'd felt as they'd wriggled among the folds of my groin and stroked me into yielding. If Bas and Benny hadn't shown up just then, I'd have given myself gladly to them and sunk into the depths of the Boiling Sea, engulfed in delirious, mind-numbing ecstasy, to my death. Benny had completed his research and, to my disappointment, had found no drug given off by snake or water that I could pin my base behaviour on. It was all me. And now the apophus was going to finish what her babies had failed to complete. I directed my self-loathing at the creature and wondered what I really felt, why I'd really returned....

>*Don't be afraid. I used to be your grandmother. I won't hurt you.*

Oh, God! I was right!

>*Please don't judge me by this form I've taken...Diana lives still.*

Unable to move, I accepted my fate. I tried to relax as the creature slipped into the murky water and swam along a narrow fjord toward a farther shore to the north. The bow wave off her slithering form surged past me, soaking me in oily water and I found myself lulled into a kind of drugged stupor. I lost track of time. This fearsome creature was once considered a sacred messiah-child by Earth's Order of the Sacred Tree; Earth's first alien-child to walk in quiet anonymity among humans. Now she was an apophus, a vulgar lonely creature exiled to this desolate place—

I was jolted awake by falling head first from the serpent-creature onto a swampy shore. I inhaled and coughed out swamp water before the serpent seized me again and secured my limp body on its long torso. It seemed that I wasn't fated for the deep and her thousands of young just yet.

>*Apologies. You slid off…*

I started to feel sick with the jostling and bumpy swaying. The pungent smell of anaerobic mud and crushed vegetation stirred my nostrils and I looked up. I saw that the serpent was lumbering into a narrow canyon toward a ghostly grove of lanky trees. They resembled mangroves in the swirling mist. Within moments the snake began to make those same lyrical sounds that had intoxicated me the first time I'd come here. At the time I didn't know who or what had made the eerie but beautiful sounds. Within moments an equally beautiful and more eerie multi-timbral chorus of feral 'voices' echoed off the canyon walls as if riding on the moving mist. I concluded against my own logic that this was some sort of communication between the apophus and…what? Surely not the trees?

I narrowed my eyes with sudden amazement. Was I seeing clearly? Were the trees *moving*?…I noticed large oval structures nested in several of the tree crowns. They resembled tree-houses, with sparkling lights running in a row along their diameter. My snake-grandmother approached one of the larger trees with a house-like structure and tall lanky buttresses. Securing me more tightly in one set of her many tentacle arms, she slithered with a jerk into a spiral up its trunk. She slid up to the house then entered an open doorway and deposited me on the straw floor of a large room with windows.

After propping my limp body against the wall, she coiled

herself and brought her human-like head close to mine. She gazed at me with tired gentle eyes that reminded me of my mother. "I'm ssssorry I had to poissssson you with my anaessssthetic," my serpent-grandmother said in a lyrical voice that clicked as though she had marbles in her mouth, "but I feared you were going to ssshoot me with that." She placed the MEC on the ground near me. I hadn't realized she had picked it up. Then she spoke again in a long hiss, "I ssso longed to ssssee you and ssspeak wisssyou, my once granddaughter."

"You can speak!" I gasped.

"Yesss," my serpent-grandmother hissed with a faint smile. I could almost imagine her as a human. "These trees are part of an ancient soul and all manner of life can communicate through them. They let me speak like I used to, through this mouth, before I became what I am now."

I took in my surroundings for the first time and stared at the soft pith-like surfaces. This was a living creature? I felt the gentle rocking and realized that it was the tree moving through the canyon! Were these the migrating trees?

She smiled kindly at me. "The Khonsus used to live in these tree-houses when they first came here, thousands of years ago. But they've since abandoned these ancient souls for more conventional dwellings and self-autonomy."

I considered that my grandmother was touted by the Sacred Order of the Trees to be the scion of Genevieve Dubois and an Epoptes through my great-grandmother's coupling with the ancient soul of the *vishna* tree; it was only fitting that she now communed with the migratory tree of Horus, another ancient soul supposedly.

"What...happened to you?" I ventured, trying to move but to no avail.

"When I came here to the Weeping Mountains twenty years ago, an apophus knocked my ship out of the sky and I fell into the water. It wasn't long before a boil of infant snakes swarmed me and took my body. Hundreds of them entered me."

I shuddered. My face tightened with the horrible memory of only seven invading me. Remembering how they moved

13

inside me, I felt a sympathetic murmur in my stomach and an involuntary stirring in my loins as a hot wave of sickness overcame me.

"I was lost to them," my grandmother hissed, her voice reverberating in my gut. I wanted to vomit but fought against succumbing. "They engulfed me in a wondrous dance, Rhea. Cleverly slid under my clinging wet clothes..." I'd been spared that much; I'd been naked. "...They whipped me with their frenzied embrace into a wanton creature of desire." I felt a flush of heat surge through me followed by a bolt of pain in my gut. "They wooed me with their sad song and erotic dance, Rhea, and I let them take me." God, I'd almost done the same, I thought with mounting dizziness, and stared at her hoary face. *That* was what I would have become: a giant snake-woman. It would not have been a final obliterating death after all, but a sort of 'death' then 'rebirth' into a living hell. "They devoured me," my once-grandmother went on, "they became me; I became them."

Like the *ouroboros* that devoured itself only to live again, I thought, staring at the swimming image of my once-grandmother.

"Diana Wood still exists, Rhea. But now, I am also one of *them*. An apophus. Each apophus is unique to its original host. The one who took down my ship was a Khonsus-apophus with a Khonsus head." She eyed me with a piercing gaze. "There's a little of them in you too, Rhea."

I swallowed convulsively in a flush of giddy heat and fought down waves of violent nausea. But the sickness overpowered me and I abruptly vomited over myself.

"Oh, dear. You're ill. You swallowed too much of the oily sea. Shallik oil is good for purging oneself of poisons, but it is a bit of a poison itself."

I fought to regain my composure and felt my breaths stutter as I coughed out the rest of the burning acid in my throat. Slouched against the wall, uselessly limp and covered in my own rank vomit, I remembered only too well how good the oil was at purging the body. It reminded me of Ka.

14

"Why did you leave Ka?" I finally challenged in a hoarse raw voice. "Why did you come here?"

"To escape his devastating control. He mind-trapped me here, on Horus, for over sixty years. I finally managed to run away when he was sufficiently distracted. He's a monster, Rhea. He manipulates with gold...You don't believe me, I see."

I stared, not knowing what to think. I imagined the old Khonsus, his infectious smile, the soothing cadence of his tenor voice and his wonderful stories. How could my grandmother say that? Ka was the most gentle, kind and wise being I'd met. I hadn't forgotten that my snake-grandmother had tried to impose her fate on me the last time I was here. *There is no victory in resistance; only in yielding without surrender* she'd advised me...I'd be an aphophus if it hadn't been for Bas and Benny rescuing me just as I surrendered to their compelling overture.

"Ka said you came to Horus to learn the music of the spheres," I pressed on.

"Yes. I learned it...and more, thanks to these ancient souls," Diana said. "But that's not why I came to Horus. I sought him out ninety years ago to confront him for what he made me do before. He almost had me convinced all over again that I'd done the right thing. He seduced me all over again and kept me prisoner."

I set my mouth in stubborn scepticism, realizing that my grandmother was blaming Ka for that atrocious thing she'd done and then for not doing anything about it after. I didn't think she was all that virtuous, remembering the baby snakes swarming me.

"Ka is a spiritual man, a Gnostic," my apophus-grandmother continued. "A great teacher. *My* teacher." She nodded, as if to herself with a deep sigh of regret. "Ka is a complex being. A great philosopher and a genius. But he's also a messianic tyrant and brutal strategist. Great beings are always complex and contradictory. He was once my mentor, Rhea, and my lover. I trusted his wisdom and intelligence. I loved him...and fell. He convinced me to submit to his mind control then betrayed my trust and mind-probed me into soul-drifting those mystics into dreaming that Gate open. He convinced me that it would connect our spiritual worlds together. I was so wrong, wasn't I? I only let in those brutal terrorists on a killing rampage."

I frowned at my serpent-grandmother and narrowed my eyes in disbelief. "Why would Ka do that?"

"You know so little, young one...You still don't know what *you* are, do you? Or the powers you have. How you can save our two worlds or destroy them so easily—"

"Whatever I am, *you* were willing to make me into an apophus," I cut her off sharply.

"Ah, you're hurt by my betrayal." She leaned back and her eyes looked mournful. "It was too late to save you, young one. My children were too many and too swift. And I...I admit that I'd grown weary of being alone and I savoured your company."

"Like you did Ka's before you abandoned him?" I said tartly. "Like you abandoned your *child*?" My mother.

That stung her and I felt cruel satisfaction surge through me like lightening. She let out a long exhale then continued in a subdued voice, "It gladdens me that your friends rescued you and that you are well." She raised her head and brightened. "My children danced for you wonderfully though, didn't they?" I felt an involuntary stirring in my abdomen and a pulsing burst of yearning between my legs. They had, I shamefully conceded. "No creature can resist their dance," she continued. "Not even *you*, young one, who have run away from love all your life." I fixed her with a look of misery. How could she torture me like this? "Ah." She sighed at my expression and looked sad. "My children..." She gazed downwards for a moment, then looked at me again. "I birth a clutch, several hundred baby apophus, every cycle of our twin moons, Rhea. I need no mate for this. But I must feed them with a suitable host, a willing host. It saddens me when they starve. I have witnessed so many of my children wash up on shore, unfed, unfulfilled. I am *their* mother now, Rhea. Your body would have fed several clutches and lived to become an apophus. One such as I."

16

I felt my teeth grind in mounting anger but kept silent.

"It is the way we reproduce," she continued. "Otherwise the apophus would die out. Do you gainsay our need to survive?" She eyed me sharply and I broke off my gaze, unable to hold her stare of challenge. "And speaking of love and children *and* your mother...Ka and I met on Earth—he was with Eclipse for many years, did you know?" I blinked with surprise. "And I fell in love with him, Rhea. When he was in the human form." I felt my stomach clench and stared at her. That meant..."Ah, Rhea," she sighed longingly. "He was the most beautiful man I'd ever seen. Too beautiful. I still love him, monster that he is," Diana continued. "He was a genius, a great philosopher and gentle humanitarian. I bore him a child, Rhea...your mother."

My heart slammed. Ka was a Vos! Which meant that—

"NO!" I screamed. "I don't believe you!" I stammered out in a thrashing voice. "You're jagging wrong. I could *never* be a Vos!" I sobbed. "I hate them! They killed my—" I cut myself off and gasped.

"You know it, Rhea. Think of all the times you probably shape-shifted for an instant without even knowing. You only have to touch them once for your body to store the potential. Perhaps a Badowin for a burst of strength or a Fauche for swiftness or hearing, or a Xhix for better sight, an Eosian to smell. You've done that a lot, I can tell. Or how about a Scandi for rapid healing? Goodness knows you've done that a few times. Like when the blenoids attacked you; anyone else would have lost their leg from the septic wound, even with Benny's help. Or when you got *dusted* by V'mer; your body should have permanently shut down long before Benny attended to you; or that awful skipboat accident; you should have died long before they reached you—"

"I've never touched a Scandi," I protested sharply, wondering how my grandmother knew so much about my mishaps and a little annoyed that she did.

"You must have," she insisted. "Without knowing it. Perhaps when you were a little child," she replied with a complacent smile. I knew I hadn't but I didn't argue. "Rhea, you were always much more than a human."

I suddenly found that I could move. Gasping with the release, I burst into motion. I scrambled to retrieve my MEC and backed toward what looked like a way out. My serpent-grandmother warily matched my movements, guarding the exit. I waved the MEC at her. "Get out of my way!"

"Rhea, beware of what appears good," she hissed. "The music of the spheres is the key to all things, good and evil. Ka is a master of its music and an impeccable dissembler. A mad genius who must be stopped. He's both your key and your doorway, young one. But don't let him rule you!"

I had stopped listening. I couldn't bear it. The discovery was too much. "Out of my way!" I shrieked. "I'll shoot!" I pointed the MEC at her with a shaky two-handed grip.

She gazed wearily at me with sad eyes and reluctantly slithered out of the way.

I hesitated at the doorway of the treehouse, gaze darting to the ground moving below me. The tree lumbered, swaying to and fro. I swiftly holstered my MEC and began to climb down the smooth trunk.

"Rhea!" my grandmother called down in that melodious voice that reminded me of my mother. "Remember the ouroboros...Remember...if you must yield, *yield but without surrender*!"

I ignored her words and focused on scrambling down. Besides, I thought, the words made no sense: to yield *was* to surrender, I decided. Damn her. I prayed she wasn't following. The trunk was covered with epiphytic vines that I could either hang onto or use as footholds. At least I thought so until halfway down when one of the vines gave way in my grasp and I fell with a shriek to the ground. I landed in a splat and a grunt of pain, legs collapsing beneath me. I'd landed in knee-deep murky water that released the sharp skunk-like stench of rotting vegetation. The tree lumbered on, ignoring me like sloughed-off debris. It continued with a dozen other trees through the canyon toward the Boiling Sea.

I scrambled up, feeling a sharp pain flame up my left leg. I realized my leg wasn't broken, probably just sprained. Both my Great Coat and the swamp had absorbed my fall. Trailing fearful glances behind to where no one appeared to be pursuing me, I dodged around the oncoming trees and bolted inland, forcing my screaming muscles and painful ankle into a hobbling run. Away from the Boiling Sea. Away from those sentient trees and my lying grandmother-snake. I stumbled and gasped across the uneven ground. My face hit the ground and I scrambled up, tasting mud, and fought into a gallop, refusing to look back. Gulping in air. Ears ringing. Nose bleeding. Eyes blurred with tears.

TWO

The mud gripped my legs as I sank and clambered through it with sobbing breaths. When I could no longer hear or see the migrating trees and I was surrounded by the damp silence of mist, I collapsed in painful exhaustion into waist-deep murky water and openly wept.

Inhaling the skunk smell of marsh plants and rotting vegetation, I wrapped my Great Coat around me for comfort. I contemplated the awful truth about myself. I'd ruthlessly discarded Serge's recent suggestion that I was a Vos. I'd rationalized that the lying scoundrel had thought that it might work in his favour. But I remembered the flutter in my stomach and the tightness in my chest at hearing his words. Truth had a way of doing that. My body had recognized it even as my mind had revolted. It wasn't fair, I concluded with a convulsive swallow and wiped my runny nose with the back of my hand. *Dress the monkey in silk and it is still a monkey*—Argentinian proverb.

I resented the Eosians—they'd taken my home and changed it. But I despised the Vos. They'd killed my father...no,

I didn't have a father...but they'd taken all that was dear to me. My world. My life. My dreams. If not for the Vos, the Eosians wouldn't have come to Earth and my life would have been radically different. Or perhaps, I reflected suddenly, I would not even have been born. Did Laura Hawke even know that her father was a Vos? And a ruthless leader of the Nihilists, bent on destroying humanity? Of course not, I concluded. Just as I hadn't known that my father was a baldie. My foolish mother didn't know her father was a shape-shifter and a murderer.

But Serge knew...the bastard had known all along, I thought, recalling my encounter with him last week....

Φ

Last week...

...I slouched in my pilot's chair, snug in Serge's old crewneck sweater, the one he'd worn—and taken off—when I'd last seen him, as I reviewed my copy of Shle She's hit list that Bas had given me earlier. I hugged myself. My right hand draped over my opposite shoulder, and I tucked my nose into my elbow, breathing in the delicious fragrance of old wool and Serge's faint but intoxicating scent. I inhaled his smell as if it were a sanctuary. While I would never admit it to anyone, including Benny, the sweater was my comfort clothing. I'd kept Benny from washing it and put it on whenever I needed to boost my spirits. Like today.

I took in a deep breath of wool with essence of Serge then read *the Rose's* hit list. Thanks to me, Rashomon, who was first on the list, was taken care of; he was dead. I was next on the list and considered a *nexus-portal* and a *ghost*, whatever they were. Instructions included taking me to the *Ancient One*. Well, the *Nihilists* were still after me, I figured. Shle She, an *anti-Nihilist* traitor and threat to Eclipse security with his worm-virus that tapped into Eclipses most secure system, the vault, was third on the list. The information pirate and broker had managed to elude them but I thought they might still succeed. I checked the fourth target and frowned in puzzlement. I couldn't understand why Barbariccia, the *dust* lord from Dark Sun, was on the list. He was already incarcerated on Sekmet. Barbariccia was described as a major contributor to the *anti-Nihilist* cause. It didn't make sense, even if he still ran his illicit operation somehow from Sekmet. What was he doing against the *Nihilists*?

The next target on the list and second to last, before Ka, was the human priest, Raphael Martinez, the rising Gnostic spiritual leader who'd started his own sect, the Hermetic Order, which was gaining a major following on Upsilon 3 in the Upsilon Andromedae system. Gnostics were major *glitter dust* consumers. Was that the connection with Barbariccia? Upsilon 3 was an arid and scorching wasteland where I'd almost been killed by a rabid pack of blenoids. It was a place I'd have preferred to forget. Martinez also maintained a large estate with a vineyard on Earth in what used to be Quebec, Canada. He ran a school and spiritual retreat there. That was where he spent most of his time. It struck a chord and I remembered: he was the sad boy that Ka had told me about, who's mother had been disgraced from the Order of the Sacred Tree. That Martinez had dedicated himself to the study of Gnosis somehow made sense to me. I glanced at the hit list again: he was listed as a *nexus-portal* and, like Rashomon, an *unlocker of future portals*. Like those spiritual people my grandmother had soul-drifted into?

"This might also interest you, Rhea," Benny went on. "Martinez is considered a prophet by the Gnostics."

I already knew. "Remind me of his prophesy?" I remembered asking Ka before and getting an arcane answer.

"Martinez predicts the coming of the *Suntelia Aeon*, a catastrophic End of the Age. He says he gets inspiration for his prophesies from the ancient souls he's connected to."

"The *vishna* trees?" I'd heard they were ancient souls of some kind with the power to influence men's thoughts.

"Yeah. The second part of his prophesy is that the destruction of our old world will be signified by *the joining of twin souls who will herald the coming of a New Age*."

I frowned and leaned my head in my hand. The first part

of his prophesy made more sense to me this time. It was the prediction of war, I thought; something I was scrambling to prevent. As for the rest..."That could mean anything." I remembered Ka shrugging the last time I asked him what he thought it meant.

"That's how a prophesy usually works," Benny quipped, equally hedging.

I leaned back and hugged myself. "Joining?...What kind of joining?" I went on, curious. "And twin souls?" Was it a reference to the two diverses? I instantly thought of Serge and I...*twin souls*...we were hardly that, I thought even as I breathed in his enticing scent on the sweater I wore. Then I stretched back and drew in a long breath, knowing I could not solve the puzzle. It was just a wild prediction by a Gnostic mystic. It wasn't as though Martinez was a god or anything, I concluded, and put it out of my mind to check telemetry.

We were presently in the 47 Ursae Majoris b system, heading toward Uma 1 to warn Ka about the traitor in his midst and the fact that he was on *the Rose's* hit list. After that I intended to chase after Serge. Where would he go first, I wondered, checking my navigational charts: after Shle in the 70 Virginis b system or Martinez in the Upsilon Andromedae system? Where would that bastard go? I thought Martinez the more urgent target, though I didn't like either destination—

Benny signalled me: "*Scimitar* class ship ahead, Rhea. I believe it's Serge."

I jerked up, feeling an irrational thrill, and eagerly checked Benny's holo projection of the ship. "What's he doing in *this* system?" I heard my voice quiver slightly.

"No idea, Rhea. But we have, I believe, a decided advantage. The *scimitar* is not a military or stealth-class ship. Its tracking equipment isn't as superior as mine. Serge doesn't have us on his sensors yet and our long-range stun cannon should take him out before he even sees us."

I let a predator's smile slide across my face. I sat back and studied the holo projection of Ka's stolen ship. I pulled out a wad of soyka gum, threw it casually in my mouth, then chewed lazily with an open mouth. "Well, then, let's catch ourselves a little prey, Benny." I blew out and popped a gum bubble then carved out a ferocious smile. "I'm hungry."

I seized the controls and banked hard toward the *scimitar*. "Lock on the *scimitar*, Benny. On my mark...Now!" My eyes lit up with the thrill of seeing the green pulson wave flicker toward the *scimitar* and watched the ship shudder in the violent concussion wave.

"The *scimitar* is disabled, Rhea. We are being hailed."

"Approach the ship for docking, Benny, and put him on," I took my hands off the controls and leaned back to let Benny handle the finicky business of docking.

The holo-com lit up with Serge's distraught face and I instantly felt mine heat. A week's beard bristled on his rugged face and he looked stunning in a grey crewneck sweater and black trousers. The sweater was identical to the one he'd worn when I'd last seen him — the one I was now wearing. As soon as he saw me, Serge's face relaxed and he gave me a rakish smile. I noticed his fleeting glance down at what I was wearing and felt my face blaze with the heat of embarrassment.

"I should have guessed it was you, Rhea," he said casually. "That your way of saying hello?"

"It is with you," I bit back, casually chewing and throwing the gum around with my tongue. "We've disabled your ship and intend to dock and take you aboard. Don't give me any trouble, Serge, and I won't have to kill you."

"Listen, Rhea," he said, leaning forward with a serious expression, "I know we parted somewhat less than amicably on Virgil 9, but I want to reassure you that I really *am* on your side..."

Of course he'd say that once I caught him.

"...and I was just trying to help," he went on with a crooked smile. It was as sincere as a blenoid was kind. "I'm concerned for your welfare because I don't think you understand what's really going on and the depth to which you're involved. I could set you straight on a few things. I could be your most useful ally—"

23

"And all your lying was supposed to teach me that?" I popped a bubble.

"Rhea, you've embarked on a very dangerous journey," he said, looking a little flustered, and nervously stroked his bristly chin. He was losing his cool. "You have no idea what you're doing."

"Yes I do. I'm taking you in and once I make a quick stop on Uma 1, I'll be delivering you to the nearest Guardian precinct."

"Chaos, Rhea." He threw himself back in his chair and raked back his grey-brown wavy hair with a brush of his hand. I felt a mean smile tug my lips. He'd lost his cool. "They don't give a blenoid's ass about me," he growled. "They'll take *you* in and let me go, then feed you to the blenoids. You think they'll even listen to you? They'll be pissing themselves with delight at their catch. You're their prize, for creon's sake. Even the mercenaries are hunting you. Your bounty's brought out all the scum in the galaxy. You're wanted dead or alive for two million credits. Did you know that?" I didn't. Was that why he was here? "Even that scumbag leader of Dark Sun didn't fetch as high a bounty."

"So, you're the snitch who helped put him in Sekmet?" I sneered.

"No," he said and glanced away from me for a moment then added darkly, "But he deserved it." I had to agree. Barbariccia ran the largest *glitter* cartel in the galaxy, with the Gnostics presumably being one of Dark Sun's major customers — until Eclipse decided to take him down for their own selfish reasons. I was sorry at the time that I wasn't one of the officers in charge of capturing him. If I had been, he wouldn't be in Sekmet; he'd be dead. According to some rumours, being in Sekmet hadn't affected his business at all and Dark Sun continued its manufacture and commerce in *glitter* like before. Serge's eyes blazed into mine again. "Don't trust anyone, Rhea."

"I'll take that advice, starting with *you*," I snarled.

"Go ahead, but at least apply it to everyone else."

"Including me, I suppose?"

"Rhea, you have no concept of the danger you pose to both yourself and to this entire world…"

"Right…I'm their ultimate weapon," I repeated the words he'd used on me on Virgil 9. I'd been hearing that from just about everyone and I was tired of it. "Well, I intend to make the world a little less dangerous, starting with you…"

Φ

I pulled myself out of the brown-stained pond and waded in a hobble through the warm swamp, Great Coat trailing like floating sails on the water. The canyon eventually opened to a wide valley, surrounded by towering oil-covered cliffs.

I considered my changed priorities as I marched aimlessly through the fen-bog. Serge was no longer my primary target now; Ka was—if my Apophus grandmother was right. I felt a twinge of irrational disappointment at the thought. There was no longer any excuse to pursue Serge and I had to admit that the thought of never seeing him again sent a deep ache through me. Damn that man for his influence on me.

I forced my mind on my present situation: how I was going to get a message to Benny to retrieve me? My allotted time had come and gone, so Benny had supposedly gone looking for Bas. Bas was a good tracker; I felt confident he could find me because—

A loud pop and crackle ahead made me skid to a halt. I watched with amazement as a ten-foot oval structure made of earth and debris emerged from the muck, creating a small wake in the black water just meters in front of me. I flinched as it snapped open at the top, releasing a sharp odour of clove and burning matches. I considered backing away slowly and took a step back then stopped dead in my tracks and held my breath as two long deep crimson 'tails' slowly whipped out. They looked suspiciously like motion-sensing antennae.

When a vicious insect-like head emerged, attached to the 'tails' and dripping slime from a long proboscis, I abandoned stealth and bolted through the knee-deep swamp, not waiting to see the rest of the creature. Oh, God! These were the carnivorous larval stage of the ammut that Ka had told me about. I'd picked a great time to return to Horus: the beginning of the 'season of the dead' when the ferocious ammut hatched and swarmed.

Within moments, I heard an ominous loud clap and buzz behind me. I forced myself to turn and dared a glance. I clamped terrified eyes on a creature rising in the air, then lost my balance and fell backward into the swamp. A twelve-foot long insect-like creature had unfurled four narrow dragon-fly wings that flapped furiously. Twelve jointed legs dangled below its thick body. Huge multi-faceted amber eyes roamed below its crimson antennae and its long proboscis twitched, hungry for its first meal. Catching my breath, I scrambled under a drowned shrub and the ammut flew past me, the machine-gun flutter of its huge wings reverberating in my gut. I swallowed down my terror and wondered what an adult looked like if this thing was its larval stage.

I backed further into the bush and heard the sounds that I dreaded—more popping and crackling. I stared at the emerging swarm of eggs in the wide valley. Like popcorn, they started with a few snaps here and there. Within moments a cacophony of eruptions and the heady odour of clove and burning matches pervaded. According to Ka these carnivorous larvae left a swath of destruction in the wake of their swarm. No wonder the migrating trees were heading *out* of the valley!

I was trapped. I grasped my useless weapon of destruction, the MEC holstered off my thigh. It only worked on a creature with a DNA signature it recognized. I had never catalogued these creatures. I was good at trapping myself, I decided, hysterical mind sliding back to Serge and those thunderstorm eyes that always ensnared me with their stormy gaze....

Φ

Last week…

26

...I kneeled down and gruffly pulled at the restraints to check their strength then rose and paused in front of Serge. I'd exchanged Serge's sweater for an Enforcer black top and Great Coat. Feeling much more in control, I leaned my hand against the wall behind his standing figure and brought my face close to his. I locked eyes with his, lips smirking, and played the gum in my mouth with my tongue. "Feels familiar, doesn't it? Only in reverse."

Serge took in a long breath, eyes roaming over me. Then he met my gaze head-on. "Go ahead," he breathed, emitting a sudden fragrance of musk and strawberries. "I know you want to kiss me."

I jerked back, face flushing with sudden anger. "Go to chaos! You're so full of shit, Serge—V'ser." I had trouble calling him by his real name. "You're so damn pompous and sure of my devotion. So hubristic about your powers of seduction—"

"Not hubristic. Not pompous, Rhea. I just know," he said calmly, inching toward me even as I recoiled. "Because my past is your future. And in my world you and I have been lovers for over five years . . ."

He suddenly raised his brows then laughed at my expression.

"Don't you think it's possible?" he teased. "Considering your initial attraction for me here on this world. Haven't you ever wondered about love at first sight?" He paused then sighed at the face I made and looked down at his manacled hands. "Okay, so you don't believe in love at first sight. Well, it happens. People feeling a strong attraction for someone out of the blue. Haven't you ever wondered why we can have such strong feelings for a stranger we've just met? Incredible attraction or revulsion?"

"Hormones," I said flatly and blew out a bubble.

"Karma," he returned.

I abruptly popped the bubble with my tongue and sucked my gum back into my mouth.

"You were wearing my sweater," he said.

"I was cold."

Undaunted he went on, "When you've known someone, your true love, in one universe, don't you think you'd recognize him or her in the other?"

I stepped back. *True love*. That was a joke, I thought. There was no such thing. There was sex and touch and the rest was hormones and chemicals: oxytocin, seratonin, dopamines, endorphins. Serge had tried my patience for long enough, playing with my feelings. He was stalling, trying to provoke me into making a mistake. It wouldn't work this time. "*Who flatters you has either cheated you or hopes to do so...*old Romanian proverb, Serge—eh, V'ser," I bit out. "We're heading back where you'll submit to questioning by the Galaxy Guardians. I'm just taking you there." I turned for the hatch door of the brig.

He made a scoffing sound. "Your precious Galaxy Guardians! They'll arrest *you* first and put you away before you have a chance to say one word about me!"

I ignored him and made for the door. He was probably right.

"Rhea, listen!" His voice was suddenly pleading. I hesitated then opened the door to leave. "Please!" he shouted in desperation. "If I were to tell you something in confidence, in confidence from the Guardians, will you promise to listen quietly?"

I stopped and turned. The mock cavalier had vanished from his face and left him weary. I couldn't quite read the complicated message in his eyes, except that he was being genuine for once. I folded my arms across my breast and let the scepticism show on my face. I studied him with narrowed eyes, sliding the gum with my tongue from one side of my mouth to the other. "What you say to me you say to the Guardians."

"I know who's after you and why."

"Oh, it's not you and this isn't all about the MEC?" I stopped playing with my gum and gave him a long hard look. "I'm listening."

"Among the Vos exists a fanatical extreme right wing group. Terrorists who call themselves the *Nihilists*..."

He'd mentioned them before...when I wasn't listening. It

28

was also the same word Asphalios used for all the shape-shifters—Vos—in Eclipse, before I'd mistakenly fried him. Shlsh's files described them as the ones spearheading the Vos invasion. According to Serge, they *were* the invasion.

"Their sole purpose is to be the only ones who control what passes between the inner and outer diverses—"

"You expect me to take you seriously?" I tilted my head with a smirk of contempt and chewed with an open mouth. "Inner and outer diverses?" I thought he'd made it all up one night during foreplay. "You told me all this garbage before."

"It's real, Rhea. As real as I am standing here. I'm visiting this outer diverse, your world, from the inner diverse, a world very similar to this one and with pretty much the same people, give or take, depending on their unique fates. Our metaverse is a tapestry of inner and outer diverses with infinite dimensions, woven together by the opposing fibres of time. We Vos aren't from some other galaxy. We live inside *you*. You're our universe, just like we are your universe."

I stared in fascination and forgot to chew my gum. Not that I believed a word he was saying, I told myself.

"Your species has always intuitively known this truth," Serge went on, settling into a cross-legged sit. "And they've sought it in your different cultures in various ways: some through meditation and prayer, or the study of metaphysics, occultism, mystery school; others through hypnotic trance and psychoactive drugs—"

"Like *glitter*."

He nodded and continued, "Yes, the Gnostics. Others do it through dance and song." He tilted his head slightly in contemplation. "So many of your species have already experienced a good glimpse of our diverse, Rhea. People like Edgar Cayce, your prophets from ancient times. Diviners, clairvoyants...the Flamenco dancer who taps into that dark music...the singer whose song surges up from the soles of her feet...the artist who feels the hair on his neck rise when he connects with a universal truth...And who hasn't experienced a déjà vu sometime in their lives."

He paused to study my brooding face. I was having a hard time maintaining my sneer. In fact I'd lost it entirely. He looked satisfied and continued, "Like I was saying before, the *Nihilists* want to close—then control—all *gates* between the diverses by first killing all humans, who are potential and actual *portals.*"

"*Portals?*" I leaned with my shoulder against the door jam, forcing out a half sneer with difficulty. *Portals* and *gates* had been used to describe people on the *Nihilist's* hit list I'd given to Ennos at the Guardian Precinct.

Serge sighed. "Remember the time I told you how when you're dreaming or meditating your essence—your soul— crosses to the inner diverse and you glimpse your outer diverse's future?"

I nodded, blinking slowly with bemused scepticism, and forced myself to casually chew my gum.

"You're being a *portal.* Virtually every human is capable of acting as a *portal.* Who hasn't had a déjà vu experience? Some people can even recall aspects of the inner diverse through their other soul-half. We call them *ghosts.*"

I swallowed convulsively. That was the word they'd used to describe me on the hit list.

"This is incredibly rare," Serge went on. "But I've heard of it. Usually scrambled in fragments of dreams that don't make sense. Sometimes as recurring, often disturbing images because they are the ones the complete soul broods over..."

I suddenly swallowed and felt my face flush with the thought of my recurring nightmare of the strange man who made love to me and the one who tried to kill me. I'd once thought it was a quirky bogus dream of Serge, but realized that it wasn't.

"I've been told that *ghosts*, if they're capable of soul- drifting—locking into someone else's dream or trance—can manipulate both the dreams and real aspects of that other person's life in the other diverse, usually in the form of a lengthy déjà vu."

I felt a chill crawl up my back, thinking back to my strange experience under the ice on Uma 1, when I thought I'd died and my other self instructed me backward in time, only to find it was all part of a déjà vu…It had been only one of several vivid occasions of life-saving déjà vu I'd had recently.

"When they are acting as portals, during dreamtime or meditation, a human opens a *gate* to the other diverse. Humans can be manipulated, even through mass hallucination, by a master soul-drifter to create a *gate* between the two diverses for others to travel through."

"Like that *gate* on Borrias?" My grandmother had presumably done that. She'd presumably soul-drifted into the dreams of a hundred spiritual leaders and convinced them to dream into reality a *gate* for the Vos. Was it still open?

"Yes, exactly!" Serge said excitedly. He moved forward as far as his chains would let him and answered my silent question, "Those kind of *gates* remain open, through the sheer force of intent by so many." Then he went on, not cluing in to the emotional turmoil rising inside me, "Some people go into this state easily through meditation or self-induced trances. They're called *nexus portals* and are basically the healers, the spiritual leaders, the mystics of humanity. The *Nihilists* want to kill all *portals* but particularly *nexus portals*, effectively closing all *gates* between our two worlds. Hence the mass murders of spiritual leaders and those people on the hit list that you and your dead partner obtained from the *Ulysses*."

"But I'm not a mystic," I objected, returning us to the topic he'd opened: me, and who was after me. And they weren't trying to kill me; just bring me to this *Ancient One*.

"No, you certainly aren't," he conceded rather too quickly for my taste. "Hardly enlightened at all." I held back a grimace at his insult. His eyes pierced into mine. "You are, however, extremely intuitive. And you're … eh, different."

I shifted, still leaning with apparent casualness against the doorway and remembering to languidly chew my gum. He hadn't really explained why the *Nihilists* were after me and what they wanted of me.

"You are, nevertheless, a *nexus portal* and a *ghost*, Rhea. At least according to that hit list. A *ghost* I was entrusted to protect, even if it was from yourself."

"Protect?" I scoffed, jerking up from the wall to stand tall and plant my fists on my hips. "By absorbing me into your diverse?"

"Between the two diverses, as a matter of fact," he said. "Absorption is a chance to save someone in the outer diverse, especially if they're doing themselves in. You're in danger of being killed by the very people you trust the most. And you risk destroying both diverses. I had the bright idea of taking you in for a while until things settled down. It was a desperate move, I know. And I hadn't counted on your melting rage."

"It saved me from the same fate that might have been my mother's at the hands of your father," I bit out. I felt my face twist with anger and pulled the gum out of my mouth to throw into the garbage dispenser. "I'm no longer sorry I killed your father," I admitted. "It ruined my life. I thought for years that I'd killed an innocent man. It made me the killer I am. And I'm not proud of that. But I'm free now from that original guilt and I feel vindicated in saving my mother. I thank you for that, at least...V'ser." I spun on my heels with a harsh backward wave of my hand and swiftly fled, door shutting, before he had a chance at rebuttal.

I heard him shout my name but the peristaltic gurgling of Benny's environmental system and my own pounding heart drowned out his words....

THREE

....Ankle throbbing, I sat in murky marsh water to my waist, Great Coat billowing up around me, and back pressed against a bush. I listened to the chaotic clamber of ammuts emerging and flying. It grew dark overhead as their swarming bodies veiled the orange sky with black. The deafening machine-gun stutter of their wings filled my head and throbbed in my gut. Any moment a stray would find me, sniff me out with its long blood-red antennae, and I'd have to run...and die. In a sudden flash of regret, I wished I'd kissed Serge one final time....

Φ

A week ago...

....I found Serge curled up on the floor, asleep, in the brig. I approached quietly with his food and bent to lay it on the ground in front of him. Seeing his sleeping face up close, I paused to gaze at him and felt my throat swell. The week's worth of dark stubble on his face somehow made him look vulnerable. My eyes flickered from his long slender nose to his sensuous mouth, relaxed and partially open in sleep, then to his tussled steely brown hair that I imagined running my fingers through. I would have liked to lay with him, nestle inside his arms, breathe in his masculine scent and feel his warm body next to mine. It drew a sigh from me. I firmed my lips and straightened, pushing my hands against my knees, and turned. Damn that man...that *alien* —

"Don't go."

I started and whirled to face Serge. He had just roused and was sitting up. He wiped the sleep from his eyes and gave me a lazy smile that warmed my face.

"Thanks for bringing the food yourself. I was getting tired of those silent droids. Please stay," he implored with a charming smile of invitation. "Keep me company while I eat. I hate to eat alone."

I obliged. I sat cross-legged on the floor several metres from him and ran my fingers through my hair to sweep it off my face. Then I clasped my hands together and watched him eat. Needing something to do, I pulled out a wad of soyka gum from my pocket and shoved it in my mouth as Serge bolted the food hungrily and glanced up at me occasionally with an appreciative smile.

I felt awkward sitting there in the silence, slowly chewing my gum as he ate. I decided to ask what was on my mind. "I'm curious." I tipped my head to one side and gave him a crooked smile. "What do you *really* look like? The Vos. What do you look like when you're not shape-shifting?"

He abruptly looked up at me with a full mouth, as if a little startled by my question. After swallowing, he surprised me with his answer: "Just like you."

I lost my smile and stopped chewing. I stared in disbelief and felt my mouth suddenly water and throat tighten with unfathomable discomfort. "*Me?*"

"Humans," he explained with an enigmatic smile.

I blinked several times, overcoming inexplicable panic. So, the Vos weren't the monsters most humans, my mother included, had imagined them to be, I concluded.

Serge looked mildly amused. "Haven't you ever wondered why shape shifters preferred the human or Eosian form? Or why you couldn't smell them out so easily in that form?"

I had. But I'd never much cared for the conclusions I'd come up with.

"In fact, I don't think any of us knows what we were in the beginning. We've looked like you for so long. I think our bodies have forgotten the original blueprint. Vos are born looking human and thinking they're human." He shrugged. "Many of them don't ever know they're Vos." He smiled like a boy and I felt my stomach clench and throat constrict again. "My home is much like your own, Rhea, made up of humans and other aliens, with the exception of Eosians and Epoptes..." Then he added, remembering my earlier remark, "...if you believe Epoptes exist, that is. For almost every person in your world there's someone like them in ours. Take you for instance..."

I swallowed suddenly, not sure I wanted to hear this. Saliva flooded my mouth.

"I told you that you existed in my world. You have an inner self in my diverse, Rhea, living there right now. It's not a mirror world but one that embraces parts of a whole, and together they're like two beating parts of a single great heart. She is your other self, your inner self. And you're her outer self.

Together, you make up the whole. That's who the girlfriend I talked about was. She's essentially *you*."

"The one in the coma?" The one who'd been brutally attacked just like my nightmare? Did that mean that I had dreamt of my double's brutal attack? But that couldn't be right. My dream had occurred in my hometown, Vancouver, on Earth. And Vancouver no longer existed, thanks to the Eosians.

Serge nodded. "The same one."

I recalled my earlier jealousy of Serge's old girlfriend. It had been me all along. I'd been competing with myself. She was also the woman that I had visions of in Virgil City. "What's her name? Is it Rhea too?"

"No, it's V'rae."

"Like the French word for truth?"

"It's spelled differently," he said.

I swallowed again, throat suddenly dry. It sounded like a shape-shifter's name. I licked my dry lips and diverted myself with another question, "Does that mean that there's another version of you here?"

As soon as he nodded, I knew: of course, the real Serge Bastion, the bookseller who lived on Beleus. V'ser's family had come through the Gate and killed the Bastion family then taken their identities—except for Serge. I swallowed the saliva pouring into my mouth. "If he's your copy then is he a Vos too?"

V'ser nodded with an enigmatic smile. "But he doesn't know it...just like—" he bit back what he was about to say and looked at me strangely...expectantly.

"Just like...*me*?"

He grinned rather smugly out of the side of his mouth.

"I'm not a shape-shifter," I said coldly. I suddenly remembered to chew my now stale gum. But my heart slammed.

"Explain how you were able to take on the shape of an Eosian, then. Twice."

"I was temporarily *tecked*—"

"There are no temporary *tecks*, Rhea," Serge said matter-of-factly. "No one does temporary *tecks* except Rava and he's a useless quack. His so-called *tecks* worked on no one except you."

I swallowed convulsively, remembering Rava's admission to this very thing. "Rava had no idea what he was doing. The guy's mad, Rhea. That's why the PDs let him have his lab. He couldn't make a *teck* to save himself. That preparatory serum he gave you was just damsel-juice. A placebo. You did it yourself, on power of suggestion. It's that simple: if you don't think you can, then you can't. But if you know you can…well, then you can. We believe what we think we know and see."

I surged to my feet. "You're wrong!"

"You know I'm right. And what about your Great Coat? How is it that you're the only Enforcer whose Great Coat lets her leap ten stories high like a Khonsus? It's not the coat, Rhea. You believed so you did. It was really a micro-second shape-shift. You've been shifting for years without even knowing it."

Damn his insufferable smile. "I'm part human and part Eosian." That was bad enough.

"And part Vos."

"Jag you!" I shrilled and stalked away.

"I wish you would," I heard him say quietly as I stormed out of the brig. "Might improve your mood."

Φ

While I didn't want to believe Serge and my grandmother about me being part Vos, it did explain why my MEC failed to kill me when V'mer set it to kill a human. But, why did it fail to kill me when it was set to kill a shape-shifter? I recalled now how that had also stunned A'ler. Did she know I was part shape-shifter? The MEC had managed to destroy that Xhix shape-shifter. Even Benny's DNA scan had failed to identify me as part Vos or part Eosian. It had identified me as fully human. What was I? A'ler had asked me the same question —

The swarm had all the while become more dense and the clatter more deafening and I had grown accustomed to the slow escalation. It was the change in the pattern that alerted me and sent my heart pumping in my throat. They'd changed their flight pattern. They were circling down. Hundreds of them directly overhead!

I threw desperate glances left and right in search of better shelter. There was nothing, save a small dense cluster of stunted trees thirty meters to my left. The rest was an open swamp of grass, tussocks and small shrubs like the one I was hiding under. I was certain that my ankle, which had been cramped this whole time, would not serve me well if I bolted for the trees. The ammuts would pick me off long before I reached them. But they were going to get me regardless, I thought as I watched the swarm descend. The sooner I bolted, the better my chances of gaining some distance before one of them reached me. Anything beat waiting here to be eaten.

Heart pumping, I dashed out from my temporary cover and fell with a loud splash as my leg gave out painfully under me. Alerted, several ammuts veered down straight for me. Heart slamming, I scrambled into a painful run as the first ammut's antennae whipped out. It lashed my face and leg with a crackling snap and drew blood. I cried out with the agonizing sting and smelled burning flesh and cloves. I immediately felt a weak numbness spread through my body. Suddenly losing all strength, I stumbled and fell backward into the knee-deep swamp with a gasp. My face plunged into the stained water. I managed to right myself, coughing out black water, and thrashed to keep from sinking in the soft mud. By then more ammuts had buzzed in. Seizing in sobbing breaths, I backed away by scrabbling on my rump, too weak to rise to my feet. The soft bottom kept giving way underneath my hands. They sunk into soft mud and debris. I watched in terrified revulsion as the nearest ammut descended upon me then I gasped as its chitinous legs poked my breast, as if testing its texture. To my horror, the giant invertebrate then settled partly on top of me and slowly pumped its body up and down, as if excited, effectively pushing me further down into the murky swamp until my head was barely out of the water.

Skin crawling with revulsion, I gazed up at the creature's head, chittering directly above mine, and fought down a moan of terror. I tried not to move. My hands constantly shifted as the muddy debris gave way. Slobber from the creature's proboscis dripped over my head then plopped, reeking of cloves and sulfur, on my face. I jerked my hand to wipe off the slime, then seized my MEC from its holster in blind panic. I aimed it at the ammut's head and, pressing the trigger, dialed through every setting I could think of with my other fingers. Nothing worked. I replaced the MEC in its holster with a shaking hand and waited to be eaten. Why was the ammut hesitating? I could hear the random shrieks of other creatures being attacked and eaten over the distant trill of the migrating trees. In fact, the swarm had left except for this one atop me. *Dear God*, I prayed, releasing an involuntary moan, *make it quick—*

Rearranging six pairs of mid and hind legs in the swamp, the ammut bent closer and curled its four forelegs under me, in a strange supporting embrace. Abruptly its antennae whipped the back of my neck. I screamed with the cloying pain of cloves and burning matches then slid into darkness before my head fell back into the water....Dreaming of Serge....

Φ

"Let me out!" Serge shouted from the brig as I piloted Benny through the angry spray of weapons fire from four Eclipse shadow trackers. "It'll save you and your ship!"

"Jag you!"

"I wish you would. It might calm you down a little."

I was just about to spit out an even more rude rebuke over my shoulder when Benny abruptly shuddered then jolted hard starboard, throwing me against my crash webbing. The emergency klaxon shrilled. Environmental systems were suddenly down to 50%. There was a breach in Benny's hull!

"Rhea!" Serge bellowed from the brig.

"I know! I know!" I shouted back, madly compensating for the hull breach. "Benny, can you manage a patch?"

"Trying a nano-hull band-aid. Louie and Huey can do a manual patch on the starboard side and Dewey's welding the aft tear." I heard the three droids clattering in a frenzy of work behind me. "It might work for a short time."

"Do it!"

"Give me your MEC design, Rhea," Serge went on from the back of the ship. "Then shoot me out in the escape pod. It's the only way you're going to save yourself and Benny. It's what they're after."

"You think I'm going for that ruse?" I barked out, still compensating for Benny's off-line systems. "It's the oldest in the book of ruses. No design, buddy boy. It might be what *you're* after but if that's what they're after then why are they trying to destroy my ship and us along with it? They won't get the design that way."

"They don't know that!" Serge yelled. "They're hired thugs. Okay, just shoot me out in your escape pod, then," he hollered. "I'll signal them and pretend I have it and they'll leave you alone long enough for you to get away."

My face tightened into a wolf's snarl.

"Rhea!"

"I'm thinking!" I bellowed back.

"Damn it, woman! You're running out of time—"

"Shut up!"

"Starboard engine in serious compromise from hull breach, Rhea," Benny announced. "We can't sustain another hit and we can't outrun them all; they have us cornered. My impact shields are down. Huey's working on it, but in the meantime, a hit would blow us apart—"

"Okay! Okay!" I shot back, relenting furiously. "Take the controls, Benny, while I secure our guest in the escape pod."

I sprang up and pelted to the back of the ship, dodging around Huey and Louie, then punched in the code that opened the brig door and bars as Serge watched from inside. "This better work," I snarled, releasing him from his manacles.

"It will," he said, smiling like a little boy at me. I gruffly pushed him out of the brig to the aft storage/sickbay, where the small escape pod was housed. I glimpsed Dewey finishing its patchwork on Benny's hull tear then turned with a dark look at Serge.

"I just want you to know that you haven't won," I said as he bent down to crawl into the cylindrical pod. "I'll come after you again and next time your little thug friends won't be nearby to rescue you."

He turned his head to look past his shoulder at me and grinned. It turned into a grimace as I used my boot to push his backside into the cramped pod. Once he'd gotten in, I swiftly closed the inner pod door, ignoring his attempt to say something, then sealed the outer door. "Pod secure, Benny!" I said. "Now!"

The pod jettisoned with a slight jerk and I watched it drift away from my ship through the small porthole with a feeling close to remorse. Ruthlessly shaking it off, I ran back to control and slid into my pilot's chair.

"I think it's working," Benny informed me. "They've slowed down and are apparently investigating the pod."

"Not shooting it down?" I asked in a voice that sounded shrill to me.

"Not yet. Shouldn't we hightail it out of here? That *was* the idea."

My face tightened with hesitation. Despite who and what he was, I couldn't abandon Serge. If they decided to react in a hostile fashion, I wanted to be there to help.

"They've locked onto the pod. I doubt that they're going to shoot it down now, Rhea."

"Okay," I said, satisfied. "Take us out of here, Benny."

Φ

I bolted awake to a pounding headache and a stinging pain in my neck and face. The acrid stench of burning matches and cloves overwhelmed me. Surely I'd either drowned or been eaten by the ammut that had stung me. But I was very much alive, tightly bound and hanging upside down by some slimy yet strong material in what appeared to be a cave. Early daylight filtered in from an opening ahead of me and I caught an upside-down view of sky and vegetation. I surmised that I'd been here overnight. Had the ammut saved me for breakfast?

My entire body, except my head, was enclosed in the beast's slime cocoon that was attached by more slime to the ceiling of the cave. I could barely wiggle inside the corded Kevlar-like material. Head slamming, I felt my breaths escalate with the urgent need to escape. I needed to get out of here before the giant insect came back to claim me for breakfast. I felt my right arm rub against my MEC holster and in a sudden flash of inspiration, bent my wrist, fingers pointing toward my head, in small nudging movements. The Kevlar-strength thixtropic material of my Great Coat had helped to give me some additional room as its flexible tissue gave way for me. I eventually felt the hard slime give way slightly as my fingers scrabbled for the MEC under my Great Coat. After what felt like hours but was likely only minutes, I could feel its cool handle and played with the dials. There were a few settings meant to vibrate with inanimate objects and I hoped to come close to the DNA that made up this Kevlar-like material. It wasn't long before the MEC singed the hardened slime—Yes! And detached the cocoon—No!

I fell. Unable to protect my head with my bound arms, I cringed as the ground rushed toward me. Then blackness took me.

FOUR

I pulled out of a deep slumber, moaning with a pounding headache. It slammed in rhythm to the throbs of my heart and the murmurs of Benny's environmental system—Wait! I forced my eyelids open against the burning light, dim though it was. Through my blurry vision I saw that I was lying on Benny's sickbay bed, dressed in my flight clothes and still slime-covered. My Great Coat had been removed.

I stretched my neck and sat up, nearly passing out again and feeling a deep throb behind my eyes. Waves of nausea rolled through me and I thought I might be sick, but it slowly passed. My face, leg and neck burned as though I'd spilled acid on them. I brought my hand gingerly up to my cheek and winced with pain and dismay as I felt a deep welt that leaked blood and clear fluid.

"Rest, Rhea," Benny said in a calm voice as I stared in a daze at my hand, slick with blood and ooze. My ears rang with every sound, including Benny's voice. "Good to see you."

"Likewise, Benny," I said in a hoarse voice, deciding to lean my elbows on my knees and rest my head in my hands. It helped against the nausea that trembled through me. I shut my eyes again. "What happened?" How did I get here? I had blurry recollections of fleeing from the ammuts, getting stung or something....

"We found you in a cave, thanks to the tracking chip on your MEC," Benny told me. "Bas said you must have knocked yourself out when you took that nasty fall from the ceiling in that cave. You've got a second to third-degree concussion, Rhea. You better take it easy for awhile."

"Oh, terrific," I moaned. I was lucky that I hadn't cracked my skull or worse with that fall.

"You were lucky, Rhea."

"I know. That fall could have killed me."

"I meant about the ammut swarm. You were taken by the queen. She alone doesn't eat right away. There were twenty cacoons hanging in there with you. She was getting ready for a real feast."

"Terrific," I groaned then forced my eyes open and looked up. "Where's Bas?"

"In the cockpit," Benny said as Duey handed me a drink of water. "Drink. You need lots of fluids. Bas is just waiting for you to wake up and get a clean bill of health so he can return to his ship. I don't see why that can't happen soon. My MRI and CT scans showed no evidence of bleeding or swelling under the skull or in your brain tissue. How do you feel?"

I reached back to my head and felt the throbbing goose egg with trembling fingers. "Like I'm going to throw up."

"That's normal. It should pass."

"That's—" I swallowed down bile. "...What I'm worried about," I added. "And my head feels like it's a bomb, ready to explode."

"I gave you a pretty strong pain killer. That's all I could do," Benny said apologetically. "How's your vision?"

Eyes narrowing, I tried and failed to focus on some storage crates that swam in the far aft corner of the room. There were far too many of them. I sighed. "Double vision without benefit of Plock Nectar...that's a real shame."

"That too will pass," Benny said calmly. I nodded slightly, realizing that it was already better than when I'd initially woken up. "Do you know what day it is?"

I closed my eyes and leaned forward again, head leaning on my hands. "I never know what day it is, Benny," I sighed. "I rely on you for that."

"Okay. It's 215.33 SGT. What's the last thing you remember?"

"Eh...the ammut swarm descending...I tried to run and one landed on me...the...queen, you say?...it stung me or something...then...I'm not sure...oh, except for being upside down in a cocoon thing and falling on my head...."

"Okay."

My fuzzy mind cleared for a moment and I remembered what I urgently needed to do. Opening my eyes suddenly, I said, "I have something to tell Bas."

I pushed down on the bed with my hands to get up but Benny's droid reached out to restrain me. "I suggest you clean up first and change. Then let me fix those nasty welts before they get infected," Benny insisted. "I just took your Great Coat off to do my tests, Rhea. You're still a mess. And you stink."

"Thanks, Benny," I said with a lame smile, appreciating Benny's blunt candour. I let Duey help me up then shuffled unsteadily to the head to shower. The nausea returned in full force and I made a mad dash, reaching it in time to lose my dinner.

Φ

"How's your head?" Bas asked, sliding over to the co-pilot's chair as I eased into my own seat with a wince.

"I'll live," I said, offering him a crooked smile. I'd showered and changed into a fresh pair of black trousers and a charcoal sleeveless top. Benny had taken my other clothes to clean. I was beginning to feel like my old self again. I healed like a Scandi, after all, I thought sullenly and now I knew why. "Bas." I leaned toward him with a look of urgency. He mimicked my move and leaned in, concern on his face. "I've discovered something very alarming," I began. I then filled Bas in on the *Nihilist* and *anti-Nihilist* Vos movements, along with my own scepticism of Serge's explanation. Still, it made sense and a part of me, a large part of me, wanted to believe him. I ended with my awful discovery that Ka was a Vos leader of the *Nihilists*.

"Did you let home know yet?"

Home was our code word for Ennos back at the Galactic Guardian headquarters. I shook my head. "We're not secure and I don't want this to leak out. I want him in the bag first."

"Ok." Bas said with a frown. "You haven't talked with home in a while, that's all."

"We can't share all our adventures with home, Bas," I said with a smirk. Besides, I was pretty sure he had been keeping Ennos apprised enough for both of us.

"Too bad this Serge Vos-guy got away," Bas added with a frown. "I can't believe that Ka is an Eclipse member and a *Nihilist* Vos as you call them." Bas shook his head in dismayed amazement. "He wasn't on that list we got of Eclipse members. You sure you have all this right?" He studied me sceptically, then let his eyes rest on my swollen cheek with a complex mixture of revulsion and sympathy. My welts still burned with a heat of their own. Benny had informed me that despite the salve he'd used on my back and cheek it would be a while before the angry welt subsided and I stopped looking like a lopsided red-faced chipmunk.

"Dead sure," I replied, knitting my brows. "I know what

you mean, though. Ka had me fooled too." I hadn't even smelled him and the Khonsus form was very different from a human, the shape-shifter's preferred shape. He must have shifted as a Khonsus for a very long time, I concluded. I felt a brief sadness fill me and weigh down my shoulders. I'd respected Ka like a father—not realizing he was actually my grandfather *and* a Vos. I'd considered him a wise and gentle creature, someone whose advice I heeded. How wrong I'd been. Of course, I hadn't shared with Bas that Ka was my grandfather and *I* was part Vos. Bas didn't need to know that. It would just complicate things for us. "We need to find him, Bas. Take him to Ennos for questioning."

"What about this Serge guy you were after?"

"He's just a scoundrel. Ka and the *Nihilists* are the key to the Vos invasion. I know it in my bones." I couldn't tell him what my grandmother had said. "I'm going to need your help, Bas. We have to go to Uma 1."

Bas tightened his lips and stood up with a slap of his hands against his thighs. Although his face wore serious concern, I thankfully noted that his eyes sparkled with enthusiasm. He knew I had a plan. "Okay," he said. "Get me to my ship and Raekwon and I will join you." Then he tilted his head to one side with a curious half grimace and unconsciously ran a hand across his mouth and cheek. "I never asked you. Did you find what you were looking for on Horus?"

"Besides swarming ammuts?" I nodded slowly. "I guess I did." More than I'd bargained for.

Φ

"Rhea, my sources tell me that Ka is no longer on Uma 1," Bas reported from his *alpha* class *twin-V wing*. He stretched back in his chair in a loose khaki T-shirt and flight pants. I frowned at his holo projected in front of me as I sat in Benny's pilot chair. "Ka caught a ride in a delta-class *shadow* freighter ten galactic days ago," Bas went on. "It's owned by BlackStar Enterprises, which the Guardians think is a front for Eclipse, but which has Bona Fide cargo, crew and passengers who may not all be with

45

Eclipse. If we go in, it'll have to be a sleuth job."

I bit down on my lip, quelling the urge to ask him who his sources were. Was it Ennos? It didn't matter as much as the veracity and reliability of the sources. And Bas could be relied on for both. He always checked his sources and did impeccable research. The Guardians were lucky to have him. So was I. "Do we know where the freighter is now?"

Bas grinned. "In the 70 Virginis system. It's scheduled for a stop on Virgil 9 to unload exotic chemicals and spices."

I grinned back with understanding. "That's also where Shle She lives," I said, absently curling a strand of my long mane around a finger. Shle was someone Eclipse might want to finish off if they knew he was still alive. I tipped my head to one side and raised a brow. "Shall we interfere?"

"Indeed, we should, Jane," Bas said, cutting a mischievous smile on his handsome violet face.

Φ

I looked up from the info-pad on the table at Bas as he entered the small cafeteria of his *twin-V*. I had docked Benny and come aboard twenty-four galactic hours ago to discuss our plan for taking Ka into custody. I had been reviewing the specifics on the info-pad Bas had given me as I sipped hot soyka from a mug.

"Makes sense, Bas," I said with an encouraging smile. Bas grabbed a chair beside me and straddled it, backrest forward, with his long legs. "We're lucky that he'll be staying aboard while they do the unloading via a transport shuttle."

"Considering the planet, it's not surprising," he said, leaning his arms on the backrest. I recalled only too well how rude and unwelcoming the Ngus were. "Only seven of the passengers are slated for transport to the planet and Ka isn't one of them," Bas went on. "The rest remain onboard. What's good for us is that there'll be less thugs on the freighter. Most of the crew go planet-side on leave, leaving a skeleton crew behind."

Bas had suggested boarding the freighter in the guise of checking out its freight. Freighters got boarded regularly by

46

Guardians, especially if illicit goods like *glitter* or some other contraband was suspected. BlackStar was used to this kind of impromptu arrival by the Guardians and usually accommodated them. Bas expected this to be no different.

"The delta-class *shadow* usually has room for eighty non-crew passengers, consisting of ten first class and remaining regular class berths. I'd expect Ka to be in a first class berth. That part of the ship." He pointed to the area shown on the info-pad in my hands. "I'll make the advance, do the official routine and draw them away. Once Raekwon scrambles their surveillance with a fake program, you'll run point and locate our parcel. Ka should be asleep and you're the best there is at breaking and entering. I'll try to meet you at first class within half an hour."

I frowned. "I'll have found him and dragged him half way to the ship by then," I said. "Can't Raekwon come with me?"

Bas shook his head. "We need him to stay with the ship and keep it primed for our swift exit once we bag Ka."

I nodded, grudgingly giving in to Bas's logic. "Okay." Then I shook my head at the info-pad. "This is incredible," I said, suddenly impressed as I scrolled to the information on security. "How did you get all this?"

He shrugged and smiled cryptically. "It's my job, Rhea. You blast the bad guys; I get and manipulate information. We've known about BlackStar and their contraband runs for years. Let's just say that the Guardians have a few moles in there."

I nodded and returned my gaze to the info-pad. Just like the *Nihilists* had a few moles in the Guardians, I thought cynically. "We'll board at midnight," I said. "Just before the next shift. They'll be less attentive then, thinking of their warm beds."

"Agreed," Bas said, tapping his lips with his index finger. Just then, my stomach growled loudly and insistently. I glanced with a mildly embarrassed smile at Bas, who looked amused. "Where are my manners," he responded, getting up. "Let me get you some food."

I smiled appreciatively at him. "Thanks." I hadn't eaten since I'd boarded yesterday. I returned my attention to the notes on the info-pad as Bas clattered at the food processor. He wasn't long, thank God.

"Here." Bas grinned impishly at me, setting a plate of unrecognizable slimy food in front of me. "I was told that you're a rather adventurous eater."

I wondered who had told him that and threw him a sharp glance of warning then returned my gaze to the plate of unappetizing food. I looked up at him, realizing that my mouth had fallen open. I'd have preferred the jelimum pastry and red wine we'd had before and re-assessed my hunger.

"Go on," he urged, eyes sparkling with amusement. "It's called *buma*." Bas pointed to what looked like slimy pale strings of worms drowning in globs of green jelly. "*Buma* is probably Eos's most cherished delicacy. It's only obtainable twice a year when the *buiuma* inverts itself."

I began to feel sick and swallowed several times. "Inverts itself?"

Bas nodded with a cheerful smile. "It's the inside muscle of the *buiuma*'s digestive tract that sloughs off during the *kelm*, our wet season," he said with a self-amused grin. "*Buma* is very nutritious and highly sought after by our gourmets who must travel great distances, at some danger to themselves, to find these shy creatures."

I stared at the unsavoury mess on the plate in front of me. I raised the fork that had rested on the food. It trailed a string of slime. "How do they find them?" I quipped rhetorically, eyes rolling, "From their slime trail?"

Bas frowned in response. He lifted his brows at me and nudged his chin forward in expectation.

"You brought this all the way from Eos?" I asked.

He didn't exactly nod but moved his head in excited anticipation with an eager smile of encouragement. Would he feel hurt if I didn't try it?

After studying the food for another moment, I intrepidly scooped some of the noodle-like intestine and jelly in my fork, broke off the slime trail still attached to the food below with finger and thumb, and brought the forkful slowly to my mouth under Bas's watchful gaze.

It didn't smell bad. I slipped the slimy food into my mouth and chewed. To my surprise again, aside from the revolting slimy texture, the *buma* was delicious. It tasted like a combination of oyster and chicken, spiced with pepper and chile.

Bas broke out into a belly laugh and slapped his thigh. "It's Eos's running joke," he said, bending over with laughter. "Most Eosians won't touch the stuff!"

I scowled at Bas and swallowed down the remaining food in my mouth despite my sudden queasiness. I remembered downing a plate full of grilled blenoid viscera several months ago on Ka's ship. It was amazing what hunger could do, I thought, glancing down at the slime trail my fork left behind as I lifted it up off the food. Abruptly dropping the fork back on the plate, I decided that I wasn't that hungry and pushed the plate away. As if in response, my stomach growled again.

Bas had already sauntered out of the cafeteria, perhaps fearing retaliation. I heard his cackling laughter echo down the hallway as I searched for some more conventional food.

FIVE

"Certainly you have permission to take port and come aboard, Officer Basileus," the BlackStar representative droned on the holo in front of Bas. He was a large gruff looking Eosian and he didn't look too happy, I thought, standing with Raekwon to the far side of the control room, so we wouldn't be seen. But he was cooperating as Bas had surmised. "You may take port in hanger ten on the aft starboard side of the freighter. We'll have someone there to meet you."

"Thank you," Bas said and shut off. He turned to me, jaw tense. "Do you think he meant that literally? *Someone*...as in *one* person?" That meant only one person for Bas to overpower. It wasn't likely, I thought.

I gave him a reassuring smile as Raekwon took his position at the helm and brought us close to the huge delta-class *shadow*. We'd left my ship, Benny, on the far side of the planet. Benny was just too recognizable, piggybacking on the *twin-V*, so to my mild consternation, I'd left Benny orbiting the far side unattended.

Sensing my concern Bas winked at me. "Benny will be fine, Rhea."

"I know," I responded then winked back at him. "So will you."

Bas tipped his head and critically assessed my usual attire of black flight trousers, top and flight jacket. With a tight frown he briskly strode to a clothes cupboard and pulled out a brown travelling cloak. "Even without the Great Coat you look too much like an Enforcer. Here." He threw the cloak at me. "Put this on. We're almost there." He then commed back in response to the hail from the freighter. Within moments the *twin-V* entered the specified freighter port and landed inside the spacious hanger.

After waiting for the doors to close and the signal of air and pressure returned, Bas nodded to us, slid into his black Great Coat and strode to the exit hatch. Raekwon gazed at the surveillance camera and saw a single Eosian standing at the bottom of the ship, waiting. I came beside the nine foot tall Fauche and contemplated that maybe we were lucky—

Three other Eosians jumped Bas from behind. Before he had a chance to defend himself, one of them slashed his legs with a kappa rifle. Bas fell and they set upon him, ripping off his Great Coat and beating him hard.

Throwing off my cloak, I pulled out my MEC and raced for the hatch. Raekwon followed close behind. Five other Eosians waited for us. One shot. I ducked to the side and the weapon pulse caught Raekwon in the belly. It seared a huge hole into him, releasing a pungent sweet gust of burning flesh. I stared horrified as the gentle Fauche's large brown eyes grew even larger before losing their focus and he fell dead.

Lips snarling in a tight purse, I leaned out and shot. I'd set the MEC to kill a shape-shifter and knock out an Eosian. I caught two of them in a slice at head-level. They lost their heads in a mass of burnt and splattering flesh and tumbled as the remaining three dashed for cover. I leapt out of the ship's hatchway four metres down and landed in a role, firing at the men crouched behind some equipment. Without thinking, I charged them. To my amazement, instead of defending themselves, they fled. I caught one and he tumbled like a burning stump to the ground. The other two disappeared through a small door.

I searched for Bas and glimpsed him being dragged by five Eosians out of the hanger through a large door made for machinery to my far right. I knew before I chased after them that it was a trap. Seeing no choice, I pursued.

I skidded through the large freight door as it closed and found myself in a vast dimly lit storage room, lined with wide rows of crates, hesium fuel cans, shelves and heavy machinery. The smell of soil, yeast and *rapture* pervaded the dark chamber. I'd fully expected an onslaught of weapon fire. I was met with eerie silence. I focused my attention on the body lying in a large space clear of materials in the middle of the chamber. It was Bas. The five Eosians had dragged him here and had apparently fled. My heart clenched. God! Was Bas dead?

I rushed to him and saw him stir. I knelt beside him and stroked his battered face. "Oh, Bas...." I breathed out as he opened his eyes and blinked at me. His face was scratched up and smeared with blood. "Can you move?"

"Can't...something broken." He clutched my arm. "You came for me," he sighed out between gasping breaths, eyes large as saucers in astonishment.

"It's what friends do," I whispered, gulping in my tears. I'd brought him into this mess. "Oh, Bas...what have we done...what have I done to you...to Raekwon...."

Bas's face went suddenly lucid and he flashed his eyes toward the door I'd just entered. "Get out, Rhea, while you still can! It's a trap. I'm sorry—"

I looked up as the door slid open and Ka swept into the room. I leapt to my feet, MEC pointed at the belly of my grandfather.

Ka raised his feathered hands without recoiling but advanced no further. "Put the weapon down, Rhea."

I kept it pointed at him. "It was you all along," I said, mouth in a tight snarl. "You were the leak I tried to warn you about."

Ka laughed briskly and I found it somehow malicious. To think that I'd once enjoyed his laugh and had found his gentle face and musical voice soothing. He'd messed with my grandmother's mind. He'd coerced her into committing an awful crime. He was responsible for the creature Diana Wood had become. An apophus. Did he know?

"So, you found her, your grandmother," he said quietly. He *did* know. The bastard. "I take it she's well."

I narrowed my eyes at him, not bothering to hide my appalled disgust. "No thanks to you."

"She chose her fate, Rhea," he said. "*Duende.*"

"You drove her to it."

"Only so far as she let me, young one. The choice was always hers."

My hands tightened on the MEC. I hated these kinds of arguments.

"As for you, young one, you never cease to impress me," Ka went on. "You really make a good weapon." He laughed with sudden amusement at his pun. "I mean that in both ways. You *make* and *are* a good weapon. Ironically, one of Eclipse's best. But that's no surprise from the granddaughter of Ka." He smiled loftily. Then a feathered brow arched. "Although, you were a little slow with the hit list...we had to help you along with that one. I needed Rashomon out of the way without tainting my own hands and you, young one, were very accommodating."

"You're style's messy, Ka, and full of mistakes."

I recognized a sneer of displeasure on his beaked face. "Yes, good help is so hard to find these days." He let out a mocking sigh. "You performed wonderfully and predictably, but that foolish A'ler set the fuse time too short—she almost killed us both in the process."

I recalled Ka tugging me violently back when Rashomon had bounded away with the MEC.

"As for Shlsh, it was his system I wanted to shut down, not him necessarily." And thanks to Bas and I, we'd done just that. "He's harmless without his network. Don't worry, we'll get him eventually. Like the rest of those worthless aliens, eh? Wouldn't you agree that we could use a little cleaning up? Isn't that really why you made the MEC? To rid the galaxy of those unsavoury races? Isn't that what you were doing on Omicron 12?"

I swallowed convulsively and tightened my hold on the MEC. It was slipping in my clammy hands. "I'm not a fascist."

"Aren't you?" Ka challenged. "Admit it, Rhea, you mercilessly killed all those Rills without the slightest remorse—"

"It was a mistake. My MEC was—I wasn't used to its settings and—"

"There are no mistakes, Rhea," Ka cut in. "There is only *duende*. And for every action a reason, and a consequence, even if unclear to the doer." Then he leaned forward. "You've long harboured anti-alien sentiments. And you particularly despise baldies."

I kept swallowing as saliva poured into my mouth.

Ka pointed to Bas with a long feathered finger. "So, why are you wasting your compassion on that one? Eosians are an abomination," he said in that same tone of condescension that I was learning to hate. "You've known it, felt it ever since you were a girl."

My stomach clenched into a tight knot.

"Baldies were created by the sinful and unnatural coupling of gods with mortal humans," Ka went on. His voice reverberated in my gut. "Baldies are self-proclaimed beings of superior intellect and physique yet they are so lowly in their lack of restraint. Their arrogance and unnatural lust condemn them to the same fate that befell them millennia ago. They corrupted Earth once already and were banished from it, but they've returned to your home and inflicted it once again with their disease of pride. Tarnished it with their version of integrity.

History is repeating itself, Rhea. It is their god-given destiny to sink into debauchery as the heinous mixture of a god's blood defiled by a lesser race feeds on their minds like an evil cancer. Rhea, you know this in your heart, felt it since you were a child."

"I might have thought it once, when I didn't know better," I said in a shaky voice. I glanced at Bas still lying on the ground. "When I didn't *want* to know better." Bas was my colleague, a man of honour and warmth who deserved to live. A friend.

"Eosians loath humans. They consider humans lowly, despicable, and useless. You owe them nothing, Rhea," he said, eyes flashing like liquid gold. "You were treated with contempt by virtually all of them."

It was true. But I could not condemn and wish away a whole race based on the vulgar behaviour of some of its individuals. Bas was proof of that.

"They have no connection with the inner diverse, Rhea. Did you know that? There are no Eosians in our world. And because of it, they lack a complete soul; they must connect to the inner soul through the *vishna* tree, the ancient souls of the Epoptes. The Eosians are their soulless tools, their archangels of woe. They can't hear the music of the spheres. *That* is an abomination."

I couldn't either, damn it! "Let him go, Ka. *I'm* the abomination, not him. Despise *me*," I bit out. "Chaos, if you want defiled, I'm the proverbial mutt: a mix of Human, Eosian and Vos, and Heaven knows what else because both my mother and my grandmother didn't care who or what they slept with."

"Why the drama, Rhea?" Ka quipped. "And why do you waste your compassion on a man who betrayed you?"

To my astonishment, Bas had risen to his feet behind me and snatched the MEC out of my hand.

"Meet V'bas, your betrayer," Ka said with a smile of malice. It was a Vos name! "He's so much worse than you," Ka said as Bas handed him the MEC. "V'bas hasn't a fraction of your spirit. He's a traitor to everyone, those he is pretending to be and those he really is. He isn't Eosian. He's a Vos, but an unreliable and truant one. One who traded sides one time too many," Ka ended with a flashing gaze at Bas—V'bas—who cowered in fear.

"I'm sorry, Rhea...." Bas choked out, looking miserable and afraid.

It all made sense to me suddenly. His fortuitous rescues, knowing things he shouldn't otherwise know, giving me the info-pod and my equipment, getting me to Horus then Paradise City. He was all part of the set up for me to kill Rashomon. Yet, he'd saved my life a few times and he'd brought Shlsh's info-pod to the Guardians.

"You helped me change my mind about what the *Nihilists* were doing, Rhea, when you turned yourself in," Bas explained with a pained expression on his face then a fearful glance at Ka. "I saw that what we were doing was wrong. But I didn't want to see you get hurt." His eyes flitted to Ka again. "Ka promised he wouldn't hurt you—he told me what you were, that you're part Vos, one of us...." I shivered at his words. "That you're actually his granddaughter! He...just wanted some information that only you had. I thought that if I brought you to him, the rest of Eclipse would leave you alone...." He glanced again at Ka with uncertain fear in his eyes. "Some of them want to kill you."

"You're a...*Nihilist?*" I whispered, staring at him in horrified disbelief. "You murdered your Outer Diverse double?"

"No!" he defended. "I...I couldn't." Terror rushed into his eyes again and he glanced briefly at Ka, as if fearing his wrath." He shuddered, probably with relief as Ka simply looked on with a scowl, then swept into what sounded to me like rhetoric. "The Vos have been downtrodden and vilified for so long, Rhea," he explained. "The Epoptes call us devils, fallen angels. But it's they who descended to sleep with the natives. We only want our chance. That's all we want. The stories the *Ancient One* left us, of what happened in ancient times are horrific. The Vos aren't so bad, Rhea...."

That's what Serge had said just before he'd tried to absorb me.

"The Epoptes sold us out, Rhea," Bas went on. "We were all headed for a renaissance in the evolution of the soul and spirit. On Earth. Through human evolution. It would have been nirvana and we were together, all of us. But the Epoptes created the Eosians instead. The Eosians defiled our world with greed and arrogance. The Epoptes blamed the Vos for it and manipulated matter to shut us out of this diverse. They trapped so many of us here to die along with the humans they'd abandoned when they created the Great Flood and left with their precious baldies to start again."

That didn't sound like Bas, I thought. He was using someone else's words, the *Ancient One's*, no doubt.

Bas continued, "The Vos who were trapped here helped save so many humans during the Great Flood, Rhea. That's the irony...it was the Vos who were responsible for the survival of the human race in the first place. But the *Ancient One* also experienced so much that he became convinced that the diverses should remain separate—"

"By killing all the humans they'd just finished saving?" I said scornfully. "What did humans ever do to you, Bas? They're an innocent casualty in your war with the Epoptes and Eosians."

"Not so innocent," Ka interjected. "Humans destroy what they fear and don't understand. Didn't they murder Azaes? And what of another peaceful superior being over two thousand years ago?" He raised a feathery brow to me. "Humans have always waged massive wars for power, greed and shallow beliefs—" He cut himself off with an impatient wave of his feathered arm. "But enough history lessons." Ka snapped his raptor's head back. "We have some business to attend to." He waved the MEC in front of me. "You've kindly informed everyone that this weapon is useless without the design that you alone possess."

Bas looked suddenly stricken that this was the information Ka was after. For a *Nihilist* agent Bas was terribly naïve, I decided. I sneered at Ka with open contempt. It was the last thing I'd divulge to him.

Ka returned me a look of challenge. "If you refuse, I'll have to mind-probe it out of you. It won't kill you but you won't much care when I'm finished either, Rhea, because your brain will be useless. And that would be a shame, young one, because I do like you. You were kind enough to save my life once. And you *are* my precious granddaughter."

"Just try it," I snarled, eyes narrowing at him in bold defiance.

Ka smiled and I snapped my eyes shut. Then immediately felt a blow to my face. He'd struck me! Eyes snapping open with an involuntary cry, I teetered off balance then recovered. So much for the legend of a Khonsus's inability to inflict physical harm. Then again, he was a shape-shifter, a Vos. I clenched my eyes shut again as Ka tried to renew eye contact and braced for another strike of his large hand.

"Don't!" I heard Bas wail. He was close to tears. "You said you wouldn't hurt her."

I reached for the *pocket* pistol hidden in my Great Coat. Ka was there in a heartbeat and struck my leg. I buckled and I fell to my knees with a grunt but kept my eyes shut. The *pocket* flew out of my grip and clattered to the floor as I flung out my hands to keep from falling on my face.

"You are too good at this game, young one. Perhaps another tactic...." Ka said.

Bas suddenly shrieked in cold fear. My eyes bolted open and to my horror I saw Bas caught in an unnatural position, arched stiffly backward and eyes locked with Ka's in the obvious grip of mind-probe. Bas's face broke into a twisted knot of pain and terror. His eyes bulged as shivering spasms swept across his face like a tidal wave crashing on a shore. Then his mouth snapped open and he screamed. I couldn't bear it.

"NO!" I scrambled to my feet and begged, "Please, Ka! Leave him alone. Take me. Take ME!"

Ka raised his great raptor wings and began to sing, an eerie piercing demon's song.

"All right!" I sobbed. "I'll give it to you! The MEC design! Please, please stop!"

Ka stopped singing and shifted his gaze. Bas grunted with the release and stumbled on his feet. He cried out, "No, Rhea! Don't give him the—"

Ka cut him off with a look of rage. Bas's face seized up again with a shriek. I had to avert my eyes from Bas's terrified open throated scream.

"STOP! I'll do it," I cried. "I'll give you the MEC design. But you have to let him go. NOW!"

Ka let a ruthless smile of victory slide across his raptor's face and finally looked away from Bas, who instantly crumpled to the floor. This time he remained there, twitching and emitting strange sobbing whimpers.

"Compassion for one who is your enemy, a traitor who betrayed you." Ka leered. "Where did you learn that, Rhea?"

"Not from you," I snarled.

"Give the design to me now," he responded gruffly. "Through the mind probe. That way I'll know you are telling the truth."

I swallowed down my terror and eyed Bas's convulsing body on the floor. Ka began his beautiful dirge. I took in a deep breath and straightened to face him. I remembered what my grandmother said to me: *There is no victory in resistance; only in yielding without surrender.* I looked directly into my grandfather's liquid amber pools and instantly felt gripped by a numbing force that made me seize in a breath. As his trilling song rang through my ears, I felt the probe cut sharply like a groping knife through my still resisting mind...razor fingers tearing through synapse, prying open memories and scattering them like shattered mirrors...my body trembled as I felt the searing flush of hot coals swelling in my eyes...I smelled the cloy of blood ringing through my ears...listened in tortured raptness to the black sound of infinite bleak desolation—

Then he released me by looking away and ceased his chant. The pungent odour of *rapture* and dirt spiked as if my brain suddenly awoke from a coma. I collapsed, sobbing out my breaths and wanting desperately to weep. I clenched my teeth and felt my face tighten, refusing to give in to sobs.

Ka folded his long feathered arms over his distended chest and looked very satisfied, like he'd just feasted on a great meal. He had. My mind. My secret. Now his. "Most interesting," he purred. "You are indeed talented, young one. A most innovative design. And a strong-willed mind, clutching your secret to the end."

I rose shakily to my feet, hands covering my mouth in horror. What had I done? God, what had I done!

"What have you done?" Ka appeared to read my thoughts. "You've redeemed yourself by giving me the design for your MEC. It will wonderfully compensate for you foiling our earlier plan to release a DNA-specific plague on humanity." He laughed suddenly at my confused expression. "Oh, didn't you know what you'd done when you killed U'clid with your eyes? He was our plague master."

I dropped my gaze and glimpsed Bas, still lying on the floor, twitching like a short-circuited machine. Blank eyes wide, he gargled out gibberish and sporadically flailed his limbs as if under an epileptic seizure.

"What have you done to him?"

"I said it would not kill," Ka said casually. "But there is nothing left of his lucid mind, I'm afraid—"

I threw myself at him.

Ka aimed his eyes on me, about to sing. A furious energy boiled up inside me and up into my eyes. Snarling with rage, I aimed full on Ka and met his gripping mind-probing stare with searing flame. He jerked aside, eyes wide with alarm, and I only singed a wing. But he'd dropped my MEC and fled. I dove for the MEC, landing in a role, and shot at Ka's fleeing figure. I missed. He disappeared through a side door.

I picked up my *pocket* then holstered the MEC and bent over Bas. "Come on, Bas! We've got to get out now before he returns with reinforcements. Bas! COME ON!"

He looked at me with glazed eyes. At least he'd stopped convulsing. There was only the remnant of it in the occasional twitch and peeping sound he made.

"Get up!" I commanded and pulled him ruthlessly to his feet. He accommodated like an automaton and I dragged him to the freight door. I opened it with a press of my hand on the exit button. The door lumbered open and I forced Bas into a sprint out of the dark storage room. As we crossed into the large hanger, the emergency klaxon shrilled and I saw men pouring in from the far side. I gruffly pushed Bas against the wall into relative safety. I charged in a dark rage. Screaming like a wild animal, I swept the weapon in a tidal wave of devastation, catching them before any of them had a chance to draw their weapons. They dropped in a mass of torn flesh and gore. Eclipse shape-shifters in the form of Eosians. I scanned for more obstacles.

Seeing none, I retrieved Bas and pulled him toward our ship. Once inside the *twin-V*, I shoved Bas past Raekwon's dead body then left him standing like a zombie in the aft hall and pounded to the large control centre and to the piloting controls. Within moments I'd started the *twin-V's* engines and swung it out of the *shadow* freighter. No one pursued us as we sailed to the far side of the planet where Benny circled.

I docked and once Bas and I were aboard, I released the *twin-V*, thinking of Raekwon's corpse inside. Then I ruthlessly forced myself back to the urgent need to get as far away as fast as possible and pelted bow-ward toward my small cockpit, pushing Bas ahead of me. I said sharply, "Prepare to get us out of here, Benny!"

I gruffly shoved Bas into the co-pilot's chair where he remained, staring vacantly into dark space, and took the pilot's seat beside him. A few well-placed moves took us out of orbit and toward the bleakness of open space.

Glancing from Bas to the vast darkness of space ahead of me, I wondered how we'd managed to escape so easily. Then I had an ugly thought that made me feel slightly ill: did Ka have something more in mind for me? Hadn't I provided him with enough? "God, forgive me. What have I done?" I murmured, glancing at Bas's vacant face, then brought my hands up to my face.

Benny startled me out of my gruesome ruminations: "Where to Rhea?"

I looked up and glanced again at Bas, still slouched where I'd pushed him into the seat. He was drooling. "Benny, we have to get him to a Med Facility fast. I think his body is in severe shock from being mind-probed. We can't let him die. Especially not after what I did to save him."

"I'm afraid that the the only Med-Facility sophisticated enough and capable of handling this kind of neurological problem is the one in Phoenix City," Benny informed me.

"Terrific." Where my mother lived. And where a few hundred Guardians lived too. I pulled out several wads of soyka gum from my black trouser pocket and stuffed them into my mouth.

"The Gleise-12 Guardian Precinct is located there. It's the one you were slated to go to when they first caught you on Horus."

I chewed slowly, inhaling the soothing soyka fumes, and muttered, "Perfect. Wouldn't they love to catch me again."

"They would, Rhea, but *you* wouldn't like it much."

"Agreed. We'll have to avoid them, Benny, along with the PD," I said, raking back the hair from my face with my fingers.

"This gives you a chance to visit your mother," Benny said, obviously trying to cheer me up.

"Sure, I can just drop in for an impromptu lunch," I said with a sneer. "Three visits in two months…she'd have a heart attack, and I'd throw up again." It was too dangerous to both my mother and I. "But you're right, Benny," I said with a sad glance at my sick friend, slumped in the co-pilot seat next to me. "We do have to go to Phoenix City. I'll have to risk it. Take us there."

SIX

Benny acquired permission to fly through the particle shield and within a few hours of waiting in orbit I landed us in Phoenix City's Spaceport.

Posing as Jane Raptor, complete with an embedded IDR thanks to Ennos, I took Bas's hand and led him out of the spaceport into the familiar permanent sunset of Phoenix City.

To my dismay, Bas had taken to placidly following me around—even to the bathroom. Just like a puppy. He followed every command I gave him without hesitation and never left my side. He even slept on the floor beside me at night. Benny had suggested that this was actually a good sign, because it meant that Bas had at least retained sufficient cognitive capabilities to distinguish and respond to my commands. I didn't like the idea that he'd somehow imprinted on me and listened only to me. Benny's voice had no affect on him.

I felt the warm breeze on my face and breathed in the rather pleasant mesquite aroma that permeated the volcanic planet. I was dressed in civilian flight clothes, charcoal pants and jacket and light grey short-sleeved top. Benny and I had agreed that my Great Coat would only draw unnecessary attention and likely prompt questions that would lead to my capture. I would have preferred to keep the coat, which provided me with additional protection, a hidden reserve of weapons and cover for my holstered MEC. But Benny had argued me out of it and I'd conceded to his logic. I'd compromised by still taking my MEC, but hiding it in the backpack slung over my shoulder. I kept my *pocket* handy, tucked under the waistband of my trousers beneath my jacket at the small of my back.

Turning to Bas, I pushed a smile and wiped his drooling mouth with a cloth from my pocket. Then I smoothed out his hair and tugged his shirt cuff straight like he was a little boy, even though he towered more than a head over me. "I'm taking you to the Med Facility, Bas. Where they'll fix you up," I said in a motherly voice then added quietly to myself, "They better or I've done a very very bad thing…."

He turned to me and mumbled. I ignored his gibberish. But this time he looked straight at me with focused eyes and struggled with his sounds, forcing me to listen.

"B-b-bad trrrrrade…eeuorrrrr…mmmec…fo…mee…."

I stared, dumbfounded. Had he said what I thought he did? *Bad trade…your MEC for me.* "Oh, Bas…I had to," I choked out. Then he was gone, the glimmer in his eyes vanished. I whispered out the rest, "It's what friends do." Then I gruffly tugged his hand. "Come on."

We reached the Med-Facility without encountering any PD or Galactic Guardians and I led Bas to Emergency. I almost stopped mid-stride when I saw the male Rill nurse at reception. His bulging head, protruding worm-like eyes and fleshy thick lips drew out an involuntary expression of revulsion from me.

I'd heard of several Rills making it off Omicron 12 and it only took two Rills to make a population, I thought scathingly. Rills were extremely prolific. I recalled what the Head Legess had told me over a year ago before I mistakenly exterminated most of their Rills: "Rills are an undisciplined and vulgar race who, if they are not kept busy mining for us, are copulating for themselves. They are animals who must be managed by a good husbandry program."

I had read that Rills made excellent healing tank diagnosticians because of their amphibious physiology and intuitive ability to discern ailments and apply treatments. Their deliberate, thoughtful and methodical outlook to problem-solving made them less likely to suggest careless prescriptions. They weren't all subversives. But somehow I couldn't bide them. They had a silly way of speaking and gave me the impression of being stupid. Despite their extreme cleanliness, they always stank like the bogs they came from on account of their particular metabolism and outer skin. I'd heard a ridiculous story that something in the odour they released acted as a sexual phermone and it didn't help that the genitals of both males and females were inordinately large. But, perhaps there was something in it, given their apparent obsession with fornication.

I found this Rill repulsive. Not quite as tall as a human, which was considered small in the galaxy, the Rill made up for what he lacked in height with ample girth. A wet sheath of glistening skin, that sloughed off daily, stretched over the Rill's rounded body. His nose was basically a big hole in his bulbous face that was covered in 'spider webs' that apparently gave him a heightened sense of smell, almost as good as mine. Three wrinkled fleshy tubes that housed lenses resembling worm-like parasites served as his eyes. For all I knew perhaps that was what they were: parasites. The Rill possessed two very different arms. His right arm was particularly large and clawed and resembled a weapon. It was tailored no doubt for digging in the bogs of Omicron 12. It had been my undoing, that weapon-like arm. He was using it now to scratch gill-like frills that dangled on either side of his thick neck.

I knew I needed to put my ugly thoughts aside and pulled Bas, drooling, to the reception desk with a forced smile at the Rill. I wasn't sure which 'eyes' to focus on. The Rill responded by raising his right arm with its uniquely huge appendage in supplicating greeting. I couldn't help an instinctive flex of my hand for a sidearm I didn't have. It was my ignorance of the Rill's gesture that had cost seventy-seven Rills their lives.

I shook off the thought and said brusquely, "This man needs immediate medical attention." I realized with an inward flinch that it had come out like a gruff command. I didn't want to intimidate or annoy this Rill. "He's been mind-probed against his will by a Khonsus," I hastily explained, hoping for compassion.

The Rill studied Bas with a face of slight revulsion. He obviously knew what that meant. "There's nots much anyones cans dos when that happens," he gargled through three fleshy puffy flaps for a mouth.

"I was told you were one of the best facilities for this sort of thing," I insisted. His pessimism wasn't encouraging.

The Rill nodded, responding to my obvious look of desperation. "Let's gets him ins and haves a doctor looks at him," he suggested. "I'lls needs some particulars. His names and yours. And a scans of your IDR."

"Mine?"

Bas's hand, which clutched mine, was sweating. Or was it my hand sweating?

"Yous wants to visits him, don'ts yous?"

"Oh, yes." I hesitated, trying to quell the panicked thought of them finding out who I was and punishing Bas on account of me. "His name is Basileus," I said, manoevering Bas's arm over the Rill's scanner. "He's a Guardian Enforcer with the Iota Hor

Precinct. I'm…eh…Jane Raptor, a friend," I ended with a hesitant wave of my arm over the scanner.

The Rill entered the information and motioned with his webbed hand for me to take Bas and sit in the waiting room. I acquiesced, feeling my breaths grow shallow. It wasn't safe for me to stay. But I needed to ensure that Bas was going to be in good hands.

Within moments, a female Rill with huge dangling breasts resembling sea cucumbers entered from a far door and motioned for me to come with Bas. When we reached the door, two very young Eosians emerged. They looked like Med security or PD and they were eyeing me suspiciously.

"Go ahead with him," one of the Eosians told the Rill and pointed to Bas. He then turned to me. "You must come with us for additional questioning." I felt a surge of alarm and knew something wasn't right. "Don't worry, Ms Raptor, your friend will be fine. You can visit him later. We just need to do some more holo work on the situation with the Khonsus."

That was a logical request. Then why did I feel the hair on the back of my neck rise? I nodded and reluctantly let go of Bas's hand. Bas grabbed my hand again.

"No, Bas," I said forcefully. He looked lost and betrayed — no, I'd imagined that, surely, out of my own guilt. His mind was gone. "Go with that Rill, Bas," I commanded, prying his hand off mine. I looked into his blank eyes. "Do as the Rill says. You want to get better, don't you? I'll come see you later." That seemed to pacify him and he finally let the Rill, who'd been tugging his other hand the whole time, lead him away. I watched him shuffle down the hall, feeling an oppressive dark foreboding. If I'd known then that I would never see him again, I'm not sure I could have let him go so easily. But I didn't, and off he went.

I turned to the guards flanking me and followed them down another hall. We entered a small room where two more Eosians sat in chairs arranged in a circle. A single chair sat in the centre, facing the others. Mine, no doubt. This wasn't going to be a questioning; more like an interrogation.

"Have a seat," the taller one offered curtly.

I pulled off my backpack and sat down, covertly opening it and sliding my hand inside until I felt the comforting coolness of my MEC.

"I'll get right to the point, Ms Raptor," the tall one said, sitting next to his colleagues. "We're with Med-Facility Security. Our senior officer is Demetrios," he pointed to the smaller Eosian seated to the far right, who nodded respectfully to me when I glanced at him. He was the youngest one there, not much more than a teenager. They were all young and they looked nervous.

"Our records show that you're wanted for questioning regarding a disturbance in Virgil City...an explosion that killed a Ngu named Shlsh Shle She," Demetrios said.

Great. They were going to pin that on me too. It was only a question of time before they connected my alias with Rhea Hawke, ex-Enforcer, murderer and subversive, wanted by the Galactic Guardians—dead or alive.

"I don't know anything about an explosion," I stalled, slowly checking the MEC setting by feel with a clammy hand as I assessed the situation: four large Eosians armed with side-arms barred the only exit. But they were no match for my MEC. "I was there on holiday for a short while."

Demetrios tilted his head and placed a finger to his ear in concentration. He suddenly paled and his eyes flickered to me. Not a good sign. When he refocused on me, I knew what he was going to say: "I'm afraid you're lying. I've just had a message from the local PD to detain you, *Rhea Hawke*, for the murder of Rashomon and Shlsh Shle She." The other officers looked in sudden alarm from the senior officer to me. "You must remain here until the PD arrive," Demetrios said in a shaky voice and jerked to his feet, grabbing for his sidearm. So did the remaining officers.

So did I. At Demetrios's first move I'd already flung off the backpack, exposing my MEC, and knocked the chair in a backward ricochet as I surged to my feet. Planting them wide, I swept my MEC in a two handed grip among the four of them before any of them had a weapon out. "I don't think so," I snarled, glaring at them with fierce challenge. "Hands away from your weapons! NOW!"

I wasn't prepared for their terrified reaction. All four of them—even Demetrios—cringed and flung out their hands for me to see. In his hysterical exuberance, one of the security officers tripped over his chair, knocking it back, and stumbled with a whimper. Did he think I was going to kill him?

What horrible thing had I become that these young men were so frightened of me? I studied each face in turn, taking in their wide-eyed terror.

I lowered the MEC and bent down to place it on the floor. Then I straightened and lifted my hands up, palms outward, in a motion of surrender. It was over. *There is no victory in resistance; only in yielding without surrender,* my grandmother had told me as I was about to drown in the Boiling Sea of Horus. But, there is a time for surrender too, I thought—

Two Eosians in Great Coats burst into the room and I gazed at the churlish faces of Borlias and Pentas, Galactic Guardian Enforcer and his side-kick mercenary.

I dove for my MEC but Borlias fired off a shot with his *pocket* pistol. It whizzed between me and the MEC. I jerked to a halt, knowing he had no qualms about where the next shot would go. I was wanted dead or alive.

The security officers stared in terrified silence as Borlias swaggered forward until he stood so close to me, I could smell his rank breath. He smiled like a wolf. "We've been looking all over the galaxy for you. And here you are, waiting for us in our backyard," he drawled in a mockingly soothing voice. Then he bared his teeth in a malicious grin. "You're going to wish you killed us, stinking human bitch."

He struck me, throwing me back. I staggered into Pentas, who met me with a low swing of his kappa rifle. It cut into my back like a MEC wave and knocked me forward, pitching me, half conscious against Borlias. My *pocket* gun clattered to the floor. Borlias gruffly pushed me off him and I collapsed to the floor and foundered on my hands and knees. I dropped my head in a daze of pain and felt sick as the world spun. The colours in the room splintered into a garish pointillist wash as I sucked in shallow breaths and tasted cloying salt in my mouth. Blood dripped from my split lip.

Too late, I thought, head swirling in remorse. Too late to save the world. Out of foolish trepidation, I'd rationalized the urgency of getting Bas here before making the difficult call to Ennos about the MEC. Now I'd lost my chance to warn him and prepare the Guardians. No other Guardian knew about the Vos infiltration because Ennos had kept my revelation about shape-shifters a secret. No one else would recognize what giving Ka the MEC design signified. These Guardians who'd captured me, certainly wouldn't believe me; chaos, they wouldn't even listen to me. I'd done the unspeakable and no one was going to know until it was too late.

"Look at me, bitch!" Borlias hauled me up by my hair, jolting me out of my daze. "Now you're going to Sekmet, where you'll learn to be humble," he drawled. Scalp burning, I met his eyes with an intensity that made him blink and let me go. I managed not to collapse.

"You have no idea what you've done," I said in a quiet voice. I ignored the blood dripping from my mouth and swallowed what pooled inside. The Vos would sweep the galaxy like a plague and wipe them all out with *my* technology.

"Shut up!" he blustered, waving a threatening hand. I didn't cower, which spooked him. He blinked several times and stuttered, "I know exactly what I've done. I'm sending you to Sekmet where you'll pay for your political subversion and all those murders you've committed."

"I've done much worse," I said. "I've killed us all...." Then I released an insane laugh of bitter irony. "Even Bas. I've killed him too as it turns out. I didn't save him after all."

I caught Borlias's agitated stare and gripped him with an icy glare. For once he looked genuinely frightened. Yes, that was the right reaction. Abject fear. *Keep it. You'll need it soon enough.*

SEVEN

I gazed out my porthole at the barren patchwork of the small wetland-dominated planet, whose surface resembled an early impressionist's painting. Dominated by sombre russet and indigo tones, the raised bog was dotted by a hasty spray of cobalt lakes and pools.

Although it was mid-morning on the planet, the mostly grey sky was saturated in low cloud and it was drizzling outside. Spates of wind drove sheets of rain hailing sporadically against my porthole. It was a wet desolate place. But then again, *"A drowning man is not troubled by rain*—Persian Proverb, Rhea," I said quietly to myself. The weather was the least of my concerns.

As the ship descended, I could make out the individual pool system of the blanket bog with its inhospitable tapestry of dark and wet shapes. I dispassionately reviewed what I knew of the planet. Its cool wet climate and rich iron deposits promoted the development of muskeg, string bogs, darkly forested swamps and wildflower-filled fens. This was Sekmet, a less than Earth sized planet that orbited the KO star, HD177830 in the constellation Vulpecula. My new home. Where I was going to die.

The past few days I had desperately tried to convince the Guardians of the consequences of my actions and the impending danger. But no one listened. The lawyer they'd appointed for me never came through with my mandatory call. He'd claimed that Ennos didn't want to speak to me; but I knew he'd never even made the call. I appeared in front of a tribunal of three judges within two days of my capture and was not permitted to speak. They'd all supposedly reviewed the evidence and summarily declared me guilty and worthy of Sekmet. I was on this AI ship within the hour.

I shook my head and with pursed lips resumed my detached review. I noted that Sekmet was quite flat but even its hills were blanketed in muskeg and fen and I saw patches of stunted forest and scrub in some areas. The dominant bog ecosystem I saw below strongly resembled Omicron 12's peatland with its associated wet and cold climate. Sekmet's ancient blanket bog had developed over 5,000 years as rain seeped down through the iron-rich soil and formed a thin impenetrable iron pan, which waterlogged the soil above. Lack of oxygen had prevented the bacteria and fungi from decomposing the dead plant material, forming peat. Brightly coloured exotic plants, able to draw their nutrients from the air or from other organisms around them, colonized the surface of pools, raised hummocks and tussocks in stiff competition. It was a ruthless plant-eat-plant world down there, I decided with sullen humour.

As the ship turned, I made out the actual penal colony with its dozens of grey tapered stacks billowing out white smoke. The facility resembled a huge factory, floating on a glistening wet mosaic of multi-textured and coloured vegetation. The facility, appropriately named Hades by its inmates, was in fact a huge peat mine that migrated across the huge blanket bog, extracting peat for sale to maintain the colony. I had already managed to get a fair bit of information from the ship, which appeared willing enough to share its database:

"Ship, who does Sekmet do its commerce with?"

"There are fifty-nine clients for Sekmet's unique peat products," the AI droned in a monotone. "Would you like all their names?"

"No, thanks. What's the peat used for?"

"Medicines, therapeutics, fuel, textiles, and filters mostly. Would you like the details?"

"No, thanks." I'd found it somewhat ironic that the colony was actually a profitable endeavour. It was probably the first time any of its inmates had given anything to society.

I let out a long exhale and leaned back in my chair, watching as we approached Hades. I reviewed the statistics I knew: Sekmet was a penal colony, not a correction centre. With the single exception of U'clid, who'd managed to leave on a technicality, no one ever left the place. Sekmet was reserved for the most treacherous and warped criminals: deviant soulless killers, cold assassins, insane murderers who felt no qualms in maiming, mutilating and torturing their victims. People I'd sent to jail; the ones I hadn't killed, that is.

I gulped in a convulsive breath and realized that I was already panicking. *Get a grip*, I told myself. *You're freaking out before you even get there*....I would have to use all my resources if I was going to live out my one to several months in my new home. I didn't give myself more. The life span of inmates on Sekmet was usually less than a year and I wasn't sure I was going to be all that tenacious. The Eosian Guardian who'd shoved me into this AI ship had offered his own prognosis with a sinister laugh: "You won't last a jagging week, human. They despise Enforcers. They'll eat you alive then excrete you as bog fertilizer!"

The ship had informed me earlier that Hades contained an inordinately high number of Rills as inmates. If any one alien race had the right to despise me, the Rill did. I'd single-handedly subverted their one and only attempt at obtaining freedom from a long life of oppression by the Legess. I decided that Sekmet was going to be my personalized purgatory.

"They will eat the fruit of their ways and be filled with the fruit of their schemes," I recited the lines from Proverbs in a quiet breath.

How had so many Rill gotten to Sekmet? I cynically concluded that they'd been condemned there, possibly undeservedly, by the administrators of Hades wishing to make a profit in addition to running a penal colony. The Rill were highly skilled peat miners. I had seen proof of that on Omicron 12, where the Legess had enslaved them to mine their bogs for generations. As a result of Hade's efficient inmate labor, Sekmet was out-competing Omicron 12 in the galactic peat trade market.

I suddenly felt the queasiness of swift deceleration as the ship banked hard for its final approach. There was no point in being nice about it, I thought darkly. I was its only passenger and not considered worthy of treating with decorum. Within moments the ship landed with a sharp jolt in the open landing bay of the floating colony. Then the exit hatch door opened and the AI droned, "This is your destination, Rhea Hawke. Please disembark."

My chest clenched. I swallowed down my fear and stepped out onto the platform of Sekmet's landing bay, catching the faint sulphurous smell of the bog. The doors of the ship abruptly closed behind me, making me involuntarily flinch. Annoyed at my reaction, I gathered my composure and swiftly assessed the empty platform, hearing only the hum of the ship's engine. My gaze rested on the endless hummocks and large meandering ponds of tea-stained water outside.

As the ship made ready to leave, I felt my heart pounding with the sudden urge to bolt. I had a panicked notion to leap off the platform into the murky bog. Swim, wade, scrabble to eventual safety in the wilderness of Sekmet in those distant hills. The ship lifted off the ground in a turmoil of dust and thunder. My face twisted with indecision as I tensed, poised to flee—

A male Azorian burst in from the adjoining chamber and I braced for an attack. He pelted right past me then leapt into the murky water. I watched him thrash through the undulating bog, stumbling, submerging and trying to swim—his left arm was amputated at the elbow. I was about to follow when laser shots peppered the water around him for several heartbeats. I flinched. As suddenly as the shots began, they ended and the Azorian slowly sank until only his head remained above the water. I stood stiff, trembling hands over my mouth, and breathing hard. I stared at the head bobbing slowly in the water.

With the ship departed, chaotic sounds drifted in from inside the colony. Faint echoes of shrill outcries, mad laughter and raucous groans filtered in with the light breeze. It sent a chill through me—

"The stupids ones stills thinks theys cans escapes thats ways," a nasal voice said behind me.

Startled, I spun around. When I saw the female Rill waddle toward me, huge arm—weapon—stretched out, I instinctively went for my MEC and caught air. My MEC was, of course, no longer holstered on my hip. That damned gesture and ominous paw got me every time, I thought and let the tension drain from my posture. I grimaced and murmured to myself, "Speak of the devil."

The Rill wore what I surmised were standard issue dull grey prison overalls that stretched taught over her ample form. The same kind of clothes the Azorian had worn. The Rill was obviously female. For their size, Rills had especially large genitals and related reproductive parts, including this one's massive mammary glands that hung like two fat sausages in plain view over her overalls to below her round belly. The Rill stopped a few meters from me and extended her three tube-eyes in a stare of cautious curiosity. Gill frills twitched on either side of her neck.

"They thinks the ship will hides them or something," the Rill went on, giving off a pungent odour, "but the AIs haves hundreds of armed surveillance cameras. No one's evers escaped that ways, not alives anyhow."

"I'll remember that," I said with a curt smile. I quelled the inclination to cover my nose with my hand.

"Evens if they could escapes the lasers, the kepries or sobeks woulds gets them soons enough," the Rill added.

I decided that I didn't want to know what a kepry or sobek was and, ignoring the Rill, brushed past her and cautiously made my way toward the entrance to Hades. As I neared the threshold, I recognized the two stone statues on either side of the doorway. The one on the right was of Anubis, the ancient Egyptian jackal god, who took part in judging a person's guilt. The statue on the left was of the lioness-headed Egyptian goddess, Sekmet, herself. I raised my eyes to a makeshift sign that had been erected above the open doorway. Words inscribed in a messy but clear scrawl read: *I am the way into eternal grief; abandon every hope, all you who enter.*

Recognizing Dante's lines, I felt my face tighten with reigned-in trepidation, and crossed the threshold into the spacious open lobby from which the Azorian and the Rill had emerged. I'd entered Hades. My home.

"Well, *Toto, I have a feeling we're not in Kansas anymore,*" I whispered to myself and fought off shivers.

The Rill shuffled behind me as I cast a wary gaze around at the radiating hallways then up to the vaulted skydome ceiling. Although I still heard the occasional distant wail or cackling, whatever had chased that Azorian to his death wasn't here. The huge lobby provided a hub for over a dozen hallways that radiated out like spokes of a wheel. Except for me and the smelly Rill the place was empty.

I turned to the Rill, who'd come beside me. She seemed harmless and I wondered what she'd done to merit being on Sekmet. Probably something subversive. "So, you're the welcome committee?" I quipped, wondering where all the inmates and those who ran the prison were. I recalled hearing that Hades was run by AI. Were there no biological facilitators? How did they manage the inmates? Or was it the lawless society I'd heard it was….Then I remembered that fleeing Azorian with a shiver.

"You'res a humans," the Rill said with a shake of her soft body, gills frilling out in excitement. The pungent smell of rotten eggs wafted off her and I tightened my face in revulsion. "Weez haven'ts hads a humans in a longs times." She circled me, inspecting me up and down. "Theys usually don't last very longs," she added matter-of-factly and without obvious malice. "Too weaks and unimaginatives."

My nose crinkled at the Rill's offensive odour and I pursed my lips, ready to deliver a rude remark. The Rill lunged forward and tugged at my charcoal grey flight jacket with her huge clawed paw. Her fleshy thick lips smiled. "Nices clothes."

I smacked the Rill's webbed hand and twitched away from her. "Don't touch me," I snarled.

"But theys won'ts lasts long here," the Rill added darkly, continuing to circle me, though more warily. "Yous best sells thems for a beds before someones rips thems offs yous themselves."

I was about to rebuke the Rill and send her on her way when a large Venik, bare-chested and dressed in ill-fitting lumi-pants, lumbered in from another hallway. The Rill stopped in her tracks like a hunted deer and focused on the reptilian-like

Venik with frightened eyes. Veniks were generally regarded as dumb brutes. It made them even more dangerous because they didn't operate with rationality. His massive scaled body resembled a Tyranosaurus with thick legs balanced by six razor poison-clawed arms, a predatory face of six mouths filled with razor sharp blue teeth and small indolent eyes. I straightened, bracing for confrontation, as the reptilian approached. I noticed the Rill cowering, trying to make herself small.

"So, *this* is our newest inmate," the Venik growled in chorus through his several mouths. "A puny ugly human!" He looked me up and down and dismissed me with prosaic eyes. "Too bad." Then he glanced over at the Rill with sudden interest. "What are you doing here, slave?"

"Sames as yous, Bondar," she answered in a timid voice that managed to convey defiance. "Checkings outs the new meats."

The Venik barked a coarse multi-timbral laugh and barrelled over to us. "There's no meat on that thing." He waved three arms at me dismissively. "But *you*...." He seized the Rill with his several arms. She cried out and he laughed churlishly, squeezing her long breasts. His sharp claws poked into them, drawing blood. "Always a thrill with a Rill!" he sung out in chorus and ripped off her overalls. "You need to learn some respect, slave. I'll teach you to call me Boss!" Within a heartbeat he'd opened a slot in his shiny pants, and pulled out an extremely long fleshy penis that curled out of his scaly body like a snake's tongue. He threw the Rill on the floor and franticly forced his gigantic body over her to her scabrous cries. No one, not even an annoying Rill, deserved that kind of abuse—not even on Sekmet.

Trembling with anger, I stepped closer. "What are you doing?"

"Scat, puny human!" he waved one hand and mauled the Rill with all his other hands as she shrieked. "This slave's mine. You can have her after me!"

"Let her go!"

"Jag off!" he growled out of one mouth while his others

were planted on the Rill's puffy lips between grunts of jerking. He hadn't bothered to look up.

I kicked him hard in his rump, almost knocking him over the Rill. It got his attention. "I said to let go of her," I snarled.

Furious at being interrupted, the Venik swiped at me with several arms in tandem, but I saw each move coming and deftly swerved. I found an opening and struck again, this time planting my boot forcefully into his side. It didn't hurt him but it knocked him off the Rill. In full combat stance, I flung myself at the slow Venik as he scrambled up in fury. I danced out a series of strategic kicks that finally ended with a lightening stab at his fleshy crotch, his most vulnerable place. The Venik fell with a thud to the ground, clutching his penis, now curled up like a coiled snake, and moaned.

After confirming that he was incapacitated for the moment, I hastily collected the Rill's overalls and kneeled beside her. "Can you move?" I asked in a soft voice of concern. "This is our exit call."

The Rill sat up and nodded, thankfully clutching her overalls. Then she looked past me in sudden alarm. I barely had time to turn when two other Veniks descended upon me, striking me several times in the face and head with open claws. I momentarily passed out then found myself lying on the floor, gazing up in a febrile Venik poison daze at Bondar's scowling reptilian face.

"You're too human for me," he said, still rubbing his crotch. "So jagging skinny and ugly. Sex with you would be like sucking blenoid poo. But those savoury clothes might sell for a few points."

He and his two thugs gruffly stripped me of my jacket, flight pants, and boots then stalked away. Their menacing laughter echoed down the hallway.

I closed my eyes and tried to breath deeply. I curled in a foetal position to stop the throbbing pain in my head and wrapped my arms around myself, willing my Scandi healing powers to wash me clean of the Venik poison. The last time a Venik had drawn blood, half my buttocks had been ripped open and I was in a fever for a week. I gingerly felt my head and decided I was lucky. I'd witnessed a suicide, an attempted rape and been beaten, all within the first five minutes of getting here. Welcome to Sekmet, I thought. Welcome home....

The Rill was beside me in a moment, stroking my blood-matted hair.

I jolted. I'd forgotten about the Rill.

"I'ms Mayling," the Rill offered as I sat up with effort.

"Rhea...." I hesitated. But the Rill was bound to find out who I was eventually. "Rhea Hawke." I braced for a negative response and almost flinched at the Rill's excitement.

"Yous that humans Galactic Enforcer. Theys saids ones was comings—"

"Ex-Enforcer," I corrected Mayling. Surely she knew that I had murdered so many of her people on Omicron 12 a year and a half ago; yet she hadn't shown any obvious affront. Only curiosity. Perhaps she'd been travelling for a long time, I surmised, and hadn't received the accurate story from anyone. It would explain why she was here, on Sekmet.

Suppressing a grunt, I rose slowly to my feet. My head slammed in objection. I glanced down at myself with an involuntary shiver. I looked very conspicuous and silly in my briefs, gray top and socks. They'd even taken my gravity boots. I turned to Mayling, now dressed, who was apparently thinking the same thing.

"Yous won't lasts long that ways. Comes with meez," Mayling urged, glancing from side to side as if afraid other thugs would come by. "I'll shows yous where yous can stays untils yous gets some points to buys overalls and a beds for yourselfs."

I nodded and gratefully followed the Rill, somehow not minding her smell any longer. Without my gravity boots, I felt the full force of the planet's gravitational field. Sekmet was considerably larger than Earth and I felt its heavy gravity pulling me relentlessly down. I glanced at Mayling. I didn't trust the Rill but Mayling was being very helpful for the moment. As we walked the whitewashed hallway, I pumped her for information,

"So, is Bondar the boss here?"

"Boss!" Mayling scoffed, slimy body shivering in disgust. "He just thinks he is. He's just a big jerk who likes to jags womens. He's one of the mevlani's henchmen."

"Can't you complain to the boss—eh, your mevlani?"

Mayling laughed, a slobbery kind of squeal that gushed out of her thick lips in a spray and made me recoil with disgust. "We're Rills," she scoffed and said no more. She didn't have to.

The fractal nature of history repeated itself, I considered wryly. The Rills seemed to attract abuse wherever they went; even their own planet of Omicron 12, which the more aggressive and galactic-commerce-minded Legess had supplanted with Guardian help—*my* help. Perhaps it was the Rill's God-given niche to fulfill. Perhaps they were born for slavery, genetically evolved for it. God, did I really believe that? I might have six months ago. But now, I didn't know what to believe anymore. Right and wrong had taken on many more shades of grey since I'd killed V'mer and met Serge. But, perhaps this explained Mayling's rather obsequious behaviour toward me.

"So, who's the boss—eh, mevlani—around here?" I asked.

"Always changes," Mayling said.

Like 'king of the hill' I thought with a nod. "I'll remember that." In a lawless society of criminal subversives, one could always expect to be subverted. Things were always in flux, always ready to explode. Being boss only made you a target, I thought.

"But for now our mevlani is Barbariccia," Mayling added.

I held back a tense inhale. The *dust* lord of Dark Sun. Perfect, I thought with new despondence. I might have to kill him after all, I thought.

EIGHT

The Rill led me through a maze of ultra-clean well-lit hallways. Eventually harsh shouts and sinister laughter filtered down the hall along with the cloying odour of body waste. I felt my steps falter. The Rill didn't seem to notice and continued her normal waddling pace and I forced myself to follow.

The hall spilled into another large hub-like lobby with soaring arches for ceiling. I seized in a stuttering breath, inhaling the pungent smells of excrement, sweat, body filth and peat. I barely took in the spacious room with halls spoking out of it, a central spiral stairway and several levels of metal catwalks that led to yet other radiating hallways above. My senses were too busy taking in its contents: inmates loitered or sprawled like opium addicts around five tall metallic cylinders, each with three bulbous tops that encircled the metal stairway at the centre of the chamber. Recumbent inmates lazily sucked on the ends of flexible hoses that emerged like multiple limbs from the cylinders. Other inmates stood by in rough animated conversation as they impatiently waited for a hose to come free. Two Badowins were shoving each other in argument while several others egged them on. At our entrance they all turned and stared at me with surly or amused expressions. All except the reclining inmates, who didn't bother to acknowledge us.

I kept close behind Mayling, eyes sharply assessing the diverse mix of aliens glaring at me. Mostly hairy gnarled Badowins, Fauches, Azorians, and even a few Eosians, all dressed in the same overalls as Mayling, only theirs hadn't been butchered into a low-cut like hers. My gaze flickered over each of their filthy faces, fearing I might recognize one of them.

A squarely-built Badowin woman, one of the quarrelling pair, cackled and pointed to me with amusement. "That's the human Enforcer that came today. Not much to look at."

I coloured and desperately wished for clothes. Amid the raunchy laughter, I heard a Fauche snigger, "I hear Bondar has her clothes for sale. Wonder if he got a Great Coat! That'd be a cash!"

Several others joined from the other hallways. More Veniks, Eosians, Azorians and aliens I hadn't ever encountered. I even saw some Rills. To my discomfort, the aliens closed in on us, shoving and murmuring insults.

An angry shout bit through the raucous, "Enforcer bitch!"

I felt my heart slam. I'd sent quite a few criminals to this place. The volatile mob jostled us as Mayling quickly maneovered me to one of the stairways.

"Hey! Puny creon! Gimme some flesh!" a wild-eyed Fauche lunged at me with a knife, his large ears flapping behind him. The crowd surged back to give him room. I twitched out of his reach then stood my ground. Planting my feet wide in a combat position, I threw my arms out, ready to strike. Where in chaos had he gotten a knife? Well, I wasn't going to go down without a fight. The crowd gave us some room and settled back with raucous hollers and hoots. They were expecting to be entertained and it was obvious to me what they expected the outcome to be.

"Screw her, Raimond!" someone shouted. "Jag the bitch!"

"Cut her into jagging pieces!"

"Cut out her tongue! I love tongues!"

"Oi, Hawkes!" Mayling shoved me up the centre stairway. "Go!" she urged and we fled up the stairs.

"Jagging Enforcer!" the Fauche railed, swiping out and missing with his knife. "Coward!"

To my panicked dismay he charged up the stairs after us and the mob followed, hungry for blood. If only I had my MEC, I thought, glancing back with disdain.

"Hey!" Mayling called down and dropped something.

The crowd scrambled for whatever it was, momentarily forgetting about me. They fell into a mad frenzy, shouting and fighting among themselves. Even the Fauche forgot his chase and returned to the floor. The mob erupted into a violent brawl.

Mayling panted up seven levels and urged me down a narrow hallway away from the frantic mob. Once we'd turned several corners and were out of hearing range, Mayling turned to me with a dark frown.

"Yous needs to picks your fights betters or yous aren'ts goings to makes it," she said with unexpected wisdom. It made me blink and stare at her.

"What was it you dropped back there that got them so

excited?" I asked, coming beside her as Mayling resumed her walk.

"Just the gateways to the gods," Mayling responded enigmatically. "Yous'll finds out soons enough I expect."

Mayling took me down several long whitewashed hallways and finally stopped near the end of one, beside a small door.

"My place," the Rill said, showing brown-stained rounded teeth in a grin.

"How do you find it in this rat's maze?" I asked, knowing I was lost.

"This tells me," Mayling pointed to the lit screen on the back of her hand. "It has a spatial tracking system specific to you." I had noticed it earlier. A tattoo of a snake eating its tail, the *ouroboros*, surrounded the rectangular screen. The *ouroboros* was some Gnostic thing about the cyclical nature of things, a single image with the entire actions of a life cycle: it beget, wed, impregnated, and slayed itself only to start all over again. The mythic *ouroboros* was a serpent of light that resided in the heavens. It was a symbol of resurrection and a harmony of opposites. I wasn't sure how it related to this hellish place though. I remembered that my grandmother had mentioned it as I fled from her. I had noticed the same implant and tattoo on most of the other inmates. It obviously served a similar purpose to the embedded IDRs of the outside world, I concluded.

The little door swung open with a wave of the Rill's slimy hand over the lit receptor on the wall beside it. The light spattered on inside, revealing a tiny cubicle no more than two and a half metres by a metre and two metres high. It was basically a cupboard with a cot, too small for even the round Rill. "Alls I cans affords," Mayling explained, following my barely disguised look of disgust.

Mayling reached below the cot and brought out a pair of rumpled battleship grey overalls.

"Heres, my others pairs," she handed them to me, and I gratefully put them on. The overalls were way too short and too wide, but they did the job of covering most of me. I glanced down at myself. The custom low-cut bib of Mayling's overall would have left my breasts exposed like the Rill's, except for my gray top, which the Venik had thankfully not taken. Watching me dress, Mayling commented with a frown, "We don't wear underwear here. No shirts. Only overalls."

I ignored the Rill. There was no way I was going to put on this clothing without my underwear. As for my shirt, I wasn't about to advertise my breasts to the world like Mayling.

"Someones usually steals the clothes off a newcomer," Mayling said, letting an amused smile tug her copious flaps for a mouth. I nodded with a smile of mock amusement as I found a ribbon-like piece of material among Maylings belongings and tied it around my slim waist to bring in the baggy overalls. "Sometimes theys can buys thems backs," Mayling added.

I pursed my lips and nodded again, wondering how I would manage that. I glanced down at my feet. Following my gaze, Mayling frowned.

"Sorry. I have no extras." She glanced down at her standard issue grey slippers.

"That's okay," I said. "You've been very kind already." Which raised the question: why was this Rill being so nice to me? I grew suspicious: a *nice* Sekmet inmate?

"Yous can sleeps heres with meez," Mayling said, as though she was adopting me.

I glanced, startled, from Mayling to the cubicle. There was barely room enough for the smelly Rill and I couldn't imagine being in the same confined space as her. I barked out a brisk humourless laugh then pressed my lips with a shake of my head. "I don't think so. Thanks anyway. I can sleep in the hall—"

"Hawkes, yous don't understands. At curfews AI cleaners sweeps the halls and anyones in thems is vaporized."

I swallowed. "Vaporized?"

"Yous needs to be inside a legal bedchamber."

I nodded then pointed to the tiny chamber. "How am I going to fit in there with you?"

"Yous can sleeps on tops of meez. I's don'ts minds." She grinned, tube-eyes dancing. "Yous cans gets your own places when yous earns points."

I glanced from the Rill to the bedchamber. Earning some points suddenly became a priority.

"How do I do that, earn points?"

'Ais...." Mayling clucked, letting her gaping nose flare. "Nots very hards. Just hards to gets lots. Yous must earns everythings here. All services excepts foods and waters. That's free."

And probably drugged, I concluded.

"Evens washrooms has to be earned. Through points."

"What do I have to do?"

"Works. The points adds up on your reads out," she pointed to her tattoo. "Then youz use thems just likes money."

"How do I get work?"

"The mevlani gives yous work."

"Show me. Now," I said a little more brusquely than I'd have liked. The Rill didn't seem to mind, though, I thought thankfully. They were used to taking orders.

"Sure." Mayling closed the room door and led me down the hallway back to the large chamber. I listened for any sign of the riot and thankfully heard nothing. As we entered the chamber, the repulsive smell of filthy bodies and excrement wafted up from below. I peered down from the upper level catwalk, noting with relief that the riot had dissipated. Except for a few inmates reclined by the cylinders, no living person remained. I felt my nose flare, noting a few casualties of the riot. Three dead bodies lay scattered in pools of darkening blood, reminding me of the incandescent and volatile nature of this colony.

For the first time I had a clear image of the five metal cylinders that rose, each swelling into three bulbous tanks to almost the height of where I stood. Small tubes in turn connected from the reservoirs up past me to the ceiling. Several dozen inmates lay like comatose invalids on the floor around the burnished cylinders, blissfully sucking with closed eyes on the tubes that extended from them.

Following my gaze down, Mayling explained, "Those are

our food and water dispensers. They don't cost anything."

I nodded. "Must taste good," I muttered, nose flaring with disgust. Each cylinder with its swollen bulbous reservoirs, resembled a three-headed cyber-beast, with flexible teets suckling its deformed young. It was hard to imagine eating in a place that stank of feces and urine. Despite that I started to feel hungry. Something didn't seem right. These were the only commodities that were free and, judging by the mellow euphoric state of these gluttons, the food had to be drugged.

"Where did everyone go?" I turned to Mayling, curious.

"Back to work. Or to the games," she said enigmatically.

"Games?" I repeated, hoping for elaboration.

Mayling pointed to the large communication holo suspended in the hall that listed half a dozen names and times. Not offering further explanation, she seized my hand and pulled me into one of the radiating halls, urging us on. "We must catch him before he goes to the games too." We hustled through yet another maze of halls. The Rill took me up a spiral stairway to the top of the building. We emerged into a spacious multi-level chamber, the largest on Sekmet I had been in so far, with a view of the towering stacks of the facility and a panorama of the colourful blanket bog beyond. Seen from this vantage point, with the sunrays slanting on it, the bog's brilliant purple and green patchwork blazed with unimaginable beauty. It provided an interesting contrast to this gloomy dark chamber whose aura made me strangely uncomfortable.

The upper and lower levels of the chamber were joined by catwalks and stairs. I rested my gaze on a hub that rose like an island in the centre of the huge room. Someone sat at a large console beneath an extravagant chandelier-like device that hung from the high ceiling. I recognized him instantly: Barbariccia.

He was breathtakingly beautiful and I couldn't help staring at him. He had the body and the face of a Greek god. a straight nose with jaw and chin chiselled in soft but masculine lines paid homage to a sensuous mouth, held in a lofty though simpering smile. The fact that he was hairless only emphasized his perfect features. Hooded intensely deep eyes languidly turned to regard me with haughty curiosity. He fingered his suit with slender hands. I noticed very long nails on his fingers.

His lecherous eyes flamed into mine and he licked his lips as if he'd just finished a delicious meal. I stifled a sharp intake of air. I understood; I was the first human female to enter Sekmet in decades and his blood ran hot with my scent. Barbariccia knowingly radiated the personification of perfection, dressed impeccably in an expensive sentient suit, the kind that looked so good on Serge. Barbariccia looked like a respectable businessman but I knew better. No one here was respectable.

Mayling leaned close to me and whispered, "That's Barbariccia. He ran the Dark Sun crime syndicate until Eclipse shut him down." Yes, I knew. Luckily I wasn't the officer in charge who'd sent him here. According to some people he was still running Dark Sun and still dispensing *glitter*. "He's the one you have to ask for a job," Mayling added. She led me to the catwalk approach to the hub then stopped shy of the catwalk. I followed her lead of bowing obsequiously with downcast eyes; except I kept my eyes focused on the Eosian—

Then hiked in a sharp inhale as I abruptly saw a vision of myself, sitting there instead of Barbariccia. I saw myself gaze back at me like a witch possessed. I looked sullenly evil. Eyes glowing like emeralds in an alien light. Tangles of wildly cropped hair framed my pale face with thrashing darkness—

"Mevlani," Mayling stammered. I jolted out of my horrific dream. "This is—"

Barbariccia cut her off with a gesture. "I know who she is, slave." Then with a dismissive wave of his hand, his face twisted into a snarl. "Get out of my sight! Leave us."

Mayling fled. I fidgeted nervously at her departure and had to fight to maintain my composure.

"I see you've found some clothes…." Barbariccia said with the touch of a sneer. He crossed his long legs. "…If not some manners." I quickly understood that I was meant to lower my gaze as Mayling had instructed me earlier; I'd forgotten in my awe-struck curiosity. Barbariccia's heavy-lidded eyes—were they blue or violet?—flickered unsteadily over me, hungry with cruel desire.

"Come here," he commanded.

I tensed. Forcing myself humble, I approached him on the catwalk, feeling the metal grids bite through my socks into the soles of my feet. I stopped a few metres from him, resting expressionless, downcast eyes on the *dust* lord. Barbariccia rose from his chair and towered over me like a purple vulture. Arms of corded muscle strained against the sentient fabric of his suit. He was very fit and large, I considered with a swallow. His condescending gaze traveled up and down my body in critical appraisal as I cast my eyes, in turn, from the large bulge of his swollen crotch to meet his indolent gaze.

He fixed cruel eyes on mine and I felt my heart beat in excited terror. "There's only one thing worse than an Enforcer," he drawled, voice swelling in a dark mixture of desire and hatred. "And that's an ex-Enforcer." He turned to his console and touched a button.

Abruptly a holo of large blood-red letters appeared in the air above us. I realized that it summarized my charges: the theft of Guardian property; the murder of the spiritual leader, Rashomon, then the information trader, Shlsh Shl She, assaulting a fellow officer and the unwarranted damage of property and vehicles, and so on. Neither my lawyer nor the so-called court had openly reviewed my charges before sentencing me to Sekmet. To my dismay the list included a charge I hadn't expected.

Barbariccia decided to pick that one too: "You even betrayed a fellow officer by luring him to a Khonsus, with Eclipse, who mind-raped him; then you brought the demented Eosian to the Gleise 12 Med-Facility to gloat. So that's how you treat your colleagues, particularly Eosian ones, ex-Officer Hawke...."

I worked my mouth in angry frustration, glaring at Barbariccia in silence. I didn't have to answer to this criminal, a man who's organization had hurt, tortured and killed more people than I could count. But, despite the one false accusation, I had to concede that I probably belonged here just the same for my many other sins. I set aside my anger and decided to get to the business at hand.

"I'd like a job."

He gave me a sinister smile. "I don't think you'll last here that long."

Was that a prediction or an edict? "I'd still like one," I coolly insisted.

"Very well," he responded curtly. He tapped another button on his console with a long manicured finger. "Come here."

I hesitated only a moment before stepping forward. As I did, part of the hanging devise above us dropped a long flexible pipe that resembled those hoses attached to the nutrition cylinders. Once lowered, Barbariccia took the end piece in his hand. Was he going to offer me some special food or force me to take some drug?

"Grab that post with your right hand," he commanded, pointing to a waist-high post beside him that thrust up from the floor and swelled into a ball at the top. It had no obvious purpose. Blinking rapidly, I placed my hand over the cool metal ball. Instantly, Barbariccia stabbed my hand with the device. I flinched, and bit back a cry, fighting the urge to recoil. Tears sprang, unbidden, to my eyes and I ruthlessly blinked them away. I tasted blood in my mouth; I'd bitten my tongue. He watched me, eyes cruelly laughing, and lips pulled back in a predator's open smile.

"You *are* an Enforcer," he said with sardonic pleasure. His indolent eyes flashed dark and I noticed his crotch stirring as he licked his pursing lips.

Forcing in controlled breaths through a grimace of pain, I watched as Barbariccia slowly removed the device that had embedded itself on the back of my hand. I removed my hand from the post, madly hoping he didn't notice it shaking, and inspected the bloody imprint of an *ouroboros* the device had left. Inside it a lit screen, smudged with my blood, was stitched into my hand. It read "2".

"It's your tracking tattoo," he explained. "You get 2 points gratis to begin. The rest is up to you, whether you are productive…and live."

He turned and punched several buttons on his console. "Now, let's see…where can we put you where you won't betray a fellow colleague…There's always room for another level five miner. Report to Iris, in Room 10 on the second level, west side. She'll assign you work, human." He'd spit out the last word with particular contempt as he handed me a card. "Give that to Iris. She'll use it to enter you in the databank to start the point-tracking."

"Thank you," I said, taking the card.

He didn't let go and I had to look up to his coldly beautiful face. His icy gaze bit into me with challenge. I stiffened with anticipation. It was obvious that he despised humans and Enforcers. And me particularly.

"When you were an Enforcer you self-righteously and viciously dispensed your version of law and order," he said in a voice of open contempt. "Death was your calling card and your answer for everything. Over a standard galactic year ago, on Omicron 12, you went way beyond your mandate with the Legess and intruded on a revolutionary meeting of key insurgents. You crushed a whole race with ruthless precision, killing seventy-seven unarmed Rills with that menacing weapon of yours."

I bit back a retort and felt saliva collect in my mouth. I'd convinced myself that they were armed, but they weren't. It was a lot easier to justify why I kept shooting even after I realized that my MEC was spitting out fatal waves rather than debilitating ones. My tormented mind had repeatedly gone over that lurid scene, trying to sort out what had triggered my tragic blunder of insanity. I couldn't help my panicked reflex of misguided self-defence; it was the rationale that I'd fed myself later that shamed me now. They were only Rills, I'd thought. Only Rills….I had wondered briefly at the time why Ennos hadn't sent me to Sekmet for my overly ambitious deed. The non-native Legess were clearly the aggressors, enslaving the obsequious Rill, and for decades had exploited their labour for keen profit…with the full support of the Guardians—perhaps the real reason I hadn't been sent to Sekmet for my act of treachery. Although it looked bad, I'd done exactly what both the Legess and the Guardians quietly wanted: I'd crushed their revolution.

"And your hatred for Eosians is becoming legendary," Barbariccia went on. "Before you betrayed your Eosian Guardian to the Khonsus, you killed another fellow Eosian officer on 215.01 SGT." He meant Asphalios. How in chaos did he know that? "And before that at 214.72 SGT on Psi-9," he went on, "you burst into the men's washroom of a drinking facility and shot and killed an unarmed Eosian with his pants down," he bit out, lips pulled back in a wolf-snarl. I swallowed hard. A brother? I wasn't proud of that one either. The Eosian's weapon lay on the floor beside him in plain view as I aimed and shot without hesitation. "You had your own rules of what was right and wrong back then," Barbariccia continued. "And who should live and die by your hand. Well, you're in *my* world now, human, with *my* rules," he bit out with narrowed eyes. They glowed like amethyst in an eerie light. "Don't get in my way. Or I'll squash you like a bug." Then he let go of the card with a snap and added with a lecherous sneer and barely perceptible nudge of his pelvis, "But not before I've had my full pleasure of you…."

NINE

Iris turned out to be a crabby old Rill, who ran the primary mining operation of Sekmet and Room 10 on the second level was the anti-chamber to the lower basement of the mine milling complex, a dingy poorly lit room covered in questionable brown slime and reeking of bog. I slipped a few times in my soaked filthy socks but quickly recovered my balance each time as I made my way down the slimy stairs into the darkness.

Smelling particularly strong of methane and peat, Iris snatched my card with a glower and processed it. She mumbled something about lazy skinny humans. She wasn't chatty or pleasant like Mayling, but I decided it didn't matter, so long as the surly Rill gave me work points. The work she assigned me was hard labour meant for a Rill, based on their amphibious physiology, very strong webbed hands and high tolerance for constant wetness and pungent bog smells. My heightened olfactory senses were going to do me in, I thought glumly.

"You need to grab the cubes of peat that come up that conveyor belt and pack them into these drying pressure containers then move them over to the curing ovens there," Iris said brusquely, pointing to the various machinery. She stopped to eye me with three eye-tubes in open contempt. "There's no human laziness on my watch, *skinny*," she hurled out the last word as invective. "And I'll make sure you work your share." It was plain to me that she hated me. I cringed at the notion of why and I strongly suspected that Iris knew what I had done to her people.

I valiantly pushed myself to do my best for the old Rill. It never seemed enough for Iris, who hounded me to work faster and carry more. I laboured for hours without taking a break and found my sore peat-stained hands eventually pucker and swell from the peat chemicals and bog water. The hand that had received the tattoo smarted particularly and became inflamed to my dismay.

Rills, all female, came and went, sullenly operating the machines and removing the dried peat blocks in carts to another part of the mine. I tried to acquaint myself with them even though they rebuffed me. I persisted, paying particular attention to how each individual Rill was unique—something I'd never noticed before—and made a point of learning their names. I discovered that each Rill was indeed distinct. Hyacinth was the smallest and quietest of the Rills and her bulging head was particularly glabrous. April was a slow lumbering Rill with a particularly large nose-hole, who liked to prattle. Orchid, almost as surly as Iris, was the largest and roundest of the Rills, with the longest breasts, almost to her knees. Her left hand, the one that wasn't clawed, lacked any appendages. I later noticed that most of the Rills lacked one or several fingers.

I kept an eye out for Mayling. She never appeared. When my assigned work shift was over in early evening, I gratefully left my workstation and waved my hand over the keypad like Iris had instructed. I noted on the lit screen of my hand that I'd earned 20 points. I now had 22 points and wondered how much that would buy me. When I inquired, the saturnine Rill curtly informed me that I needed to earn 20 more to get a place of my own and then keep up with 40 a day. Catching her surly hint of a smile at my disappointment, I deduced that it meant I needed to accomplish at least twice the work I'd done today on a daily basis just to maintain a place of my own. And that didn't include using the washroom, I thought as I inspected my cracked and swollen hands. Several fingers had begun to bleed at their joints and stung as if burned with acid. An angry red rash had formed around the tattoo. I caught Iris's malicious grin. I was going to have to toughen up real fast, I thought savagely.

Φ

When I emerged from the lower levels into the main chamber, squinty-eyed, exhausted with muscles aching, I coveted the burnished silver cylinders with sick longing. My belly ached with intense hunger and my lips were dry with thirst. I hadn't had anything all day. Despite the vile smell and secretions, I was going to have to eat or starve to death. "Okay, Cerberus, I'm all yours," I mumbled to one of the cylinders.

The sharpness of human waste and boggy sweat cut through the all too subtle fragrance of contentment given off by the two dozen inmates sprawled around the cylinders. None of them paid me any attention or seemed in the least bit bothered by the odour; they all had their eyes closed in a feeding trance, sucking languidly on the hoses. I curled up my nose and stepped over several bodies, looking for an outlet that wasn't occupied.

I gave one sad body a wide birth: an Azorian who'd obviously wet himself, his body curled, twitching and whimpering in a pool of his own urine. After stepping around him I abruptly retreated and nearly slipped and fell when I encountered two Eosians copulating. Both were still connected to the hoses, hungrily seizing in gasping inhales of pleasure between convulsive gulps of mash. I briskly turned then flinched again and backed away when I encountered another dazed inmate, a Badowin, who was shivering, writhing and moaning with his gnarled hairy hand dug deep and wriggling in the crotch hole of his overalls.

I glanced down at my pair of overalls and with a shudder noticed the easy-access buttoned flap over my crotch. I'd initially concluded that it was for the bathroom. God, they were all so pathetic, I thought, suddenly appalled. I backed away in disgust and bolted, then slid on something slick on the floor and fell on my rump with a startled grunt. I felt suddenly faint as a sharp hunger pang overwhelmed me. Feeling my repugnance subside, I relented and rose shakily to my feet, feeling the wetness on my socks and rump but not daring to investigate. If I didn't eat, I'd be worse off. I'd be dead.

I forced myself to step over bodies and eventually found a tube that was free. I stood for several moments, before taking it out of its slot and bringing the nozzle to my mouth with a long breath of hesitation. How many other mouths had touched it? After a hard swallow, I pressed my lips against the nozzle and lightly sucked. I was delightfully startled by the squirt of incredibly tasty thick mash in my mouth. It was sweet with a musky oily after taste, reminding me of mangos. Forgetting my surroundings, I gulped in the mash like an addict. I decided to sit down and was soon reclining like the others in the bliss of sensual gratification. My eyes closed and I was instantly transported to Benny. Piloting him through the brilliant blue cobwebs of a scintillating nebula—

I felt a tap on my shoulder and opened my eyes. It was Mayling. Happy to see my friend, I gave her a goofy grin, realizing that I was content for the first time since I came here and considered wryly that I hadn't thought that was possible on Sekmet. The Rill was frowning at me.

"You need to leave now," Mayling urged me in a

commanding voice.

"But I don't think I'm finished. Just a bit more," I insisted. I'd talked around the hose without removing it and resumed sucking, eyes fluttering shut again.

"No, you've had enough," the Rill scolded, gruffly pulling the hose out of my mouth. I watched the nozzle longingly as Mayling replaced it in its holder on the cylinder. "It's not good to keep eating," Mayling went on. "And it's getting close to curfew. We need to be out of the hallways by then."

I looked at the others. "What about *them*?" They looked like they weren't going anywhere too soon. Especially that copulating couple who were still actively engaged.

"They're lost," Mayling said sadly then insisted forcefully, "Come, Hawke."

I grudgingly assented and with a backward glance at the others, followed Mayling.

"What do you mean?" I asked Mayling once we were in the hallway leading to her bedchamber. "What do you mean they're lost?"

"They've given up, Hawke. They'll be there when the vaporizers come and take them."

I swallowed hard.

"Some of them have no place to go," Mayling went on. "They've lost their bedrooms because they stopped working. They end up spending the whole day there. Some wet their pants, or even have bowel movements, because they don't want to stop. They've lost the will to do anything else. The food is dangerous, Hawke. You must have it but you must not let it take over. It takes your dreams and nightmares and sets them on fire inside you."

I swallowed the saliva flooding my mouth and knew that the images of the copulating couple, dreaming Azorian and masturbating Badowin would haunt me....They were each committing suicide in their own way. It seemed impossible for anyone to last even a month here. Still, I considered, Mayling seemed to be doing not too badly.

As Mayling opened her bedchamber door with a swipe of

her hand over the sensor, I turned to her inquisitively. "Why are you here, Mayling?" The Rill didn't seem to belong with all these insane murderers. And why weren't her eyes dull like the others?

Mayling fixed all three eyes on me. "I blew up a peat mining factory, not too different from this one. On Omicron 12, where I'm from. I killed seventy-nine Legess and thirty of my own kind, unfortunately," she said. "It was the seventy-nine Legess that I was sent here for. They didn't care about the Rills. I started a movement against slavery. Until then we were abused by the Legess for generations. We were treated worse there than we are here. My action started the revolution, gave other Rills the courage to do the same and rise up against our oppression." She then fixed on me an intense stare with all three eye-tubes. "I'd do it again."

I stilled my breath and fought to keep my composure. I couldn't face Mayling's three eyes and dropped my gaze, pretending I was intent on adjusting my overalls. That explained why she didn't know what I had done. She'd been carted off to Omicron 12 before I had come to deliver the final blow to their movement. Had Iris not told her?

"Why are *you* here?" Mayling asked in turn.

I flicked my eyes at the Rill and looked away as quickly. "I betrayed a friend."

Φ

Utterly exhausted, I overcame my repugnance, stripped to my shirt, which was the only clothing not soaked with someone's urine, and climbed on top of the Rill's naked bulbous body. I had finally managed to accept the unsavoury feeling of her slimy wrinkled body under my naked flesh and was just dozing off, when she shuddered and gurgled out growling moans then let out a puff of sharp bog odour. When Mayling continued her moans and farts, I challenged her in a sharp voice, "Why don't you go to the bathroom if you have gas."

"It's not gas," Mayling admitted. "I'm pleasuring myself.

94

It relieves the tension. I can do you too—"

"NO!" I snapped back, now wide awake. "Thanks. I'm trying to sleep."

"Could have fooled me," Mayling grumbled. Within moments she was snoring loudly in deep sleep, her rotund body rising then descending with blubbering sighs. It was a long time before I fell asleep. My busy mind kept me awake with persistent thoughts of escape. Surely there was some way out that these criminals hadn't considered, something only an Enforcer could think of....Whatever it was, it eluded me that night. Out of sheer exhaustion I finally succumbed to a restless sleep, bobbing like a sailor on a rough sea.

...*I feel my heart pounding with the thrill of knowing I successfully infiltrated the secret meeting of Rill terrorists. Just as the Rill traitor informed me, the leaders of the dozen bog clans have gathered here, together under one roof, to discuss strategy and attempt amalgamation—just what the Legess feared and the one thing that has prevented the Rills from being successful so far in their insurrection. As I lurk in the back shadows of the large chamber, I make out the various clan leaders at the front, responding to each other in didactic tones, followed by enthusiastic moans and calls by the rest. I make a decision: they will never all be here in one place like this again. I must act NOW! Heart pumping, I surge out from the dark, MEC pointed in a two-handed grip and shout, "You're all under arrest for treason! Stay as you are!"*

One Rill moves, right arm aggressively swinging forward. With a weapon! I open fire—

I jolted awake with halting breaths in pitch darkness. For a panicked moment I didn't know where I was. Then I remembered. I was in Mayling's sleeping cupboard. I'd somehow slid down between Mayling and the wall and now found myself clutching the Rill's sloughed off skin as a blanket. I yelped in startled disgust and threw off the dead skin. Mayling grunted half-awake and stirred, squishing me against the wall until I could hardly breath. I felt suddenly ill and my breaths shattered into shallow stutters.

"I need to get out," I uttered my muffled words beneath

the pungent Rill. Then more urgently, "I need to get out, NOW!"

Mayling grunted then finally signalled the door open, flooding the room with artificial light from the hall. She then shifted, spilling me out onto the hallway floor. I hungrily gasped in the sweet air. After a moment, I scrambled onto all fours then pushed myself giddily to my feet.

"It's very earlys in the mornings stills," Mayling informed me with a loud yawn.

"Have the AIs gone through yet?"

Mayling checked the hallway. "Yes."

Covering a yawn, I thanked Mayling for the use of her bedchamber and bent down to fish under the cot for my clothes. I caught the reeking odour of strong ammonia and after a sniff of my socks and underwear, I concluded that they were the offending articles and decided not to put them on. Somehow, my overalls didn't smell and I suddenly realized that they were made of self-cleaning sentient material. My underwear and socks weren't. Leaving them on the hallway floor, I pulled on the baggy overalls, cinched them in at my slim waist with my makeshift belt, then with a stretch I took leave of Mayling and wandered down the hall as her door shut behind me. I couldn't believe I'd actually slept. Shivering from exhaustion, I wrapped my bare arms around myself for warmth and walked on. I could have used a cup of soyka right now, I thought. Or at least some soyka gum.

I decided to report for work early to get a head start on earning points; I knew that the mine extraction never stopped. I hoped to afford a room of my own by the end of the day despite being not that fast at the job Barbariccia had allotted me. He'd purposely given me a job less suited to a human and I understood that it would take me twice the effort and time to earn the same points I would earn in a job more suited to my abilities. Precisely what Barbariccia had intended. He'd probably had a good chuckle about putting me in with Iris and her Rills too.

I hesitated at the cylinders. The place was clean and didn't smell too bad. A few inmates were already enjoying Cerberus's bounty. I spotted a Fauche, two Badowins, a female Rill I didn't recognize and a Xhix, all lying blissfully on the clean floor and sucking on their hoses. Most of them, I noticed with dismay, had lost a finger or more. None of the inmates I'd seen last night were there now. This group didn't look too far-gone and the place smelled fresh compared to Mayling's bedchamber. No harm in a quick breakfast, I considered, thinking it might help quell my early-morning trembles. I settled by a hose next to a contented Rill and pulled it out to sip on the tasty mash. As soon as I tasted it, I desperately wanted more. It didn't seem to quench my thirst or satisfy my hunger. Within moments I didn't care and slid down in a slouch to enjoy my meal. My eyes flickered shut in soporific numbness and I forgot about work.

I was startled out of my contented stupor by the boisterous arrival of three Veniks. They'd entered the chamber like predators stalking gazelle at a watering hole. They settled on the young Rill to my right, tearing open her crotch flap and groping out their long curling phalluses in unison. The Rill screamed sporadically, shivering and farting, then gurgled out muffled moans as two Veniks pressed on either side of her, silencing her by crushing her mouth with theirs, and chortling and hissing out insults with their other mouths.

I recognized Bondar, their leader. After a long swig of the Rill's mash, he joined the dog pile. The Venik facing her hadn't disengaged, though; he continued to pump her as Bondar rolled out his curly phallus with a wet hiss then forced it deep into the Rill's mouth while the other two jerked into her, front and back.

Bondar abruptly turned and aimed a challenging stare at me. Defying me to interfere. I inhaled sharply and coughed out my mash. I'd already noticed that all three of the burly Veniks were armed with knives, and concluded that I was powerless to interfere. I turned away as Bondar barked out a sinister guffaw then panted out his lust as he jerked over the Rill, smothered under his reptilian belly. After emitting a delighted howl of release, he straightened, phallus curling like a snake's tongue neatly back into his lumi trousers. Then he kicked me in the side. Stiff with shame, I looked away. I noted that the other users chose to remain oblivious.

The Veniks lumbered off, laughing and shouting like drunkards. Cured of the intoxicating mash, I replaced the hose in its socket and bent over the Rill. "Are you okay?" I asked solicitously. "I can help you to a medic if you need one."

The Rill's tube eyes shook in all directions and she scrambled up, grabbed what was left of her overalls and fled. I pushed myself up slowly with a puzzled sigh. The Rill appeared more frightened of me than she had been of the Veniks. I shrugged then strode toward the lower levels to my workplace. On my way I spotted the women's washroom and, feeling my bladder full from a full breakfast intake, I entered after a wave of my hand over the monitor by the locked door. I'd pulled aside my crotch flap, thinking it a handy design, particularly now that I wasn't wearing underwear, and squatted over the toilet to relieve myself—

Φ

The door opened with a bang and I flinched. Barbariccia, followed by three Veniks, sauntered in. His startling eyes pierced into me with a look that filled me with terror. They were uncommonly bright and gleamed of malice. I suspected that he smuggled *glitter* in and partook regularly.

Barbariccia licked his lips with a mocking smile. "Where's the gun, slave?"

I hastily bent to pull up my flap but the Veniks lunged forward at the snap of Barbariccia's fingers. One kicked my legs out from under me, throwing me backward. My back and head collided painfully with the toilet. They seized my arms and legs gruffly, chuckling maliciously, as one rested his boot on my exposed neck, painfully choking me. Barbariccia came forward to peer down at me with a sneer. Breaths gasping, I flared my nose in a snarl and flashed him a defiant look—

The Venik's boot stomped my face and blinded me with pain. "No one looks directly at the Mevlani!" the Venik growled. "Specially not like *that*, bitch!"

Barbariccia pushed the Veniks aside to stand over me. They still held me down as his blurry image swam before me. I fought from shrinking back. I had no place to shrink back to; I was already slammed up against the toilet and lay spread-eagled on the floor, arms and legs pinned by the Venik brutes. My breaths came in a shallow pant but I managed a glare.

"I told you not to interfere," Barbariccia said in quiet contempt. The tip of his boot slid into my flap and roughly grazed my exposed crotch. "Leave the Rills alone. They're the slaves of the galaxy. *Our* slaves. To do with as we please."

He pressed down with all his weight and I sucked in the pain. "That's for rescuing that filthy Rill when you first came." Then he lifted his boot off me and squatted down, arms leaning on his knees.

"She has a name." I glared at him through a film of tears. "It's—"

He struck my face so hard my ears rang. "Not here!" My face burned. "They're all the same here. They're *Rills*. Slaves. Slaves don't have names...*slave*," he addressed me. I understood. I was one of them, less even. A slave's slave.

*There is no victory in resistance; only in yielding....*I thought it my personal irony that I was not permitted to do even one kindness in this place. It was not, it seemed, for redemption that I had come here...only for punishment. So be it. Let it begin....

Barbariccia stood up in icy calmness. He unzipped his expensive tocanai trousers, let them drop, and stepped out of them. His swollen phallus bounced up erect like an escaping inmate. Barbariccia laughed maliciously, looking from me down to himself, and stroked his large phallus lovingly. He was particularly well-endowed, even for an Eosian. "*This* is what you want, *tutsak*," he said almost tenderly. "This is what you've wanted since the day you first came to Hades. I saw it in your eyes, when you glanced down at my prize. I saw your mouth water with desire. And I almost took you then." He sneered with his own demented thoughts. "Every human female dreams of this." He stroked himself.

He was probably right. The Eosian cock was a human

female's fantasy. My mother ought to know; she'd tested enough of them. Barbariccia took his phallus in his right hand and pinned his eyes on me in ominous expectation.

"This could be for you now, *tutsak*...if you were a good girl...." After a few strokes his eyes darkened and grew heavy-lidded and his mouth went slack with arousal. "But you aren't a good girl...not yet," he drawled. "So, until then...." He threw a scowling glance at his henchmen. "Wipe the insolence off her face."

He snapped the fingers of his free hand and the Veniks pounced on me like dogs let loose. They eagerly pulled out their curly phalluses with grunting laughs. Sharp blue teeth flashed as they argued among themselves about where to position themselves on me. I watched their scabrous penises curl and uncurl in pulses of swelling excitement.

I panicked and tried to slither from under them. A reptilian paw struck me hard on the face with a sharp clap. I bit my tongue and blacked out for a moment. Blood pooled in my mouth. My ears rang and my vision returned in a blurry daze. My damaged eye had swollen shut. Luckily the Venik had kept his claws in; or my face would have been slashed to pieces.

They stripped off my clothes, gruffly pulling me this way and that, bound my hands behind me and forced me to kneel just as Bondar and his cronies had done to the Rill at the food cylinders. Then I was pressed between two hulking unwashed bodies in a strangling embrace of warm damp flesh and the cloying smell of lust and sweat. I shuddered out jagged sobs as they forced their snake-like phalluses into me.

There is no victory in resistance; only in yielding without surrender...How could my grandmother ever have advised me so? There was no victory in this. Only pitiful surrender. Barbariccia was right. This was why I'd come here; and braced for punishment.

...No, embraced it.

I glimpsed Barbariccia, eyes dark, laughing. He played with himself vigorously and blissfully watched the Veniks rape me. Then he ejaculated a wide arc of creamy semen that spilled onto my shoulder.

I clamped my eyes shut to the humiliation and pain. My heart beat like a drum. I was seized by the sema percussion that had stirred me on Horus; it beat through me and out of me with the rising chorus of the Venik's climaxes. Emptying me. They were tearing me apart from inside and I submitted completely to it...delirious with it...until there was no longer anything left of me...only blistering flame in a swirl of tumult and annihilation...a pure darkness that embraced my dissipating self in a million directions through a cacophony of discordance—it became my mother's gasping cry as she lay with her legs spread wide, giving birth—to me, I assumed—flesh and muscle tearing, blood flowing...my head protruding...

When the thugs had pushed themselves off, phalluses curling neatly back inside their pants, my mind returned. Unsupported, I wavered on my knees, facing the line of sinks swimming against the wall. The sinks reeled crazily in my vision as I forced myself not to vomit. Then everything hurtled up in a slow arc, and I understood that I was falling. I don't remember hitting the floor.

I awoke from a dark daze, looking up at the swimming image of Barbariccia, leering down at me. It was then that my body began to shiver convulsively and I finally understood what my grandmother had meant. I thought of the Khonsus whirling dervishes I'd seen on Horus and Ka's words about the sema...*the rapture of dissolving into love and the sacrifice of the mind to love, to complete submission, unity and the annihilation of self in God.*

I drifted into a kind of surreal release that came with punishment deserved, perhaps even sought for from all the deaths I'd ruthlessly claimed and even exalted in. I felt my eyes roll back into welcome darkness with thoughts of deliverance...*to yield without surrendering....*

Something cold and wet touched my lips and my eyes snapped open. Barbariccia crouched over me, eyes dark with lust. It was his tongue I'd felt. He was licking the blood spilling out of my mouth off my swollen lips and chin. In some ways this was the worst. I closed my eyes to his tormenting face and felt him stroke my eyebrows and gently push the hair from my face and curl it rapturously in his fingers. Eosians adored human hair and Barbariccia, it seemed, exalted in mine.

He whispered like a lover, "My *tutsak*...the flower of magnificent pain blooms inside you." I thought him absolutely mad.

He rose to his feet. "Leave the Rills alone. Consider this a warning," he said in garish cheerfulness and glanced at his three guards. Their laughter rang in my ears as I sank in and out of consciousness. "Behave, *tutsak*, and you'll be rewarded," he ended.

Then they burst open the door and left me to my misery as someone sidled by them. I heaved my gaze up. It was Orchid. I barely met her eyes through my convulsive tremors and involuntary whimpers. She skirted around me with a look of fearful contempt. Then, after a halting moment, she relieved herself on me.

TEN

Despite my initial intention to go to work early, I was late that day. When I finally got to my work station after cleaning myself up and visiting the medic-station, the only sign of my encounter with Barbariccia's thugs was my stiff gait, a bruised and half-swollen shut eye and a bruise on my forehead from blacking out and knocking my head on the shower head. The Veniks had thankfully not used their sharp claws; they'd left no outward scars. My experience with five of their slave traders on EpsEri 2 had taught me to appreciate those poisonous claws. Only one of the slave traders had reached me and slashed his claw across my buttock cheek before Benny had swooped down to rescue me. But that was another place and time, so far away and so long ago.

I'd dragged myself to the medic station by focusing on my steps, one at a time. I could barely walk and had to lean several times against the wall to keep from falling. There, I availed myself of a fine array of medical aids: a numbing foam of nano-agents that dulled the raw pain, helped stop the bleeding and promoted healing of torn tissue; a topical salve for my torn outer flesh; and lastly, an anti-infection/nutrient mixture that I swallowed. The rest was up to my Scandi-healing ability, which I prayed would kick in.

Upon entering the main chamber of Room 10, I caught site of Orchid and levelled a long hard gaze at her; she met my steady gaze with a defiant but flickering challenge. After a shrug she finally made a rude gesture at me and shuffled off.

Despite feverish chills, I laboured in a full work day as Iris, refusing to recognize that I'd been hurt, pushed me even harder than usual to complete tasks thoroughly ill-suited for a human. As I set myself to work, I felt a convulsive tremor run down my back. The Eosians had done well to cloister themselves on Eos among the wise *vishna* trees, I considered. They'd lived in isolation and self-enforced ignorance for centuries—as if knowing that to re-enter the world was to unleash their inner cruelty as no other sentient race could. Intelligence and cruelty were the most terrible of mates. The suffering they wrought was bottomless and unthinkably cruel in its genius.

By the end of the day, deep bloody fissures ran through my blistered hands. My inner thighs felt tacky with blood that had seeped out from the wounds of deep and grinding penetration that no human was meant to endure.

Faint from exhaustion, I stiffly ran my hand over the key pad, noting that I'd gained enough points to get a place of my own. I then turned to Iris, glowering at me, with a begging look. I couldn't speak. But I made her understand with gestures and a pleading look. Her eyes gleamed with cruel satisfaction. I followed her gaze down and saw a large dark stain where blood had soaked my clothes. When I met her eyes she was grinning. I must have looked truly pathetic because she relented and brusquely instructed me on how to get a place.

I couldn't find Mayling to tell her I had my own place and at the end of the day, I retired to my tiny cubicle on the fifth level, after pulling myself with difficulty away from the relieving mash, treating myself to a hot though painful shower, then revisiting the medic station for more painkillers. I'd thankfully had the bathroom and hallways to myself and surmised that everyone was at the games that Mayling had mentioned. A glance at the com-holo showed that there was a full slate tonight.

I closed the door of my cramped cubicle, feeling like it was a sanctuary, then sat on my cot and undressed. The slight cloy of peat bog permeated my cramped sleeping quarters and I knew it was me I smelled. The shower hadn't succeeded in ridding my body of the smell of the bog or in removing the persistent brown stain on my hands. In fact, I came to realize that the shower water smelled faintly of sulfur. I was beginning to smell like a Rill.

After a careful inspection of my bruised body and wounds I leaned back with a long sigh. I'd stopped bleeding and thanked God I healed like a Scandi.

I'd witnessed a suicide and rape and been beaten on my first day here; today it was *I* who was raped and verbally abused. What was next? There were rules in this place but they were made, and apparently remade, by lawless criminals with their own agenda. The laws of logic and fair play didn't apply here. I knew that everything I'd learned outside was useless inside Sekmet.

I crawled under the musty covers. With a wave of my hand to extinguish the light, I curled up and shut my eyes.

Then, like a wheel falling into a rut, my unruly mind settled on Serge….He was a Vos agent who'd shown that he didn't care a quintle for me despite his overt sexual advances; but chaos only knew why he'd become the source of my strength and resilience right now. My dreams of him, of being with him, seemed to give me hope for the next day. Out there, in a world doomed by my MEC, Bas was a vegetable, Serge was the enemy, and Benny was melted at the scrap yard. Memories were all I had now—until I died, which would be soon, I thought. I recalled something Ennos had said to me at the Iota Hor-2 precinct some time ago: *you don't belong to this world; you haven't a clue how it works.*

"That's why I'm here," I murmured and wished I'd kissed Serge the last time I'd seen him.

Φ

The days continued much the same way. When did yielding become surrender? When did hope abandon me? Not then. I still resisted; still thought of escape, even if only subconsciously, mind ever-scheming with observations, deductions, self-deliberations. I'd convinced myself that I still had a reason to live, still had a purpose to fulfill: I needed to warn the world. No one knew what I'd done...what I'd started. The chain of events I'd begun would go on after I died. I had to live to stop it all. Escape remained paramount.

I struggled out of bed when the light automatically spattered on at the appointed time in the morning for me to leave and go to work. I walked with my head bent low, avoiding anyone's direct gaze, especially when I heard taunting shouts or laughter. If the Rills were the slaves of the colony, I was the Rill's chattel. I was everyone's plaything to abuse, including the Rills. Mash was thrown at me as I passed by the cylinders; profanities slung at me. Inmates tripped me or purposely collided into me. I concluded with dread that the only reason I wasn't abused more thoroughly was that I was being saved for Barbariccia. I bore it all quietly, head bowed and thoughts bent inward in penitence: *yielding without surrender...*

I laboured hard, hands swelling, cracking and bleeding each day until they eventually toughened like leather as I ruthlessly attacked my tasks under Iris's cruel gaze and Orchid's brusque taunts. I worked a long day, pushing myself to my endurance limit, and by the time I emerged from the lower levels most of the inmates had thankfully gone to the games. That suited me; there was less chance of meeting any of Bondar's crowd or any other of Barbariccia's thugs. Since that first disastrous encounter, I had managed to avoid inviting their wrathful attention and punishment. I went directly to the cylinders for delirious mash and numbness of mind. Every time I ended up dreaming of Serge and forced myself off the tube. Sometimes I had enough presence of mind and energy to take a shower in the empty washroom while the rest of the colony attended the games. Most of the time I simply retired to bed, barely noticing—and no longer caring—that I smelled like the rest of them: filthy, sweaty and like a bog.

But my Guardian-trained mind noticed other things. I watched and schemed of how I might use the information to escape. There was a kind of hierarchy to the lawless society, which consisted of two main types of inmates: dullards who worked hard and looked desperate like me; and sharp-witted clear-eyed individuals like the Mevlani and his thugs who didn't seem to work. They just wandered the floor, apparently unaffected by the soporific affect of the mash. The latter group seemed to use the former group as playthings for their bored amusement, to rape, injure, torture and intimidate. I noticed them everywhere, the Mevlani's victims. I saw Azorians with large burn scars on their hides; Fauche with only one ear; even a Khonsus with most of his feathers removed. I saw mutilated faces and severed limbs. I witnessed Rills with an eye tube torn off and guessed that Orchid's mutilation had occurred here, in Hades. And once I noticed them, I started seeing them everywhere.

The Rills were berated and mistreated by both groups. They seemed destined to be abused, I thought sadly and recalled with shame how I used to dismiss them as a lesser race.

The game, I finally discovered by piecing together from fractured discussions I'd overheard, was a treacherous contest for points played by dullards like me and sponsored by the clear-eyed inmates. The game was played in an arena in front of an audience eager for blood. It was apparently not for the faint of heart. But, then again, who was faint of heart in this place? Most of us were cold-blooded murderers, myself included.

I watched and worked hard at being invisible. I missed Mayling and wondered where she had gone. For all her annoying traits Mayling had become my friend, someone I could talk to. Perhaps she had finally succumbed and been vaporized or some Venik had done her in.

Φ

The days drifted into weeks and I found it harder and harder to drag myself out of bed to work in the mine. Although I'd managed to evade most of the scornful inmates by travelling during the twilight hours, the workplace was something I couldn't avoid. Iris relentlessly berated me no matter how hard I worked. She shouted insults at me about my human weaknesses every opportunity she had. I mutely bore her invective as something I deserved for my previous ill to her kind. But my willing subservience seemed to infuriate her the more and she eventually relied on physical violence to satisfy her anger, smacking me over the head now and then to drive home a point: "You think humans are superior, eh, *skinny*? You can't even do this simple task right!"

I let her strike me with her great webbed hand while the other Rills chuckled.

"You worthless idle scum of the galaxy!"

The other Rills, taking her cue and seeing my submission, began to molest me; they shoved me out of their way, tittering and growling abusive words, and sometimes spit at me. Orchid, who had been harassing me already, escalated her own brand of abuse. I endured it all quietly without any thought of retaliation. Only months ago I would have thought it the hardest thing to do; I succumbed to it willingly, almost gratefully, now. *There is no victory in resistance...*I was no longer looking for victory.

...Not even when Orchid deliberately sabotaged my peat cubes by urinating over them then complained to Iris that I had done it. Iris, of course, gruffly took my hand and subtracted twenty points for every cube that I had supposedly defiled, including additional ones in the curing ovens that had been infected by the tainted ones. I was forced to work twice as hard and long to compensate for the loss to my point count, or lose my dwelling.

107

...Not even when Orchid and April opened the drying pressure container and broke all my morning's work, leaving dishevelled piles of peat everywhere for Iris to find. In response to her inquiring glower, Orchid shrugged and pointed to me, remarking that she'd noticed me being particularly careless that morning. Iris believed her, of course. I submitted without argument to the subtraction of points and, after cleaning out the pressure container, began all over again to the sniggers of the other Rills. I worked until near curfew and missed my dinner that day.

Φ

I lost track of time as the days bled into one another. The nights were always the same; I wet my pillow with silent tears, dreaming that Serge would rescue me...until I stopped dreaming and stopped crying. That was when hope died inside me and the dangerous numbness of despair came like a dark wave. And swallowed me whole. It left me empty like a husk, with nothing to fill its space, so I caved in.

One day, unable to face the hard labour, insults and physical abuse, I ignored the light spattering on and, pulling the smelly blanket over my head, slept in. Not heeding my lesson of avoiding breakfast, I surrendered to Cerberus and sucked back mash. When I finally made it to Room 10, I suffered Iris's gruff reprimand with my head bowed in silence and winced as she smacked me sharply on the head several times with her large paw then shoved me to my workstation at the end of the hauler. She snarled about lazy skinny humans as I set slowly to work. April sidled close to me and I thought for a foolish moment she was going to speak to me. Then she sucked in a great breath and spat on me. I flinched and watched her waddle off with a pile of peat bricks in her arms. I didn't bother to wipe the spittle off the side of my face and out of my hair.

Once Iris left the room, Orchid waddled over to my small pile of cubes and waited until I noticed to squat and urinate over them. I sighed with defeat, briefly meeting her gaze of challenge with slumped shoulders and hooded eyes, and started all over again. By midday, April had gathered enough courage to stoop over and defecate on my stacked peat cube pile as Orchid laughed behind her good hand. When they'd sidled off together, cackling maliciously, I stole to a corner and squeezed behind one of the curing ovens. I curled on the floor and shivered to sleep. Eventually I heard the Rills looking for me. They shouted profanities and insulted the human race. But they didn't find me.

"Where's skinny?" I heard Iris ask very close to my hiding place. There was no way anyone was going to find me here, I thought. No Rill could even come close; they were too rotund. "That no good lazy human jag! I'll beat her ugly little butt for slacking off again!"

I didn't emerge until the end of the workday, after Iris, Orchid and the others had left for the evening crew. Ignoring the curious gaze of the Rill in charge of the evening shift, I glanced at my hand and saw that I'd only earned 10 points. That wasn't near enough to keep my place. Instead of feeling alarm, I just took solace in Cerberus. I barely got to my room before curfew.

Φ

The next day I slept in again. I didn't have the heart to face Iris and her Rill thugs again. If I didn't work very hard, my place would be vaporized and I'd have nowhere to go that night. Defying common sense, I stopped at the cylinders. A quick one, I told myself, not caring that I didn't believe myself. When I started to suck down the food, I knew I was staying.

Almost instantly, I drifted into drowsy apathy. Expelling a long sigh, I reclined on the floor.

...My mouth fell open and I found myself softly crying, shoulders shaking with soundless tears. I replaced the tube in my mouth and sucked harder and was about to close my eyes when I gasped and choked on my mash at who I saw striding toward me.

Serge! He'd shifted into a purple Eosian, but I recognized his stormy eyes, that feral grin and his confident loping gait. He scrambled over several recumbent inmates and crouched over me, pupils dark with lust, and licking his lips with a mischievous smile. His eyes searched mine for understanding. And consent. Assenting with my eyes, I took the nozzle out of my mouth to speak. He shook his head and replaced it in my mouth with an impish smile. Then he nodded to me with a wink, indicating for me to continue eating.

"Oh, Rhea…You've been a good girl," he said, grinning. "A very good girl…"

I clutched my nozzle with both hands and sucked on mash as Serge reached up and grabbed another nozzle and put it to his own mouth. He sucked deeply, eyes fluttering shut for a moment in deep euphoria. After a few inhales, his eyes snapped open with a feral intensity and, gripping the nozzle in his mouth to free his hands, he frantically undid both our flaps.

I took in a sharp inhale of mash at his revealed manhood, already swollen, erect and glistening with pre-come. I breathed in his enticing sexual smell with growing excitement. Strawberries and musk. His penis was very large, typical for most Eosians, and I decided that this was a dream. I seized in shallow breaths as Serge leaned on the floor with his hands and straddled me with his thighs. His pelvis and stiff manhood pressed hot against the flesh of my stirring loins.

Recalling the coupling Eosians, I wondered fleetingly if I was emulating them with some inmate who I'd given Serge's identity or was I the sadder case of the dreaming Badowin, masturbating myself into oblivion. Either way, surely I was imagining all this: Serge, particularly—

Then he entered me in a splintering surge of ecstasy and I didn't care. I was going down in a wonderful flame. He thrust deep, filling me and reaching the core of my burning arousal like a MEC wave. It flamed through me and I arched into him with urgency, then rocked my pelvis to feed his thrusts, escalating us to a frenzied rhythm. He grunted and spluttered in convulsive gulps of mash, trying to keep up. He was less interactive than I'd remembered; but, no matter, I could do it for both of us—especially if this was all a self-induced dream. I continued to pump and matched Serge's gasps with my own convulsive intakes. Then his swelling moan of excitement signalled that he'd reached his precipice and I pushed us over the edge into a violent shudder.

I congratulated myself on my realistic vision—

The nozzle wrenched out of my mouth and hands. I snapped open eyes that I hadn't realized I'd closed and saw Serge sauntering away, his hose left dangling beside me. Then he turned his head—I gasped. It wasn't Serge. I stared at Barbariccia, sneering at me with cruel eyes of wicked satisfaction. He was buttoning up his trousers. "I'll see you later, *tutsak*," he said.

I let my head drop back and, seizing my nozzle, closed my eyes and sucked in my mash in deep inhales. Tired and hopeless, I felt myself slide willingly into the darkness of despair.

Φ

...As I lurk in the back shadows of the large chamber, I make out the various clan leaders at the front, responding to each other in didactic tones, followed by enthusiastic moans and calls by the rest. I make a decision: they will never be all here in one place like this again. I must act NOW! Heart pumping, I surge out from the dark, MEC pointed in a two-handed grip and shout, "You're all under arrest for treason! Stay as you are!"

One Rill moves, arm aggressively swinging forward. Holding a weapon! I open fire. But they don't just fall. Their bodies explode in bloody strings of flesh and organs. A receding wave of shrieking Rills falls away from me, arms swinging toward me, with weapons my panic-stricken mind tells me. As if driven by some demonic force, as if to stop would be to admit to what I've begun, I kill them all. I don't stop until a single Rill remains...Mayling stands there with eyes of recrimination and horror—

Mayling was shaking me.

"Stop that now!" Mayling shouted at me with a glower. "You're giving up, aren't you?"

I spit out the hose and seized Mayling's overalls in a tight grip. "Mayling! You're alive!" I was both thrilled and mortified at the sight of my Rill friend. "I never told you what I did. I'm so sorry!" I gripped her in a slobbering embrace and wept convulsively.

"I don't cares what youz did," Mayling said, gruffly pulling my arms off her. "Rights nows youz needs to gets up and leaves. It's evening."

"But I killed so many—"

"I told youz, I don'ts needs to knows," Mayling cut me off, then checked my tattooed hand and expostulated. "Youz haven'ts worked all days! You've beens here since mornings." The Rill then looked me over and grunted with disgust. "You even wets yourself. You're pathetic!" She discreetly buttoned up my flap and pulled me by the arm. "Come ons. Gets up!"

"Leave me, Mayling. I have no where to go," I sniffed and leaned back, wiping my runny nose with my bare arm. "There's no way I can earn enough points now. It's too late." I had no strength or will left for anything.

"Yous can sleeps with meez again."

"No!" I shrilled. I couldn't bear her kindness. "You've been too kind to me. Leave me here. I can't go on anymore. I deserve it. I really do. I'm ready to go. I've done enough harm for one person."

Mayling's face softened with pity. She fished in one of her bulging overalls pockets and, pulling out a package of soyka gum, handed it to me. "Here, this will helps clears your minds."

I sat up and gladly took the package. "Where did you get this?"

"I stoles it off the new meats today," she said with a grin.

I stuffed several wads into my mouth and chewed slowly with an appreciative inhale. My mind drifted back through the haze to when I was the new meat. It seemed so long ago. When I was a different person.

"There is ones things you might try." Mayling smiled slyly at me with a hopeful face. "The games." She glanced at the small com-board on the far wall. "There are stills somes open slots tonight."

Already invigorated by the soyka gum, I listened attentively with interest.

"Every nights, inmates plays the game while others bets on whos will win. They plays for points. If youz play and wins youz gets five hundred points for yourself and your sponsor gets a thousand points because they puts in the five hundred for youz in the pot."

"What kind of game is it?" What I'd heard so far hadn't been good.

"A games of survival. Youz plays against another opponents in a game of strength, courage and wits."

I felt my heart sink. Right now I possessed none of these. I might have been able to contend when I'd first come to Sekmet but I wasn't in any shape right now.

Mayling sensed what I was thinking. "You still thinks like an Enforcer, Hawke. Most of these guys are stupid brutes with no minds for strategy. They're in heres not because they're intelligents or cunning but because they're dumbs as well as insanely violents or annoying. You'd haves your brains on your side, Hawke. Besides, there's a second reason for youz to play. That's the only ways you gets enough points to be ables to affords the root."

"The root? Why do I want the root?"

"The wakesh root makes you immunes to that," Mayling said, pointing to the hose hanging off the cylinder that Serge—Barbariccia—whoever, perhaps I myself had left hanging; even I could have knocked it off in my wildly random movements.

It was awfully tempting to have a chance at kicking this devastating addiction.

I noticed Mayling staring at me expectantly. "Don't I need a sponsor?" I asked. "Where am I going to find one?"

Mayling nodded. "I already founds youz one."

I looked at her in puzzled astonishment. "Who?"

"Bondar."

"What?" I started back, appalled. "Barbariccia's own henchman?"

Mayling smiled knowingly.

"Why would he?..." I trailed.

"Wants to sponsor youz?" Mayling guessed my thoughts with a smirk. "He was impressed with your performance and spirits the first days youz came."

I wasn't that person anymore.

Mayling seemed to guess my thoughts again. "Besides, he's desperates for a candidate. No ones wants him as a sponsor. Youz fits together."

"Yeah," I nodded glumly. "Two desperados." I tightened my lips with understanding. The Venik was making his move. Was Barbariccia's time already up? He seemed at the pinnacle of his rule. Then again, that was usually when they fell, I reflected. I hated to have anything to do with that Venik or be indebted to him, but how else was I going to play? After some meditation, I said with apprehension, "Okay. I'll give it a try."

"We must hasten then," Mayling said, helping me to my feet. "I'll takes youz to Bondar." I followed the Rill, barefoot, down the hall. I chewed my gum harder as thoughts of doom nudged my mind.

Mayling turned and remarked casually, "Your flap was open. Did someone...or were you just?..."

I coloured. "I think...I imagined it all...a man, someone I eh...like from the outside, appeared. But he turned out to be Barbariccia. I think I made it all up, to torture myself..." I ended, dropping my gaze restlessly to the floor.

"Maybes nots," Mayling remarked, drawing my curious gaze. "You're nots too bad lookings and he *is* an Eosian," she pointed out, directing all three eyes at me. She was referring to the Eosian's particular weakness for human females.

"I thought that he might prefer men," I observed.

"Maybe so, but you'res pretty and he's cruels and likes to see sufferings." I thought back to the Veniks raping me while Barbariccia masterbated with sadistic pleasure. Then Mayling's already thick lips pouted and she resumed looking forward. "We all gets jagged here eventually," she casually added. "Might as wells enjoy it."

I turned to Mayling in horrified amazement.

"How can you say that?" I challenged her. There was nothing remotely enjoyable about being raped.

"Survivals," she said with a shrug. "Copulation is still...well, copulation." She then farted with obvious pleasure at the thought. Expressed as only a Rill could express it, I thought.

ELEVEN

I stood in the centre of the five hectare blood-stained arena, facing the semi-circular bleachers where Bondar and Barbariccia and an audience of several dozen aliens sat, packed like blood hounds smelling death.

I inhaled the rank smell of unwashed bodies, sweat and old blood and privately wondered what I was doing here. Bondar seemed to think I was capable enough; he'd gleefully accepted me as his candidate and now looked smug, seated not far from Barbariccia, who ignored him and studied me with a look of amusement on his calm face. Had he ravished me or not? Suddenly aware of my soiled clothes, I grew self-conscious and nervously fidgeted as I waited for Barbariccia's candidate to enter the arena.

Bondar abruptly stood up and held up my original jacket in one hand and my slacks in the other.

"I'm still looking for a buyer for these!" he announced happily in a multi-timbral chorus. "Great clothes of impeccable quality. Original Enforcer clothes."

Which they weren't, I thought scathingly. They were just ordinary flight clothes. Damn that Bondar! The bastard was selling my clothes right in front of me, his own candidate. It showed me what kind of team we were...and what he thought of my chances.

"Are they intelligent?" someone in the audience asked.

Bondar brought both my jacket and pants up to his reptilian face and buried his snout in them with a deep inhale. All he smelled was me, I thought, wincing inside. I felt my face tighten to a grimace as I watched him smear my clothes over his face: it seemed that *essence of Rhea* was a perfume for him because his doleful eyes flickered dreamily shut and his many mouths smiled lecherously. Several inmates cackled.

"You can't tell by smelling it, creon!" someone scoffed.

"They're far too small!" said another. "She's just a puny little pip."

My gaze involuntarily flickered down my own torso. I wasn't that small, I thought petulantly. I was almost six feet tall.

Bondar bent down and lifted up my boots. "What about these? Real gravity boots. They instantly adjust according to the weight of the wearer to the gravitational pull of any planet you travelled to—"

"No one's going anywhere, you buffoon!"

They started booing him and shouted for him to sit down.

I dropped my gaze to the dirty blood-stained floor as the jeers and slanders spread to me. I heard several pointed insults aimed at the human race. What *was* I doing here besides inviting abuse?

Mayling had sagely waited until just before I entered the arena, when it was too late to back out, to fully explain the game to me: "It's a simple contest: just find and take possession of the wakesh root, hidden in the obstacle course of the arena, before the opponent does—and keep it by immobilizing the other contestant. This is usually done by killing the opponent but you don't have to..." I had repeated the part about *usually killing the opponent* and Mayling ignored me to continue: "Whatever you do, don't let yourself fall into the pit."

"Pit?" I had repeated with a hard swallow.

"No one ever gets out. Usually youz just hears a lot of splashing then a lots of silence. Sometimes a sobeks wanders in and manages to eludes the peat saws and turbines, then youz also hear thrashing and lots of awful cries of terrors and pains as the sobek bites off a limb and—"

"I get it," I cut in.

"There are two ways to plays the games," Mayling went on. "Defeats your opponent first then looks for the root ats your leisure, or finds the root first and use its to defeats your opponent. Which way youz goes depends on your personal strengths. Considering your present status and your humans abilities, I suggests youz first finds the root, then takes a bite of the root immediately to gives yourselfs a decided advantage over your opponent."

That only worked if I got it first. And that was unlikely, given the wave-sensitive eyesight of the Xhix, who'd just entered the arena through an adjacent door. Wonderful, I thought with growing despair. Xhix could see through objects.

Holding a mining shovel in one hand, the Xhix waved to the cheering crowd with his other. I dismally recalled the crowd's jeers and catcalls when I'd entered the arena. It was obvious who they thought would win.

I was contemplating the misnomer of Mayling's use of the term obstacle course, when Barbariccia stood and shouted, "Let the contest begin!"

I kept a sharp eye on the Xhix, who stood poised several meters from me. Maybe I could outsmart him. I might be more swift, if I let him lead me to the root. The Xhix seemed to realize what I was thinking. He faced me with a smirk and turned black, tapping his shovel with his paw. He wasn't about to give away the whereabouts of the root.

The floor rumbled and, just a meter from where I stood, it abruptly separated, giving off a strong waft of sulfur. The gap in the floor groaned into a long chasm that continued to widen. Both the Xhix and I stepped back. This must be the infamous pit Mayling had referred to. I carefully leaned over to catch a glimpse of what lay below. I made out murky bog and peat, moving slowly across the gaping opening as the penal facility rolled along, churning up peat and mire some ten meters below—

Something hard and painful struck my head, throwing me off balance into the gap with a startled grunt. I briefly registered the Xhix's victorious laugh as I pitched forward and blacked out.

I jerked awake, inhaling water. I'd plunged into black cold churning water and broke the surface with gasping breaths.

The Xhix had swiftly made his move with the shovel as I had foolishly let myself be distracted. I struggled against the strong current. The roaring sound of the moving facility was deafening from this vantage and I discovered that I had to swim deep sections and scramble over floating hummocks to keep from being swept underneath the huge penal colony. The current kept tugging me back from the advancing wall toward the back wall. I tossed a fleeting glance up the shaft to the arena's opening and thought I caught the silhouette of the victorious Xhix standing at the edge. Then he disappeared and the floor began to close over me, dousing me in darkness. The crowds were no doubt roaring with laughter at the Xhix's victory as the massive engines roared my defeat. I'd proven as buffoonish as Bondar. The groaning engines pushed the lumbering facility like a giant creeping bear along the bog as I thrashed in the cold water, trying to keep up, throwing panicked glances up to the narrowing shaft of light.

Strength swiftly ebbing, I saw the advancing aft edge of the hole gain on me. I scrambled over tussocks of floating peat with grunts of effort only to have them give way under me and plunge me into the roiling murky water. Spluttering and gulping in black water, I struggled to maintain the pace of the shaft opening but I ran across more churned up peat that I had to negotiate around. Each time I saw the far wall move farther ahead and the back wall gain on me. Then, as the ceiling drew closed, the back shaft wall was upon me in the frightful darkness. Throwing out my arms in desperation, I fought the current, wailing and sobbing out my struggles. The current swept me underneath into utter blackness.

Panic hit. I was under the two kilometre long colony, underwater, in pitch darkness.

It can't end this way, I thought, savagely clinging to my last breaths of life. No wise words from my snake-grandmother came to me. And no vision or déjà vu availed itself from my soul-double in that other diverse. I was drowning this time for good. In Sekmet's blanket bog, beneath a giant moving penal colony that would in its wake eventually spit out my body in a dead-man's float. If only I was a Rill, I thought desperately, as I lost consciousness. Rills were bog creatures with gills and capable of swimming underwater for long periods of time. It made them particularly suited to collect still submerged peat—

I abruptly felt myself painfully straining against my belt and had the presence of mind to undo it. I felt my body bloat and fill out my overalls. I suddenly found myself able to breath! Was I hallucinating or dead? The pitch black opened into shades of darkness and I found myself able to see small shafts of flickering light here and there. I intuitively understood that I needed to swim with the current but not directly with it, diagonally with it to avoid the turbine rotors and the peat saws that would rip me to shreds. But to either side, directly behind the saws, lay slanted shafts where the mined peat was retrieved by Iris's team. It would be difficult to negotiate around to the shafts without being caught in the saws but I managed against the current with my strong webbed arms and legs and soon found myself carried up out of the dark murky water and eventually into one of the mining chambers where I worked.

Once inside the building, I stumbled off the moving conveyor and let myself fall ungracefully to the floor. I gasped in my breaths and laughed and sobbed at the same time. How in chaos had I done that? I should be dead. Was it possible that I'd...no, that was too much to believe—that I'd shape-shifted for a short while into a Rill...I was part Vos, after all...I held out trembling hands in front of me and after turning them over to check, I inspected the rest of my body then ran my hands along my throat to check for remnant gills. Nothing remained to suggest I'd turned into a Rill; I was all human again.

Φ

I heard some voices and shuffling feet; Rill workers. I scrambled to the far side of the chamber, leaving a trail of bog water and pieces of peat, and scrambled to my hiding place behind the large ovens to hide. I waited in trembling silence, pulling back rogue strands of hair that had plastered over my face. They must have gone past this chamber into the next one because no one entered and the chamber grew quiet again. Shivering with unruly emotion and cold, I felt my mind drift feverishly from my miraculous recovery to my possible future on Sekmet. Why had I survived? For what? For more of *this*? The human spirit to live was a strange thing, I reflected finally. Even when being tortured or irreparably debilitated, most humans chose to live...Did Bas?

Suddenly reminded of poor Jaz, my tappin, my breath hitched. I'd asked Bas to look in on my tappin while I was away. With Bas a vegetable in the Gleise-12 Med-Facility, who was going to take care of Jaz? Who would feed him, pat him, love him?...I burst into desperate tears.

"Crying won't helps."

I jerked into silence and scanned the darkness. "Who's there?" I choked out, swallowing down my sobs.

"It's me, of course."

Mayling! I slid out from behind the warm ovens.

The Rill came forward and leaned back on her haunches to regard me critically. "Sekmets is a cruels society, based on whos is the cruelests."

I wiped my eyes with a frown. "Then I'm a fool to go on."

"No youz aren't."

I flinched at her words. Was she calling me cruel? Did she know what I'd done to her people, after all? Had Iris told her? I swallowed and gazed searchingly at the Rill. "What do you mean?"

"Youz survived the pit. No ones has ever done that. Everyones thinks you're dead, Hawke. But you'res an Enforcers. Youz didn't drowns or get eatens up by the turbines or peat saws or sobeks. You'res clevers."

"No I'm not clever, Mayling," I objected with a self-mocking laugh and brushed the hair off my face with a brusque sweep of my hand. I didn't share that I'd likely shape-shifted into a Rill to survive. "And that's probably why I'm an ex-Enforcer," I added. "I'm not smart, not like you. I've seen how you Rill manage in this place. If anyone should be dead it's you, yet you thrive here. You're treated like slaves by the other inmates. Everyone abuses you, shows you no respect. They rape you for sport, you have no privileges, no protective allegiances. Yet you're all mostly healthy and content with your lot, and you seem to move about easily throughout the facility. How do you do it?"

Mayling smiled and looked suddenly wise. "Weez looks invisible to thems. Excepts when they wants to take pleasure from us, no ones notices us mosts of the times."

I nodded with a wry smile. A lesson I hadn't learned yet.

"But you'res human," Mayling continued. "Youz can't be invisibles. You'res uniques. Uniques is valuables in the universe."

I firmed my lips and bowed my head in despair. "We're back to my doom, Mayling. I...just can't...continue in this place..." I trailed with and put my hands to my head. "I'm so...tired."

Mayling leaned closer, her bog-smell wafting over to me. "The tricks is not to wins in the game; yous haves to wins *before* the games."

I looked up, wiping wet strings of hair off my face. "What are you saying?"

"Yous needs the wakesh root to wins."

"But I don't get the wakesh root until I win."

"Ais..." Mayling chortled. "Withouts the roots yous loses."

This was like getting a job, I thought sullenly. "Okay, how do I get the wakesh root *before* I play the game?"

"Ais..." Mayling nodded. "Nows youz are askings the right questions." She gave me a naughty smile, which suggested that she knew. "Follows meez."

Φ

She led me to a door that she opened by using her handprint. It led down a long clammy stairway. As we descended, I felt the air grow cool and dank. The rankness of sulphur, excrement and general filth grew strong. We must have descended at least two more levels. This was the world of the Rill: the bowels of Hades. The sewers. Mayling led me through several chambers, one of which I noted contained the AI cleaning units, and we ended up in a tall chamber with diagnostic machinery and several cylindrical structures.

"Youz wondered why we Rills are still so healthy and contents in this jagging place, despite how ill-treated weez are," Mayling said, pointing with her large clawed arm at one of the cylinders with a hatch in the middle of the chamber. "That's because we leaved Hades from times to times. Through the sewers. We're in charge of sewage maintenance, because no ones else wants to do it. It's our escape route. We digs tunnels in the peat while we're minings for Hades. Then weez uses thems to escape into the outer bog laters. Sometimes weez connects with the natural tunnels of the sobeks or theys finds our tunnels; that's when weez encounter thems and a Rill doesn't return."

"Why would you want to come back?" I asked.

"The bog is no place to lives and we haves no way of leavings the planet."

"Then why do you bother to go out?"

"To find this," Mayling replied, pulling out from her overalls pocket a long gnarled bright yellow root the thickness of my thumb with several knobby branches. "We sells it to inmates who cans afford it."

I eyed it with laconic curiosity. It smelled spicy like nutmeg and pepper. "What is it?"

"The gateways to the gods," Mayling responded, all three eyes focused on me.

"That's what you dropped into the mob that first day I was here, isn't it?"

Mayling nodded and handed the mildly earth-scented root to me. "This is the wakesh root. Yous chews it."

I took the root in my hand. "What does it do?" I figured it was the natural source of either an antidote for the drugs in the food and water or some stimulant that counteracted the depressants. "Will it pick me up? Clear my brain?"

"You'll see." Mayling urged me with a wave of her

webbed hand.

I hated the idea of taking a drug. Particularly something whose properties I didn't know. But I trembled with desperation and weariness. And I was already drugged, I told myself. The bottom of it was I simply wasn't going to make it if I didn't get help. Glancing nervously at Mayling, who nodded reassuringly, I bit down on the root and gnawed it with my teeth. It was quite woody on the surface but, once I broke through, the fleshy part beneath was easier to penetrate and chew. It tasted of yams, walnuts and chilli pepper and had the texture of an unripe apple.

"I don't feel any different," I said despondently. "I feel nothing—"

A knife-sharp pain bit into my gut and sent me doubling over. My mouth gaped open in a silent scream.

"What have you done to me?" I cried out, eyes blazing at the Rill. I fell to my knees in dizzying pain.

"I'm sorry, I didn't tell you that it comes with one side effect. It makes you sick, but you'll get used to it. They all do."

Mayling was right. With the pain came a sudden wave of confidence, clarity and purpose. It swept through me like an exotic wind that cleared away my cobwebs of weary and fearful doubt. The room took on a new brightness and everything in it sparkled with sharp colour, texture and contrast. I sucked in my gut, calmly ignoring the gnawing pain, and straightened. I turned to Mayling, observing her texture, pores, hairs as if for the first time, and bared my teeth in a feral smile. I could do anything. I was invincible. Why hadn't I known that before? I'd wasted so much time languishing in useless despair. I was capable of so much and I knew exactly what I needed to do.

Mayling grinned, seeing the obvious effect on me. "That root will last you a day or two. The narcotic acts rapidly, but it also dissipates quickly. You'll need a fix—a mouthful—every couple of hours. That one is free. The next one will cost you two hundred points. Then all the ones after are a hundred each."

I nodded, eyeing the root in my hand with a broad grin. I'd never felt so tall. The sour pain in my stomach had already subsided. I could handle its remnants.

I placed my hand on the Rill's shoulder. "Thanks for the root, Mayling. You've proven yourself a worthy friend. Excuse me now while I try to be one back." I found some chord to cinch in my baggy overalls. Then, after a quick nod at Mayling, I sprinted to the hallway that would lead me up the slimy stairs to the upper levels.

TWELVE

I wandered the hallways with a purposeful stride then let a feral smile pull back my lips as I both smelled and saw the Venik. Bondar was still in the place where he regularly languished and I had learned to avoid. He was doing what he liked best: raping a poor squawking Rill as two other Rills watched, fidgeting in fright.

Catching a glimpse of me, Bondar betrayed initial shock at seeing me alive, then scoffed in a growling chorus, "Get out of here, human bitch, before I have a mind to jag you just because you don't want me to. You cost me everything, slave. You jagging humiliated me."

"You did that for yourself, Bondar. Let her go."

Bondar sneered with malice. Still glaring at me, he bared his sharp blue teeth in a snarl and grunted in a hard jerk as he sank his razor teeth into the Rill's neck. With a snap he tore her head off. Blood spurted out like a green fountain.

I stared in shock. My face tightened in a snarl of rage and I surged forward in an adrenalin rush. I flew into a cartwheel leap that caught Bondar by the throat between my taut thighs. I brought him down in a painful headlock. I heard him gulp in choking breaths. The other Rills scrambled to the far side and watched with terrified curiosity.

Bondar struggled hard to get loose and grunted with frustration, his many arms flailing out at my steely legs. I knew what he was thinking: how could this puny human hold him like this? Bondar, of course, had no idea I was part shape-shifter and was tapping into the Venik strength to contain his struggles. But it had been too short a tap to manifest itself in visible form. It was the first time I'd consciously tried to shape-shift and it worked like I knew it would.

"You murdering scum," I hissed.

Bondar growled and struggled against my steely grip.

"Where are my clothes?" I demanded. "I want them back."

"Jag you!" Bondar choked out.

"Just what I intend to prevent..." I snarled. Then with a forceful twist of my legs, I snapped his neck. "...Permanently," I ended, letting his lifeless corpse drop between my legs to the floor. His massive body thudded to the ground with a finality that brought out a hush from the onlookers followed by excited murmurs.

I turned to them with a look of feral challenge and found to my surprise that the few onlookers had swollen into a large crowd. Very well, then, let them look, I thought ferociously. Death was a spectator sport in Sekmet.

Recognizing no challengers in the crowd, I ignored them and bent down on one knee to remove Bondar's sheath, knife and belt. I cinched the belt on my waist then pulled the knife out of his sheath and ruthlessly sawed off Bondar's right hand. As I got up, holding the knife in one hand and the severed hand in the other, both dripping black blood, I caught Mayling's face among the crowd of onlookers and our eyes met. Mayling's three eyes extended as long as they went in an expression of...what? I still couldn't totally gauge expression on Rills. Was it terror? Terror of what she'd unleashed?

I swiftly looked away and, after a last brief glance at the decapitated Rill lying in a spreading pool of dark-green blood, I turned to leave. The crowd parted respectfully for me as I strode past them toward the hub chamber.

Φ

Using the position setting on Bondar's tracking screen, I found Bondar's sleep chamber and waved his severed hand over the sensor. The door opened, releasing a stench of body filth. I ditched the Venik's hand and dropped to my knees to search under his cot. I found my charcoal grey flight clothes rumpled in the very back along with my boots. Pulling them out with a ferocious smile of satisfaction, I got up and found a women's washroom. I waved my hand over the sensor and entered as though I owned it. Two Rills were cavorting on the floor like dogs in heat—I recognized one of them as April. She flicked startled eyes at me and they rushed out in frightened confusion.

I stripped and showered then dried off and put on my old clothes and grey top, overlooking that Bondar had slobbered all over them. The sentient trousers and jacket rearranged themselves on me, crumples and folds vanishing. I then bent over the sink and washed the blood off the knife. That done I stood in front of the mirror and ruthlessly grabbed a skein of my long tangled mane. I sawed it off level to my chin with the knife. After a fierce glance at the clump of hair in my hand, I dropped it to the floor then continued until I'd cut all my hair to that length. When I'd finished, with a brisk satisfied glance at myself in the mirror—my eyes glowed fiercely like a *glitter* addict—I replaced the knife in its sheath and left.

Φ

"You can't play," Barbariccia quipped lazily as he eyed me up and down with ruthless appreciation. I watched his razor eyes appraise my expressionless face, now framed by a spreading dark veil of chaotic short hair. His gaze traveled down my body to where my hand loosely rested on the knife sheathed on the waist of my flight slacks. "You killed your sponsor. Should have thought of that before you went into that violent tirade of yours." He scoffed by making a clicking sound with his tongue. "That's quite a temper you have." He let his gaze drift over me again with obvious lust and shifted in his chair, spreading his long legs out to free his bulging crotch. "Normally

I like temper on a woman. It excites me."

"I don't need a sponsor," I responded coolly. I stood facing him in his control chamber with three Venik thugs so close behind me that I could smell their body odour. Keeping my hand poised over the haft of my sheathed knife, I went on, "You'll play me just the same. Send in your best and I'll beat them. You know you want to," I taunted then added in a snarl of confidence, "You know you *have* to." I had already heard the buzz; the inmates were itching to see me in action. My survival of the pit and then dispatching Bondar had amazed and excited them. Barbariccia had no other choice but to respond to the call to uphold his reputation. The night was still young.

Barbariccia sniffed with disgust, but I knew I had him.

"You failed miserably last time," he said, resisting. "My Xhis beat you in the first minute with his first attempt. And he was far from my best. You were laughable."

"That won't happen again," I replied coldly.

Stalemated, he stared at me with frigid eyes for a long moment. "Very well," he snapped. "For the amusement value, it'll be worth it. You can sponsor yourself. Come here."

I quelled the urge to hesitate and came forward immediately.

"Put your hand on that peg."

I met his eyes with challenge and kept my arm poised but not moving.

He smirked, amused. "It's just to give you some points so you can enter them in the contest as sponsor. You haven't nearly enough now to do much of anything, slave," he ended with a churlish grin.

I placed my tattooed hand on the post where I'd first received my tattoo and implant. Barbariccia placed another device on the back of my hand, over the implant and I felt a mild vibration; no piercing pain this time. When he removed it, I noticed that my readout was 510 points. It cost 500 points to enter the game.

"The twenty-one slot," he said. "I'm already broadcasting it on our boards." It was the most popular time, I noted. And only forty minutes away. I thought I heard a sudden raucous in the distance. Our eyes met in recognition. The colony had reacted to the posting. "Be there," Barbariccia bit out.

"You can count on it." I nodded curtly. Then, without another word, I spun on my heels and left him, brushing past the towering Veniks. Only once I'd made it out of his large chamber did I let a fierce smile curl my lips.

Φ

I stood once again in the centre of the arena, facing Barbariccia. I was dressed in Mayling's baggy overalls and my stretchy top as a contingency to possible shape-shifting.

This time, upon my entry, I was greeted by instant cheers amid the jeers and catcalls. I felt a strange calm descend on me as I waited for Barbariccia's candidate to enter and searched the stands for Mayling. Just as I spotted the Rill, an Azorian lumbered into the arena to loud applause. No doubt another favourite, I thought, turning my attention to my opponent.

The Azorian grimaced at me, showing large brown-stained teeth in a lipless mouth under his long snout. His face resembled a feret's. He stood over eight feet tall with lean limbs and rippled torso. A tough sandpaper hide served as his main thermo-regulation. On Azor, his home planet in the Beta Hydri system, and where temperatures ranged between 40ºC and 45ºC, his outer skin was apparently supple but out here, where temperatures were cooler and fluctuated far more, Azorians developed a tough hide. But it wouldn't protect him in water, I thought. If he fell into the mire below, he'd die of hypothermia in the cold water before the wall or a sobek had a chance to claim him. His body would seize up in a dying coma and he'd be sucked underneath the floating colony within moments.

As I expected, the floor suddenly gave way and a crack that spanned the diameter of the arena opened to a pungent bog smell. Now that I recognized the wakesh root's subtle but unique aroma, I used my sensitive olfactory senses to find its position in the large arena. I could see the Azorian using his heat-sensitive senses to distinguish the root's signature over other non-biological items in the arena. We both found it at the same time: across the gap, not far from where Barbariccia was seated. Chaos, it was probably in his pants pocket.

The Azorian ignored me, ditching combat for speed, and made a run for the still growing gap: he was going for the root first! I pelted after him. We both cleared the gap at the same time. The Azorian landed with a grunt on his huge flat feet then stomped into an impossible run straight toward the grinning Eosian. Right behind him, I landed with a roll that progressed into a leaping run.

Before I realized it, the Azorian came to a dead stop, turned and lunged for me. He swiped at me with one of his huge flat paws and caught me in the shoulder, throwing me to the ground. I hit my head and blacked out momentarily, hearing the crowd cheer. Shaking my head to clear it, I scrambled up, realizing that the Azorian could have easily finished me off but had chosen not to. In that time, he'd retrieved the root behind a ledge on the arena bleacher boards just beneath where Barbariccia was seated and was brandishing it triumphantly to the audience.

The crowd cheered madly as I threw myself at the Azorian, striking out in a veltic kick. It was like striking armour. The Azorian grunted with the impact but remained unaffected. He turned to me and swiped out again. I jerked back to avoid another blow and lashed out again with my long leg, using the weight of my whole body. The Azorian recoiled slightly. Clutching the root in one hand, he swiped repeatedly with the other as I dodged and kicked out. The Azorian fled suddenly and it was obvious to me that he was going to attempt to leap over the gap. The gap had grown very wide and I doubted that the Azorian would clear it. He didn't and fell with a terrified shriek.

Heart pumping, I leapt in behind him, hearing startled cries from the crowd.

I plunged feet first into dark freezing water and rose quickly to the surface with gasping breaths. I immediately spotted the Azorian, floating with his face in the water, already unconscious under severe hypothermia. The swift current was carrying him toward the wall. I swam hard with the current to reach him and, by chance, found the brightly coloured root he'd been holding floating on the surface nearby. Snatching the root then sticking it in my mouth and clutching it in my teeth, I seized the large Azorian and wrenched off my belt, hoping my oversized overalls and stretchy top would stay on me when I shifted. With a deep inhale I shifted to a powerful Khonsus. Just as the wall was about to take us, I pumped with my powerful legs and spread my Khonsus wings, rising out of the water while clutching the Azorian by his armpits. I pushed with all my might in a burst of speed to soar like a jet in an arcing trajectory. Just before we cleared the opening and were about to reappear in the arena overhead, I returned to my human form. I let go of the heavy Azorian, who thudded to the floor, then landed in a roll.

The arena was silent for a brief moment of shock. Then the astonished crowd broke into a thunderous raucous of cheering and applauding as I stood up in my baggy oversized overalls, soaking wet and covered in sludge. After a glance at the already stirring Azorian, I drew myself tall and took the root gripped between my teeth in my hand and raised it to the crowd.

They shouted with delight and I felt a tremulous smile tug my lips, already drawn back in panting breaths. Despite this place, I felt a brief thrill in my personal triumph. I'd beaten the game and I hadn't killed anyone.

Still holding my smile, and chest heaving with deep inhales, my gaze finally rested on Barbariccia and I nodded to him. He returned me a stony glare then narrowed his eyes.

Φ

Each evening for a week, I sponsored myself against one of Barbariccia's candidates. Another Xhix, a Delenian, two Badowins, and even an Eosian. Each time, I found a way to outwit or out-maneover them by playing to both their strengths and weaknesses. And, of course, using brief invisible bursts of critical shape-shifting. Each time, to my pride and satisfaction, I managed not to kill my opponent to achieve my victory. Eventually, I realized that this, alone, was enough to enrage Barbariccia. It seemed to humiliate him more than it humiliated his contenders.

Several of them simply demonstrated new respect for me and one of them even defected from Barbariccia's fold of henchmen to devote himself to my well-being: the Azorian I'd saved. His name was Tat Mol. I discovered that he'd been incarcerated here for a major embezzlement scheme against the Galactic Bank. No one fooled around with the Galactic Bank and he was sentenced to Sekmet to send a clear signal to anyone else contemplating a similar crime. Although he'd shot a law enforcer during the coarse of a wild chase, I felt vindicated in my intuition that Tat Mol was not a natural killer. He'd played the game because he was desperate, just like me. I'd first taken notice of Tat when he began to follow me around like a fan would a superstar. Initially annoyed, I finally took pity on him and shared my wakesh root with him. I had plenty. I won a new one each day during a game and had points enough to buy lots more from Mayling. Although I didn't think I needed one, Tat dedicated himself to being my bodyguard. It gave him something useful to do, he'd said.

THIRTEEN

I savoured the black longing pain in my belly as the wakesh root wore off. I prolonged the burn in my gut for as long as I could, until it splintered up and made me shiver with unfathomable desire. The timing was just right, I thought, pulling the root out from my overalls pocket with a shaky hand and biting hungrily into it. I instantly felt its euphoric energy throb in my veins. I felt the dull nausea crawl inside and settle like a great bear in my stomach as strength and drive surged through me like white lightening. Then my lips pulled back and

I released a feral smile of pure manic energy.

I'd waited until the last possible moment after feeling the root's effects wear off to achieve maximum effect. Now, as I stood poised to enter the game arena, my body surged with power. I was wired for action.

As both sponsor and player, I stood to gain 1500 points and a wakesh root in this game.

I took in a deep breath then entered. The stands were crowded as usual. At my entrance they broke out into boisterous shouts and cheers and I realized with a burst of self-conscious pride that I was now the crowd's favourite. I made out a large number of Rills, including Mayling, as I cast my gaze around the circular arena. I even spotted Iris, Orchid and April seated together below her. Tat stood at the very back, keeping watch. When I spotted Barbariccia, already seated in his favourite spot near the arena floor, I sauntered toward him.

"Are you sure you want to sponsor yourself in this one, slave?" Barbariccia challenged with a leer when I was within a few meters of him. "Fifteen hundred points is meaningless when you're dead...or worse," he ended diabolically.

I gazed at him calmly. This was my seventh game and I remained undefeated, save the first one. I didn't bother to answer but levelled a steady gaze at him.

"So, why do you keep ditching your sexy clothes for that jagging sac of shit?" He laughed maliciously, a stuttering cackle I found revolting, then licked his lips slowly. "Thought you might get them dirty? You won't care when you're dead. You're so pathetic, Hawke."

"Appearances can be deceiving," I said quietly then let my lip curl up on one side. "*Under a ragged coat lies wisdom*...old Romanian proverb." I raised a brow and firmed my lips. "I'm sorry I toasted that Eosian in the men's washroom." My voice softened to a surprising gentleness as I felt unwanted compassion flood me with sudden understanding. "He was your lover, wasn't he?"

I knew I'd guessed right, watching him draw in a shuddering breath and bring a hand up blindly to his face. I'd obviously rattled him with my remark. I hadn't intentionally meant to unbalance him, but now that I had, I'm sorry to say that I felt inward satisfaction.

"You should have told him to think twice before selling *glitter* to innocent Creons so he could rob them later," I added as an afterthought. "He had no honour."

"You're one to talk of honour...*traitor*," he spat out.

God knew I probably deserved to be here but not on that charge. But I kept my thoughts to myself.

Barbariccia's snarling mouth turned into a sneer and he added very loudly for everyone to hear, "Oh, by the way, you're a great jag, slave."

I winced inside at the sordid truth and felt my face flush with shame and anger. I'd never been quite sure. It was obvious that Barbariccia had intended to humiliate and unsettle me with that remark. He'd grown desperate. I hid my shocked revulsion and calmly replied in a voice meant only for his ears, "It was easy when I pictured you as someone else."

"Still," he pressed on loudly, "You liked me well enough." He sneered with disdainful pleasure and I saw his pupils dilate. He then cackled maliciously. "I was just about more than you could handle, eh, human?"

There were several sniggers in the crowd.

"Not really," I responded coolly, "considering that I did all the work." I had the satisfaction of seeing him colour and heard more sniggering from those close enough to hear. I let my tongue brush lazily over my upper lip in mock seductiveness. "I got myself off. You were just along for the ride. You could have been a bed post for all you did."

Amid a few guffaws, his face went dark purple and he abruptly lashed out at me. I jerked back out of his way.

"You always get others to do your jobs, even the pleasant ones," I said more loudly. "It's your moniker, isn't it Barbariccia. That's why you're going to lose." I sneered with demonic inspiration. "I know why Eclipse put you out of business so easily, because you're a petty thinker with no imagination and no courage to raise the stakes. Well, I'm raising them now." I turned to the crowd. "We play for the Rills!" I announced.

"What?" Barbariccia grunted. The crowd had also gone quiet in shock. I glanced at the Rills. Iris, Orchid, April and Hyacinth. They stared in bewilderment, Mayling too.

I turned to Barbariccia with an intense glare. "If you win, you get all the Rills as your personal slaves as well as their normal duties working the mines. If I win, the Rills are free. No one is allowed to touch them or order them around. *No one.*"

Barbariccia tossed his head back and cackled loudly in sudden understanding. "You're a jagging bleeding heart! You killed so many Rills; now you want to make up for it?" He barked out another stuttering laugh. "Now, that's choice: an assassin with a conscience...a little late for that now, don't you think?"

"It's never too late, until you're dead."

"Well, you will be soon, slave. You're more pathetic than I thought you were, Hawke. The Rills are already mine to do as I please." Then he eyed me wickedly and nodded. "And talk about raising the stakes, I accept only if we change them to this: if my candidate wins, *you* become my personal slave, remaining at my side as my courtesan, to do whatever and whenever I may please with you—that's *if* you survive, of course."

I kept my face impassive but felt myself swallow convulsively. I thought of his Venik thugs and their perverse ideas of fun and Barbariccia looking on, masturbating. I didn't want to imagine the possibilities. "Very well," I forced out the words quietly. "I agree to your terms."

"You've all heard the terms!" he leapt up and shouted to the crowd, hardly containing his glee. It made me suddenly uncomfortable. "If Hawke wins we leave the Rills alone; if my candidate wins, Hawke is mine," he ended with a diabolical sneer. "Then let us begin." He raised his hand. "I have chosen as my candidate, Ra!"

Φ

Even before the Khonsus entered the arena, I flinched with

alarm at the name, which had given away what he was.

The other door opened and I heard the trilling as a huge tawny-feathered Khonsus emerged, wings already spread, and floating toward me, mouth open in song. Eyes shining like liquid gold. The crowd cheered. I quickly averted my eyes and thought desperately about my alternatives. How could I fight this behemoth with mind-raping eyes? If I couldn't face my opponent, how could I strike? Despite his lack of agility, the Khonsus had me beat on the offensive.

It was just then, as I quickly looked away from the Khonsus and directed my gaze toward the bleachers, that I saw him and started. Serge! In the form of an Eosian. Our eyes locked and his spoke volumes. Of sad longing and anguish…and hope. Suppressing a sharp inhale, I unthinkingly brought my hands to my face, fingers cool against my burning cheeks, and stared back, caught in his gaze. I forced a glance at Barbariccia to make sure he was still there and sure enough he was, gazing at me with a sneer spread across his smug face. Blinking hard, I returned my gaze to where I'd seen Serge. He was still there, watching me intently. I felt the sound erupt from my lips before I had a chance to stifle it, a kind of moan. It couldn't be. It had to be a wild hallucination, some side-effect of my drugs and my foolishly longing heart. Another one of my cruel visions…

Then Serge abruptly looked past me with alarm. Alerted, I darted out of the Khonsus's striking range, pirouetted with closed eyes and jabbed in a side-kick. I landed it and heard the Khonsus grunt with surprise. I followed with a hand-stand back flip kick to his chest, sending him staggering back. Then, shifting briefly—imperceptibly—into a Khonsus, I opened my eyes and caught the golden gaze of the stunned Khonsus. In that brief second, I bit sharply into his dazed mind before he had a chance to recover. He screamed.

I sprang into a whirling dervish leap, ending in a wide-arcing kick to his head. The large Khonsus thudded to the ground, knocked out, as I landed on my hands and feet then stood up, desperately searching the crowd for Serge. He was gone. Had it been a cruel vision? I hadn't realized how much I needed to see him there and felt my heart plummet. Oh, God! I couldn't bear it, the misery of letting hope invade me again only to dash my heart against the rocks in its swell. Of all the sensations I'd tried to quell, hope was the cruellest.

Blinking back tears in a slight shudder of stifled weeping, I forced myself to the task at hand. Smelling out the root, I found it and held it up for the audience to see. They stood and cheered wildly as I once more scanned the crowd for that face I longed to see again. As the cheering subsided and the crowd sat down, I finally turned to Barbariccia. He stared at me with open scorn and fury.

"My, my, my..." he drawled. "Mercy towards your enemy and a conscience for the downtrodden." He glared at me with a shake of his head. "You've gone jagging soft, Hawke," he growled with obvious ill-temper at having lost his elusive prize: me. "And your luck can't hold out for long. Those traits you've recently cultivated won't do you any good in here." Then he decided to be vastly amused by me and let out a peal of sinister laughter. "It's actually quite ironic, really, Hawke, your tragic sense of timing..." Yes, that was *my* moniker. "...You apply cold-hearted assassin's rules in the outside world when you could have used some compassion; then you cultivate compassion and mercy in a place where cold calculation and swift dispatch works best. You really have no idea how this world works, do you? You're pathetic, Hawke, and you can't beat me."

"I'm not trying to," I admitted and saw his face briefly betray confusion.

"You should be," he said, sneering. "Because I am."

"That'll be your downfall." Then, noting that the next slot was open, I lifted my head high and projected my voice to the crowd as well as to Barbariccia, "I challenge *you* in the very next contest. You, Barbariccia. No one else. You and I. Right now. Or are *you* too soft?"

The crowd shouted in mad excitement. They stood up again and waved in frenzied enthusiasm. I'd called out a milestone contest. And despite his obvious reluctance, the haughty Barbariccia had no choice but to accept.

"All right. But only if we fight for the same thing as this contest."

I glared at him. I'd won the Rills their freedom already. But the crowd went wild with enthusiasm. "Very well," I said, realizing that one of the reasons he'd accepted so quickly was a second chance to win the other part of the bargain: *me*. "I accept."

Φ

I wasn't prepared for Barbariccia's bold and sudden move. Without ceremony he leapt onto the arena and slashed at me with a large knife. I barely ducked out of his way and felt a sting of pain on my torso where his blade had caught me. I swiftly drew up the blousy overalls and flicked my gaze down at the bloody eight-inch long slash. Gnashing my teeth, I focused back on Barbariccia, who'd shadowed my retreat and paced around me with a predatory grin. He ran his finger against his knife blade and brought the finger, dipped in my blood, to his lips. He licked off the blood with a carnal smile. It seemed his intent was to get me any way he could, dead or alive.

We paced around one another like two snarling animals. I lunged forward a few times to gauge Barbariccia's reaction speed and his movements. On one move, he unexpectedly slashed high and caught my upper arm. I cried out, more from surprise than pain. The crowd stood and shouted. Someone started stomping his feet. Soon the whole arena throbbed in a rhythm that matched my pounding heart.

Emboldened by the inmates' enthusiasm, Barbariccia charged at me in a frenzy of multiple lunges. Each time I managed to dart out of his reach and each time I saw him grow more furious.

By now, I had analyzed his movements and commanded myself into calmness. Although swift, Barbariccia was sloppy and had no method. He was just another thug, I concluded, watching his undisciplined lunges and attacks. I led him toward the opening chasm behind me. He didn't seem to notice or care. Perhaps he intended to push me into the pit. I had other plans.

I boldly rushed him and pirouetted with a low kick to his legs. He stumbled off balance but quickly recovered. He was a giant Eosian, after all, and much stronger than me. I leapt out again with a high kick and he ducked out of my way with a follow through slap of his hand to my solar plexus. I fell, turning, with a hard thud onto my stomach.

Barbariccia snarled and pounced, knife held up in a killer's swing to stab me in the back. But I had feigned my weakness. I spun around and kicked out with all my strength—and a little more, thanks to my flicker of shape-shifting—landing my boot against his chest. I lifted him off his feet and threw him toward the gap.

He landed in a slide and let out a terrified girl's screamed. The crowd went wild with thunderous shouts and shrieks.

I scrambled up and saw Barbariccia dangling over the edge of the platform of the yawning chasm. He'd slid over the edge and was scrabbling the ledge with his arms in a losing battle. His hold was slipping and one arm slid off.

"Please!" he shrieked with real fear. "I can't swim!"

Without thinking, I rushed to him and lay spread-eagled for balance. Digging my feet into the rough arena surface, I held out my arm. "Grab my hand!" I commanded. He swung his arm up and seized my hand. I pulled him back.

Barbariccia scrambled up with my help. Then, in a strangely familiar moment that forced me to seize in my breath, he savagely clutched my leg, dislodging me. For an eternal moment, our eyes locked: his blazing with sinister victory; mine widening in the final realization of how mad he really was. Barbariccia snarled, "You're coming down with me!" Then tugged fiercely. I lost my hold and slid.

We both fell.

I plunged into the icy black water of the bog and surfaced with a harsh shake of my head to clear my vision. I spotted Barbariccia quickly, thrashing in the water, head going under with panicked splutters. He'd told the truth: he couldn't swim!

He was drowning and the current was carrying him to the edge of the wall.

I swam over to him.

As soon as I reached him, Barbariccia seized my head and plunged me maliciously underwater. "Die, bitch!" I heard him splutter between gasping breaths and intakes of bog water. He wound his powerful thighs around my waist, effectively holding me underwater.

In cloying panic, I realized that Barbariccia wasn't interested in being saved; he was obsessed with killing me. I didn't have a chance as a human against his powerful rage. Swiftly losing my breath, I shifted briefly to a muscular Badowin and swung with all my might, fist connecting with his face. Barbariccia momentarily loosened his vice grip with a grunt.

Just as I wriggled free, I felt something large brush past me. I knew it wasn't Barbariccia and felt sudden alarm at the obvious conclusion: a sobek had gotten in! I surfaced in my returned human form with gasping inhales. Barbariccia was already metres away from me, carried by the black current to the wall.

"Look out! There's a sobek in here!" I yelled between gasping breaths.

"Save me! Help!" Barbariccia shrieked between gasping inhales of water, arms thrashing out madly. We watched the powerful wake of the huge sobek, circling toward him. For the love of Creos, the thing had to be at least twenty feet long! Barbariccia snagged on a solid tussock and scrambled on. The tussock didn't give way and Barbariccia barked out a victorious laugh. "I'll enjoy watching you get eaten!" he shouted gleefully. He *was* insane, I thought as I tread water and glanced from the sobek to Barbariccia. Then I saw the wall looming toward him.

"Look out!" I yelled. "Let go of the tussock! The wall behind you! Let go!"

Barbariccia sneered at me in defiance, distrusting my warning as a ruse. It was the last thing he did. I watched in horrified revulsion as the wall first knocked him down then relentlessly pressed him into the dirt and flayed his body sheer along with the tussock-top. Dark blood spread everywhere. The sobek thrashed around then disappeared under the wall along with what was left of Barbariccia. I didn't have to worry about the little blood I gave off from my flesh wounds. Barbariccia was providing much more for the hungry beast.

Holding down a grimace, I shape-shifted into a Khonsus and flew up with enough momentum to let me land as a human in the arena to surprised raucous and cheers. They'd all sat down earlier in bewilderment but now surged to their feet. Amid the clatter I heard them shout: "Mevlani! Mevlani! Mevlani!"

I stared at them in astonishment. Then I bowed my head in complicated shame and excitement. When I raised my head again, I inhaled deeply then announced in a loud commanding voice, "The Rills are free!" The crowd's animation dimmed. Taking advantage of their momentary quiet, I continued, "No one is to enslave them, abuse them, insult them or take advantage of them again. Or there will be punishment." My eyes challenged the crowd. I saw stunned disbelief on the faces of Iris, Orchid and April. What they must have thought at that moment I had no idea. I was sure they thought me quite mad. Even Mayling stared in amazement. Disbelief swiftly transformed into distrust. I saw Iris look suddenly very suspicious. She had every right to be leery; she and her colleagues had done nothing but mistreat me. How could they expect kindness in return? I could not help wonder, as my breast swelled with pride, if God—*my* God—had placed me here for this reason.

After a moment of quiet, the crowd cheered and surged toward me like a tidal wave. I recoiled briefly, but at the sight of their exuberant faces and hearing their cheering sounds I forced myself to stand my ground. It took all my control to keep from backing up as the mob descended upon me. They swept me up and, hoisting me on several pairs of shoulders, flowed out of the arena. I eventually understood that they were carrying me to Barbariccia's old control room upstairs. They took me right to Barbariccia's central hub chair and there dropped me gently to take my seat on his old thrown.

Seeing that they expected it of me, I sat down and realized the crowd expected yet more. Tat Mol came forward and Mayling pushed her way through.

Mayling bowed, eyes riveted to the ground. The crowd followed, murmuring, "Mevlani…Mevlani…Mevlani…"

Overwhelmed by strong conflicting emotions, I held my face tight, lips drawn back in a complicated smile. I was still breathing hard from my ordeal and the present situation made me extremely uncomfortable.

"Please get up," I said when I found my voice. "You're not my slaves. Get up! Now leave me."

The crowd backed away.

"Mayling, please stay," I said. Tat Mol hesitated, obviously hoping I'd ask him to stay as well. I added to him, "Watch the door, Mol. Let me know if anyone comes." It was a redundant request, I realized, noting that my holo readouts included surveillance of every part of the penal colony. Happy with his task, Mol trotted to the main doorway of the large chamber and stationed himself there.

I turned to Mayling with a sigh. "What now?"

"Youz defeated Mevlani. Now *youz* Mevlani," Mayling informed me. "This is your news place. Youz controls everything from here. Points. Jobs for new meats. Rules. You'll see. Best things is youz can give yourself as many points as youz want. And youz don't haves to works anymore ins the mine. Mevlani gets as many roots as theyz wants." Then she pointed up to a set of wire-mesh stairs. "You gets a nice big bedrooms with a view too."

"Thanks, Mayling. What about you? Can I give you anything? A better room, or—"

"I have everything I need right now," Mayling cut me off enigmatically, then turned after another bow and walked away. With disappointment, I watched my friend leave, my friend who didn't want anything from me. I let out a long exhale, then leaned back on the powerful chair and gazed at nothing, feeling alone.

FOURTEEN

I sat leaning slightly to one side and resting my arms on the armrests of the comfortable chair. I inhaled Barbariccia's lingering scent in the upholstery. I was showered and dressed in my original clothes—charcoal grey sentient flight trousers and jacket, gravity boots and grey top. I coolly regarded an Azorian who, though he cowered in front of me, looked unremorseful.

"You enslaved a Rill to do your bidding," I said. "Don't deny it. I saw you on my surveillance holo." I'd used it a lot initially, looking for Serge. Hoping beyond reason. Chasing ghosts.

"I forgot the new rule. It was a mistake—"

"There are no mistakes. There is only *duende*," I said, quietly repeating the cruel words Ka had used on me so long ago. "And for every action a reason, and a consequence, even if unclear to the doer." With those cold calculated words, I instructed the Azorian to place his hand on the post and removed all his points. "Now, go and earn your life."

After sending him on his way, I leaned back and raked back my unruly shoulder length hair with my hands. I frowned darkly. Since my ruling not to harm or abuse the Rills, spates of insubordination were running rampant. Inmates didn't like my rules. I even felt Mol looking at me strangely at times. The only person I could trust was Mayling, who stood next to me.

But I didn't even tell her about my search for Serge. Despite my new position of power, I dared not make overt inquiries. My power was fleeting at best and then only at the whim of the colony's inmates. Even now, as Mevlani, I was not liked and no friend of mine was safe from retaliation. I only drew Mayling close to me. If Serge was indeed here, we'd eventually find each other, I decided and ceased my dangerous search. I wasn't exactly invisible. Had I really seen him? Had he come to rescue me? More like he'd been caught in some unsavoury crime and was here on legitimate terms...More like

I'd imagined him there and it was I who was caught…in some unsavoury madness of longing.

Φ

Mayling stood before me, bowing obsequiously with eyes directed down.

I leaned forward on Barbariccia's old chair. "Oh, for creon-sake, Mayling, get up," I chastised my friend. "You don't have to do that."

Mayling looked up and met my gaze head on. "I'ves heards a bad rumours, Hawkes. Theys wants to kills youz. Most of the colony."

I pushed a half-smile. "Like that's news."

"Since youz banned the games, everyones is mad."

"You too?"

"Doesn't matters if I ams."

I leaned forward. "It does to me."

"The morales is very lows. Everyones is in a very bad moods and most of thems blames us for it. The Rills."

I swallowed suddenly. "I started all of this for the Rills. For *you*. I think I made it better. Didn't I, Mayling? Chaos, if I could shut off the drugs the AIs feed us I would but I can't control that. So, I give everyone enough points to afford a root shared among two people every day. We don't need the games anymore. No more killings on account of that cruel sport. You still get your points for the root. It's a win-win combination."

Mayling remained silent. She didn't seem to agree but she wasn't talking.

"Well, isn't it?" I prompted.

"Weez can'ts bring back that many roots. There's a shortage and inmates are gettings mads at us for it. The games served the purpose of a fair lottery, Hawke. What you've dones. It's backfiring on us."

I hadn't considered that. My mouth went dry with thoughts of failure.

"The inmates are bored, Hawke. Everyones looked

143

forwards to the game. The excitement, even the killings."

I met my friend's steady gaze with a faltering one and felt my face tighten at this news. It amounted to more than the lack of root supply. "I was just trying to prevent more killings than necessary," I went on, trying to justify myself. "Of course there'll still be killings. They're all murderers, after all. But the games were cruel. I'm just trying to make it more fair."

"In this place?" Mayling said, barely hiding a scoffing voice. She abruptly straightened. "Just watch your backs. And don'ts trusts anyones." Did she mean herself too? Then she turned and left, brushing past Mol at the doorway. I found him giving me a dirty look before turning quickly away when he saw me watching him.

Φ

I wake out of a febrile dream to catch the rancid smell of something disturbing and unfamiliar. It flares with the cloying smell of a sudden spike of pain. I do not question how I can smell the pain that is not mine, but I know it's real and that it belongs to my mother. This is confirmed as I hear my mother's plaintive wail—

I pelt to my mother's room and halt, stiff with fear. My mother lies naked with her face buried in the pillows of her bed, hands tied to the bed posts like a prisoner, and a naked baldie hunches over her. He gropes her buttock cheek with one hand, while holding a round device in the other, and rocks himself over her as she moans in pain then plaintively grunts out: "No, please! Oh, YES—

I scream, "Stop hurting my mom!"

Both my mother and the baldie turn abruptly to face me. My mother looks shocked. The baldie trades surprise for amusement and jeers, "You little fucker—"

I scream in terror and rage. What happens next is even more terrifying. A glowing energy flares up inside me. It concentrates behind my eyes into a seething flame and bursts through my eyes at the alien. He barely has a chance to utter a guttural cry before his body melts like putty.

I stare in shock at what I have done. I see the horror in my mother's eyes. Then she screams. This time the agony is unquestionable. They are the screams of one who has lost something precious—

I bolted awake in a cold sweat to the pungent odour of methane. Mayling was shaking my shoulder. "Yous haves to hide! They're coming for youz! Mol let them in!"

"What?" I mumbled, still groggy and disoriented from the awful nightmare I hadn't had for a while. My heart raced in alarm.

"Hurry!" Mayling whispered. She fetched my clothes flung over my dresser and threw them at me. My grey top flopped into my face. I snapped up my black trousers in the air before they did the same.

"Okay, okay," I grumbled, swinging my legs over the side of the large bed and sliding into my clothes. I was wide awake now. "Where can I go?" I asked the obvious as I pulled on my boots.

Mayling's three eye tubes focused on me. "My place. No ones will expect the Mevlanis to snuggle in with a lowly Rills."

I nodded, feeling a twinge of guilt at the spacious room I'd enjoyed since becoming Mevlani. The retreat to Mayling's would only afford me a few hours at best. Then what? I'd have to face the mob. And they'd probably kill me. For sport.

To my astonishment, Mayling knew a back way out of my penthouse bedroom and led me safely to her old sleeping chamber. We crawled inside the little cupboard of a room. None too soon the sounds of loud shuffling and shouting came and went: my posse.

"Sorrys for the mess and smell, Mevlanis," the Rill apologized.

I almost laughed at the obsequious words. "Oh, Mayling!" I said, tapping the Rill I was lying on top of. "I offered you more and you wouldn't take it. You saved my life. And please don't call me Mevlani anymore. I'm not your mevlani, or anyone else's, for that matter."

"Ais."

After a long moment of silence, in which neither of us

slept, I finally whispered, "You know, this is only temporary. In the morning I'll have to make my presence known."

"I knows," Mayling agreed sadly. She'd come to the same conclusion. We were just drawing out the time before the mob caught up with me.

"I have a plan. For escape, that is." I finally announced quietly. With that remark, I jolted with the sudden realization that, except for a brief moment when I thought I'd seen Serge, I hadn't once considered escape since I'd become Mevlani.

Mayling shifted under me. "What's your plan?"

"I'll leave the same way you do, out of the sewers and through the underwater tunnels. I'll catch a ride down with the AI cleaners, when no one else would dare be out in the halls." After a glance at the luminous dial of my watch, I added, "That should be coming through any minute now." I'd observed earlier that the AIs parked on the fourth level, where the sewers were.

Mayling remained quiet.

"Well?" I prompted.

"Hawke. This is a suicide plan. Youz won't make it."

I ignored Mayling's objection. "Do you mean the sobeks and koppies—"

"Kepries."

"Okay, kepries. What are they?"

"Kepries are large flying invertebrates that grows and hatch in the dung piles made by the sobeks. The sobeks, in turn lays their eggs in the dungs and when they hatch, the youngs feeds on the kepries."

I nodded with a grimace. Kepries couldn't be nearly as bad as the twelve-foot long ammuts I'd encountered on Horus. "What about the sobek adults? I just caught a glimpse of one in the pit with Barbariccia."

"They'res ferocious blenoid-like creatures but huge and with scales and sharp teeth whos lives in the deeper parts of the bog. Theys can grows up to twenty-five feets long and cans hold their breaths for up to an hours. If they're hungry, they chops up their preys into little pieces and eats them. But usually theys

146

drowns their preys then wraps them in a kinds of mucus for later eatings."

"Great," I muttered. The crocodiles of Sekmet. "And they find your tunnels?"

"They *makes* tunnels," Mayling corrected me. "Our tunnels sometimes merge with theirs, giving thems access to ours."

"Terrific. What about the kepries? What do they do?"

"Yous don't want to know."

"I *do* want to know," I insisted.

"No, you *don't*. It's all moot, Hawkes. Because yous can'ts survives the first legs of your escape plan. No ones excepts a Rill can swims the peat tunnels. They're a maze and some of thems are kilometres long…You'll drowns before you finds a way out to the surface, where the kepries lives, or gets eatens by a sobeks."

I smiled quietly. "Don't worry about the tunnels, Mayling. I'll manage."

"No, yous won'ts. It's nots like Omicron 12, Hawke." Mayling blurted out.

I stared at Mayling's dark shape and felt my heart slam. I whispered, "You…know."

"I'ves always knowns who youz weres," Mayling admitted darkly. "I's knews whats yous dids to my peoples on Omicron 12. Iris told me before you set foots in Hades. She was your informants on Omicron 12."

I stared in confused distress, wishing I could see Mayling's expression. I could just make out the silhouette of her bulbous head and tube-eyes; the left one was a little smaller than the others.

"Oh, God." I breathed in a hollow whisper of shame. I hadn't even recognized Iris from Omicron 12. All Rills had looked alike to me then. I surmised that after her act of treachery in betraying her own people, Iris must have attempted something to redeem her self-respect, which had resulted in her sentence here. I stared at Mayling. "You—why did you help me, then? Why didn't you let me perish the first day? And why did you give me the wakesh root?"

Mayling bowed her head and let her eye-tubes dangle. "I'ze was selfish. Iris wanted to throw youz to the sobeks but Ize wanted revenge," she admitted, a single eye bending up to peer at me.

"Revenge? By *helping* me?"

Mayling focussed all three tube-eyes sadly back on me. "Its woulds have been too easys to lets yous die the firsts day or the first week. I 'ze wanted yous to suffers for a longs times, as longs as possibles…"

I swallowed hard and we were silent for a long time. I finally said, "Why are you helping me now?" Or was it simply more of the same? I glanced at the door, imagining the bog beyond. What would I find out there? Or was it even simpler? Was Mayling executing me? I imagined her supporting my flawed plan…the vaporizers taking me to a place where I would be destroyed.

Mayling sighed. "Yous isn'ts whats I thoughts yous weres. What any of us thoughts you were. Yous are kinds, unselfish and honorables. Yous saved meez from Bondar ons the firsts days yous were heres when you didn't even know me. Before we became…friends. Then you tried to help us all, after we were all so mean to you, even when it meant risking your own freedoms and having the whole colony rebel against youz and them now wanting youz dead. Youz tried to stops the killings and made the games honourable. Hawkes, I thinks that maybe youz changed from what youz were and youz don'ts belongs here."

I stared at Mayling, unable to speak for a moment. Emotion lodged in my throat. Then I seized her slimy hand. "You don't belong here either," I insisted in a shaky voice. "Come with me."

"No, I *do* belongs here. More than youz know." Then she tensed. "Get ready! I hear thems coming!"

FIFTEEN

Immediately after the AIs passed Mayling's door, I opened it and leaped onto the top of one and scrabbled madly, almost sliding off. Once I had a good hold, I glanced back but Mayling had already closed her door. I swallowed down my misgiving and felt sorrow for my Rill friend. Good bye, *friend*. She'd called me that, *friend*. Well, I'd find out soon enough if Mayling was really my friend.

The vaporizers travelled past the main food cylinders and, sure enough, a few dazed patrons lingered. I shut my eyes and grimaced with sad revulsion at the jolting grind and sparking crackles and pops, followed by the cloying sweet smell of burning flesh. I gagged briefly, keeping my eyes closed, and commanded myself not to be sick. The victims hadn't made a sound, I thought in sickened grief.

Then the vaporizers continued on their journey, sweeping the hallways of bacteria, fungus, mildew and dust. After an hour, they took me down to the fourth level, rank with the cloying sweet smell of sulphur and sewage. To the bowels of Hades, where they finally rested. I hopped off, limbs stiff from holding on, as the last AI turned itself off for the night. I crept out into the rank sewer chamber.

Save for the thrumming of machinery, it should have been totally quiet; it wasn't. I heard sporadic bumps and the sounds of two Rills grunting and farting. God! They were making out down here!

I skirted around the anti-chamber from where the sounds of moaning pleasure emanated and remained unseen as I reached the main utility room where the hatch to the main sewer line was located.

Remembering how V'mer had ripped out of his clothes when he'd shifted into a larger form, I pulled off my boots then stripped and rolled my clothes into a bundle, cinching them with Bondar's knife belt. Just as I was about to lift myself onto the hatch lip and pull the hatch open, I heard the shuffling of feet and shouts from the slimy stairway. Chaos!

They were coming this way and I had moments before they were upon me. Had Mayling given me away, after all?

Then I flinched in alarm as a tall Eosian abruptly stepped from behind a large pressure container. In the instant that we made eye contact, I knew who it was and inhaled a sharp breath. Serge! This time there was no mistaking him, even as a purple Eosian. He was standing not more than three metres from me and I inhaled his heady scent. His thunderstorm eyes went dark as his pupils opened and he stared at me in amazement and miserable longing. I wanted nothing better than to rush into his sweeping arms. I didn't move. It all happened in a moment but it encompassed eternity. He took one step toward me then shifted in a jerky movement, as if controlled against his will, and dashed through the doorway into the hall toward the rabble.

I heard them arguing.

"...We found the jagging Rill alone!" one shouted. "She wouldn't tell us anything. I jagged her good! She's not talking to anyone now!"

I sucked in a sharp breath of self-rebuke for not trusting Mayling and let bitter sadness clamp my heart. Mayling had been my friend to the end. I hoped they hadn't killed her.

"Let's kill that jagging Mol! He sent us to that Rill on a wild blenoid chase!"

"Fami saw the bitch riding the vaporizers!" another shouted. That would lead them right here, I thought with alarm.

Serge's voice cut in: "I just saw the bitch go that way! Hurry! She's getting away!" I heard them scramble then run away.

Realizing that he was giving me the precious few seconds I needed, I slung my boots by their laces around my neck then hopped up to the ledge of the hatch and made ready to pull up the hatch door—

I came face to face with Iris. She'd just emerged from the anti-chamber, obviously alerted by the sounds of my pursuers. We stared at one another in a giant pause. What she would have said or done I don't know because just then two Veniks entered the chamber. As Iris turned to face them, I ducked down to crouch behind the cylinder, with my bare back against the cold metal. They hadn't spotted my fleeting figure—they'd seen Iris, who'd stood in front of me to the side, and were eying her with eagerness—but I'd recognized them in my brief glimpse: two of Barbariccia's former thugs, the same ones who'd violated me in the women's washroom soon after I arrived. I hadn't had them killed when I became Mevlani—live and let live, I'd thought.

"What are you doing here, Rill?" one of the Veniks growled. "We have a mind to teach you your place. The human bitch isn't going to be Mevlani much longer and you're still a slave no matter what she said."

Giving off a strong scent, Iris sidled forward as if to greet them and I felt sure she was going to give my presence away in concession for freedom from their abuse. The Veniks responded by eagerly pouncing on her. They pressed her between them and fumbled with her clothes. She said nothing, except to utter guttural moans, sandwiched between their jerking bodies.

I shivered with outrage and, without thinking, I unsheathed Bondar's knife, grabbed it by the blade then bounced to my feet—instantly assessing the situation—and threw. The blade caught one of the Veniks in the throat. He stiffened and raised four of his hands up to grapple at the knife, then went slack and toppled to the floor. Iris and the second Venik stared at me in shock. I stood naked before them, heaving great breaths, realizing that I had no other weapon. The Venik came to the same conclusion. After a brief glance at his dead colleague he charged me.

Everything happened so fast. Orchid leapt out from the anti-chamber with a banshee's yell and tackled the large reptilian. Iris jumped on him as well and they all struggled to his violent growls. I sprinted to the fallen Venik, pulled out the knife, then hurled myself at the struggling Venik and pushed the knife deep into his chest, piercing his main heart. He struggled fiercely as all three of us held him down. Then he slumped unconscious or dead.

I rose to my feet, regaining my breaths, and glanced at the two Rills. Iris and Orchid were obviously lovers, I thought. Drawing in heavy breaths of exertion, they both grinned at me, looking very pleased with themselves. I didn't know what to say and simply stared. They'd helped me. *Me.*

Iris pushed me gruffly toward the hatch. "Go! Go, before the others return!"

I nodded to them in silent appreciation, suddenly overcome with inexplicable emotion and not trusting my voice in a reply. I bent down and pulled my knife out with a swift wipe of its blade on the Venik's tunic. I hastily retrieved my bundle of clothes then leapt up on the hatch lip and pulled the door up with a glance back. The Rills had already slunk away. The two Veniks lay in black bloody pools on the floor. I had no time to hesitate at the foul stench released from below and, hugging my bundle, I lowered myself down a ladder then closed the hatch, shutting out all the light, behind me.

Φ

I climbed down in the pitch black and quelled the urge to shift into a Rill. The climb would be much harder as a Rill. I suppressed a grimace at hearing the trickle and plopping of sewage from the several conduits that led into this main vertical tunnel. The sharp rankness of alien excrement and urine overpowered the almost sweet methane aroma of the bog as I felt my way down the slimy rungs. I imagined myself a pilgrim in the frozen Cocytus, descending Lucifer's shaggy back toward the centre of the Earth. Looking for Purgatory.

I continued my blind descent, shivering with more than cold, until my foot plunged into frigid water. At that point I concentrated and soon bloated into a Rill. I submerged myself in the bog water, knowing I could breath underwater.

Now that I was a Rill, it didn't feel as cold and the pitch black resolved into several shades of grey. The maze of dark peat tunnels seemed endless. I could only trust in my new capacity as a Rill to compass myself in the right direction. There was no way of knowing if I was going in circles. I just had to trust in my Rill's homing ability and hope like crazy that I didn't run into a Rill-eating sobek. Rills, Mayling had told me, had a keen sense of direction, thanks to a small gland in their brain that acted like a compass. In truth, all I really needed to do was remain in one position sufficiently deep and let the entire facility overtake me as it crept along the giant bog. Not content to stay put, I headed in the opposite direction of the facility.

Φ

It wasn't long before I'd swum out from under the moving Penal colony into the natural darkness of the early morning. I remained submerged for some time, until the low drone of the facility dissipated to nothing.

Still clutching my bundle, I pulled myself out of the water and crawled onto land. I shifted back into my human form and shivered. The air ached with a complicated mixture of sulfur amid sweet and acrid aromas that reminded me of my travels with Benny. I reclined naked on the prickly turf to rest and breath in the bracing scent of freedom. The cold breeze wicked away the wetness on my shivering body. I'd been lucky, I thought; I hadn't encountered a sobek and I'd made it to the surface.

Rising on my elbows, I lifted my head and watched dawn break to the west, lighting the sky in intense shades of ochre, russet and indigo. It was so beautiful, I reflected. I'd missed the outdoors, its complex fragrances and wild beauty.

Directly overhead, dark clouds wept a fine mist that gently wet my face and made me blink. My muscles ached from my several hours long swim but otherwise I felt good. Goosebumps rose over my skin and I felt waves of shivers pass through me like a freezing surf. But I was free and, at least for the moment, it didn't matter how cold it was.

I took a quick bearing and saw that the colony was still visible in the distance. If I could see it, the AIs could still see me, I figured. Surmising that my dark clothing would afford me more cover than the light skin of my naked body, I wrung them out and pulled the damp clothes on with difficulty. Once dressed, I scrambled up with a shiver and bolted into a hunched run as the growing light of day defined the earthy shades of the bog.

By mid-morning the wind had picked up and the cold gusts sent the rain pelting down, spattering my face like wet missals and plastering my hair across my face.

Continually blinking the rain out of my eyes, I negotiated the hummocky terrain with difficulty, sometimes having to make major detours around large open bodies of water as I headed east. I eventually discovered to my dismay that my pace was swiftly faltering. My breaths began to labour as I pushed myself through thick wet scrub, past gnarly drowned trees,. I plunged with gasps into surprisingly deep crevices filled with bog water.

A glacial wind wailed through my shivering body and whipped my hair about my face. I was losing sensation in my legs and lower torso, which alternatively got wet and exposed to the cold wind. Sobbing in my breaths, I struggled over islands of soggy hummocks. Some turned out to be floating mats that abruptly caved in under my weight, plunging me into deep frigid murky pools. I was forced to thrash my way across deep bog water, grunting with effort.

How was I going to survive? A convulsive tremor ran through me. I needed to find some shelter and get warm. I gripped my waist with my arms. Where would I find that in this forsaken place? Even the hills were covered in bog; I'd observed that from the air when I'd first arrived. Then there was the question of food, I contemplated, reminded by my grumbling belly. With the exception of a few bird-like creatures, I hadn't seen evidence of any wildlife yet. Mayling had warned me about the sobeks and the kepries. But I hadn't seen any giant dung piles or flying invertebrates. Maybe Mayling had made them up. Poor Mayling....she'd been punished for being my friend. Just like Bas.

My mind drifted.

It wandered feverishly into places I didn't want it to go. To Serge. What had he been doing there in the penal colony? Why was he there? He'd never approached me, although he had helped me get away in the end. Perhaps I'd conjured him then just like I had in the arena and my hopeless sexual encounter with Barbariccia. I'd had so many crazy visions lately, I didn't know what was real anymore.

A deep ache in my belly made me halt for a moment and I felt my breaths stutter with black longing. My gut burned deep with need. It splintered through me and sent me shivering with despair. This wasn't just hunger. I knew what it was: it had been several hours since I'd had the last of my wakesh root. I was coming down hard.

...Killing U'clid with my eyes was the only good thing I'd ever done in my stupid miserable life, I considered. First there was the war, then U'clid's human plague, then *me*. It was the ultimate irony that Ka had set me up, I who'd thwarted their previous plan, to hand him the best weapon of all: my MEC. The ultimate weapon of destruction. God! They were all right: V'mer, my grandmother, Serge: I was a menace. Why had I bothered to escape? It wasn't as though I could do anything about my folly here, on this forsaken planet.

I let myself fall on my rump in the wet bog and broke out into convulsive sobs of total despondency. I recognized the drug-induced source of my emotional instability but couldn't help myself. Rain drummed my body relentlessly, merging with my tears. I should go back, I thought suddenly. There was nothing for me here. Mayling was right; I'd never survive. I *had* to go back. Maybe I could beg someone for a wakesh root.

I turned back for the colony and halted with a sharp inhale. I was face to face with a snarling fifteen foot long crocodile-like creature. A jagging sobek! I recoiled in a stagger. The sobek slithered swiftly toward me. I missed a step on a hummock and slipped. I wrenched my leg sideways with a sharp snap of pain and an outcry. Just as I scrambled up, the sobek pounced with powerful legs. I slashed out with my knife and caught the creature in the belly. The knife ripped through flesh and lodged, spurting greenish blood. The sobek shrieked then reared up, knife tearing out of my hand, and fled.

I stared, bemused and panting out my breaths as the creature slithered away and disappeared into a deep pond, leaving a thrashing wake in the direction of Hades. The sobek could easily have just bitten off my head. Mayling hadn't told me that sobeks were much less aggressive out of the water.

I leaned back in the muck and lifted my leg out of the murky water to examined it. The ankle was swollen and already visibly bruised. Probably sprained. It was the same ankle I'd sprained recently on Horus. The same one I'd broken on Mar Delena close to a year ago and sprained again on Virgil 9.

I rose and, glancing in the direction where the sobek had disappeared, resolved to put as much distance between me and the angry creature by heading toward the open fen of grassed hummocks, reeds and floating vegetation.

I stumbled several hours through putrid ankle-deep black water and soft mud, past islands of tall mud mounds. Succumbing to fatigue and shivering from cold, I tripped on a root and sprawled face-forward into the water and black mud. Spluttering and shaking my head, I sat up and coughed out water and mud. My ankle throbbed. I examined it and saw that it had swollen to twice its original size and was tender and hot to my touch.

I wasn't going to make it, I thought with dismay. I shivered in the cold muck and let a wave of hopelessness overtake me—

My head jerked up at the smell and I inhaled sharply: the wakesh root! It was close by, somewhere underfoot, underwater. Shivering my need, I frantically clawed the mud underwater for it, chest heaving with sobbing breaths. There! I'd pulled up a long gnarly root out of the black water and recognized its bright yellow flesh. Hastily wiping off the mud, I pulled hard at the exposed root, wishing for my knife, and feeling my insides crawl with desire. After some resistance to my tugging, a piece abruptly snapped off, throwing me suddenly backwards with my prize. I didn't bother to clean it thoroughly of the mud stuck to it, before franticly gnawing at the root.

Tasting dirt and metal, I leaned back and felt the drug course through me in a pulsing lance of dark elation. I moaned in a mixture of exhaustion and feral gratification. When I felt the familiar nausea cloy inside my stomach I knew I'd hit nirvana and let a sickly smile crawl over my face. I breathed in renewed strength. Maybe I would make it, after all—

A twig snapped behind me and I jumped, heightened senses inhaling musk and strawberries.

Serge!

"Rhea."

Relief and panic competed inside me. Serge was the last person I wanted to see me this way: filthy, junked-up, vulnerable...and longing for him. I hadn't heard him approach; I'd been too loud and distracted to hear anything else. Suddenly tearful, I scrambled to my feet and pocketed the root. I fled in a staggering run, tripping and stumbling over a tangle of roots in the muck. My ankle flamed. I didn't look back.

"What?" I heard him quip. "No warm welcome like: 'It's so good to see you Serge, I missed you so much.'" Then after a pause of huffing breaths, he added in exasperation, "Rhea! Wait up!"

"Why are you following me?" I threw a withering look over my shoulder at him. He'd gone back to being a human, those ugly lumi pants recklessly low-riding his hips and revealing taut abdomen muscles and the alluring curve of his pelvis. I noticed with some satisfaction that he was having a hard time negotiating the underwater root tangle as well.

"What do you think?" he answered in a sarcastic tone.

"I don't need your help!"

"That's a matter of opinion. You're hurt and you're crying—"

"You're the one making me cry." I glared at him. I hadn't noticed I was crying. "This is all your fault. I never cried before I met you."

He barked out an exasperated laugh then added, "That's because I woke up your senses. I made you alive."

"You made me miserable!"

"Alive and miserable, then," he conceded. "Let me help you." He broke into a sprint, splashing in awkward steps.

"I told you, I don't need help from a lying scoundrel," I

huffed and threw myself into a frenzied lopsided gallop to keep ahead of him. "I don't need help from a God-damned Vos, *Nihilist, anti-Nihilist,* spy, thief—whatever you are!" I tripped and fell. Serge was bending over me, pulling me up, even as I struggled to get free. My chest heaved. Black bog juice dripped off my face. I turned to face him and caught his intoxicating smell: a cottonwood forest in spring cut by musk and a hint of strawberry. It overwhelmed my senses and made me dizzy with desire. I stared up into his face and longed to fling my arms around him and kiss him. I bit out, "I'm perfectly fine on my own."

"Oh, you are, are you?" he retorted. "In case you didn't notice, I saved your scrawny flat butt." His face was close to mine, eyes blazing and breathing hard.

"Where were you the rest of the time? Sun tanning in the penthouse suite? Get off me!" I twitched my face from his and pushed away. I didn't like how he'd described my butt.

"It took me over a month just to get in," he huffed out, clinging to me and fighting off my struggles. "By then you were already running the place. I was stunned. I'm amazed at your talents, particularly in escaping. Frankly, Rhea, I didn't expect you to be in any shape to do anything—"

"Well, thanks for the encouraging thoughts and incredible faith in my abilities," I said tartly. "I had a little help from several friends and none of them was you." I thrashed out furiously to get free. "I didn't ask for your help back there. I could have managed, damn you!"

"You ungrateful little witch!" he growled, pinning my arms in a forceful embrace. He glared at me. "You're too jagging proud to admit that you need my help."

Lips snarling, I jerked out of his grasp but slipped in the wet sod with a shriek and took him down with me. We fell with a splat, black oily mud oozing over both of us. He scrambled on top of me, straddling my hips, and pinned my flailing arms with his hands.

For a hesitant moment I inhaled his heady aroma and felt myself tumbling dangerously into his tempest eyes. He held my gaze and I drew in a shuddering breath. So much passed between us in that gaze and for a moment we were staring at each other like the time when we'd first made love. It was an exquisite moment of infinite devotion, wonder and tenderness. And mutual surrender. And I felt as though I'd loved him and trusted him all my life—

Desperate, I shifted with a shrill grunt into a massive Venik, realizing too late that my clothes tore to shreds off of me. I struck out. Within a heartbeat, Serge matched my form, lumi-pants ripping off, and countered. I tried an Azorian. He matched. A Khonsus—he was already one! I finally returned to my human form and Serge followed suit, barking out a laugh and breathing hard like me. His dark eyes grew large. We were both naked.

"Good try," he panted with a rough laugh. He glanced down my body before locking eyes with mine. "Just look at you...You've chopped off your beautiful hair. The drugs have wasted your skin, done something to your eyes...But you're still so..."

I dreaded what he saw and met his thunderstorm gaze with my own vulnerable gaze. I knew I was a spectacle: wet and bedraggled hair plastered over my face in tangles of mud—yet I returned him a plaintive thirsty look...How I'd missed those eyes.

They blazed into mine. "...so beautiful," he finished in a hoarse voice. Then he slammed his mouth against mine in a crushing embrace. Like a spring released I yielded and we kissed. I flung my arms around him, clasping his neck and pulling him close, feeling the hard heat of his response. I savoured his body stirring over mine as I rocked my hips up against him. His lips flamed over my face, defining every feature, and I trembled at the tantalizing rasp of his whiskers. His hands mauled my body with uncontrollable ardour. I was all his...except—

"No!" I slithered out from beneath him and kicked out. He barked out a yelp. I scrambled to my wavering feet, slipping, and stuttered out in a shaky voice, "I won't let you take advantage of me."

"Advantage!" he exclaimed and rubbed his thigh. "You want it too, damn it. You were kissing back."

"I'm not...myself," I warbled, staggering back, and threw out an arm to lean on a stunted marsh tree. "I'm...I don't feel at all well," I said in a voice that sounded far away. I slipped and fell backward on my rump with a grunt. Serge surged forward to help then stopped himself.

A craving for more root seared a hole in my belly and burned up my throat like bile. I hadn't had enough. That explained my continued emotional wretchedness. Suddenly remembering the root in my jacket pocket, I scrambled on all fours in the mud. I frantically searched for shreds of my jacket, forgetting my state of undress and unaware that I was showing Serge my muddy backside.

"Looking for this?"

I jerked around and saw him holding up the yellow root. My eyes narrowed at him. "Give it to me," I commanded.

He sneered and pitched it in a hard throw into one of the deeper pools to my wail of objection.

I fell back into the mud and glared dejectedly at him. But it was an empty defensive glare. I felt sudden shame and fought down the intense aching need that gnawed my belly. I was keenly aware of my vulnerability and wished myself away from Serge's piercing gaze. I shivered sporadically from both cold and withdrawal, blinking back the rain that dripped from my eyelashes as I locked my gaze with his unerring one with difficulty. I broke off first, fighting from whimpering.

Serge sighed and I caught him watching me with a mixture of amusement and pity as I shakily wiped the hair plastered across my eyes and smeared my face with mud from my filthy hand. Then he tilted his head to one side with a sad smile.

"Listen, Rhea, I have an interstellar ship waiting not far from here. I've slaved it to my portable controls." He tapped a device in his other hand. "I promise I won't take advantage of you. I won't come near. Just let me help you get off this cursed planet. Then I'll leave you be. You can go wherever you want after that."

Damn Serge. And his beautiful body. I didn't want him to leave—I just didn't want him to know I felt that way. The memory of his kiss flamed still on my lips. The rain didn't help, washing the mud off our slick bodies and revealing him in all his magnificence. He was the last person I wanted to help me. Right now I didn't have a choice. I swallowed my pain and shame with closed eyes and finally nodded. I desperately wanted to leave this place.

"Good. Nice to see you've finally come to your senses," he said. Then his maverick smile returned. "And look, I've stopped your crying."

I barked out an exhausted laugh. It released more sobs. Damn him for seeing me this way, I thought, unable to stop my uncontrollable weeping. At least he had the sense not to approach me and looked away until my sobs abated.

We waited in awkward silence, sitting beside one another in the mud and careful to avert our eyes as the cold rain sluiced down our bodies and hissed and spattered on the ground. Shivering from cold, I brought up my knees and folded my arms around my legs. I fought the urge to crawl over and snuggle up against Serge's body for warmth.

I blinked back the rain and rested my gaze on the expansive blanket bog. For all its harsh inhospitability this wet habitat held an aching beauty...perhaps because I finally had some hope; I was with Serge and finally free from Hades and expected to be off this forsaken planet soon if all went well. There was no sign of Hades or anything that didn't belong to the bog as far as the eye could see in all directions. We could have been the last—or the first and only—humans there...like Adam and Eve.

Rhea! I'm coming!

The voice in my head had sounded like Benny's voice. I was starting to hallucinate...or...could it be the com implant in my ear?

When I saw the ship approaching, I gasped and wept

convulsively, forgetting my state of undress, and rose to my feet.

It *was* Benny!

I wiped the tears from my eyes and tongued on the mouth com I hadn't used for so long: "Benny! Can you hear me?"

Loud and clear, Rhea. Make way. I'll be landing.

Within moments Benny's welcome silhouette appeared over the horizon and I gasped out my joy and flung my hands to my mouth to keep from crying more than I was already. When Benny landed, Serge helped me limp up the ladder and as soon as he followed me in, Serge commanded Benny to take off. Benny had two blankets waiting for us. After grabbing one for himself, Serge wrapped the other around me. I accepted with an appreciative nod. The hatch closed and I seized hold of the closed hatch handle to keep from falling as Benny lurched up into the upper atmosphere.

"Oh, Benny, I never thought I'd ever see you again," I gasped out with a giddy smile at Serge. Then I cast my gaze around at Benny's interior, smelling and touching. "It's so good to see you, Benny." I found it hard to contain the emotional surge in my voice.

"And you, Rhea."

"I missed you so much."

"I missed you too, Rhea."

I gulped in a hitched breath and had to bring a hand to my mouth to quell the sobbing gasp that wanted to burst out. I never thought I'd see any of this again.

"Well," Serge muttered, "I guess we know who she likes best…"

He wandered to the brig and opened the hatch door. "Come here," he said to me. "Look at this." He pointed inside. I hobbled over, looking for something unusual. All I noticed was some additional equipment. Benny had also installed a shower. "What's this, Benny?"

"Now, Benny!" Serge commanded, quickly stepping back.

The barred door slid shut, locking me inside. Serge tilted his head to one side and smiled smugly at me.

"You son of a creon!" I shrieked, seizing the bars and

ignoring the blanket falling off me. "Let me out!" Serge didn't move. "Benny! Open the door!" I commanded.

"Benny knows this is for the best, Rhea. Welcome to your personalized detox unit."

"You bastard!"

SIXTEEN

"You have to take me back!" I insisted, glaring at Serge through the bars of my prison. How long had I been here? I'd lost track of time. I dropped to my knees, hands clutching the bars of the brig. "I command it! Benny! Don't listen to that Vos bastard!"

I abruptly started shaking uncontrollably and felt a dark sickness wash over me. I thought I might vomit...Shrill nightmares lapped on the shores of my consciousness, wearing away my sanity, like surf on a sandy beach. Staccato visions of my own vile acts.

"Please, Serge," I pleaded, sinking to the floor and weeping. "Please take me back. I *want* to go back," I sobbed. I lay on the floor, crying in convulsive shudders, craning to see him. "Please, please. I can't stand it! Don't let the fire take me again!"

He remained silent, standing stiff and gazing at me through the bars with pain in his eyes.

A violent shiver convulsed my body and I burst into a sweat. Serge's face and body broke up in front of me. Cold flames consumed me from inside and Serge disappeared as I burned up into a delirious oblivion.

Φ

I found myself lying in Serge's arms with the cold water of the shower spattering my shuddering body. We were both naked and I felt suddenly self-conscious. He'd seen me nude plenty of times before, but somehow this was different. I was vulnerable. He seemed to sense this and was uncommonly gentle with me while remaining detached as he directed the cold water over us.

I looked up at him with clammy fear and met his dark gaze, smelling his compassion—a gentle, sweet aroma of a cottonwood forest in spring—

Violent spasms wracked through my body like vicious waves smashing a rock face. Feeling my mind splinter, I clutched his neck with an involuntarily moan and tried to hang on to my mind. To Serge pressed against me, murmuring to me in a soothing voice. To his wonderful aroma and those strong arms snug around me.

Then my muscles seized up painfully and I felt my body abruptly stiffen like a hard board. I locked my eyes on his and knew with despair that he couldn't hold me. The wave swept up and shattered my mind. It fled in a million directions as I vaguely heard my own piercing screams of terror.

Φ

I roused as if from the dead, tongue thick and plastered against the roof of my mouth. I pushed my heavy lids open and found myself lying snug under warm covers in Benny's sickbay bed. I stretched like a cat with a lazy sighing breath and noticed that I was wearing a soft long nightgown I didn't remember putting on—or having.

"Good morning, Rhea," Benny's pleasant voice made me smile. "Welcome home."

"Mmm," I sighed out with another long stretch. "Thanks, Benny."

I sat up stiffly, partially still under the covers, and glanced down at my hands. I brought them up in front of me and turned them slowly to inspect. Although still mildly stained, they were no longer swollen or cracked. The back of my right hand contained a long rectangular scar where Benny had obviously removed the sensor that had been stitched there. No nuyu, I thought with wry humour then felt my throat swell as I made out the faint remnant of the ouroboros tattoo that Benny had not totally succeeded in eradicating. I remembered Serge asking me, soon after we'd become lovers, why I hadn't had my scars removed with nuyu. They were a part of me, I'd answered.

I blinked several times and ran my fuzzy tongue across my slime-covered teeth. They needed badly to be brushed —

"There's a toothbrush and toothpaste there for you, Rhea," Benny said.

"Thanks." I smiled. Benny was always anticipating my needs. I grabbed the brush on the small table beside the bed and added toothpaste then, after a dip of the brush into the water glass on the table, I brushed my teeth and inhaled the refreshing mint in my mouth. I spat out the waste froth into the dispenser Benny had left on the table, took a drink and spit some more then drank the rest of the water.

"Would you like some soyka gum?" Benny inquired.

For the first time in my adult life, I felt sick at the thought of soyka or soyka gum. "No thanks, Benny. Not now anyway." Not ever, I thought with sudden revulsion.

My stomach growled with hunger. As if on cue Serge entered with a tray of food and I immediately coloured, noting the suave cut of his intelligent tocanai suit on his long muscular body. My gaze flickered appreciatively over his masculine form, defined by a light blue open-collared textured shirt, comfortable-fitting grey trousers and open jacket. My eyes finally rested on his rugged though clean-shaven aristocratic face. His dark grey eyes sparkled like dew in the morning as he flashed an open smile at me, setting my face afire. He was so wonderful to look at. A few rogue curls of his steely-brown hair hung over his forehead, begging for my hand to sweep them aside.

"Benny said you'd be famished when you woke up." His voice was like dawn breaking. I could listen to him talk all day. Serge set the tray down beside me but didn't sit himself. I proved him right by seizing the tray and bolting the food down, avoiding his gaze. It was my favourite Earth dish, synthesized by Benny: Japanese sushi, tempura, salad and miso soup. When I finally looked up at him, staring at me with a half-amused, half-bemused look on his face, I barked out an awkward laugh, soup spraying out of my mouth. It made me laugh more and I brought my hands up to my mouth in embarrassment. Despite intense shame at my pathetic performance in the Sekmet swamp, I let giddy happiness surge through me. Serge had come for me. For *me*. And I dared hope that he'd done it because he cared for me.

"How do you feel?" he asked with a gentle smile and attentive eyes.

I swallowed down what was left of my Ebi Roll before speaking. "Good, thanks." Feeling still awkward with him, I turned back to my food and bolted more, chop sticks deftly snagging a Tamago Roll and stuffing it whole in my mouth. I wasn't sure but I recalled some rather unsavoury memories during detox. I finally gathered the courage to look up at him again and say, "I don't remember much during detox. You took care of me..." I swallowed convulsively. "—Helped me get past some awful moments and I'm sorry if I said anything offensive to you. I wasn't myself." I gave him a tight smile of appreciation. "I have a lot to thank you for."

He nodded to me in silent acknowledgement, dark eyes smiling tenderly. They suddenly sparkled. "Does that mean you won't put me in the brig this time?"

I smiled crookedly to his rakish grin. Then I let a brow furrow slightly in inquiry and pulled up my knees under the blanket to hug with my arms. "How long have I been..."

"Detoxifying? Twelve standard galactic days," he said, sitting next to me on the bed. "We've been keeping out of any major systems and only touched down once for supplies and to get you some warm bedclothes."

I smiled in gratitude and hugged my soft nightgown: Serge's taste, no doubt. I normally just wore a t-shirt and men's briefs to bed.

"Benny helped speed up the detox process by using an air mix that helped counteract the drugs in your system. Benny's analysis suggested that you got a mouthful of human-specific psychoactive drugs, mainly depressants, each time you ate on

Sekmet. Benny thinks that every time your mouth touched the hose, the DNA signature in your saliva triggered a specific mixture suited to you. Very clever, considering the mix of species there and their individual physiologies."

I frowned. "Yes, very," I muttered back and thought how unsanitary the whole thing was.

"Benny identified a nasty and very addictive mixture of opiates and benzodiazopines that you would have eaten daily in that mash cocktail. The counter drug in the wakesh root was, of course, a powerful and dangerous stimulant, a complicated hallucinogenic amphetamine mixture. If used for too long, it would have driven you mad and eventually killed you."

Hence the sudden collapse of the leadership that Mayling had referred to. Perhaps that was what happened to Barbariccia in the end. He'd gone mad.

"We were lucky. Your strong constitution and quick healing abilities helped. We should have taken you to a Med-Facility but we couldn't risk it, so Benny had to replicate a detox tank. The brig worked well as a holding area. And the shower was good for your delirium and fever shakes..." He smiled a little like a rogue. I remembered being naked in his arms. "You kept fluctuating from one state to the other," he went on, nudging my memory, "coming down hard each time in severe withdrawal. It sent your body into shock and jagged your endocrine system and your thermal-regulatory system among a host of other things." That brought back some memories I'd rather not have had, of desperate things I did and said while coming off the drugs. "Benny can list them all for you later. Benny knew what to do each time. He's the one you need to thank, Rhea. Benny saved your life."

I nodded and gazed up at the ship's walls. "Thanks, Benny."

"You're most welcome," Benny responded. "Glad to have you back, Rhea."

I smiled weakly. "Glad to be back."

"I guess the wakesh root, ironically, kept you alive during the three months you were on Sekmet," Serge said.

Three months! Was that all? I was certain I'd been there longer. I glanced from Serge to my food and took another bite, nursing thoughts of Sekmet. "I'd have perished in a few weeks if Mayling hadn't introduced me to the root," I admitted. "I only wish I could have saved those poor Rills..."

"The Rills? Don't worry about the Rills," Serge quipped in a puzzling cavalier tone. He waved his hand in the air as if to dismiss them. "They run the place." He laughed briskly at my startled look of disbelief. "They're the unofficial custodians of Hades. They've had the contract from the beginning. Their ingenious proposal even beat out the Eosians."

"But—that's not—" I spluttered, trying to gather my wits. "Mayling...she was brutally attacked by that Venik when I first came. And I saw them gang-rape another Rill soon after." I didn't mention my own gang rape.

"All part of their ruse and definitely part of the risk, a casualty of doing this kind of business. I'm not saying it wasn't real. Quite the opposite. But that's how they play that game, for keeps. Don't forget, they were used to being abused on their own home planet by an aggressive colonizer. This isn't so different except they get paid big currency for it."

"But, Mayling was...was..." I felt my face tighten.

"Not killed, as it turns out. They beat her up but she'll be fine, Rhea." He patted my hand. Then he tilted his head. "I'm also compelled to point out that the Rills probably didn't mind all that sex as much as you think," he went. "The Rill are intensely sexual beings. What you thought was a rape was probably just a healthy dose of rough sex between consenting partners."

I blinked. "I...I...really..." I trailed, mind revisiting each supposed act of sexual assault and trying not to compare them to my own. Serge might have been right, I thought at length, recalling Mayling's rather casual dismissal of it all. But then there was Bondar: "But I saw a Venik kill one of them..."

"Doesn't happen often," Serge said, frowning slightly in reflection. "Your presence there probably provoked it—"

I felt my heart race. "Are you saying it was my fault?"

"No, of course not." He reached out as if to touch my hand then seemed to think better of it. "But you know Veniks. They're easily goaded to violence, especially where their pride is involved."

I had to concede to that and felt my lips tighten with the thought. Bondar had a thing for me and it made sense that I'd pushed him to that violent act.

"The inmates might have thought they were running the place," Serge went on, "but it was the Rill all along. They made all the decisions, like who got to play the game and who didn't."

I thought of Mayling's help in that matter. She'd manipulated me from the start. Mayling had as much as admitted it too.

"Not bad for an otherwise oppressed sub-dominant race who've never risen from slavery except on one short occasion when a certain Guardian Enforcer put them back in their place, eh?"

I forced down a hard swallow of shame and Serge swiftly lost his smirk. I tried to hide my shame by pushing out my tight jaw and found myself desperately glaring at him for his hurtful reference to my previous act of treachery.

"I'm sorry," he apologized, leaning suddenly forward and obviously wanting to take my hand but stopping himself. "I shouldn't have made fun."

I briskly pulled off the covers and swung my legs out of bed. Then I stood up barefoot in my long nightgown, holding the empty plate, and pressed my lips tight with a forced half smile. "That's okay," I said with icy calm, "I deserve it. I just wish it wasn't you who said it." I turned to leave. "Good night."

"Wait, Rhea," Serge implored and stood up with me. "I'm really sorry I said that. Besides, this is your room. I'm the one who should leave. But, come and sit. We've both said some things lately that we shouldn't have...."

I turned and sat down beside him on the bed. Truth was, I didn't want to leave his company just yet.

He offered me an open smile, eyes twinkling like miniature galaxies. Obviously hoping to cheer me up. It did.

And drew out a half smile from me.

He gazed deeply into my eyes, touching my fluttering heart. My tremulous smile blossomed into a broad grin. How long since I'd smiled? For an eternal instant we grinned at one another and I felt a brief moment of peace in that elation. In that moment it seemed as though so much more passed between us: an understanding of friendship and trust. Of love. And for that instant I knew what it was like to be home.

Then Serge's smile faltered and he looked away, face darkening and shattering that precious moment. "You did it, didn't you?" He dropped the smile and turned back to gaze at me with a pained look. "Gave Ka your MEC design."

I swallowed and firmed my lips, then looked down and nodded, unable to meet his eyes any longer.

"God help us all," he murmured. After a long silence I glanced furtively up and found him watching me in sullen contemplation. He pursed his lips. "Our ghosts didn't always see everything clearly but it became obvious once we'd entered your diverse that my father's virus wasn't likely to wipe out the human race." He looked past me deliberately. "But we also knew from our own past that a new weapon of mass destruction would become available. One that would selectively kill any DNA type...like all humans for instance," he ended grimly.

"The MEC," I breathed. "You're referring to *me*."

He nodded soberly. "We knew what you were going to do before you did. There was talk of a human who walked among Eosians for years before Ennos signed you on with the Guardians. I made the connection after I met your inner diverse self. Her dreams were...very revealing," he ended with a grim smile. It turned into a grimace and he pursed his lips sternly. "Unfortunately, others made the same conclusion and you became Plan B and everyone's prize...Ka's prize. Almost everything that has happened up to now has happened out of his devising. And all of it involved you in a major way."

I sat back and expelled a long breath. I'd been a pawn for so long without even knowing it. It made me furious. I felt sparks of anger flame through my blistering shame. "Why didn't you tell me this before?" I challenged. Would I have listened? Probably not. "God, what else does Ka have in mind for me?" I sighed.

"Haven't you done enough already?" he said sharply, and rose to his feet. He said sternly, "This was *exactly* what I was trying to prevent..." He paced like a lion and rubbed his temples wearily, then added in a grumble, "Among other things." He was, no doubt, alluding to all the other *faux pas* I'd managed recently. "You should have given *me* the MEC design...You should still give it to me," he ended gruffly. He slid one hand in a trouser pocket and let his cold steel eyes pierce into me. They sliced into me with cold deliberation, expecting me to naturally acquiesce.

This was too much! I surged to my feet and glared at him with rising anger. "*Other things*? Why don't you go ahead and say it: like everything I've done since I scorched your father with my eyes."

"I told you before, this isn't personal."

"So you keep insisting. You want it just handed to you? Why don't you ask your sister, then. She should have it by now."

He firmed his lips in frustrated anger and grabbed the collar of his shirt then waved his other hand at me. "I told you, we're on opposing sides."

"You want me to give the design to *you*, though. So that your two competing sides can take turns killing humans and blowing this galaxy up," I said, crossing my arms over my loose-fitting nightgown.

"Haven't you listened to a word I've said?" he growled. "Our group doesn't—"

"As though I believe you." I tilted my head to one side with a cold smirk. "You two groups need to settle your differences and harmonize if you're going to succeed in taking over this galaxy—"

"I told you!" he shouted, losing his temper and stomping a foot. "We aren't from another galaxy! And I'm on *your* side!"

I barked out a sharp laugh. "More stories to suit your circumstance. Like you're doing this out of the goodness of your heart. You're just a snide, lying arrogant thug with false allusions of appearing a gentleman. You're the rudest and most disrespectful man I've ever met. You don't fool me, Serge—V'ser, whatever you call yourself. You've been after the MEC and its design since we first met and you've charmed, lied, and bullied your way to get it since. I'll *never* give you the design." I watched his expression change from startled dismay to mild affront as I berated him.

He narrowed his eyes at me and blew out a sigh. "Then we're all doomed," he said quietly. He followed with a sneer of contempt. "Congratulations."

"Sure. Blame *me* for what *you're* going to do."

He glared back. "I can't believe this!" he expostulated. "Didn't you learn *anything* on Sekmet? I would have thought that the penal colony had mellowed you, taught you some humility. You're so—" He cut himself off and shook his head. He waved his hand animatedly at me, opening and closing his fingers. "Always snapping back like a baby blenoid. Why can't you just accept for once that you've made an incredible mistake, the greatest mistake in your entire miserable little life, and swallow the jagging thing!" he scolded. Then, with a sound of exasperation, he turned to leave the room.

"And where dare I ask was my greatest mistake?" I taunted. He halted and swung around to glower in angry disbelief, planting stiff fingers on his hips. I went on, "Was it in giving Ka the MEC design and not *you*? Or was it in saving a *Nihilist* traitor—"

"You *didn't* save him—"

"Or was it in not submitting to your pathetic seduction attempts!" I shrilled out in defensive anger at his pointing out the awful irony of my misplaced heroics.

Face reddening, Serge twisted his mouth with a sound of frustration and I braced for a furious rebuke. His hands clenched but he spun around to leave. Then he reconsidered and, unclenching his hands, turned back with glacial calm. "Oh, and you can stop flattering yourself about how you helped the Rills," he said dryly. "They wanted you out of there as much as the other inmates. Your little personal mission for 'Rhea justice' spoiled their whole system and made the Rills conspicuous. It increased animosity against them and ended up putting them at higher risk of being killed. Sekmet's a permanent penal colony, Rhea, not a correction centre. Its inmates are virtually all incurable lifers. They're there for committing atrocious crimes. The Rill had a finely balanced system that played to their cruel motivations, a system that not only worked and paid for itself but was extremely profitable. It'll be months, perhaps years before the Rills have it all normal again. Maybe never…"

I felt my throat swell with his cruel revelation and stepped back, wavering, as if he'd struck me.

"…now that their usual vehicle for wakesh export is nonexistent…" he added grimly. *What?* I couldn't speak but my expression must have said it all. Serge released a cold laugh that chilled through me. "Yeah, the wakesh root is their main export."

I found my voice, "But…I thought the peat—"

He waved a hand dismissively. "Just a sideline product. It barely brings in enough to keep the lights on. And now that you've killed their main client—"

"Barbariccia?" I stuttered in confusion.

"The *dust* lord of Dark Sun." He shook his head at my expression. "It's *dust*, Rhea. Where did you think *glitter dust* came from? It's refined from the wakesh root." I realized with a flush of heat that he was right and I should have guessed from the symptoms. *Gateway to the gods*, Mayling had called it. I still didn't understand the problem, though. I'd messed up Dark Sun's *glitter* enterprise by killing Barbariccia. Wasn't that a good thing? Serge glowered at me, sensing my thoughts. "The Rills were selling wakesh root exclusively to Dark Sun to refine to *glitter* on Nexus and your precious Guardians let them. Why, you wonder? Because they had a good thing going with the growing peat market and at least this way the Guardians knew where the *dust* was going. And they were right. Now with Dark Sun effectively decapitated, it's an open market. The Rills will sell to the highest bidder, including Eclipse. That's why

Barbariccia was on the Eclipse hit list. As long as he was alive on Sekmet, his little kingdom, *glitter* distribution and availability was essentially in his hands. Barbariccia was just a petty drug dealer pushing a product. Sure, he used a lot of people, but he wasn't interested in killing his clients. Chaos, a lot of his product went to the Gnostic movement. However, Eclipse—the *Nihilists*, rather—are terrorists. They'll use *dust* as a weapon, Rhea. To kill. Just like they'll use your MEC."

A shiver ran through me at the memory of being *dusted*. God! I'd upset the balance…again.

Serge shook his head. "You have no clue how this world works." That was Ennos's line, I recalled. Serge pursed his lips into a kind of sneer. "You're so distrustful and fearful of the very world you're trying to save, Rhea. It's no wonder you blunder from one disaster to another. You're nothing but a string of dreadful accidents waiting to happen." With that last stinging rebuke, he turned on his heel and hastily strode out, leaving me alone and shivering with my guilt.

I wanted to shout an angry rebuttal, but stopped myself. I saw the truth in his cruel words. It drained the anger from me and left only despair. It was a bitter pill he'd made me swallow. It had not escaped me, the terrible irony of what I'd done: free a people who didn't need freeing and opening a possible scenario worse than the one I'd entered. I thought of Mayling's apparent kindness to me. How she'd steadfastly helped me, first out of cruel vengeance, then out of apparent compassion. Had it all been self-serving? I thought of Iris and Orchid, how they'd helped me get away in the end. What I'd mistaken in my foolish pride as their giddy triumph against those cruel Veniks was an unbridled relief and rejoicing that I was leaving. Serge was wrong; Sekmet *had* changed me. But too late. Too late to fix anything.

"Oh, Bas…" I murmured, sinking onto the bed. "I've changed, but the world hasn't…What have I done…." I covered my face with my hands and breathed deeply. I'd given my weapon of mass destruction to the enemy in exchange for what? Bas wasn't likely to recover to the point that he'd be even aware of what I'd sacrificed for him: a world. Serge had pretty much summed it up: I'd ruined everything.

Φ

When I had dressed and entered the cockpit, Serge greeted me tersely from the co-pilot's chair. The ship was small. There wasn't any place for him to go to get away from me.

He looked lost in thought, absently stroking the stubble of his chin. I felt the tension in the air. Serge finally turned to me with stiff politeness and announced that he'd asked Benny to drop him off at Digamma 2, where he could purchase a used *falcon* class ship for the next leg of his journey. Did he really have to leave?

"I said I would let you be as soon as you were recovered," he said, showing no emotion. Then after a pause, he added with an ironic grimace, "As long as you don't intend to press on with forcefully detaining me to take me to a Guardian precinct, that is."

"No, of course not," I quickly assured him. I was still unclear about whose side he was really on. But somehow, I'd lost the heart to put him in the brig and take him in. Things had changed for both of us. And I wasn't sure who the real enemy was anymore…apart from my own stupidity, that is. Somehow, despite being a rude scoundrel and a liar, Serge had turned out to be my ally, fighting for the same thing. At least for now. I was fairly certain that he wasn't *the Rose*. He wasn't even a *Nihilist*. And, despite obvious motives, he *had* helped me escape from Sekmet. I could never repay him for his gentle and steadfast assistance in overcoming my drug abuse.

I cleared my throat. Trying to hide the pain in my voice, I stumbled on, needing to hear what I already knew: "Why…*did* you help me get off Sekmet?"

He turned to me with frosty eyes. "Isn't it obvious? I needed to find out what you did and then get the MEC design from you if possible."

"Well, your mission failed," I said miserably. "You

should have left me there."

"Yes," he cruelly agreed, looking away. "I should have."

SEVENTEEN

I fidgeted by the door, watching Serge gather his things in a small backpack. It had been next to impossible to physically avoid the other in the cramped *ray*-class ship. But we'd painstakingly avoided each other's gaze or any conversation during the two-day voyage here. I'd restricted myself most of the time to the cockpit and had slept in the pilot's chair, while he'd spent most of his time aft in sickbay, reading. It had been awkward a few times during mealtimes or when both wanted to use the facilities. Serge had always swiftly relented and backed off. Now there was no way out, though. Our eyes met briefly. Neither could hold the other's gaze and Serge awkwardly extended his hand, keeping his eyes slightly off my face. I took his clammy hand and shook it, eyes flicking to him and looking away as quickly.

"Well, good bye, Rhea," he said, finally meeting my eyes and betraying a pained expression.

I had to swallow before returning my farewell. "Good bye, Serge."

He brushed past me, accidentally bumping my shoulder with a muttered apology, and stepped out of the hatch to climb down Benny's short ladder. He hastily hopped down, skipping the last rungs, to the platform of the Digamma 2 Spaceport. As if rushing to get away from me and my ship.

I watched with a tight throat as Serge walked away. He abruptly turned his head to look over his shoulder at me and I caught my breath.

"Watch your back, Rhea," he said, looking at me strangely with sad eyes. "Be careful of who you trust. If you're not going to give me the MEC, then at least don't give it to anyone else. For the love of Creos, please don't," he ended imploringly. Then he turned and strode quickly away.

Benny closed the hatch. The tension drained from my shoulders. I backed away from the hatch in a stumble, suddenly feeling light-headed.

"Rhea, I have something for you," Benny said. "It's in the aft stores."

I wondered with a hollow smile if Benny was trying to distract me, and strode to the aft storage next to sickbay. I inhaled sharply at the sight of my Great Coat draped over one of my food crates. My MEC and its holster and belt were coiled on top of it.

I rushed to the coat and touched it. "How did you get these?"

"I'm not sure, Rhea. All I know is that Serge had them both when he came aboard to rescue me from the scrappers. He left them here for you."

I swallowed hard. I absently stroked the soft thixtropic material of my Great Coat and let my gaze drift from it to the MEC. How had Serge managed to get these from the Guardians? Not to mention Benny from the scrappers. I'd never asked. Never had a chance. I sighed a long breath. No matter what else, I owed Serge a great deal. But I was likely never going to see him again and swallowed down my empty sadness.

Φ

I piloted Benny out of the turbulent higher atmosphere of Digamma 2, searching for distraction.

"Okay, Benny," I said, pulling my feet down from the console and sitting up in my pilot's chair. I raked back my thick hair with two hands. "I've put it off long enough. Put me through to Ennos, on his secure private line."

"Okay, Rhea."

Within moments, a frozen image of Ennos's face appeared in front of me. Not him personally, just his answer holo. "Leave a message," he said.

I seized in a breath and began my message: "It's me,

Rhea." I forced a smile of greeting. "You might or might not know that I was caught by the Gleise Guardian Precinct and sent to Sekmet for the murder of Rashomon. Anyway, I managed to escape and I need to relay some important developments to you…"

I then proceeded to tell him about how I'd given away the MEC design to *Nihilist* Vos in exchange for Bas's life, ruined though it was. "I sure hope this is a secure transmission…" I hesitated then went on, "Anyway, things are a little different than they were before. I no longer think that V'ser is an enemy, at least not one worth pursuing. He isn't a *Nihilist* Vos and, for the moment, appears to be an ally in some ways. Our real enemy are the *Nihilist* Vos led by someone called the *Ancient One* who was trapped in our world since millennia. The same one in those communications we intercepted, the one who directed *the Rose*. At present, I have no tangible leads to either *the Rose* or the *Ancient One* but one of the *Nihilist* leaders is a shape-shifter posing as a Schiss priest named Ka."

I hesitated, face tightening with shame, then forced myself to continue, "I gave him my MEC design, Ennos." I swallowed convulsively. "I'm so sorry. I was trying to save Bas…" Oh, God, this was harder than I thought it was going to be and felt the heat of tears pooling in my eyes. I forced on in a shaky voice, "I know it was wrong, but it seemed right at the time…" I didn't volunteer that Bas was a Vos *Nihilist*. It wasn't as though he was going to hurt anyone in the near future…or ever.

"Anyway, Ka poses as a Khonsus mostly these days and he masterminded getting the MEC. I know Ka is on the hit list but he might also be *the Rose*, in which case his being on the list is a decoy. It's because of him that Bas is in the Gleise-12 Med Facility with no brain." I swallowed the bile rising in my throat. "I'm still singly responsible for the next possible galactic war." I let out a guilty exhale. "Me and my MEC. You should have locked me up when you had the chance." I dropped my gaze for a moment to take in a deep breath to collect the composure that seemed to want to desert me then looked back at the holo with imploring eyes. "You've got to tell the rest of the Guardians,

Ennos. Warn them of what's coming. The *Nihilists* have had three months to prepare. I think they're making MEC weapons for a new siege and we need to find their weapons-making facilities before they have enough for a full-scale attack. I can only guess what kind of assault they're planning..."

I thought of all the Vos who'd already infiltrated human colonies like the Bastions and shuddered. Were they all going to arm themselves then wage a simultaneous attack? Or did they have a larger concerted effort in mind?

"I'm betting that A'ler and the *Ulysses* are involved. I'll see what information I can dig up and let you know. And—" I swallowed my words suddenly, then cleared my throat and continued, "I'll send you the design for safe-keeping so you can prepare a defence. It's on this info-meg I'm sending with this message. It's encrypted as you and I earlier agreed." I attached an info-pod to the holo unit and saw the holo flicker with faint images over the frozen image of Ennos, indicating successful uploading and transmission. "That's all. Rhea out."

I severed the connection with a flick of my finger and leaned back in my pilot's chair with a long sigh. I'd embedded a lock-and-key code in the MEC design to prevent it from being shared without my knowledge. If Ennos sent it to anyone else without entering the second part of the twin-code, which only I knew, the design would self-destruct. But indiscreet sharing wasn't what I feared right now. It was that Ennos would just sit on all my information again. It would be devastating for him to contain it now. The safety of the galaxy depended on his fast action. He wasn't known for fast action. I narrowed my eyes and stared into the darkness of space. I couldn't rely on Ennos. Who else could I send this information to?

In the meantime, I needed to prepare for my next move. Before I visited my surly friend, Zec, on Ogium 9, there was something I needed to do first...

Sitting up from my slouch, I said, "Benny, take us to Beleus. We can fuel-up on kappa particles on HD28185b."

"All right, Rhea." Then after a pause, "Are you okay?"

I absently let my gaze drop down to my hands and I

ended up gazing at the scar on the back of my right hand. God...*my* God was a cruel and unforgiving god...After a moment of thought, I found my lip curl up in a sad but determined smile. I had a plan. "I will be, Benny."

Φ

I walked the leaf-littered street of Beleus City's Earth-town with surging emotions. I inhaled the complex aroma of salt sea air together with the musty-sweet scent of oak and beech trees. It smelled like home. Beleus City was actually built on a giant floating platform on the vast Beleus Sea. One of its suburbs, Earth Town, resembled a small coastal town in New England. As sea birds cawed overhead, I cast my gaze down the length of the street, lined with eastern seaboard native trees and shrubs. Even the buildings were made to resemble the classic clapboard, grey-stone, and brick buildings of a coastal town in Maine. I felt like I'd been here before. Perhaps I'd dreamt about such a place.

There were a few people walking the streets, like me. An elderly man shuffled ahead of me down the street. A couple with arms linked skipped in a youthful pace toward me. I gave them a brief glance, eyes locking with the girl's, and wondered suddenly how many of these 'humans' were Vos *Nihilists*, like V'ser's family who had killed their outer-diverse counterparts and were posing as something they weren't. Heart suddenly racing, I broke eye contact as the couple passed me. I fought from looking back and shrugged off shivers. Was the girl's look one of fearful recognition? I moved on and eventually the prickles lifted off my spine when nothing happened.

When I came to it, I recognized it immediately. The old book shop resembled something out of my youthful dreams and looked exactly as I imagined it would. The façade was a delightful mixture of quaint decrepitude and old 20th Century art deco. An old painted sign of earnest artistry swung precariously from a rusted iron gabble over the heavy wooden door with a window. A giant deciduous tree spread its crown over the shop, dropping copious amounts of yellow and brown leaves on the roof and entrance. Humble yet avant-garde.

I slowed and swept my hands down my flight jacket to straighten it, hand automatically plunging into a pocket in search of gum that wasn't there. Hoping for anonymity, I'd left the Great Coat and MEC behind and had dressed in regular flight clothes, black slacks and gravity boots, grey top and dark grey flight jacket. Then I'd run a brush through my hair in a hasty effort to look presentable.

I swallowed down my hesitation and strode with long steps to the entrance. When I opened the door, getting a brief glimpse of the inside through the door window, I was greeted with a slightly musty smell and old dishevelled shelves crowded with even older books. They were stacked haphazardly, giving an air of disorder. But I knew better. That was just the nature of the book collection. I inhaled the delightful smell of old paper and pressed book jackets and felt my nervousness dissolve as I pulled out a short slim book and regarded it.

"Can I help you find something?"

I jerked and almost dropped the book. It was Serge's voice. I turned with a sudden swallow and came face to face with Serge...that is, Mr Bastion. He stood watching me with a professional smile, vacant of recognition. I stared and tried hard to maintain my composure. My heart was slamming.

Bastion's long unruly hair was pulled back from his clean-shaven face into a ponytail. He was casually dressed in tan cotton trousers and a loose denim shirt. Although he was decidedly Serge's—V'ser's—double, Bastion displayed little of V'ser's aristocratic stature, confident smile, or probing eyes. There appeared no impudent flame behind those grey eyes, no faint smirk of sexual appreciation, no cavalier stance of his muscular torso. Bastion was a harmless version of my nemesis, a simple man who lived in earnest. But he looked sweet, enticing dreams of home, and I felt longing ache through my whole body.

"Are you a fan of Lorca?" he posed with a hopeful smile.

I fumbled to replace the book in its spot and forced out a casual answer, "No, not really, never heard of him. I'm just a fan of ancient Earth books generally. I have a few and I'm always looking to add to my collection or to trade...."

He smiled more openly in genuine appreciation. "Well, if you like poetry you'd like Lorca," he continued, reaching past me to pull out the book I'd just hastily replaced on the shelf. "He writes wonderful poetry about the human condition. Very passionate."

God! Was he blushing? Then I realized that my own face was heating. But he'd already buried his face in the book, flipping pages frantically as if looking for a quote to vindicate his claim.

"This book is actually a collection of his essays on the elusive concept of *duende* as well as some of his poetry," Bastion said hastily, flicking his gaze up at me and then looking down as quickly. He closed the book with a nervous snap and passed it to me to take another look. "Lorca was born in 1898 near Granada, Spain, and executed in 1936 during the Spanish Civil War."

"Oh," I said, accepting the book. I studied the cover: it was titled, "In Search of Duende". The poet's name was Federico Garcia Lorca. As Bastion continued filling me in on the history of Lorca and his romantic poetry, I reflected that he was something of a connoisseur of this man's work. Or a consummate salesman.

"Despite its price, you're certainly convincing me about the merits of the book," I said, offering him a crooked smile.

His eyes lit up like a lightening storm and he said with new intensity, "I have to admit a fascination for this often misunderstood and elusive concept, *duende*..."

"A compelling earth-force, an inner spirit that fires the heart and connects the soul to the essence of life," I said, remembering Serge's explanation of the Spanish word.

"Why, yes!" Bastion exclaimed, very pleased and obviously impressed with my knowledge. He grinned brashly and I felt my throat tighten, reminded of Serge—V'ser, that is...I couldn't get used to thinking of him as V'ser...

"I'm Serge Bastion." He smiled shyly and extended his hand to me.

I accepted it and felt his light press. Not overly confident but definitely warm. I gripped his hand firmly and smiled back. "Rhea Hawke."

He beamed. "Like the magnificent raptor of Earth."

"Same one," I said with a husky laugh. It seemed to send him spiralling into an intoxicated state and, noticing his eyes dilate, I commanded myself to curb my smiles. The other Serge seemed to have a particular weakness for my open smiles too.

Bastion shuffled his feet and looked suddenly awkward and nervous. "Listen, if you're inclined, we could go to the park next door and read some of this...to see if you really want to buy it...that is, if you have time...I can close the shop for a while. Hardly anyone comes anyway." He smiled like a boy skipping school. "...I hope I'm not being too forward..."

There was that blush again. It seemed that when it came to inviting a girl on a date both Serges were equally brash and inept. I felt the glow of friendship warm my face. I wanted so much to stay with him and to flee at the same time. Then I convinced myself by remembering my mission.

"I'd be happy to, Mr Bastion," I said, feeling an impish smile tug my left lip up.

"Please call me Serge," he implored. I couldn't.

Bastion locked up the shop and eagerly led me to a small urban park nearby. We walked side by side, careful not to walk too close. The same feelings stirred in me as the ones I felt the first time I'd walked home with Serge on Iota Horologii. My heart hammered in a storm of excitement. I could smell Bastion's own excitement and attraction for me. I thought of my mission here: to inform and warn him of impending personal danger. How was I going to break it to him? What would he think if I told him that someone posing as his sister was also presently running one of the most treacherous crime syndicates in the galaxy...and had murdered his real sister.

Blissfully unaware of my inner dilemna, Bastion found a bench beneath the overhanging canopy of a large sinquin tree, one of the few non native-Earth trees in this section of town, and sat down, already studying the book. I inhaled the enticing aroma of blooming sinquin flowers that dangled down like orange tassels and sat next to Bastion, eyes peripherally studying him. The sinquin barely masked Bastion's own powerful scent for me, of raspberries and musk.

As he flipped the pages, I felt my mission falter. I'd come here to enlighten Bastion about what really happened to his family and warn him of possible attempts on his life by his doppelganger, Serge—which I considered highly unlikely—or by other members of Eclipse—which were much more likely. But as I studied Bastion's face of sad innocence—that slightly crooked nose, those honest eyes and vulnerable mouth—I faltered. How could I plunge this naive man into a world of intrigue and paranoia? Inflict him with dark doubt and destroy his faith in the world? On a possibility. No one had touched him yet. Perhaps no one would.

"Ah, here's a passage," he said, beaming with a quick glance at me. *"Angel and Muse approach from without; the Angel sheds light and the Muse gives form…But the* Duende, *on the other hand, must come to life in the nethermost recesses of the blood."*

Realizing that Bastion was watching me expectantly, I smiled self-consciously. "Interesting choice of words," I said, thinking of the Vos and what Serge had said to me long ago during our rather heated discussion in front of a controversial thermal artwork that portrayed a Vos as noble god.

"Here's another one," Bastion went on, *"Through the empty arch enters a mental air blowing insistently over the heads of the dead, seeking new landscapes and unfamiliar accents; an air bearing the odour of child's spittle, crushed grass, and the veil of Medusa announcing the unending baptism of all newly-created things."*

"It's beautiful and raw at the same time," I said, suddenly reminded of my grandmother.

He was staring at me with a strange look then blurted out, "Why do I get the feeling that we've met before?" he asked innocently.

"I don't think so." I laughed briskly and looked quickly away, pretending to study the flowers of the tree. I had to stop looking at him that way, I rebuked myself. It was inviting him to make those kind of remarks. I abruptly realized what I was doing: it was exactly what Serge had done to me when we'd first met and it was written all over my face: *I love you; kiss me.* I was unfairly transferring my longing for Serge onto Bastion. On the heels of that realization, it dawned on me that Serge's longing looks had never been for me but for his lost beloved, V'rae. And I wasn't V'rae. Not in the least like her, according to Serge. Just like Bastion, for all his similar mannerisms and sweet looks, wasn't Serge.

Bastion smiled suddenly out of the side of his mouth, reminding me of Serge's brash grins. "Will you have dinner with me?"

"I don't think so," I said too quickly and saw his face fall with dismay. "I have some previous engagements that I can't break off," I explained, hearing the lame words make me grimace inside. I just couldn't do this, I thought with some anguish. Maybe, if I'd never met Serge-V'ser, I might have had a better chance with this man. That is, if I ever met him. I might have never come here and noticed him if I hadn't met the inner diverse Serge...either way, it wasn't going to work and I owed this man that much... It was obvious that he was attracted to me; I could smell it, see it. Chaos, I could practically touch it. In fact, I suddenly realized with simultaneous thrill and dread, that he was falling in love with me right there and then. Seeded, no doubt by the shared dreams of his soul-double, V'ser with his beloved, V'rae.

Bastion was an innocent man, not a Vos agent on a mission. He was just a man making a living as a bookseller in an ordinary world...one I didn't belong in, I realized. Because I wasn't innocent. I was a convicted criminal who'd escaped from Sekmet. Someone who'd caused many deaths, and who was responsible for the coming end of the world. Bastion had the right to live his remaining life in the bliss of ignorance. I owed him that. He didn't need to know he was a Vos. It meant nothing in this world. And with that decision I made ready to leave.

"You said you had a book you might like to lend," he prompted, desperate and not wishing me to leave just yet.

"Yes, one I recently acquired." I gave him a small smile.

"Milton's *Paradise Lost and Regained*."

"Excellent choice," Bastion said with an approving smile. "Funny." His smile turned whimsical. "I just sold a copy of that book to *another* beautiful woman." His eyes burned into me. Then he suggested, dark eyes imploring, "Maybe you can bring it by sometime for me to look at."

"Sure," I said, knowing I wouldn't. "Maybe."

"Here." He held out Lorca's book. "A trade."

"No, no," I recoiled.

"I insist," he said, placing the book in my hands and resting his hand on mine. His touch flamed up my face. Seizing in a breath, I surged to my feet.

"Thank you, Mr. Bastion," I said.

"Serge, please," he insisted. "Call me Serge."

I nodded, unable to say the word. "Thanks for the book. It was nice talking with you. I must go now. Goodbye!" And fled.

"Until we meet again!" I heard him call after me.

EIGHTEEN

"Are you sure you want to do this?" Benny asked in a sceptical voice.

I slouched in my pilot's chair, boots on the console, and ran my finger along my thick mat of dark hair. I gazed out with a blank expression at the darkness of space ahead of me.

"I don't see any other way," I responded. I hated to go back to Zec for information. He was a mean-spirited crook who was as likely to slit my throat as give me any information, even if I paid him upfront. There was an outside chance that if I agreed to sleep with him, he wouldn't have me killed and would give me what I needed: the coordinates to the present whereabouts of the *Ulysses*. He'd been sweet on me for years and my final submission would likely shock him into gleeful magnanimity. But I refused to sacrifice my body to that rogue. The thought of it made me feel sick.

"What about Shlsh Shle she?" Benny suggested.

I pulled my feet down off the console and blinked. He had likely set up shop again somewhere. It was worth a try. It also gave me a chance to actually board the *Ulysses* undetected. I knew Zec would leak my intentions to Eclipse. I'd keep Zec as a last resort.

"I think he's back in business, Rhea," Benny added. "I'll show you."

Benny displayed a recent data transaction regarding recent ZetaCorp ship building practices that he'd acquired on the net. It had Shle's style all over it. "The transaction was discreet and parties remained anonymous but payment was in the six figures. Shle deals a lot with the Fauche."

"It's got to be him," I said, peering at the data holo with a frown of concentration. "Where did the payment go?"

"Thought you'd never ask," Benny said. "Virgil 9."

"The bastard's still there." And obviously set up shop again. I let a predatory smile crease my face. "Let's go visit our good friend."

Φ

"Maybe I should try Zec first," I said with a long frown.

"Why?" Benny said in a voice that sounded astonished. "We're almost there. Virgil City is right in front of us. Are you hesitating because they might catch you and turn you in?"

I sighed. "I've caused the death of two out of three targets on Eclipse's hit list, Benny. Rashomon and Barbariccia."

"So you think you'll trigger Shle's death somehow?"

"Well, I've been managing to kill them off one by one for Eclipse so far," I bit out sarcastically. "I should put myself on their payroll."

On the tails of that statement, dark thoughts of Serge nudged forward. Had that been the real reason he was on Sekmet? To ensure that I killed Barbariccia? If Barbariccia had maintained his galactic crime organization from inside Sekmet, it was reasonable to assume that Serge could also have manipulated Hade's organization. He'd managed to get in and out, after all. And he knew an awful lot about its structure and who ran what. Considering my history of fascist thinking, baldie prejudice and my combat abilities, I was a natural to take Barbariccia out. Serge had already admitted that the Rills manipulated what went on, like who got to play the game and likely with whom. It was an easy step to convince the Rills to give me every chance to fight against Barbariccia and let nature take its course. The other inmates and the arena did the rest. The Rills had no apparent allegiance to Barbariccia or Dark Sun. And there were plenty of other potential clients for *glitter* out there to keep them happy.

"Are you okay?"

I stretched my neck and closed my eyes for a moment. After briskly running my hands through my hair, I opened my misty eyes and admitted in a quivering voice, "No."

I took in a deep stuttering breath and exhaled slowly. Suddenly light-headed, I leaned forward and dropped my head down between my knees. What did it matter? He was gone anyway. He'd never loved me, I thought. I'd been his business all along—he'd as much as told me that too—whether it was the MEC design he was after or to placate his sister.

"Listen, Rhea," Benny said, "I know you're distraught about the possibility of acting as unwilling assassin again, but Serge isn't around this time. So, you might be lucky."

I sat up slowly. "Are you sure he isn't there?" I said fretfully.

"I can't be 100% certain but there's no signature of any used *falcons* from Digamma 2 at the Virgil City Spaceport right now."

I swallowed and took another deep breath, snapping into calm professionalism. "Okay. Let's do it."

Φ

Getting into Virgil City wasn't going to be easy. Rhea Hawke, former Galactic Guardian, was a fugitive with a price on her head. Dead or alive for two million credits, according to Serge. And that was before Sekmet. As Jane Raptor, I wasn't any better off, blamed for the explosion that had totally destroyed Shlsh Shle She's information facility. I figured that the only way I was going to get in was through stealth and good old fashioned walking.

"Time to break out the sunblock," I quipped, leaning back in my pilot's seat with one leg up on the console.

"Rhea, you don't understand," Benny said. "The timing is all wrong."

I sat up and stared out into black space with a frown. "What do you mean?"

"It'll be pre-dawn in Virgil City when we arrive."

I blinked. "So, it'll be dark." Then I remembered. Virgil 9's rotation was locked by the tidal forces of the planet around which it orbited. Day and night lasted several weeks. Water in the atmosphere rained down on the cool night side, forming significant bodies of water that evaporated in early daytime, leaving behind a lifeless desert as the surface warmed to 85ºC.

"Oh," I said, placing a finger on my lips in realization.

"Yes. Virgil City will not only be in darkness but it'll be under fifty meters of water."

I'd read about it, seen the holos. It was remarkable, an entire city that cycled from being submerged under water to burning in blistering heat. Its residents, the Ngus, remained safely ensconced inside the constant temperature and humidity of their underground city. When I had first seen the city, I'd thought it resembled a huge gray-green bunker with criss-crossing corrugations and thrusting outcrops of rough organic material in a swelling shifting desert. Now it lay under fifty meters of water.

"Great," I muttered.

"We'll have to wait."

"Two weeks?" I expostulated. "We don't have that kind of time, Benny. We'll go in." I let a roguish smile crease my face. "It's perfect. They'll never suspect anyone of entering."

"But Rhea, that's because no one can."

I narrowed my eyes in thought and frowned, tapping my lips with my finger.

"First you have to dive deep to the bottom and find your way in the pitch darkness and not get noticed," Benny droned on as I called up the holos I'd seen of the moon. "Then you must penetrate the inner city, which will be secured from incoming water—"

"There!" I pointed to the holo of the submerged city. "See those bubbles? Something's getting out. Vents for waste products, Benny. Under pressure. That's how I'll get in."

"But, Rhea, you still have to swim all the way down…"

I grinned, thinking of Mayling. "That's the easy part."

Φ

As Benny hovered over the great temporary sea of Virgil 9, I stood naked at the hatchway, a large water-proof backpack slung over my shoulders, and peered into the dark water. Goldilocks's ruby reflection glistened and broke up into thousands of tiny neon lights on the choppy surface of the water, the only light I could see in the pitch black sea.

"I'll signal you when to get me, Benny," I said. "Don't go too far."

"I won't, Rhea. Good luck." I heard scepticism in his voice, but Benny knew better than to argue with me once my mind was made up.

"Thanks, Benny." Then, without hesitation, I leapt down, feet first into the very warm black water. Once submerged, I shifted into a Rill and could see. I used my powerful webbed arms and legs to get me down into the dark waters below. It actually wasn't as dark as I thought it would be. I'd expected it to be murky and thick with microscopic plankton. The water was surprisingly clear. Perhaps it was toxic, I suddenly considered with alarm. But my Rill body sensed nothing. I soon made out the underwater city, glittering like phosphorescence in the water. It was brilliant! The city's dull colours under the harsh sunlight had blossomed into bright oranges, crimsons, blues and yellows. The whole city pulsed with colour. I stared in fascination for several moments before looking for a vent. I soon found one by its telltale bubbles and swam toward it.

Waste products of the photosynthetic Ngus, of course weren't quite like those of secondary consumers like me. Less ammonia, urea and feces and more gaseous oxygen, some carbon dioxide, nitrogen and a few other elements unique to the Ngu metabolism. The Ngu actually recycled most of their waste products. The city acted like a giant organism with arteries and veins carrying nutrients and waste products alike to be filtered and re-used. But it wasn't a perfectly closed system, I reflected with some gratification. Part of that stemmed from the fact that Ngus weren't the only race that spent time in Virgil City. The city was known for being a discreet meeting place for those out of pace with the Galactic law. There was always a small contingent of off-worlders—traders, dealers, gamblers, bohemians, and the like, making use of the place and requiring their form of sustenance and waste-removal.

I found my way through the waste conduit and finally broke the surface of swirling wastewater inside a large metalloid tank. A loud thrum of engines clattered and roared. It was very dark inside. I remained in Rill form to take advantage of their superior eyesight in darkness and spotted a natural set of rungs that led up to what might be a hatch. Thinking this was perhaps for maintenance purposes, I swam to the rungs and when I reached them, shifted back to my more nimble human form to climb by feel. The hatch easily opened to a rank wave of rotting compost and fermenting vegetation.

I peered out and saw several more cylinders like the one I'd emerged from and realized that I was in the room Serge and I had made love in. Trying to shake off the haunting memory, I dropped down onto the spongy pith-like floor. Still dripping, I pulled off my backpack and bladed myself dry. I squatted to open the bag and quickly dressed into my Enforcer clothes: black top, trousers and gravity boots. I shrugged into my Great Coat, fastened my utility belt and holster then slid my MEC snug into its holster.

Shlsh Shle She wouldn't be very happy to see me, I thought with a cruel smile as I strode with long steps out of the pungent waste room and looked forward to a little playful banter.

Φ

I was right: Shlsh Shle She had essentially re-built his technological informatics room to the point where it was difficult to tell that anything had ever happened to it. And he wasn't happy to see me.

When he caught sight of me, as I let myself in with the old code—hubristic of him, I thought—Shle She shrank back and tried to slither to safety by merging into the far metalloid-cellular wall. But I anticipated his move, skirted around his hulking protoplasmic form and cut him off. My MEC pointed at his belly, or at least what I thought was his belly.

"What do you want, piss-for-brains," he hissed out, eye-tentacles bobbing around nervously. "Haven't you done enough?"

"Hang on to your bloomers, Shle," I snarled and put my MEC away. The more nervous he was the more rude he got, I reasoned, and I didn't relish hearing anything more vile than he was already dishing out. "I just came for some information. I want to know where the *Ulysses* is parked these days."

"Why should I tell you, blenoidshit?"

"Because I'll pay you well."

That seemed to satisfy him. At least he was considering. He finally said, "All I know is that the *Ulysses* has an acting-captain now by the name of K'vur."

"What? Where's A'ler?"

"How should I know, blenoid's ass?"

I pushed the front of my Great Coat aside and let my hand rest on my MEC again. I narrowed my eyes at the Ngu.

"Okay, okay," he slurred out and slithered over to a holo console and merged with part of it. "A'ler's been re-assigned to some planet in the HD222582 system," he announced. "Kraal, a moon of HD222582b, a ringed gas giant with a highly eccentric orbit."

I felt my breaths escalate. I kept my voice calm, "And you're going to tell me what kind of supply ships go to that planet. Where they go on the planet and when."

Within a moment, Shle She had the answer: "Mostly BlackStar delta class *shadow* freighters. I can't speak for unofficial supplies, but official inventory showed lots of building equipment four months ago." That was just after I had given Ka my MEC design. They hadn't wasted any time while I languished on Sekmet. Shle She continued, "Now its mostly maintenance stuff for the only colony on Kraal. Otherwise the moon is uninhabited with extreme seasonal cycles."

"What about kappa particles?"

"What?"

"Shipments of quintle?"

"Oh, yeah…There's the odd huge shipment of it. What's it for?"

"I'm the one paying for the information, Shlsh," I said. Then I aimed a steady gaze at him. "You told me last time that your worm-virus gave you access to the vault…"

"Got destroyed along with the system. I'm betting that's what they were after," he said. I was betting he was right. Then he made that strange laughing sound again. "But I had back-up. How do you think I got up and running so fast, eh? The whole city is an organic-AI. They would have had to destroy the whole city to really shut me down."

Very clever, I thought, and I bet the *Nihilists* didn't know it either. I levelled a hard gaze at him and decided to be honest, appeal to his sense of justice and honour…if he had any. "Listen, Shlsh, the *Nihilists* may not stop with the human race. They do call themselves *Nihilists*, after all." He didn't move. "You're still on the hit list as an *anti-Nihilist*, Shlsh." I let him chew on that for a moment before adding, "And since you are, do you believe in their cause? Because if you do, now's the time to help."

He surprised me by actually considering what I'd said without a swift rebuke. "You bring up a good point, creon.

Perhaps, if I cracked the vault again, I would find something that would help you," he offered.

I smiled at him with delighted surprise. It was what I was hoping for but didn't expect from him. "That would be very helpful Shlsh."

His body jiggled and I wasn't sure what that meant but decided that it was an expression of pleasure and smug pride. "Just don't go and advertise that I did this for you, creon," he warned.

I grinned and nodded. "You have my ship's com signal. Let me know if you find anything of value for us." Then I gave him a wry smile and nodded, happy enough that I almost patted him with my hand. "Thanks for your time and efforts." I waved my arm over the IDR on one of his consoles and punched in a thousand credits from the bank account of Jane Raptor. "Don't spend it all in one place," I said then left.

Φ

"Set course for the HD70642 system, Benny," I said, back inside my ship.

"I thought we were heading for HD222582b," Benny said. Had I detected a squeamish tone to his voice?

"We have to make a slight detour to visit an old friend, Benny." I sat slouched in my pilot's chair with my head resting on my hand.

"You don't mean…"

"I do—"

"Oh my God!"

"Splendid City's not that bad, Benny," I said, a little annoyed. I thought Benny was being a little dramatic, using *my* expletive.

"Not that, Rhea. I've just registered a tremor associated with a subsurface explosion through my sensors."

"What?" I pulled my hand down from my head and sat up from my slouched position. My chest tightened with a dreadful thought. "Not Shlsh…" I moaned.

194

"Yes, Rhea. I'm sorry. He's gone. I'm intercepting emergency communications within the organic-AI community. It would appear that a recoil from a non-authorized signal caused the explosion."

"Oh my God..." I whispered to myself. Shlsh had sent his worm-virus to the vault and they'd booby-trapped it, returned his signal with a vengeance.

"Half the city's gone, Rhea," Benny went on. I hardly registered what he was saying as I realized that I'd done it again. Triggered a hit, but this time with so many innocent casualties. The horrible irony was that I'd caused Shlsh's death by appealing to his compassion and sense of honour. I leaned forward and pressed my hands over my face then breathed deeply, barely hearing Benny, "Rhea?...Rhea?..."

Φ

As always, Splendid City was splendid. I gazed down past my gravity boots on the transparent pedestrian air tube over a thousand meters above the ground to the buildings below. The multi-shaped, rounded and spiked rooftops blushed in the rose-coloured sky. Swarms of air vehicles buzzed around the towers and the gossamer walkways connecting them. Splendid City was a monument to the art of architecture and I had to confess that I quite liked the texture and look of the city. It was only its inhabitants that I had a problem with. And then only some of them.

I had hoped that I wouldn't need to return for a very long time; yet here I was, less than a Standard Galactic year later, back in the place I'd once called home.

Unfortunately, Zec was the only person I knew who could supply me with the perfectly configured Q-bomb material I needed with no questions asked. If I'd been home on Iota Hor-2, I could have whipped them up easily but that was out of the question. I could never go back. Neon City wasn't home anymore. And Jaz, my wild tappin, was on his own. Last time I'd visited Zec, I'd barely managed to slide out of his way with a promise I hadn't kept. Now I was back without the payment I'd promised. Despite the truth of it, I knew he wouldn't suffer another hard-done-by story without some dispensation. I glanced down at my Great Coat and the MEC holstered on my right thigh. Last time I didn't have my tools, I thought with a wry smile.

Φ

I entered Zec's casino like I had the last time, through the front door. No one challenged me in the smoky bar or elevator. When I stepped out of the elevator on Zec's private penthouse floor, two Azorians bearing Q-guns jumped me. I quickly despatched them with my MEC, watched them thud, unconscious, to the ground, then stepped over them and casually strode down the hall to Zec's luxury office.

"What are you doing, Hawke?" Zec's voice reverberated in the hall. "Why'd you kill my men?" He sounded nervous. Good. This was going to be a different meeting from last time. Last time it was I who was nervous.

"I just knocked them cold," I said, snarling up at the small cameras above me. I reached the door and tried it. It wouldn't open. "Let me in, Zec." Then after another moment, "I won't hurt you."

"Did you come to pay me?"

"Sure," I lied. "Let me in."

The door clicked and I pushed my way inside. Two Xhix bodyguards threw themselves at me from behind the door. I'd anticipated them and swerved out of the way then used one against the other and had them both on the floor, unconscious, within a few heartbeats.

I straightened, breathing a little harder than when I'd entered, but otherwise unscathed, and turned to Zec with my MEC pointed at him. He stood in front of his huge gadpie desk, with the rose-coloured backdrop of the city behind him. He held a fat cigar of pungent poi mash between thumb and fingers. Dressed as usual, in bright blue lumi-trousers and a flowing open collar Scandi shirt beneath a black silk jacket, Zec managed to look both ridiculous and dangerous at the same time. He didn't appear armed; he usually left that to his bodyguards.

Zec gave an admiring whistle and an oily smile slid over his handsome face. Dark, slick hair was drawn back in a loose ponytail. He drew in a long inhale of poi mash then blew brown putrid smoke out in my direction, heavy-lidded eyes appraising me. "You haven't lost it."

"Pray that *you* don't lose it." I pointed my MEC a little lower and he instinctively covered his crotch with his hands, eyes widening.

He glared at me with new respect and some fear. "What do you want, Hawke? I know you didn't bring me my payment."

"For what?" I challenged him, sauntering closer to him with my MEC still levelled at his crotch. "You're half right, though. I do have payment. But for a Q-bomb, fifth quintle level with a five hundred charge. And I need it now."

He threw his head back and laughed. "Whose ship are you blowing up this time?"

I smiled wryly. "Do you want the credits or not?"

I'd never known Zec to say no to a potential deal to make money. "Five thousand," he said with a sneer. "Up front."

"That's..." I began in a flustered tone, feigning affront.

"Particle-stream robbery?" He grinned. "That's the deal."

I looked directly at him with a hard gaze. "I pay only on delivery. And only if it's within the hour. *That's* the deal."

He leaned back on the desk and crossed his long legs and we stared at one another, as if in stalemate. Then I saw his eyes waver and stray from mine; I'd won. His eyes roamed me up and down, appraising with a sneer. He flicked his poi mash cigar at me. "Okay, Hawke. Wait in the Sky Lounge. Paz will bring it down to you." An Azorian, I thought. "I have an IDR there for your payment."

I nodded and made it to the door, stepping over his still unconscious men, before he called, "Hawke!" I turned with some inkling of what he was going to say. I gave him a demure smile. He sneered at me like he knew what I was thinking. "I still want my payment for the MEC sale to A'ler. I don't care what happened. I held up my end of the deal and I expect to be paid."

My smile soured. "You also told her who I was," I argued. "I don't owe you a thing."

He took a long inhale of his poi mash and blew it out in my direction. Pungent smoke coiled around him in a brown haze. "I need to keep *all* my clients happy. You're here, aren't you? No harm done then, eh?"

He pulled a smile out of me. Good old Zec. Always playing both sides and never seeing the problem with it. The irony of the situation was that I did get the MEC to Eclipse but I never got paid for it, of course. Unless sparing Bas could be counted on as payment. "No harm done," I echoed in a hollow voice. I needed to keep Zec relatively happy; I wasn't sure when I'd need him again. I added, "I'm still waiting to be paid for that one myself. You'll get your payment when I get mine."

"That's not how it works—"

"Actually, it is, Zec," I said firmly and rested my hand on the MEC handle in my holster. I smirked. *"You can't pick up two watermelons with one hand…*old Persian proverb."

He leaned back suddenly and waved his hand at me in a grand gesture, smiling like a salesman: with his mouth, not his eyes. "I'm content, Hawke. I know you'll get yours."

That was what I was afraid of. "One hour," I reminded him.

He nodded and repeated it with an oily smile.

I raised my brows at him then left. I'd have to trust Zec. That was the hard part.

I waited nervously, sipping Plock Nectar for forty-five minutes in the *hedon*-filled Sky Lounge, and absently watched two Sporians do the Y-step to a funky tune. An Eosian and a Xhix were sparring in a lively card game at the table in front of me. I found my gaze straying to a young human couple kissing in a booth to my right. My thoughts wandered to Serge and a long sigh escaped my lips. Too much Plock Nectar, I thought, and pushed the unfinished drink away.

When the Azorian came with the package, I leapt up, almost knocking my drink over, and greeted him coolly. A swift check of the merchandize confirmed that Zec had come through. I nodded to the Azorian, hiding my astonished pleasure, and paid my seven thousand credits on the IDR then hastily left with a last glance at the kissing couple.

NINETEEN

Snug in my white thermal suit, I sprawled on my belly in the thick powder snow of a large mountain top. Feeling my legs burn from the tortuous climb, I could only hear my panting breaths as they slowly regained their normal rhythm inside my protective helmet. Above me, the sky shimmered a deep electric blue, thanks to an orbiting field of microscopic ice particles. The hazy crescent shape of HD222582b, its thin white ring looking like the mistake of a painter's brush stroke suspended not far from the horizon. Below me, somewhere in the deep silence of the bleak valley, lay the installation I was searching for.

I opened my face shield and felt fresh cold air flood in. It bit at my face and made my eyes water briefly. I inhaled the crisp fragrance of old snow. It left the taste of metal in the back of my throat and I suspected I was smelling my own cauterized nostrils. I then raised the long-range field mag to my eyes and tracked my gaze over the snow-swept valley below. I almost missed it: a cluster of round-roofed buildings that spanned several hectares about twenty kilometres away. They glinted like a few gemstones amid a whitewash glare beneath the crisp blue sky. Snow had piled itself several stories high on mostly one side of every building, signifying the direction of the prevailing wind. I'd almost missed the place in my initial sweep.

I crept back from the crest of the hill with a frown and replaced the field mag on the utility belt of my thin thermal suit. I watched my breaths coil out of my mouth and rise like smoke then dissipate into the frigid minus 40º C air. Kraal was an unforgiving ice moon, not unlike Uma 1, I thought; only, luckily for me, not quite as cold. Though, Benny had informed me that during Kraal's ice storms, the wind-chill factor could drop the temperature to nearly 80° below zero and ice particles flew like salvos of sharp glass that punctured and sliced everything in their path.

Without full protection, no one would survive for very long. But today, the day was thankfully calm and the sun shone in a bright blue-sky. I also had a lot more protection on me than I'd had on Uma 1, I considered as I closed my face shield. The air, though cold and thin, was just breathable. It allowed me to open the face-shield of my thermal suit from time to time to get a whiff of fresh air; although it burned in my throat and made my nostrils stick shut. The gas giant that Kraal orbited traveled an eccentric path, wobbling a distance from 0.39 AU to 2.31 AU in its 576-day orbit around the G3 star. As a result, the moon underwent severe seasonal cycles of melting and refreezing. We were definitely in its winter season.

Benny had deposited me on the other side of this mountain range, well out of sensor range and I'd hiked up the mountains on snowshoes, leaving Benny secure in the far valley. We'd maintained com-silence and I'd given Benny instructions to wait two days for me—far more time than I needed, after which he was to return to Iota Hor and report to Ennos.

After taking in a deep breath, I headed down, snowshoes crunching in the dry snow. I knew I was disguised visually in the blinding white snow of the harsh sunlight, but I hoped that the sensor-jamming device Benny had provided me would keep me as hidden from the facility's sensors as it did from Benny's own sensors. Otherwise, this was going to be a short mission.

Φ

I reached the outer perimeter of the facility without apparently tripping any alarms. So far so good, I thought with an inward sigh of relief. The first building I reached was one of the largest and tallest. I suspected that it either housed the hanger bay for off-world vehicles or the kappa energy coils to fuel the facility. The tallest building would be the energy reactor. I found a small utility exit door and grinned. Maybe this was going to work.

I keyed myself in easily, using a trick I'd learned on Ogium 9. After opening the door a slit and checking for occupants, I slipped inside and took in a sharp breath at what I saw. I smiled. This was the facility's hanger bay for vehicles. And what I was looking for. Before me stood over fifty mid-sized *seed phantom*, long range one-man missal-type ships originally of an ancient alien technology that had been used in the past in suicide missions. I recognized ZetaCorp's hand in replicating the design. The bow was a sharp conical shape, built for ramming and the mid and aft sections were built of a flexible ballooning material that puffed out or shrank according to navigational needs.

After checking for any guards, I quickly boarded one of the vehicles and to my dismay recognized my MEC technology moulded into the console. I drew in a shuddering breath. This ship was a giant MEC and they were producing a massive fleet of them!

I disembarked hastily and set to work by first pulling off the thin thermal suit. Then I pulled out the MEC, Great Coat and Q-bombs from my backpack. I'd made five Q-bombs out of Zec's one. After stuffing the thermal suit into the pack, I holstered the MEC then strung the five cylindrical Q-bombs on my belt before I shrugged into the Coat. I pulled out my thick hair caught underneath—it had already grown past my shoulders—and lashed it back with an elastic tie that I'd fished out of my MEC pocket.

I placed the first Q-bomb inside one of the centre ships. I inspected the cylinder then carefully set it for 'ricochet'. Only one Q-bomb would be timed. The one I would place in the power reactor room, where both quintle and kappa particles were first harnessed and converted into fuel energy. Where an explosion of sufficient magnitude would set off the others.

As several guards returned from the outer perimeter I

slipped out then crept on silent feet down the corridor. I found the power-feed chamber, thrumming with the sounds of kappa and quintle particles, and set the next Q-bomb there.

I set the remaining ones except one on my way to the main power reactor room. I realized that I hadn't met anyone in the hallway when I heard a shuffle around the corner of the hall. I ducked into a recess of the corridor and hid. No one passed. I frowned and crept out, frustrated and impatient. I pulled my MEC out and aimed a two handed grip ahead of me as I crept forward. When I made it to the corner, I hiked in a breath of startled relief.

"Rhea!"

It was Serge! Roguishly handsome in a brown pilot's AI jacket, tussled hair and several-days old bristle. He pointed a Q-gun straight at me. The thrill of seeing him surged through my body. But, apart from my face colouring involuntarily, I wasn't about to let it show. He, on the other hand, grinned with surprised delight. He lowered his Q-gun and looked genuinely pleased to see me. Which was unexpected. When I'd last seen him, he couldn't stand being in the same room with me. No doubt he'd relented and was trying a new approach to obtain his prize, my MEC design.

I lowered my MEC and found my other hand automatically search my pocket for the soyka gum I'd sworn off—a habit I found hard to quell when I was uneasy and craved it the most. Abandoning the useless search, I cavalierly tilted my body, leaning on one leg, and threw Serge a withering look. "What in jagging chaos are *you* doing here?"

"Same as you, trying to fix the mess *you* made," he quipped. "And hello, by the way. I see you've found your Great Coat and MEC."

Despite wanting to thank him for the coat and MEC, the glare for his wanton insult won out: "Well, stand aside and let a professional do her job, then." I holstered my MEC and resumed my stride, keeping a peripheral eye on him. I didn't trust Serge. He'd been on Uma 1 when I'd killed Rashomon, on Virgil City when I almost killed Shlsh Shle She, and on Sekmet when I'd failed to save Barbariccia in the pit.

"You seem to have a natural talent for finding trouble," Serge said, replacing his Q-gun in its holster and coming beside me. "And, by the way, did you take a course or were you just born rude?"

I tossed a sideways glance of annoyance at him without slowing my pace and brushed my tongue across my upper teeth in mock seduction. "Your outer diverse copy, Bastion, he's a lot sweeter than you," I said tartly.

"Oh?" Serge looked contemplative then added, "I guess he hasn't known you for very long, has he?" The implication was obvious.

"And a lot more polite," I muttered, stepping up my pace.

"No, definitely hasn't," he muttered back, keeping up with me.

"Seen your sister lately?" I said snidely.

"No, of course not," he responded gruffly. "She doesn't know I'm here."

I sneered at him, not bothering to hide my disbelief.

He decided to ignore my reaction and pointed to our left. "This way." Bending into a light crouch, Serge started for the low-ceilinged hall. After a few steps he turned to me with expectation.

I hadn't moved. I stood where he'd left me, watching him with a slightly annoyed look on my face.

"Well, come on!" he urged, waving his hand at me.

"You can go that way if you like. I'm going this way." I pointed in another direction.

He retreated back to the main hall and frowned at me in exasperation. "What? Why?" He pointed to where he had been heading. "This is the way to the power-feed chamber. Where we can cause the most damage. I can rig a short in the quintle particle conduits..."

I didn't tell him I'd already been there and had hidden one of my five bombs. "The main power reactor is in a separate chamber," I said. "If it's set off, a chain reaction will do the job much more efficiently and completely, giving us a chance to get out before everything goes. I don't know about you but I intend to get out of here alive."

He thought it over for a moment. "But how do we set it off? We'd need—"

"This," I said, pulling up the last of my Q-bombs hanging off my belt. His eyes grew big.

"Okay," he promptly said. "I'll go your way."

"And try to keep up," I said sharply over my shoulder then sprinted down the hall.

Φ

I found what I was looking for: a small door to a low utility access shaft we could use as a shortcut to the main power reactor chamber; we'd avoid the heavily armed security station that way. Instructing Serge to keep watch, I used my MEC to silently drill into the locking device and hinges of the metre-high shaft door.

Serge was instantly there, bending down to pull the shaft door open.

I ruthlessly pushed him aside. "I'll do it," I snapped.

He came beside me again and watched me pull to no avail. It seemed stuck despite the damage my MEC had done to it. Serge finally said, "Have I pissed you off or something? I mean, aside from insulting you pretty badly the last time we were together—"

I glared at him over my shoulder without saying anything then grimaced as I resumed my attempts to open the door.

"Here, let me help," he offered. Before I could refuse his help, he pushed himself beside me and grabbed the shaft door. With his added strength, the door gave way abruptly, throwing us backwards with a sudden recoil. I fell hard onto my rump with a grunt. The door landed on me and I gasped. Serge was instantly removing the heavy metalloid door off me with a look of concern and bent down to help me to my feet.

I hesitated only a moment to touch my chin and look annoyed at the blood on my fingers. Then I took his hand. As I rose, I glanced briefly at him then quickly let go of his hand. I brushed myself off and reluctantly accepted a small cloth he'd pulled out of his pocket for my cut. I pressed the cloth to my chin and gave him a long hard look then decided to respond to his question. "You might have admitted the real reason you were on Sekmet, your actual mission there," I challenged him.

He looked genuinely puzzled. "I thought I told you already."

"Right," I said shortly and bent low to enter the shaft. "Like it had nothing to do with me killing Barbariccia."

"What?" he said, brows knitting in bewilderment. He looked genuinely puzzled.

"And just like you were going to save me by absorption back on Virgil 9," I muttered with a shake of my head, then proceeded to crawl inside the narrow shaft. "Get the door behind you."

"Okay," he said, shuffling right behind me and pulling the door up against the shaft from inside. "I'm not sure I get your drift. I already told you what I think of Barbariccia and it sounds like you two hit it off like two starving blenoids. But as for absorption, you need to know the real story. My father was actually trying to save your mother when he tried to absorb her. My guess is he'd fallen for her and wanted to save her from the virus he was making. Makes sense; he was a sucker for beauty. Just like me."

I forced my steps not to falter. Could that be true? And what if it was? What did that mean about what I had done as a child?

We remained quiet until the shaft abruptly took a 90° turn and I stopped suddenly. Serge, who'd taken to following rather blindly, collided into my backside, knocking me forward so I struck my head against the wall with a clunk.

"Oh, sorry," he quickly apologized. "You okay?"

"Yeah," I said curtly, glaring at him and rubbing my head. "Just fine." Not really. But I wasn't about to admit that to him and found myself sitting back and fumbling in my pocket again. Damn that habit! I needed some soyka gum!

"Well, you don't look okay to me," he volunteered, sitting beside me. "Here." He'd pulled something out of his jacket pocket and handed it to me. I gaped at the small bar of genuine Earth chocolate. "It might cheer you up a bit," he offered with a crooked smile. He always seemed to know what I needed.

My eyes lit up, despite my foul mood, and I was about to take the bar then retracted my hand.

"Please take it. I've got more," he said, pushing the bar forward. "At least have a piece then."

I couldn't resist the compromise. I took the bar and undid the wrapper then broke off a portion of the creamy chocolate for myself and gave him back the bar. He watched me savour the smooth chocolate and smiled. I must have looked a lot less menacing, I concluded and found a half-smile creep across my mouth.

Serge took a piece of chocolate and chewed slowly. "I know you're really pissed off with me for something. And it's more than for those nasty things we said to one another the last time we were together."

I swallowed down the rich chocolate and gazed at the floor with a sigh. I said wearily, "I just wish all the lies would stop, Serge." I looked up at him. "I know I haven't always been very forthcoming with things but at least I haven't lied about myself. Not knowingly anyway…not like you have."

He met my gaze with a sad smile. "Perhaps I don't deserve your trust. But stop listening to your mind for a minute and ask your intuitive self. Your intuition. I know it will tell you that I'm your friend, Rhea."

Friend. I didn't want him to be my *friend,* my mind screamed back. I dropped my gaze, feeling my face heat. Maybe that was the real problem. None of his lies had come as close to hurting me as the one about loving me. And I knew that his love for me was one thing I could never have.

"Humans have always shown the highest intuitive capacity in the galaxy," Serge went on rather blithely. "That's why we chose them for our *Great Experiment.*"

I looked up, smiling and frowning at the same time, but

thankful he'd steered the subject away from the personal. "We?"

"The Vos and the Epoptes," he said, handing me another piece of chocolate and throwing another piece into his own mouth. I watched him enjoy the cocoa melt in his mouth and stifled the urge to wipe off some that had smeared over his lower lip and chin. "In ancient times we were together, Rhea. One in the same."

Bas had said the same thing to me.

"...In ancient times we—"

"Shhh!" I hissed, clamping my hand over his mouth. I'd heard footfalls and desultory laughter. "Shut up!" I whispered hoarsely. "I hear the patrol." They were making their rounds in the power-feed chamber.

Chaos, if I didn't know better, I'd have thought he was purposely trying to compromise our mission with his incompetence. But Serge was no stealth expert. That was certain. He'd been too awkward and inattentive. His terrorist work for Eclipse and the Vos *Nihilists*—and/or *anti-Nihilists*—had been at the social and political level. He was an intellectual. A smooth talker, a powerful salesman. And a charming seducer of willing victims...like me.

When the patrol had left and I couldn't hear them anymore, I crept forward with Serge directly behind me. After removing the shaft door we entered the chamber. I heard Serge draw in a breath. I was impressed too: the giant reactor chamber towered with tall cylinders of bubbling liquid of several irredescent colours. A huge circular coiling apparatus encircled the room and connected with the tall cylinders to a rhythmic throbbing and crackling. The room smelled of burning metal; kappa and quintle charging each other.

I glanced furtively at Serge and felt terrible misgiving. I wanted to trust him but I just couldn't.

He turned to me in expectation. "Aren't you going to—"

I swung hard and struck him in the chin. The blow threw him backward, head snapping back like a whip, and he dropped, out cold, on the floor with a thud. I felt my face tighten into a snarl of regret. He was going to be awfully angry with me when he woke up. But I couldn't let him see where I was planting the bomb. It was insurance in case we were caught, I told myself. At least he could say with total honesty that he didn't know where I'd put it.

I sprinted to the very centre of the cluster of cylinders and looked around me. There was no place where I could hide the bomb...except. I'd raised my head and was looking up at one of the cylinders. No one would find it up there. In sudden inspiration, I grinned and quickly stripped. I took the last Q-bomb in my hand and set it for ten minutes from now, then shifted into a Khonsus and flew up to the top of the cylinder. I attached the bomb on the top of the casing with self-adhesive then dropped down and quickly dressed.

When I reached Serge, still sprawled on the floor where I'd left him, I bent down with a puzzled face. I'd half-expected him to have roused by now. Throwing a quick glance around, I shook his still body. "Come on, Serge. Wake up, dream boy."

I knelt and after several attempts to shake him awake, then several taps to his cheeks, began to feel alarm. Had I hit him too hard? I knew I'd shifted briefly into a brawny Badowin to gain sufficient strength to knock Serge out. Badowins were built like ZetaCorp freighters. They were small but, like a cornered blenoid, packed with ten times their weight in strength. Had I hurt Serge? His nose was bleeding. "Come on, come on," I repeated in a hoarse whisper. I felt urgency crawl up my spine. Any minute the security patrol would return on their circular rounds and catch us there.

I was shaking him hard and keeping watch in the hallway when Serge made me flinch by jerking awake and seizing my wrists. Painfully. My gaze shot down and I met his glare with an inward wince.

"You hit me!" Still clutching my wrists, he sat up and slowly shook me.

I finally pulled away from his powerful grasp.

"Get over it, Serge," I said. "We don't have time for this. They're coming." I threw a glance behind me to where I thought I'd heard the return of the patrol in the hall outside.

"You knocked me right out with the power of a Venik—"

"A Badowin, actually," I corrected between glances behind me to the door.

"You could have killed me—"

"But I didn't!" I cut him off in a loud whisper. "I'm sorry. Can we go now?"

He gripped me in an ice-storm glare of recrimination. Then the moment was over. He released me and looked away, still glowering. I scrambled to my feet then offered my hand to help him but Serge got up on his own.

As he dusted himself off, I knew it was already too late and felt alarm surge up my gut and constrict my chest. I reached for my MEC—

"Hands off the sidearm, slave!" a baritone voice commanded behind me. "Get your hands up where we can see them."

I lifted my arms and saw Serge do the same. We turned together to face a half dozen Eosian men at the door, dressed in black fatigues with pulse pistols aimed at us. I didn't bother to try for my MEC. My eyes gravitated to Serge, who glanced at me in silent inquiry. He was probably wondering how long we had before the bomb went off. Not long enough to escape, I thought. We were all going to die.

TWENTY

"Well, isn't that choice," A'ler bit out, eyes flicking from me to Serge. She held a kappa rifle, aimed steadily between us. The guards had herded us to A'ler's private office, where she'd waved the security guards off except the one who'd disarmed me of my MEC. "The perfect pair of lovers."

"We're not lovers—" we both fervently insisted at the same time then trailed with a sharp glance at the other.

"Like I give a blenoid's ass," A'ler cut in. "You've got nerve coming here in the first place, V'ser. But bringing *her* here—"

"He didn't *bring* me here. I came on my own," I retorted.

A'ler turned on me with a glare of pure hatred and pointed the rifle at me. "Look, slave, if you don't shut up, I'll shoot you right now," she snarled. Then she cast a furious gaze back to her younger brother. "You're pathetic. You were supposed to get her design and instead you fell in love with her, you stupid idiot! You messed up every mission I gave you and now you're actually plotting against me. Did *she* put you up to this?" She pointed the kappa rifle at me.

I hung on to the bit about 'falling in love' like wine. Why had A'ler said that? Didn't she know about V'rae?

"I've been an *anti-Nihilist* for a lot longer than I've known *her*," Serge admitted with a scornful glance at me. "You figured that out."

"Yeah, I did, traitor," A'ler spat out. "I knew you were soft. You're the only one who didn't kill your double. I have a mind to kill him myself!"

"Leave him alone!" I shouted and was immediately furious with myself. Now I'd given the shape-shifter another reason to go after Bastion. A'ler obviously relished the idea of hurting someone I cared for. For reasons unclear to me, A'ler despised me. Or was it the obvious? I'd killed her father and her brother…

A'ler laughed menacingly. "Or maybe I'll just let you kill him for me instead," she added with a sinister smile of amusement. God knows I'd done enough of that for Eclipse. A'ler turned to Serge with an amused sneer. "Chaos, brother! She wants you both! You *and* your double!" She cackled out a churlish laugh. "You're not enough to satisfy her!" Then she snarled, "We're running out of time, V'ser. I know you've planted a bomb to disable this facility. My men searched the power-feed chamber and couldn't find anything. Tell me where it is and I won't shoot you or the girl."

Of course A'ler knew about only one bomb, because Zec knew about one bomb, I considered with inward satisfaction. Of course, Serge had only seen one bomb too. But it was the main bomb. Without it, the others would not explode.

"You know I won't tell you, sister," Serge said calmly, keeping his eyes on hers. "What you're doing here is very wrong. This weapon-making facility is all wrong," he said, waving his arms around him. "It won't solve anything. You'll just cause another war that will never end. We have to stop it all, sister. Start getting along with the world. Inner and outer diverses. Why can't we just live together?"

I stared at him and felt my throat catch. At that moment, as I gauged the sincere exchange between brother and sister, I instantly knew that everything he'd told me was true. He'd always spoken the truth. Beneath the cavalier rogue lived a noble man of honourable purpose. A hero. He'd been a victim of circumstance—and my prejudice.

A'ler sneered. "You're full of blenoidshit, V'ser. These humans will never accept us. They're as bad as the bloody Eosians and their high and mighty Epoptes. If we don't stop them they'll try to destroy our world. *This* diverse should be destroyed. But we'll settle for annihilating humans with your pretty lady's toy first...for now." With those last taunting words, she glanced at me with malice in her eyes.

I felt rage boil inside me. Rage and shame at what I'd begun. I balled my hands into tight fists. It was all I could do not to throw myself at A'ler.

"If you don't care about getting yourself shot, maybe I'll shoot *her*, then," A'ler swung the rifle at me. "Your sweetheart who *isn't your lover*," she bit out in a mocking voice. I recognized a filial resemblance in her crooked smile. She looked a lot like Serge, I thought as I tensed and saw Serge's agony through my peripheral vision.

Eyes flicking from the kappa rifle to A'ler's snarling face, I challenged, "What about your directive to take me to the *Ancient One*?"

A'ler glared back. "Don't push your luck, slave. I don't always do what I'm told."

"Your brother doesn't know where the bomb is," I countered quickly. "I planted it. After I knocked him out."

A'ler barked out an amused laugh. "I wouldn't have trusted him with such a delicate job either. Now, tell me where it is," she said, pointing the rifle back at Serge.

I stared at A'ler in quiet defiance. I was counting on A'ler not to shoot her own brother.

Obviously Serge was thinking the same thing. "Don't tell her, Rhea," he said, keeping his eyes on A'ler.

"What makes you think I would?" I snarled, drawing on my former mean-spirited banter with him and hoping it would convince A'ler.

Serge gave his sister a confident smile. "You wouldn't shoot your own brother—"

The loud report of the kappa rifle made me flinch. Serge's eyes widened in shocked disbelief then he looked down at the small wound in his chest.

Feeling a sympathetic stab of pain in my tight chest, I stifled a shriek and helplessly watched Serge fall to his knees then lose consciousness and flop over into a heap on the ground.

"NO!" I rushed to Serge's limp body and knelt over him. I opened his shirt and gaped at the very small but deep wound. It leaked a small bit of blood mixed with kappa-induced fluid. The wound didn't look like much now but already the flesh surrounding the small hole was reacting. It raged like an angry red boil. Serge's face was grey with shock. Kappa particles didn't usually kill right away but they were relentlessly deadly as they ate away the flesh of any creature they entered. It was a painful, long, but usually inevitable death.

"Enough blenoid crap!" A'ler shrilled. "He'll die for sure if you don't tell me where you put the bomb. Right now!"

A'ler knew what she was doing. There was still a chance to save him—if I told A'ler right away. The implied promise was immediate medical aid for her brother.

I touched his ashen face. It felt cold, dangerously cold. Dear God, I thought, why did I keep having to make these awful decisions? Gauging right from wrong—and choosing my actions—had been so much easier before I'd let the world in.

I looked from Serge's unconscious face to A'ler's face of

shocked exhilaration. Last time I'd chosen Bas over the galaxy. That had been a mistake. But how could I let Serge slowly die an agonizing death? I had no choice—

The answer came from elsewhere. An explosion. First one, then a stuttering series of blasts that shook the room we were in. The emergency klaxon shrilled. I glanced at my watch. I hadn't realized how much time had passed. Saved by the bomb, I thought. Or not...I'd rigged the bomb series to cut off the hanger bay with all its vehicles, effectively trapping any survivors on planet. I'd meant to be out of there before the bombs went off. Any chances of treating Serge were nil, unless I got him to Benny.

A'ler swore loudly. Then, with a last glare at me, she charged off, abandoning us to attend to more pressing matters. I instantly leapt at the guard who'd been distracted by A'ler's hasty departure. I caught him in a flying kick and knocked him out before he realized what had happened. After swiftly retrieving my MEC, I turned back to Serge, lying pale on the floor. He'd begun to smell of burning metal.

With a grunt of effort, I pulled him up by his armpits and heaved him over my backpack onto my shoulders. He stirred slightly and moaned. "That's it," I said, baring my teeth in a feral grimace. "Stay with me, Serge." I half-carried half-dragged his heavy body toward the nearest exit. I managed a stumbling sprint under his considerable weight, periodically shifting for an instant into a Badowin for a boost of strength. People rushed madly to safety and paid us no attention. Crowds milled through the corridors, looking for any exit. Fire and smoke erupted everywhere as stuttering explosions continued to pepper the air. It was every person for himself or herself.

I nudged my way through the panicked crowd, looking for any exit to the outside as the hallways shook with thundering sounds. The whole place was going. And soon. Then I found an exit. It was already open and people were spilling outside without thermal suits. I dropped back into a less used side corridor and laid Serge on the floor then rustled through my backpack for my thermal suit. I struggled to put it on Serge, knowing it's sentient fabric would stretch to fit him. When I'd gotten the headgear on him, I hooked the snowshoes on my utility belt, closed my Great Coat and heaved Serge back onto my shoulders. Then I pushed my way outside, into the biting frigid air. I turned off the jamming device and gasped out, "Benny! Get here on the double! Use my positioning sensor. I'll be in the open."

Coming! Benny's voice came over my ear-com.

I shivered as the freezing wind howled around me and I clamped the snowshoes over my gravity boots. My Great Coat would protect me well enough for a short time. But it was Serge I was worried about. Despite being warm inside the thermal suit, he looked deathly pale. A sob caught in my throat as I continued to drag him in the deep snow. Then I heard Benny. He crested the mountain peak I'd stood on earlier and swooped down straight toward us. Now I recognized another problem. Serge and I would be exposed to a rabid crowd who desperately wanted to get out of the cold and into a safe vehicle.

I deliberately ran back toward the building, dragging Serge on my back. There were fewer refugees where I was heading. It was also where the most danger lay from building destruction.

Within moments, Benny was beside me and the hatch immediately opened. I hoisted Serge and myself up Benny's ladder and pushed Serge inside the open hatch. Huey and Dewey hauled him inside from the hatchway. By then several men tried to force their way up and I kicked at them ruthlessly with my boot.

One grabbed my boot, even as the ship lifted off the air. He clung hard, pulling me down as I scrambled for a hold on the ladder. He was pulling me down! In a flash of inspiration, I shifted into a tappin and both boots, including the one the man grasped slipped off my tiny feline feet effortlessly. He fell with a scream to the snowy ground as I shifted back to human form and scrambled inside.

"Benny!" I gasped out, breathless. "It's Serge. Help him!" But Benny was way ahead of me: Huey and Dewey were already gently hauling Serge onto the retractable medical table of the infirmary.

"Get us out of here!" I shrilled, eyes flickering to the outside monitor that showed the rabid crowd. The whole place was going to blow soon.

Φ

I was thrown into the wall as Benny soared up. I quickly recovered and helped role Serge's unconscious body flat, face up on the table.

"He was shot with a kappa rifle," I said in a shaky voice.

"Oh, dear," Benny said.

Benny was already high in the atmosphere when the whole facility exploded in a giant fire storm. I stared only briefly at the towering conflagration shown on Benny's exterior scanners before turning back to Serge. I pulled the thermal suit off him, catching a whiff of burning metal, then worked on his shirt and exposed the wound. I sucked in a breath. The wound had grown since I'd last peeked at it. A wide swath of festering bubbling flesh surrounded a gaping hole the size of a large man's thumb that oozed dark fluid and smelled of smoke and metal. It was mostly blood but also something else, a mixture that formed inside the body from the kappa particles. Kappa rifle wounds were disastrous. And usually fatal. The kappa particle acted like a chemical weapon that essentially ate flesh. Even if the wound was minor, the secondary effects of kappa particles inside the body slowly ate away the victim until he or she died an awful death. I flung my hands to my mouth. I breathed out, "Oh, God..."

"Rhea," Benny said brusquely, "stay if you're going to be helpful but go if you're going to get in my way. Do something useful."

I pulled in a deep breath to centre myself and pulled off Serge's shirt. The blackened skin around the puncture flaked and bubbled like an angry burn. I glanced up several times at the ship's scanner reading. We hadn't been followed. I wondered if

A'ler had escaped the devastation. If she had she had a lot of regrouping to do before she posed any kind of threat again. We'd succeeded in destroying the weapon facility. But at what cost?

"Might as well take everything off, Rhea," Benny advised.

I tried not to show my agitation and, after a hard swallow, proceeded to remove Serge's boots and socks. Huey set up Benny's apparatus for removing associated waste particles from the kappa particle weapon discharge as I struggled with Serge's belt for an inordinate amount of time before managing to unbuckle and loosen it. Then I hauled his pants off his long muscular legs. Without hesitation I pulled off his briefs, making an effort not to glance at what was exposed.

"Okay. Now what," I said.

"Fetch those appliances in the tray on the counter and bring them here beside him. Don't touch them. Just the tray."

I jumped to the counter and brought the tray with long and short forceps and other barbaric surgical appliances. "What are you going to do?" I said in a voice hollow with dread. I grimaced as I watched Benny's laser apparatus lower from the ceiling and inhaled the cloying stench of burning tissue as Huey cut away strands of boiling flesh around the wound. Huey had used that same laser a few times to cut away a projectile or two from my body.

"He should be in a healing tank, Rhea," Benny said. "I'm not sure I'm going to be able to stop the process of kappa disintegration. It's like a swift cancer. It's rapidly eating him from inside."

My throat swelled and I glanced at Serge's deathly pale face. Feeling utterly helpless, I felt the heat of desperate tears threaten the back of my eyes and blinked several times to clear my vision.

"The laser surgery will help slow the process, but I can only cut away so much of his rotting flesh," Benny went on. "The key is to stop the process from the inside. Huey's given him a strong anti-kappa medication. Unfortunately, it's almost as dangerous as the kappa itself and may have some nasty side-effects. But, aside from a healing tank, it's the only thing that will stop the chemical reaction and the flesh from rotting."

I swallowed hard and brought a trembling hand to my mouth. "What are the dangers of the drug?"

"High fever, delirium, possible brain-damage. The patient usually undergoes several stages. The worst is the first stage: a high fever with accompanying delirium and some hallucination. Some never get beyond that or if they do, their brain's so jagged up they might as well not have. If they survive that first very dangerous stage, a long period of mixed wakefulness and restless sleep follows for an indefinite time. It's accompanied by a lot of confusion. I've heard of some victims who never come clear of that stage. Then there are complications related to the side-effect."

"Oh." I pulled in a long breath. "And the side-effect?"

"Possible sterility. I'm sorry."

My face burned and I wondered briefly why Benny apologized to *me*. It wasn't as though I was married to him or anything.

"Help me get him to a bed," Benny said. "No point in putting any bed clothes on him. He'll just soil it one way or another."

I grabbed Serge's legs while Huey and Dewey hoisted him up by the shoulders and together we laid him on the sickbay bed. I covered his pale cold body with a thermal sheet and stood watching him in silence. I watched his chest move slowly with deep inhales and rested my gaze on his face. My hero.

"Where to, Rhea?" Benny finally broke the silence. I gasped out a sobbing breath, rousing to look up and check ship readouts on the overhead screens.

I found my voice: "Let's lay low for awhile, Benny. Find a star system and a planet where we can hole up for a while."

"Okay. I'll let you know when I find a suitable candidate."

"Thanks," I said as the two droids moved back. I grabbed a chair and placed it next to the bed. Then I sat down and tucked my legs underneath keeping my knees drawn tight. I leaned forward with a long sigh, placed my elbows on my lap then clasped my hands and watched over the man I loved.

TWENTY-ONE

"He's burning up!" I called in a voice on the edge of being out of control. I struggled with Serge, who was writhing on the floor with the thermal sheet caught among his thrashing limbs. He'd fallen off the bed in a sudden jerky movement and hadn't stopped. As I grabbed one arm, Serge flung out the other strong arm and struck me full in the face. It knocked me backwards in a daze and I landed on my rump. I shook my head to clear it and thrust myself back onto Serge, trying to contain his convulsions. He appeared to be enacting a living dream, or nightmare by the look of his tormented flushed face. His eyes flashed open periodically and he stared in alarm but he didn't recognize me.

Although the wound in his chest had started to heal over the past two Galactic days, it now burned a deep angry red and I saw a large rash spread over his whole torso. His body glistened with sweat and he was incredibly hot.

"It's me! Rhea!" I screamed. "Let me help you!" I seized one arm and was struck by the other. "Stop, Serge! STOP IT!" I didn't even realize I was in tears.

"Rhea!" Benny shouted. "Rhea, I know he's your beloved," He added gently. "Let me do this. For you."

Stunned at his words, I let go and stepped aside as Huey and Dewey seized the delirious Serge and administered some drug into his arm. I stumbled and fell backward, exhausted. I hadn't slept in three Galactic days. I'd relied on a few cat naps on the chair while Serge thrashed, fidgeted and moaned on the bed.

"He needs cold," Benny informed me. "Help me get him to the shower in the brig. We have to bring down the fever fast. It's climbing dangerously. He'll have a full blown seizure any moment." I helped dumbly and watched as Huey lay Serge in the stall and propped his convulsing body against the wall then turned on the cold water. Serge jolted and immediately went from thrashing to shivering.

I climbed out of my clothes and stepped into the shower, braced by the shock of freezing cold water. Shivering, I pushed Serge forward and manoeuvred behind him then sat with my legs spread out behind his rump. I folded my arms around him and hugged him close to me, gently stroking. It might have been my imagination but I thought he calmed down a little.

Φ

Once Serge's fever came down, he settled. Benny turned off the shower and I dried Serge with Huey's help and we put him in bed again. As I helped Huey administer intravenous fluids to Serge, I noticed that the angry red rash had vanished with the fever and his wound appeared to heal again.

"I think it's working, Rhea," Benny announced, optimistic for the first time, as I covered Serge with a clean thermal sheet. "The anti-kappa drug appears to have stopped the rotting and we're over the worst of both drugs. He just needs to heal now. He's lost a lot of tissue and fluid but I think he's going to be okay."

I clamped my hand over my mouth and felt my face contort under a series of overjoyed grins, sobbing laughs and weeping. I cleared my throat to speak. "Benny, do you remember telling me that you knew Serge was my...beloved?" I gazed at the floor self-consciously and felt my face warm. Just uttering the word felt both exhilarating and uncomfortable. "You're right. He is my beloved...But I don't think I'm his."

After a moment of silence, Benny said gently, "Did I ever tell you about how Serge used to sit all day with you after Sekmet when you were delirious during detox? He used to lie down with you for hours and wrap himself around you to soothe you and keep you warm, Rhea. It seemed to be the only thing that kept you from the jitters. I'd say that was love."

I felt my breaths hitch and swallowed at Benny's beautiful words. He was a bit of a poet, I decided. I absently studied the metalloid wall beside me and brought my lips together in a tight purse. "He loves V'rae," I finally said.

"That may be so, but he also loves *you*."

Φ

I had squatted beside Serge's sleeping figure for a long time, gazing at his passive face. He looked so vulnerable, with his lips parted slightly in sleep and several days growth of stubble on his face. I let my eyes rest on him like a tired pilgrim rested on a grassy meadow and felt braced. As my eyes traced every curve, pore, blemish, and stubble, I recalled the first time, back on Iota Hor, that I'd had occasion to study him this closely, uninterrupted. It was when he lay asleep beside me one morning after a night of exquisite lovemaking. How I adored every noble feature: from his long straight nose and confident jaw to his trusting mouth and delicious lips so wonderful to kiss...

I found myself gravitating toward him until my lips were almost touching his —

Serge's face abruptly tightened into a frown and he flinched then moaned. I jerked back and pushed myself up on my knees to stand. I watched his face constrict and body curl up tightly into a ball. Then he shuddered briefly before relaxing again.

"Rhea," Benny said quietly, rousing me from a state of mindlessness, and I jerked as if from a fall. "Are you sure you don't want a cup of soyka? Or at least some soyka gum? It would help you stay awake. You just about fell standing on your feet."

"Thanks, Benny. No," I said, hearing my hoarse voice crack. I'd repeatedly refused any stimulant and had sworn off soyka products. They were too close to those mind-altering drugs I'd taken on Sekmet. But Benny was right. I was a basket case. I'd relentlessly watched Serge for three days straight. And during that time, just as Benny had predicted, Serge had partially roused several times. Each time he appeared very confused although he did seem to recognize me. He murmured several words, but I couldn't recognize any of them.

I let out a long sigh. I was so tired. Giving in to my exhaustion, I stripped, dropping my clothes on the floor, and pulled up the blanket then slid underneath. I lay down on the bed behind Serge, spooning him with my body, then folded my arms around his warm chest and sighed instantly to sleep.

Φ

...It always began with a stranger coming to my bed. He crept over the foot of my bed like a great lion, naked and smelling like a forest in spring. His face was veiled in shadow but it didn't matter; I recognized his muscular body— he was my noble lover. I let him pull off my nightdress. He caressed my thighs with gentle hands and I opened to him, body aching for his like a muse for a long forgotten poem. Then he lay upon me like a Great Coat, warm skin moulded over my yearning body, and his lips touched mine. It coaxed me to stir and join him...but I already mourned what would follow when he disappeared and my heart throbbed with dread...already alone...alone with another man brandishing a knife...

I woke with a sharp inhale, facing Serge's smiling face. He'd obviously turned to face me and appeared awake. I suddenly realized that Serge had been my lover in the dream. And V'mer had been the man with the knife! He'd put Serge's beloved, V'rae in a coma. Oh, God! I swallowed down my choking breaths.

Serge was half-awake, lazy eyes glinting at me with lust. He looked so vulnerable and sweet and moved gently against me. I felt his hard heat and my body responded with its own moist heat. I folded my arms around his neck, letting the covers slide off my shoulders. Matching his rhythm, I rolled my hips into his warm flesh, lips nearing his for a kiss.

He murmured, "V'rae...my V'rae...you've come back..."

I stiffened and pulled away. Serge was obviously still confused and slightly delirious. He thought I was his real beloved. But I wasn't. I just looked like her.

"It's just me," I said to him quietly. "Rhea."

Benny interjected, "I apologize for interrupting, Rhea."

"What?" I seized the cover and pulled it over my bared breasts, suddenly self-conscious, and looked up annoyed. Benny was usually so discreet.

"It'll help against the side-effects, Rhea. Sterility, remember? If you were to help him along…"

"Really," I grunted, looking back at Serge's happy face. His eyes were glazed with desire. He thought I was his beloved, V'rae, returned from her coma. Well, I supposed I could be his surrogate V'rae one more time. No doubt all those previous times we'd made love, I'd served the same handy substitute.

With sudden dark inspiration, I thought of the one remaining 'truth' I hadn't yet accepted from Serge: the truth about absorption. Was it what he'd said it was? A transforming journey to where souls were born? Or was it the end? Or was it just kinky sex?

Heart slamming, I gave him a brief grin then turned my back to him and pushed out my backside in invitation. He responded, eagerly digging his strong shaft into my buttock cheeks. He wrapped his strong arms around me, hands stroking and fondled my aching breasts. Oh, to have him touch me this way! I sighed and trembled with a deep ache. The ache to have him inside me. Any way. Even this way.

Overwhelming desire trembling through me, I reached back and grabbed his hard phallus, already snug against my butt cheek, then directed it in between my cheeks until the tip of his member was teasing my anus. We inhaled sharply together and he seemed to know what to do next.

He repeatedly slid his shaft forward over the folds of my moist heat then back to my rear, trailing a wet path of desire. Each time my arousal escalated until I uttered a low moan and thought I might even come. As if sensing my readiness, he abruptly thrust into my tight orifice and I seized in a stuttering breath. After a moment of great discomfort, my insides seemed to explode with sparks of incredible ecstasy as he moved inside me. Like a sparking ball of fire, its burn licked through my belly and pulsed in my loins. I wanted to wail—did wail—

Then found myself suddenly falling into a vast darkness...It opened up into a galaxy of stars of unimaginable beauty. Was this Serge's universe? Was I inside him? No...It was *my* galaxy, the Milky Way, stretched out in a remarkably beautiful multi-coloured spiral. A Fibonacci spiral...

God! Where was I?...

TWENTY-TWO

Oh, God! I'm there! I was no longer with Serge inside Benny. In fact, I was no longer in a body. I was an incorporeal floating consciousness witnessing God's miracle of tumultuous, aching beauty. Before me shone a most spectacular sight, the galaxy as a ring of fire, an *ouroboros* eating its own tail at the galactic central point near Sagittarius...

It should have been eerie and frightful but somehow this vast cataclysmic phenomenon spoke of incredible peace and...home. This was God...*I* was God...a loosely assembled mosaic of fluid particles and fields flowing in synchrony to the beat of my divine song, a single harmonious note in the prodigious concert of the universe. And for a brief moment, an instant made eternity, I understood it all...

The heavenly motions were a continuous song for several voices, perceived not by the ear but by the soul, a figured music that set landmarks in the immeasurable flow of time and space...This was the music of the spheres as I would never in my corporeal life have understood or accepted. And I could 'hear' it all. The fractal stirring of souls finding their rhythm and harmony. The unknowable synchronous motion of life within an autopoietic network of soul-filaments. The discordant harmony of paradox and cruel beauty in a cycle of death and rebirth. From the creative destruction of a single forest fire to the galaxy tearing apart its neighbouring galaxies and eating their stars as it grows and breaths. The *ouroboros*. The fractal mathematicians, the whirling dervishes of Horus, the Hermeticists and Gnosists of Earth, the Khonsus singers…they all felt it in their hearts and knew it in their souls. I now did too.

…The grand revolutions of fractal bodies were made in unimaginable silence. My human form hearing the concert of the universe stirring was no less incomprehensible. As I had closed my eyes against the blinding sun, so I'd shut out a harmony too vibrant to endure…Until now. The cosmos was God's instrument and I'd found my song.

I knew that by sheer will, I could place myself in either diverse. Just point my soul there. I knew instantly where I wanted to go. The solar winds were a vast sweeping deepness that enchanted and uplifted every molecule of my existence, as I rode the spectrum of light through the resonating, breathing galaxy, braced by the high velocity clouds that roared in my turbulent wake….

Φ

…I lay in my bed, in V'rae's bed, the same one in which I—V'rae had made love with Serge not long ago. It was still warm and I could smell them both. I rose, naked, and wandered to the window where early morning sunlight streaked into the familiar room. What I saw startled me. This was Kitsilano in Vancouver. The sun touched the city in gold brilliance. Golden flecks glittered in the bay and blazed on the glass towers. How could I be on Earth?

It took me a moment to realize that in the inner diverse, Earth had not changed. This was Earth as it would have been in my diverse if no *Nihilists* had attacked and no Eosians had rescued and evicted humanity off the planet. And this was exactly where I'd have chosen to live.

I felt a giddy smile seize my face. It was all so beautiful! Then I saw something below that made my stomach clench. An ambulance.

"Oh, no," I breathed out. I swiftly glanced down to the small patio just two floors below the window and my nose flared as I recognized a pool of smeared blood.

Grabbing a pink robe hanging by the door, I raced out of the apartment and found the exit door. My heart slammed as I pounded barefoot down the stairs two by two, twenty floors to ground floor. As I burst out the exit door, I saw two ambulance attendants leave the building, pulling a wheeled stretcher. Trailing behind, hunched over a body on the stretcher, was Serge. I caught my breath and ducked behind a decorative column then peered around.

Serge was crying. He held V'rae's limp hand that dangled out from under the sheet. He leaned over her, murmuring to her unconscious figure. I had never seen him this broken and tortured. It pained my heart to see him so forlorn and lost. I burst into sympathetic tears.

I set my mind to return to the outer diverse, knowing what I must do…

Φ

I opened my eyes. I was lying in the sickbay bed, alone. Serge was gone! I flung off the covers and sat up then caught him sitting at the table, dressed in khaki trousers and his charcoal wool crewneck sweater. At my movement, Serge turned to face me with surprised joy as I stared at him, shaking off my previous vision of him.

"There you are," he said, rakishly eying my bared breasts. I grabbed the blanket in sudden demureness and covered myself. I was naked. I'd been dressed in the inner diverse. A plate full of food sat before Serge and he held a forkful poised in front of his mouth. "Benny says I just came out of a delirium moments ago. Where were you?" he asked, puzzled. "I didn't see you pass me just now. I guess I was too busy stuffing my face. Benny actually thought that you'd vanished off the ship." He looked up in the general direction of the ceiling. "See, Benny, she was here the whole time. Probably just using the loo." Then he turned glowing eyes back to me, grinning through dark stubble. "I had the craziest dream that I was back home in my diverse… then I thought you and I were having raunchy sex."

He chuckled. "That's when I woke up, and you obviously weren't there so I guess I imagined it," he ended with a crooked smile. Then he barked out a hoarse belly laugh. The kind that always incited me to join him.

I laughed giddily with heady joy. He was alive and well. Colour had returned to his face and his eyes were lucid and bright. "You're better," I said, mouth opening to a broad grin. "In fact, you look great!"

He beamed back at me. "So do you." He leaned back with a sigh and gazed at me, looking entranced. "God, how I love your unabashed smile, Rhea." I knew my mouth was large and when overcome with great joy my smile opened to a wide grin that dominated my face. He somehow didn't think less of me for it. Quite the reverse. "You light up a whole room with that smile," he ended raptly. Then, with a brash smile, he leaned forward and added, "Chaos, it makes me want to grab you, woman!"

My grin faltered and closed to an awkward tremulous smile as I swallowed sudden discomfort and broke off my gaze. I would have preferred his previous anger, coldness and sarcasm to this. It felt as though we were betraying his true beloved, V'rae. Because I wanted him to grab me too.

He sensed the wall of tension that I'd put up and said in a subdued voice, pointing to the food in front of him "I was really hungry when I woke up. Care to join me? I'm afraid I was a little over-exuberant and chose with my eyes, not my stomach. So there's plenty here." He waved a hand over his over-full plate of brazed blenoid legs, crisp steg chips, dhap weed salad and roasted poms.

I smelled the poms and smiled.

"But you were just heading to bed to catch up on sleep, weren't you?" he quickly posed in an apologetic tone. "I'm sorry I took your bed. It's all yours if you want it."

"No, that's okay," I said. "My bed's your bed." I immediately blushed at the inference and quickly explained, "It's really the infirmary bed, so it's for anyone who needs it."

He nodded with a rakish smile. "Well, I seem to have put

it to good use. Thanks. You might be wanting it for some quality rest, though. Looks like you need some."

"I think I will, but I'd love to join you first." I tossed the blanket aside and got up, naked, to collect the clothes I'd left scattered on the floor earlier. As I pulled my trousers on, I glanced up at Serge and noticed his eyes grow dark as he shamelessly watched me. I couldn't help a smirk at his blatant enjoyment.

"Benny tells me that we succeeded in destroying the weapon-building facility," he said as I pulled my sleeveless black top over my head. "Okay, I mean *you* succeeded," he amended as I sat down on the bed to put on my socks and boots. "You didn't need me," he went on. "In fact, I got in the way. I got us caught and almost compromised the mission with A'ler. It was good that you didn't show me where you'd put the bomb. You had a right not to trust me. I don't know if I could have stayed quiet when she pointed the rifle at you." He sighed as I pulled on one sock then glanced up at him. "My temper just about spoiled the mission. You should have left me in the control chamber hall."

"The thought had crossed my mind," I admitted darkly, letting my previous frustration with him colour my voice. I caught him wincing at my cruel words and was reminded with vindictive satisfaction of Serge's earlier mean words about leaving me on Sekmet.

"What about my sister?..." he hesitated. "Did she..." he trailed.

I met his hopeful gaze with a pained look. "I don't know, Serge," I said. I honestly didn't know if A'ler had escaped the blast and made it off the ice planet. I thought it both admirable and crazy that Serge still cared for the sister who'd shot him and left him for dead on Kraal. I pushed a reassuring half-smile. "She may have escaped on a ship outside the hanger," I offered. "I'm sorry about what happened." I resumed pulling on my other sock, recalling Serge's stunned look of pained grief at his sister's reprehensible act. "I really didn't think she'd shoot you," I ended in a grimace.

"Neither did I," he responded sadly. He briefly inspected where the wound in his chest had mostly healed. "Thanks to you and Benny, I'm okay." Then he gave me a curious look. "But, Rhea, in truth you look like...well...like..."

"Shit? That's what Bas would have said," I said with a self-mocking smile. It turned maudlin and I held a boot absently in one hand. "I miss him. I often think of Bas and those awful vacant eyes where there used to be a sparkle of humour and wit. I can't visit him, though." I dropped my gaze to the floor, suddenly remembering to secure my gravity boots. Then I got up and sat across from Serge at the table and helped myself to a roasted pom with my fingers.

"Actually, I was going to say that you look *different*," Serge said. "More complicated than you were even before. Your eyes have a look to them that's...I don't know how to explain it...otherworldly."

I grabbed another pom and stuffed it ungracefully into my mouth, narrowing my eyes at him. "It's called sleep deprivation for several days straight."

"No, no," he insisted. "It's not that kind of look. Not spaced out. Not like when you were drugged on Sekmet. More like the opposite, as though you'd experienced some amazing thing, some epiphany. You're...*glowing*."

Apart from a reflexive swallow, I kept my gaze steady and offered no explanation. In response to my silence, Serge looked away in thought for a moment then returned his gaze on me with alarming intensity. "You're not...pregnant, are you?"

I hadn't expected that and barked out a sharp laugh then helped myself to another pom. Had he done some quick math? It couldn't have been his if I was. "No," I said, but had to avert my eyes as I thought of my galactic out-of-body experience and the horrible scene I'd witnessed. I chewed and swallowed the tasty pom then finally returned my gaze on Serge with dark curiosity. "Who was the man with the knife? The one who attacked your girlfriend, my double?"

"What?" He looked stunned by my question.

"It was V'mer, wasn't it? Your brother. He stabbed V'rae

and pushed her out the window."

Serge suddenly looked ill again, and I relented my intrusive question. But he recovered and said quietly. "You're right, it was my brother. How did you know?"

I didn't answer his question. "Why did he do it?"

His gaze expressed pain. "To torture me."

He then shifted his gaze from me and put his full attention on the food. I took the last of the poms with my fingers and slid it into my mouth. I followed with a blenoid leg and we ate in silence for several moments. Then, feeling obstinate curiosity nudge me, I put down the blenoid leg bone I'd been gnawing on and licked my fingers then pursed my lips for another hard question.

"Why did V'mer and A'ler hate me so much—aside from the obvious, my killing your father. *You* don't seem as cut up about it…" Then I amended as he looked up at me, "Or do you just hide it better?"

He glanced away with a mocking smile for a moment and I braced for more of the anger he'd displayed earlier toward me. When he returned his gaze to me, his eyes shone with dark intensity. "Five years ago I did hate you as violently."

I swallowed. I hadn't expected that reply.

"I was a rebel and, like my siblings, eager to embrace the idealistic legends handed down by the *Ancient One*."

Just like Bas had, I thought. This *Ancient One* must have been an accomplished politician. He'd convinced them all with powerful rhetoric to pursue violent anarchy on a world that had little to do with them.

"Then I met someone who changed everything for me— *you*."

I blinked in astonished confusion and swallowed down emotion rising in my throat.

"Your inner diverse self, that is," Serge explained.

I nodded in sudden understanding. "On Virgil 9," I added in a subdued voice.

"Yes. That meeting wasn't by chance." He put his fork down and leaned forward with his arms resting on the table. His eyes blazed into mine and I saw a million stars in them. "I used to be a *Nihilist*, Rhea. One of their most fervent agents. You were my mission—well, V'rae was and *you* indirectly. She'd gone to Virgil City on holiday to study the symbiotic architecture of the Ngus."

I remembered my vision of being V'rae as she got off the shuttle in the huge Virgil City Spaceport. I remembered her fascination and keen appreciation for the artistry of the photosynthetic colony. And I'd easily shared her wonder at the time.

"We all knew what you'd done to our father in your diverse, *this* diverse. We'd also pieced together your role in weapons development—the MEC—and the deaths you'd cause." I stiffened but kept my face impassive. "I wanted to kill you myself. But I'm not a warrior. Besides, I had another mission. My mission five years ago," Serge went on, gazing deep into my eyes and threatening to unsteady me, "was to get close to your inner diverse self, pump her for information about you from her dreams and visions then get close to *you*."

I swallowed. "And get the MEC design—"

"Anyway I could."

He looked down at his hands for a moment and let out a long breath, as though he didn't want to continue but was compelled to finish what he'd started. I waited patiently, seated with my hands stiffly placed on my lap. He looked up at me with a sad, almost apologetic look. "It was so easy. Too easy. Probably why I was such a dumb blenoid with you. V'rae fell instantly in love with me. I guess I thought you'd do the same."

I recalled the vision I'd had of colliding with Serge in Virgil City and experiencing the scary but exhilarating sensation of falling head over heels in love with a stranger. True love, I thought. Something that had eluded me all my life....

"She was so sweet and forgiving and her outlook on life was beautiful and innocent," Serge went on dreamily. "She saved my soul. I fell in love, Rhea," he said, eyes piercing deep into my soul. I winced inside. "First she taught me about unconditional love, then she taught me to forgive you. And I

230

saw the error of everything the *Nihilists* were doing. Right then I gave up on the *Nihilist* movement and secretly changed my allegiances." He raised his hands emphatically. "I researched the *anti-Nihilist* movement and devoted myself to keeping the two diverses open and to the protection of the human race from annihilation. Oddly enough, my mission with you remained the same, only I was trying to get the design for other reasons. My brother and sister picked up on my change. They suspected that I'd gone weak, that V'rae had turned me. I guess she had," he ended with a maudlin smile that stirred my heart. My mind re-enacted the heart-breaking image of Serge crying over his comatose lover and I felt my throat swell.

Serge gazed at me with new intensity. "There's another reason my brother and sister hated you. They knew you'd kill them."

"What?" I recoiled in my chair, stunned.

"That's why V'mer attacked V'rae. He thought that if he killed V'rae, she wouldn't be able to help you through some critical déjà vu experiences. He thought he'd kill two blenoids with one shot. I think it backfired on him."

I was still digesting the inference that I would kill A'ler. Perhaps I already had. Maybe A'ler hadn't made it off Kraal.

Serge slowly shook his head and aimed a dark gaze past me. "For V'mer it was always personal. He didn't care about the MEC. He just wanted you dead...and to hurt me. My sister's more practical. She's a Splinter Leader and dedicated to the *Nihilist* cause. She was willing to wait until you did...what you just did," he ended in a dark wincing smile.

We remained silent for some moments, avoiding eye contact, picking at the food. Serge finally roused. "Glow aside, you do look tired," he insisted, pushing the chair back and standing up. "The bed's all yours, Rhea. Get some rest. Benny said you stayed up far too long, tending me. I'm thankful but you need to rest now. We can talk some more later, after you've slept."

I nodded with a smile of gratitude and shuffled to the bed where I sat down to pull off my boots. What I'd witnessed during my 'absorption' refused to go away. It forced me to look away from Serge's warm smile. It was V'rae he'd fallen in love with. V'rae he loved with all his heart and soul and body. I was just a copy. A handy one. Well, I was going to change that, I thought, finding my gaze on him.

Its look prompted him to ask, "What?"

"Nothing," I said, quickly pushing a nonchalant smile. "I'm just glad you're okay."

He laughed, though obviously not sure why.

After an awkward moment of silence Serge added quietly, "Get some sleep...*chérie*." His eyes sparkled like dew in the morning and he gave me a tremulous smile that warmed me from head to toe. "I'll douse the lights for you and go up front for a while. Benny told me you stayed up round the clock for several Galactic days with me. Thanks."

"It's what friends—" I involuntarily gulped down the rest of what I wanted to say. Then, pushing a smile, I lay back down on the bed, not bothering to undress.

Serge came over and placed a thermal sheet over me with a warm smile. Then, as promised, he shut off the lights and left. *It's what friends do*, I finished my thought as I clutched the pillow and slid my arm underneath in a loose hug. Then I closed my eyes. I sighed into the pillow and breathed in Serge, already feeling the tendrils of slumber embrace me....*And I'm trying to be a good friend....*

TWENTY-THREE

...V'ser crept over the foot of my bed like a great lion, naked and smelling like a forest in spring. I let him pull off my nightdress. He caressed my thighs with gentle hands and I opened to him, body aching for his like a muse for a long forgotten poem. Then he lay upon me like a Great Coat, warm skin moulded over my yearning body, and his lips touched mine. It coaxed me to stir and join him. We made tender love then curled together, falling into deep slumber.

I soon roused, while he still slept soundly, and pulled on my nightgown then stole to the north-facing window of my bedroom. The dawn was breaking over English Bay in shades of gold glitter and lit the towers one by one like torches. Suddenly inspired with an idea for a painting, I left V'ser sleeping and took the stairs up and wandered the familiar hallway toward my art studio.

...Heart suddenly throbbing with inexplicable dread, I knew that when I'd turn the last corner into my studio, something ominous would occur and felt the hair on my neck stand up.

I know it's V'mer lurking behind the door. He's going to rush me with a knife. I have to be ready for him. He's going to try to push me out the window!

V'mer suddenly appeared from behind the door that was ajar, violently slashing out, and manoeuvred me to the open window.

In a sudden adrenalin rush I sidestepped one of his lunges and grabbed his knife hand in a jerky vizion grip. He grunted in painful surprise and dropped the knife. In a rage, he twisted out of my grip and I lost my balance. It gave him enough time to retrieve the knife and charge me again. I barely had time to scramble to my feet and dodged his slash then inhaled sharply with pain. I glanced from his venomous grin down to a bloody gash cut across my waist. He hissed with manic pleasure and attacked in victorious frenzy. I ducked with a sweeping sidekick and he sailed over me, propelled by his own weight. He sailed through the very window he'd meant to push me through. I heard him fall with a hard crash —

Φ

I roused with a long satisfied sigh and was about to stretch when a sharp pain in my belly forced me to stop. Muscle spasm, I thought. I yawned lazily and contemplated that I hadn't slept so well in days. When I finally opened my eyes, I jolted. Serge's face was inches from mine, staring at me with a confused and stricken expression. He stood up from his crouched position with alarmed concern.

"What have you done?" he said with urgency, stormy eyes slicing into mine.

I blinked up at him, pushing the hair out of my face, and gave him a sleepy smile of truce, not sure what I'd done wrong this time to agitate him. Still under the drowsiness of awoken sleep, I blurted out, "I...saved... V'rae."

His stricken expression transformed to incredulity. I sat up and threw off the thermal sheet. It was wet and I looked down. The sheet was covered in blood. And so was I! I felt a renewed stab of pain and stared at the tear in my black top. Blood flowed from a gash on my torso the size V'rae had received. Heart pounding with alarm, I clutched my wound to staunch the warm, slick flow of blood. I stared up at Serge with terrified confusion and suddenly felt faint.

TWENTY-FOUR

"I don't know what to say," Serge stammered, holding the smart bandage in place as it settled on my wound. "Why'd you do it?"

I just stared at him; I couldn't answer.

Benny had instructed Serge to help me shuffle in a slight daze to the infirmary table where he'd awkwardly helped me strip off my top and blood-soaked trousers and briefs. He'd then helped me recline naked on the table. Huey had cleaned up my wound and the rest of me. Benny informed me, to my relief, that it had been fairly superficial, though I'd lost a lot of blood. After administering a nutrient-blood mixture, Huey pulled out a smart band-aid and had given it to Serge to put on me.

He'd been awkward and I inordinately self-conscious. The band-aid had tickled me at first and we'd both laughed giddily. Then he finally got it right and it stitched itself on after administering a local anaesthetic.

This was the first time, apart from when I'd embarrassed him with my abusive words, that Serge appeared at a loss for words, I thought with an inward smile. He should have looked happy. Did, in fact, betray astonishment and gratitude. But it was a confused kind of happiness. A giddy nervous sort of joy.

"It's incredible," he said between halting breaths as I painfully tried to sit up with a grimace once the band aid had stitched itself on. Serge jerked forward and brought his arm under my bare back to support me. "Vrae's no longer in a coma," he went on deliriously, making a point of not looking at me. "I sensed right away that I was living a different reality. Then Benny urged me to look in on you. Rhea," he said, turning eyes toward me with new intensity, and seized me by the shoulders. "You've changed the course of events by soul-drifting into V'rae's life. Through your déjà vu intervention—and more than a suggestion, obviously—she, you, fought back and sent V'mer to the hospital. All she got was a gash, just like the one you have." He shook his head in bewilderment. "It was you too. You were there and you put yourself on the line. If you'd made a wrong move and he'd succeeded, *you'd* be in a coma too, Rhea."

He was staring deep into my eyes, right into my heart. Could he see what was there? Suddenly uncomfortable under his intense gaze, I leaned back on my arms to ease the tight pain and broke my gaze from him. "But I didn't."

"You're very talented. And lucky. He's very mean. And fast. Why did you do it?" It was the second time he asked me; and the second time I evaded his question.

I swung my gaze back to his eyes. "Did she—I—we kill him?" I asked in sudden concern.

"No. It'll be a long time before he's up and about, though. He broke both legs and suffered internal injuries. Rhea, I can't thank you enough for this. I don't know why you did it." He leaned forward and grabbed me in a bearhug. I'd wanted to melt into it, savour the warmth of his body against mine in bittersweet happiness. But the sudden pain made me flinch with a squeak. "Oops," he said and quickly retracted with a goofy smile.

"It's what friends...do," I choked out past my swelling throat, feeling suddenly very self-conscious about my state of nudity. I couldn't tell him why I really did it.

As always, sensing my need, one of Benny's droids

handed me another black top and I took it gratefully. When I raised my arms to put it on it sent a bite of sharp pain and I silently grimaced.

"Here," Serge quickly offered. "Let me help you."

I felt my face warm as he took the top from me and gently drew it over my head. He slowly pulled my hair out from underneath, hands trailing my neck. My skin tingled and my eyes fluttered shut briefly at his touch. He helped me with each arm, supporting it as I slowly manoeuvred through each sleeve. Then he was looking at me quietly, for longer than made me comfortable.

Just as I was about to draw away, he burst out in a sigh, "Selfless, beautiful Rhea. *Ma cherie...*" He leaned forward with a broad smile as if to kiss me. Then stopped the same instant I recoiled.

We stared at one another in the awkward silence of a painful understanding. I was the first to move. I mumbled something about checking Benny's readouts and moved stiffly off the table to my feet. Benny handed me a new pair of briefs and trousers and, not able to bend down, I was forced to ask Serge with an embarrassed laugh to help me with those as well. He kneeled gladly down and held the briefs so I could slide each leg in then he pulled them up, fingers trailing my long legs and rump. It made my pulse leap. He did the same for my trousers. Then he moved to fasten them on me, hands traveling my abdomen, dangerously low. I snapped a restraining hand on him and gave him a stubborn look that stopped him. He looked up with a crooked grin and stood up as I quickly secured the trousers and fled the infirmary for the cockpit.

TWENTY-FIVE

"Why have we landed here?" I growled at Benny, very annoyed.

After several hours of sitting uncomfortably in my pilot's

chair, though diverted by wonderful conversation with Serge seated next to me in the co-pilot seat, I had finally acquiesced to Benny's continual suggestion to recline on the sickbay bed and let my wound heal by getting some needed rest. I'd just roused and after a routine glance of Benny's holo readouts on the wall I'd discovered that I'd slept for over thirty Galactic hours—I suspected that Huey had given me a sedative in my nightcap. During my lengthy dreamless slumber we'd jacked the particle-wave stream to Borrias, 6,500 light years away and had just landed moments ago. What in chaos were we doing here!

"For the love of Creos!" I muttered hoarsely and flung off the covers then surged to my feet with a grimace of sudden pain. I threw out my hand to the bulkhead wall to steady myself. To chaos with Serge if he saw me in my briefs and t-shirt, I thought, ready to storm the cockpit where he likely was. He'd seen me in much less recently. "Benny, I didn't authorize this—"

Serge stood at the door, looking at me strangely, hesitant and refusing to enter. He was dressed in his travelling clothes: loose beige slacks and shirt and brown flight jacket. I noticed a backpack slung over his shoulder. "I'm sorry, Rhea. I authorized it," he admitted quietly.

"What?" I was ready to rebuke him but curbed my instinct. Something was wrong. He hadn't even raked his eyes over my lower torso and bared legs in appreciation. He kept his gaze steady on my face.

"The *gate's* here," he explained, glancing past me through the starboard window at the greenish landscape. "I'm not a *nexus portal* or *ghost* or even a *soul-drifter* like you. I can't just go there in my dreams. I have to use the physical *gate* that others built."

I swallowed. "Why?" I knew the answer.

"I have to go back." He shuffled his feet. "To my diverse. It's in grave danger from the *Nihilists* now, particularly since V'rae wasn't immobilized and V'mer's in hospital." It was V'rae he was concerned about, I realized; not so much the safety of his diverse; he was spouting hyperbole for my benefit. Why didn't he just admit it? I'd saved her for him, after all. "It's caused a repercussion. And we're not prepared like you. Now that we destroyed their weapons facility and your people are alerted and mobilized, I need to return and help mine." But they *weren't* alerted and mobilized, I thought in objection. How could he think that? And it was naïve to believe that Kraal was the only MEC weapons facility the *Nihilists* had established, albeit it had to be the largest and most advanced. "We can't let the *Nihilists* terrorize our world too. Besides," his voice cracked. His eyes lit with passion and burned briefly with the deep truth, "She needs me, Rhea, now that she's back. She's weak, hurt and scared." The flame in his eyes died under the frost of formality. "You don't really...*need* me. Not like her. You're strong. You don't need anyone."

He was wrong, dead wrong, I thought, fighting down the tears. And cruel to say that. But he was right to go back to his life with V'rae, I told myself. The woman he really loved. The woman he'd deeply loved for five years and who was no longer in her coma, thanks to me. I'd done it, after all, for him. For *them*. For this.

"Your people will do just fine, even if there's a war," he continued in a stiff voice, eyes now cold and formal. "You've got the MEC," he ended with a wry humourless smile. "And they've got *you*." Right, my mind rapped out sullenly, they've got me, a fugitive without a home or allies. "I'm not worried about you, Rhea. You're tough, resilient. Independent...A warrior."

Couldn't he see that I wasn't, I thought as hot tears scalded my eyes and I had to swallow down my swelling emotions. But even as my lips quivered with restraint, I stood quietly like a rock, proving Serge right.

"Good bye and good luck," he said, not approaching me.

Perhaps that was a good thing, because if he had just touched me or even looked at me with any warmth, I would have thrown myself at him and tearfully, selfishly begged him to stay.

Serge skirted past me to the hatch and Benny opened it. Serge stepped out into the cool air of Borrias and was gone. The cool breeze brought with it an exotic scent of fermenting vegetation and methane. I remained still, realizing that I hadn't said goodbye and that he hadn't waited. The hatch closed. I bowed my head, not interested in the planet, and shivered suddenly. Seizing the Great Coat I'd draped over the bedside chair, I shrugged into it for warmth and tried to imagine being in Benny without Serge as we travelled in the void of cold and empty space.

TWENTY-SIX

"Are you sure you want to do this, Rhea?" Benny questioned me as we neared the Gleise 876 system. "It's not too late to turn back. This is very dangerous."

I checked my holo readouts and smiled calmly to myself. "It's okay, Benny. I don't intend to get caught. I'm only going to see my mother." It might be for the last time, I thought, but kept that to myself. "I won't go anywhere near the Med-Facility," I assured Benny with a tight smile. As much as I pined to visit Bas, I understood the futility of that effort.

"Okay, Rhea," Benny conceded and fell silent.

I did some quick math and deduced that my mother would have had her baby shortly after I went to Sekmet. If all had gone well, I now had a little brother or sister. And, for reasons I could not fathom, I grew very excited at the prospect.

Φ

When I saw my mother waiting for me at the front door, I rushed to her and we hugged. I was close to tears and hung on to her for longer than normal to give me time to gather my composure. I don't think I could have broken off and looked at her and not broken out into sobs. When I finally pulled away, I found her eying me with concern and some consternation.

"I thought you were...well, in jail..."

"I was. I..." I tightened my lips. "I escaped, Mom." And

gave my mother a big empty smile.

"Oh, sweetheart!" She understood. And, to my mother's credit, she just swallowed and seized me in another embrace. "I thought I'd never see you again, after they took you to that horrible place. Oh, my baby!"

At her last words I came apart and couldn't keep in the tears. I shuddered out my sobs as my mother held on to me firmly like she would a child. I wanted to stay there forever, embraced in memories of childhood innocence. How far I'd strayed.

"There...there...." my mother soothed, stroking my hair. "Oh, Rhea, my sweet darling....I know they hurt you. I know they hurt you badly. I felt it. It brought on my labour pains. You couldn't scream—so, I did for you."

I pulled away and stared at her, dumbfounded.

"I was early," she said, then seized my hand and led me eagerly to a darkened room, where her baby was sleeping. She bent over the bassinet and gently drew out a bundle. The baby stirred with a sleepy whimper then settled in her arms. Without waiting for me to prepare, she thrust the swaddled child into my arms. "Meet Ben, your little brother," she said with obvious glee as I looked down in wonder at the sleeping child clasped in my arms. He was beautiful! Of course he was—his mother was. A spray of dark hair covered his round head. His nose was tiny and perfectly shaped and his eyes had the longest lashes. His mouth was a pink flower in a pale chubby face, smooth as a flower's petals. He was about a year old in biological Earth time, though owing to the decimal system of standard galactic time, only five months SGT had gone by.

I couldn't help beaming back at my mother. "He's beautiful," I breathed out raptly.

"Just like you were," she said.

I gave her an inquiring look as I instinctively rocked back and forth with the child in my arms. "Ben?" I raised a brow.

She laughed softly. "After the brother you always wanted."

I pushed out a breath. She'd been more attentive to my

unspoken desires than I'd thought. I grinned at her and cuddled Ben. My very own brother! Then I forced my mind on my current mission and with a sad smile, returned Ben to my mother's arms. "I can't stay long, Mom. This is dangerous for both of us."

"I understand," Laura said, putting Ben back into his bassinet. "Come, sit." She led me back into the living room. "Let's talk. You have a few moments, don't you?"

"I just wanted to see you...and Ben." I hesitated. "And to ask you a favour."

"Anything, darling."

"I have a good friend in the Phoenix City Med-Facility. His name is Bas. His brain was damaged during a skirmish and...I was hoping someone would visit him from time to time and just sit with him..." I trailed, searching my mother's eyes for a positive response. "He's Eosian," I added.

"Oh, my dear," my mother leaned forward, picking up the importance of this request. "Of course I'll do it. I'd be happy to."

I sighed audibly with relief. It took a large weight off me.

"Do you think I could bring Ben along?"

I thought it over for a moment. "It probably wouldn't hurt." Bas was basically a brainless vegetable with rare moments of apparent clarity. Ben might bring back some of that to life, I pondered. Then I stood up. "I better go." I hadn't told my mother that a war might happen. Perhaps I would be able to avert it. Or I might be dead soon. And so might she.

Φ

"You can't be serious, Rhea," Benny said as I leaned forward and pulled up the sleeves of Serge's charcoal wool sweater to adjust course. "This is so illogical. So..."

"Stupid?" I smiled grimly, checking the navigational readout. Benny had managed to intercept an Eclipse message that indicated that A'ler had survived Kraal and had returned to the *Ulysses*. After sharing my plan with him, Benny had tried to dissuade me from setting course for the HD222582 system.

"Yes, that's a good word. Why are you doing this?"

"Because it's what I do best, Benny." I leaned back in my pilot's chair and folded my arms under my breasts, hugging the soft wool of Serge's sweater and gazing out into dark space. "I'm a trained assassin. And someone needs to take the *Ancient One* out. He's the key to all of this, to the *Nihilist* attacks on human colonies. He's the instigator. It's perfect, Benny. I'm supposed to be delivered to him. I'm just going to make it easier for them to catch me and take me to him."

"But you'll never escape…"

Escape wasn't my plan, I thought soberly. The *Nihilists*, aka Eclipse, had put me to good use for their brutal mission. It was about time I did the same in return for the galaxy. I had two plans. Neither involved escape.

Φ

It was easy getting on the *Ulysses*, I thought, stepping off the shuttle with the crowd of crewers who'd returned from planetside. It was the getting off that was the problem. But I had insurance, I thought, gently feeling the device I'd strapped to my torso, well hidden under my flight jacket.

I'd left my Great Coat behind, on Benny—I wouldn't need it where I was going. But I holstered on my MEC. I'd dropped Benny off on the small moon where I snuck onto the ship's supply shuttle, with orders to surrender himself to the Iota Hor 2 precinct and a detailed message of my plans. I prayed that Ennos wouldn't send him to the scrapper.

I glanced at my watch and smiled. I knew where to find A'ler this time of the day and headed for the ten kilometre-long park. When I found Pod Door 200, I took in a deep breath then opened it, instantly braced by the complicated scent of hay, wood and freshwater. I stepped onto the grass and strode to the meandering river at the centre of the long park, toward the gazebo café where I knew I'd find A'ler.

As I expected, she sat at one of the three tables, eating. Even from this distance I recognized her instantly; her upright haughty posture, the long sable hair that flowed like silk over her shoulders.

I was within a few meters from her when she finally turned her saturnine face to mine and looked up. Her wide eyes told me that I'd caught her by surprise this time. Before she had time to react, I surged forward and clamped a handcuff to her left wrist then to my right wrist.

She surged to her feet and pulled gruffly on it, pulling my arm with hers so I stumbled after her.

"You and I," I said, managing to sound slightly amused. "We just can't seem to get away from each other. Maybe we shouldn't fight it."

"What do you want?" A'ler hissed out, inspecting the coded handcuff with a glower then returning her scowl to me.

"The *Ancient One*. Just carry out your orders to deliver me to him. That's all I want."

A'ler laughed sharply, nervously. "You're insane! Why would I do that?"

"Because it's your mandate for the *Nihilists*," I bit back. "And if you don't, I'll kill us both."

"With what?" she scoffed, lunging out and snatching the MEC out of my holster with her right hand then pointing it at me.

"If you shoot me, you kill yourself too," I said steadily. "I have a bomb-device strapped to me that monitors my heart. If my heart goes, so do I...and you along with me."

"You wouldn't kill yourself," A'ler barked out in nervous disbelief, eyes frisking me. They settled on my waist and narrowed.

I let a cruel smile curl my lips back into a snarl. "My best friend—my only friend—is a vegetable thanks to one of your agents; I'm a fugitive with no home...my time is limited..." I didn't mention that the only love of my life had returned to his diverse, but A'ler didn't need to hear that. She probably already knew that her brother had gone back. "And I'm not in a very good mood. Just try me."

A'ler seemed to size up what I'd said. "What do you want

with the *Ancient One*?"

I smiled grimly. "My business with him is my own affair. He wants me brought before him. That's all you need to know." Surely she knew what I intended.

"No one knows who the *Ancient One* is," she said. "We never see him."

"But you're a Splinter Leader and you communicate with him. You must know *where* he is." *And you might still be the Rose, and therefore in tight with him*, I added to myself.

"Maybe...and maybe not..." She sneered in defiance.

I jerked my arm, pulling A'ler's arm with mine, to press her hand against my left breast. "It's linked to my heartbeat, which I can regulate to a point. If it slows down too much like when I'm unconscious—or dead...boom! If it speeds up too much like when I get agitated with the wrong answer...BOOM! Get it?"

"You're blenoid," she said, shaking her head and blinking at me with dawning fear.

I steadied my intense gaze on her. "I might be blenoid, but I'm not blenoidshitting you. Don't push your luck, A'ler, or I might get real excited and you and I will be blown to bits all across this wonderful plain," I growled hoarsely. "Somehow I hadn't pegged you as having a death wish. In fact, quite the opposite."

"All right, all right," she grumbled and surprised me by giving me back my MEC. Then, with a strong tug, she led me out toward the hanger bay. I had to give her credit. Once she was of a mind, all went swiftly. A *shadow tracker* was prepared for stream-travel and we set off within two hours.

I watched through my starboard-side window as A'ler's ship entered the darkness of space then turned to A'ler in the pilot's chair for distraction. She ignored me and tended to her controls single-handedly with a scowl; we were still handcuffed to one another. I sighed and glanced down at the bomb strapped below my breast. It blinked faithfully. This was going to be a long trip.

TWENTY-SEVEN

The trip on the particle-stream took us twenty-eight standard galactic hours and neither of us slept. I didn't trust her and she certainly didn't trust me. Handcuffed together, A'ler and I remained in the cockpit of her *shadow* tracker the whole time except twice to eat and a few times to use the bathroom.

By the twentieth hour I realized that we were headed for the Upsilon Andromedae system and guessed our destination: "You're taking us to Upsilon 3." It was one of the moons of Upsilon b, a ringed gas giant. Upsilon 3 was about Earth-size, an arid wasteland that diurnally shifted between extreme temperatures. During the height of midday, it easily reached 45ºC, an Azorian's dream, and in the deep of night it was often below freezing, an Azorian's nightmare. And speaking of mad blenoids, the planet was full of them.

A'ler gave me a sidelong glance of pure disgust and I knew I'd guessed right.

I'd been there before. I'd tracked and dispatched an Azorian assassin to the small ephemeral town there once—but at the cost of a blenoid attack. In his desperation, the Azorian had fled the ghost town into the arid wilderness, and if I hadn't shot him, the blenoids would have torn him apart. If they hadn't, he would have died a horrible death of severe hypothermia. As it turned out, my shot infuriated a pack of sleeping blenoids and I became the subject of their fury instead.

Ferocious and unpredictable, with dull brains and razor sharp teeth, blenoids were the galaxy's most dangerous predators; but beneath their tough hide, blenoid meat was considered a galactic delicacy, so long as you stayed away from their organs. Their eating habits made them akin to the seagulls of Earth; they ate everything and anything, including their own and what came out of them. And they were prolific. Blenoids weren't very large. They stood about a meter long and almost that high but with the anatomy and mad tenaciousness of a pit bull and the rough ochre hide of a rhino.

Adapted to the arid heat of the Upsilon desert, they resembled hyenas with extremely large ears and paws to increase surface area and promote heat loss. Five beady eyes, two on either side of their massive head and one centrally located, were adapted to the harsh bright sunlight of the Upsilon 3 dessert. Their massive powerful jaws contained three layers of razor-sharp teeth. Once they bit down on a prey, the jaw locked into a vice-like grip that either ground deeper or tore out deep muscle. Blenoid saliva contained a powerful narcotic and poison that dulled its victims and caused severe infection that spread swiftly. My grandmother was right; most blenoid attack victims died from shock. Those who'd survived, and there weren't many, had only done so due to drastic measures like having a limb immediately severed to save the rest of their body. Blenoids attacked anything, no matter what its size and tore it to shreds. They were even known to rip one another apart in a frenzy of aroused anger or if they sensed any weakness. It was natural selection at its cruellest, I considered.

I felt an involuntary shudder at the memory of their furious chase and one catching me by the leg in the pincer-grip of its massive mouth. He took me down in a blaze of pain and I would have been flayed alive by the angry pack if Benny hadn't frightened them away. As for the one that had clamped his razor mouth into my thigh—his toxic slobber already sending a prickling soporific flame through my leg—Benny had opted to decapitate him with his laser cannon to spare my leg. After I'd somehow managed to scramble aboard with the severed head still attached to me, Benny had to apply a topical muscle relaxant to the blenoid to extricate the scissor-sharp teeth embedded in my leg without tearing flesh and muscle needlessly. I'd somehow managed not to faint until after Benny had removed the blenoid's head.

I'd heard a theory—perhaps Benny had told me—that blenoids had actually been bred as fierce fighting animals for sport by some previous civilization, then they'd somehow gotten out of hand and began to run in packs, killing everything in sight.

In any case, some ancient civilization had abandoned the planet to the blenoids ages ago. They'd left a series of clustered large spiralled shell-like structures that used some arcane energy, which defied physics. Venik slave traders and other criminals looking for a brief respite from Galactic Enforcers made use of the buildings. The buildings still functioned and provided food, warmth and shelter. And most importantly, a constant and comfortable temperature. I thought it rather apt for the *Ancient One* to make one of them his Enclave.

By its own right, Upsilon 3 wasn't the most hospitable of planets. Its thin atmosphere, heavy gravity and hot, fluctuating temperatures made it uncomfortable for any species for any length of time, save its own indigenous small creatures and the blenoids that ate them. Maybe this was one of the reasons why blenoids were so surly, I considered. Even Azorians, who would have enjoyed the over 50ºC seering temperature of the day, couldn't survive the plummeting freezing temperature at night. The Galactic meat-traders didn't stay beyond the time it took to hunt and prepare the blenoid meat for galaxy-wide sale. Apart from the Gnostics who'd claimed one cluster of the ancient alien buildings as their temple of worship, no one lived here—except the *Ancient One*, that is. So, between the Venik slave traders, the blenoid meat traders, the Gnostic priests and the *Nihilists*, this backwater planet was actually getting crowded.

Bleary-eyed and very cross, A'ler took us down to the arid planet, piercing the cerulean atmosphere with a view of mostly ruddy sand dotted with grey-green scrub below. I caught a glimpse of the town, Zibar, abandoned now to the swirling red sands until the next hunting party arrived. It consisted of a dozen ramshackle buildings, made from off-planet corrugate and several dug-out compounds; to house the blenoids awaiting slaughter, I presumed. The buildings were mostly used to render and package the blenoid meat and there were several barracks for sleeping and eating. The meat-traders seldom stayed for more than a few days; blenoids were plentiful and dumbly responded to the traps the hunters laid out for them.

Aler received coordinates to land from the *Ancient One's* guard and suddenly banked hard to port with a sinister smile. My stomach lurched with the strong gyrating force of her hairpin turn. I grimaced down my supper and focused on the view below, knowing she'd made the sharp turn just to discomfort me. We left the dusty town behind and presently neared a small cluster of snail-like structures with ancillary buildings of corrugate, together forming an enclosed courtyard next to the largest of the ancient structures: the Gnostic Sanctuary, I surmised. Gnostics tended to choose some inhospitable place to make their retreat, I thought. The Schiss Order had chosen the frozen ice planet of Uma 1. This Hermetic Order had located their retreat on this forbidding desert planet.

We then crossed a vast expanse of open desert. I gazed down at the waved pattern of cresent-shaped dunes, obviously formed by a constant wind. It was a harsh and miserable environment, I thought.

"Barkhans," A'ler offered, pointing to the dunes and breaking her taciturn silence. "That's the *West Ghouroud*. No one's ever crossed it and lived." She eyed me with a dismissive look of disgust as much as to imply, *especially a puny like you.*

I didn't respond and let my gaze stray back to the dune sea. The dunes looked like the capped waves of a red ocean, the deep ochre of their shaded slipfaces contrasting with the harsh bright windward sides, still baking in the sun. The dunes looked small, but I guessed that some were at least three hundred meters high.

Φ

We continued some 250 kilometres south, mostly over *ghouroud* territory, to the next cluster of ancient snail-like structures, glowing in the setting light of Upsilon Andromedae. The *Ancient One's* Enclave. A'ler slowed in preparation for landing. With a sideways glower at me she set down on a small platform beside the largest of the snail-like structures. I couldn't blame her mood: despite her reputation for being something of a renegade among her own, what she was about to do—deliver me to the *Ancient One*—might be the last thing she did for them. Once I dispatched him, A'ler would naturally be blamed and dealt with. I didn't think the *Nihilists* would let her live. I glanced at her stern face as the ship jolted in a hard landing on the circular platform. I felt a little sorry for A'ler. I seemed fated to hurt her family; now it was her turn.

She turned to glare at me and shook her hand-cuffed hand. "Shall we?"

I nodded and we rose together, shackle-bound, and made our way to the aft exit. A'ler opened the hatch and a blast of furnace-hot air knocked me gasping and recoiling. A'ler shouted a laugh of defiance and pulled me gruffly outside into the harsh sunlight.

"Puny slave!" she snarled.

Even at sunset, I could feel the stifling heat as we awkwardly disembarked. I inhaled a cloyingly sweet fragrance, reminiscent of cabbage, sewage and rotting flesh: blenoids, I concluded. And remembered; they stank.

I saw A'ler wrinkle her nose and bring her free hand up to cover it. She glanced at me with a glower, as if I was to blame for the smell, and tugged me in the direction of the large spiralled structure, eyes darting from side to side in search of wandering packs of blenoids. I followed her gaze and let mine take in the wide expanse of shifting red sands, dotted with islands of low creeping grey-green scrub. My gaze settled to the east.

Upsilon Andromedae sat poised over the horizon. I could manage only a glance at the large bluish sphere of Upsilon b above the sun, its huge-diameter ring extending vertically down beyond the horizon and cutting a knife-sharp blade through the sun that cast a long shadow of the ring across the russet expanse. I stared, struck by the terrible beauty of this harsh landscape and just made out what looked like a dust storm on the horizon.

Then A'ler tugged me into a scrambling jog and I caught her expression of harnessed fear. The blenoids tended to come out at night, when it was cooler. I tripped but quickly recovered. She scowled at me and grunted something I couldn't make out.

It was probably just as well. I caught the words *stupid slave* amid her stream of invective.

It was only as we got closer that I realized: the grey-green structure was surrounded by a mote, of sorts, filled with deep indigo water that sparkled under the glowing light of the setting star. Blenoids hated water; they couldn't swim. But how were we to get across? I watched A'ler hesitate at the water's shore. Was she contemplating swimming across? I knew from my previous trip to this planet that swimming wasn't an option; microscopic algae-like creatures that resembled green slime colonized most of Upsilon 3's ephemeral water bodies. They swarmed then flayed their victim within minutes with their toxic microscopic bodies. And if you managed to swallow any of the water...I shivered at the thought.

I was about to tell A'ler about the killer-plankton, when a sharp howl not far behind us made me flinch. I felt A'ler jump beside me. She glared at me, eyes sparkling like cold sapphires. I smelled her fear. The blenoids were on the hunt; they smelled our fear too. Just as a pack crested the hill behind us, A'ler leapt into the water, tugging me in a sharp jerk behind her.

"What are you—" I cried then swallowed my wail of objection.

Where she'd thrown out her leg, a replica of the snail-like structure had suddenly appeared just below water-level and some kind of greenish force field pulled back the water. I thought it reminiscent of the shield used in Paradise City on Uma 1. I landed on the solid structure in a sprawl and skinned my knee. She pulled me up gruffly and glowered at me.

"Come on!" she spit out, throwing a frightened gaze to the blenoids pelting toward us. She leapt again, pulling me along. This time I was ready and leapt with her as another step appeared before us. I landed more gracefully and threw a backward glance to see the step behind us disappear. We had a good gap between us and the blenoids, now crowding the shore. They growled and spat, but refused to enter the water. A'ler stepped out again. Each time a 'step' appeared where it was needed and the previous one disappeared.

When we reached the far shore, where the two buildings were located, a dark entrance appeared in the larger structure. I didn't think it had been there before. We were obviously expected. I noticed the Greek letter phi etched over the door. It then struck me that the snail-like structures spiralled in what was likely Fibonacci's golden ratio: circular arcs connecting the opposite corners of "squares" in a sequence that ran 0, 1, 1, 2, 3, 5, 8, 13, 21, 34, 55, 89, and 144... each number being the sum of the previous two...The snail spiral, like many other naturally occurring spirals conformed to this sequence; like the branching of trees, arrangement of leaves on a stem, flowering artichoke, the uncurling fern and arrangement of the pine cone. The series converged on phi, the letter I was staring at above the doorway.

A'ler glanced down at the bomb strapped to my torso and scowled. Then, unflinching, she led us to the entranceway and we plunged into the darkness.

It was like walking into a tomb. The cool moist air wicked away my sweat as my eyes adjusted. It was not actually dark, only dark relative to the scorching brightness outside. We'd entered a wide corridor of smooth foreign material that appeared lit from within its walls. A'ler hesitated only a moment before continuing down the corridor. We reached a large door without meeting anyone. We stopped in front of the door and A'ler appeared unsure of how to proceed for the first time. Within a few heartbeats a voice resonated in the hall: "State your purpose, A'ler."

She jumped, startled. I thought she was more nervous than I was. "Tell the *Ancient One* that I have Rhea Hawke here for him as requested," A'ler said, masking her fear with disdain. She didn't mention that I was armed with my MEC and that a bomb was strapped to my belly, which baffled me. Surely it would target her as a willing accomplice.

"He's expecting you," the voice boomed as the door clicked open. "Enter."

I exchanged a glance with A'ler. She returned me a look that betrayed puzzlement. I'd been with her the whole time and she had not disclosed her mission to anyone, including the

Upsilon 3 enclave.

I gave A'ler a crooked smile. "This is the end of the road for you."

I unlocked the handcuff by pressing the code and gruffly pushed her aside to enter the chamber alone. As I shut the door behind me, I whipped out my MEC in a two-handed grip and took in the spacious circular room in a sweeping gaze. Tall smooth walls lit from within swirled in dynamic relief that appeared to tell a story of epic proportions; of great wars, with creatures of all manner and shape and angelic flying beings that beckoned my gaze. Though compelled to study them, I focused on the only other thing in the room, a stepped dais at its centre with an opulent glittering thrown, its back facing me. At my entrance, it turned, revealing a seated figure and I inhaled sharply—

Φ

It was Ka. I stared. Ka was the *Ancient One*! This changed everything. How could I kill my own grandfather?

"So, you are my intended assassin," he said with slight amusement, voice rich and dark like deeply brewed soyka. His liquid amber eyes glinted like gold. Then he raised a bird eyebrow and smiled in sudden enlightenment. "You've changed, young one." He rose from his throne as if to take the steps down to me. I jerked my arms out straight, pointing my MEC at him and hoping he didn't notice my imperceptible shake. Ka smiled tenderly. "You were an empty vessel before, grasping at worthless Guardian rhetoric to fill your vacant soul. But you've found something much better now...Love."

I felt my face constrict with painful acceptance of his words. Why was he saying this to me now? He always seemed to touch my heart in the most painful way.

"You've filled yourself with love, young one," he said gently. I swallowed down the emotion that crept up my throat as he continued, "And although I see in your eyes that you'd be willing to sacrifice your life to save those loved ones...I also

252

know your great secret, Rhea…the one you're trying so hard to hide…that you wouldn't kill your own grandfather." He took a step down.

"Just try me," I snarled, tightening my grip on the MEC. My hands were slipping.

"Perhaps I will," he said calmly, stepping down again. "But consider this first, young one: all things are of the one, the whole." Was he suggesting that if I killed him I was killing part of myself? He was probably right, I considered and felt my hands tremble and grow clammy as he went on, "Do you know of the sacred sand mandala ceremony carried out by your Earth's Buddist monks of Tibet?" He didn't wait for my response and waved his hand at me. "Of course you do, you're extremely well read for someone who avoids doing research," he smiled sideways. "But let me fill you in just the same: the sand mandala is an ornate, highly detailed geometric design symbolic of the universe. It is painstakingly created over many days by these Tibetan monks and represents their sacred world of balance held together by spirit. Once this incredible work of art is finished and revered in a short ceremony, they destroy it." He took another step down, knowing I wasn't going to shoot him. "Form comes out of nothing and returns there, like the elements that move through our living world, making and unmaking life. Rhea, we are the raw material of reality, matter and energy transformed to life, an impermanent one, as the Buddist monks demonstrated in their sand mandala. Our corporeal selves are impermanent. It is the spirit of the *ouroboros* that endures in us all, young one. But, of course, you know all this. You've felt it, experienced it, haven't you? The relentless, often violent, but necessary cycle between opposites, life and death and rebirth, all sliding across one another like the two diverses—"

"Which you wish kept separate," I reminded him.

"Yes, young one. Two complementary entities, two separate worlds sliding past one another like the tectonic plates of the Earth's crust. Let them grow too far apart and they release an inner fire of devastation; let them draw too close and they destroy each other and the whole world of which they are a part.

It is all a sacred balance, often embracing paradox. Like you, young one…You are a paradox: an assassin with a conscience. I know what you did on Sekmet. Rhea Hawke, Guardian Enforcer, would never have acted that way. She would have blasted everyone there like those low-life murderers deserved. You demonstrated compassion and mercy far beyond your years. You still believe there is good in the world, in all of us, even those murderers. Even in *me*…" His eyes stroked my heart in a cruel caress. "Rhea, you're not a killer. You weren't born to kill, you were born for love…"

A sob caught in my throat, barely audible, and I felt my whole body shudder with the effort of staying in control. I was coming apart. Why did he always have that affect on me?

My grandfather stepped off the dais and approached me slowly, gliding as if on air, long purple robe trailing behind him. "You've seen it, you've been there," he smiled with open joy and pride. "I see its glow on you. I see it in your eyes, how you look upon your world. And mostly, I hear it in your voice and the rhythm of your movements. You've discovered your song, Rhea. And how your soul can sing it!" he ended, rejoicing. Proud.

I gasped at his words. As if they'd sliced deeply into my heart, I fell to my knees and let the weapon drop from my shaking hand. It clattered to the floor. He'd called my bluff. He knew I couldn't shoot him, couldn't trip the bomb attached to me. I was out of options. I ripped off the heart monitor and removed the bomb harness then threw it on the floor. Tears burst out of me. The room—along with my last chance to right all my wrongs—swam out of focus.

"There, there…" Ka was suddenly kneeling beside me, soothing. Then he pushed the bomb aside and picked up the MEC and stood. His voice cooled, "We have come full circle, young one. What am I to do with you?"

I stood up shakily, finding my MEC pointed at me and wanted to laugh. A hysterical laugh of defeat. I smothered it and instead gazed back at my grandfather with wounded eyes of anguish.

"You thought you were clever, destroying the Kraal

weapons facility. And assuredly, it was a set back for us. Kraal was our largest and most advanced facility, but the other two facilities are catching up..." Ka laughed lightly at my reaction of dismay. "We anticipate that within a few months we'll have enough ships equipped with your wonderful MEC design. A ship for every major human colony in the galaxy." They were aiming for a simultaneous hit, the ultimate in surprise. The ultimate in devastation.

"The Guardians won't let you," I said, though not believing it. It had been over a month since I'd sent my message to Ennos and I wasn't sure what he'd done with it. It was possible that he'd mobilized a full force by now. It was more likely that he'd done nothing, paralysed with fear.

Ka smiled at me as though I was a wayward pupil who'd disappointed him. "You are so naïve, young one. An interesting combination for a trained assassin, don't you think? But not a very good one. Haven't you wondered why your precious Guardians haven't done anything yet?"

My face must have given me away, because he leaned back and shouted out a peel of laughter that made me wince. I'd always suspected that there was at least one Vos spy among the Guardians. Someone besides Bas. Someone he reported to. Ka had just proven my fears. And my heart slammed. It followed where my mind raced: was it Ennos? The man I'd trusted the most; the man I'd told everything.

"Now that I've dashed your hopes for a Guardian retaliation, let me add that no one knows you're here either. No one will come to rescue you, much less be inclined to. You might as well rethink your priorities, young one. You're still a wanted criminal. You have no allies or friends here...they're either gone, dead or worse. You are a Vos, after all," he reminded me. "Consider your options, granddaughter." He lowered my MEC and gave me a smile of pity. I hated him for it.

As if he'd silently commanded it, the door opened and two large Eosian guards entered.

"Take her to the detention," Ka said dismissively to them. As they gruffly took me by my arms to lead me away, he glanced at me once again. "Think it over, young one. You can still accomplish a great deal. Study with me, learn to master the music of the spheres. Together, we could make a galactic symphony."

I remembered my grandmother's words of warning and met Ka's amber eyes with a steady glare of incrimination. Our eyes locked for just a moment but so much passed between us. It was finally he who looked away first. With a flick of his hand the guards ushered me out.

TWENTY-EIGHT

The guards took me outside, into the sun's beating heat, one ahead and one behind me. The setting sun threw long shadows of us ahead as they led me along a dusty path and eventually over a gully on a bridge that led from the large spiral building to a smaller one. As soon as we set foot on the bridge, I heard vicious snarls and barks and glanced below to a dug-out compound and a mêlée of snapping blenoids. A dozen upturned massive heads snarled and barked at me. *Fresh meat.* That's what I was to them. But *they* were the fresh meat, I thought. Ka liked his blenoid viscera, I reflected with a snarling frown. And he liked it fresh.

I glanced behind me and caught a glimpse of my grandfather, standing on an outside balcony of the building we'd just left. He watched me with a dark musing raptor's face. My heart beat faster as I contemplated a terrifying idea: my grandmother had told me that all I needed was to have touched a being to be able to shape-shift into one. I'd done it several times on Sekmet: Khonsus, Azorian, Badowin and others. Thanks to the blenoid's earlier attack, I had more than I needed, I thought as I studied the growling animals below. They paced nervously in a loose pack, snapping and snarling at one another as much as up at me. They were waiting, hoping, for something to happen. I intended not to disappoint them. Glancing back at

Ka, I loosed a defiant smile of unalloyed victory. Then, feeling the pumping thrill of fear, I leapt. The guard behind me shouted.

In the brief instant of my fall I glimpsed the horror on my grandfather's face. It was probably the first time I'd truly surprised him—and probably the last. I fought the panic to shift right away. They had to see me fall—and land. I wanted them to think I'd gotten eaten, without actually getting eaten. That was the trick.

I landed with a painful thud on a blenoid and it yelped under me. For an eternal instant, I was face to face with another blenoid, its massive russet head inches from mine, toxic saliva dripping from its open mouth and insane slit eyes staring into mine like I was its next meal.

I centred my mind and shape-shifted into a blenoid.

In the confusing mêlée of snarls, snapping growls and scrambling bodies, I shrugged off my clothes and forced myself to bite the animal who'd broken my fall. The others instantly set upon it and I winced inside as they tore the blenoid apart, along with my clothes. Blenoid flesh flew between snarling snapping jaws along with bits of strewn clothing. I entered the fray, stealing a leg of my trousers in my sharp teeth from another blenoid as Ka, breathless, reached the platform. He peered down in shocked dismay and flung his feathered hands to his mouth, uttering a cry of pure torment. It stung me with guilt for my cruel deception.

I hadn't realized that I'd released the trousers and my face was upturned until he dropped his hands and studied me with a dark look. Our eyes met. Feeling suddenly vulnerable, I challenged another blenoid with vicious snarls. It was a risk because if I showed any weakness in the conflict, I would be the next victim. I found the smallest blenoid, probably a female, and bit her haunch. She yelped then spun around with remarkable speed and snapped back at me, baring three sets of sharp teeth. Saliva, metallic blue-green blood and gore dripped off her massive snout. I leapt in a sideways motion onto her back, like I'd seen other blenoids do, and sank my teeth through her tough hide into her sinewy neck, tasting cloying flesh, fur and the warm acrid metal of blood. Two other blenoids joined my attack once the female faltered slightly and as they finished what I'd begun, I saw Ka turn away and berate the two guards. He abruptly spun around to one of them and struck him hard on the head. So, my grandfather had a temper after all, quite a bad one. I then recalled how he'd hit me in angry frustration aboard his vessel when he mind-raped Bas. A Khonsus who inflicted physical abuse; but then he wasn't a real Khonsus, I reminded myself.

Once his party had retreated back to the main building, I struggled out from the pack of ferocious blenoids and stole away, sore and feeling the slick wetness of blood on me and not sure if it was mine or the female's I'd attacked. I retreated quickly to the edge of the compound into the hiding shade of several thin-leaved thorny cozu shrubs and shifted back to my human form.

Crouching naked under the already cooling evening shadow of the bushes, I shivered and peered at the blenoids, snapping and barking at one another in the aftermath of the kill. I felt the sticky drumming ache of my own wounds and glanced down at myself. I spotted several angry welts, where teeth had grazed my skin on my thighs, torso and arms. My flesh had reacted to their toxic saliva. After my first encounter with blenoids my body had created its own immunity to their toxic saliva. A few deeper scratches oozed with blood. Still, I'd been lucky it wasn't worse. Most creatures didn't recover from the simplest blenoid scratches. I knew I'd survive.

I turned to inspect the wall behind me. It was designed to hold in four-legged blenoids, not a human with prehensile hands and feet. The short twilight of Upsilon 3 would swiftly give way to darkness when I would climb up out of the compound. I hesitated at the thought; I wasn't worried about the blenoids inside the compound—they were calm and sleepy after the kill. It was the blenoids outside the compounds that concerned me. I'd be virtually escaping the frying pan into the fire. There was the moat to consider first. One step in it and I'd be skinned alive. Ka already thought I was dead—wait! Of course...I had many options in my shape-shifting abilities. I'd shifted as a Khonsus before...I didn't have to get across the moat; I just had to fly over it. In fact I could fly over the desert and the blenoids until I reached the Gnostic Sanctuary, about a hundred and fifty kilometres to the north.

Within moments the darkness closed in and I shifted into a Khonsus and took flight out of the compound. It was too easy, I thought with a grin, peering down at the compound receding behind me and then at the wide expanse of dark desert that lay ahead. Braced by the cold air streaming past me, I exalted in my alien bird-form and soared over the alien landscape below.

Φ

I'd been flying north no more than two hours when I spotted a dusty commotion below me. It was A'ler, running for her life from a pack of blenoids. The *Nihilists* must have turned her out into the desert for bringing me armed to the *Ancient One*. Without thinking I veered from my flight path and landed nearby and shifted into a blenoid.

Closer to her than the blenoid pack, I pounded toward her and she veered from me, terrified. I barely reached her before the others and pounced on her, knocking her to the ground. She shrieked and slashed out with panicked arms, a useless ploy had I been a real blenoid. I twitched my face from her clawing hands then swiftly shifted to my naked human form.

She suspended her actions and stared. "*You!*"

"Take your clothes off and shift to a Khonsus!" I hissed out.

"I can't!" she wailed. "I've never touched one!"

I gaped at her. She'd never touched Ka? I might have shifted to a Khonsus and pulled her up with me like I'd done with Tat Mol on Sekmet—but I didn't think of it right then. For the life of me, I don't know why, but I didn't. Instead, I suddenly remembered what Ka really was and felt a pang of confusion at my own ability to transform into a Khonsus; Ka was the only Khonsus I'd ever touched before I'd shifted into one that first time on Sekmet, and he—like me—wasn't a true Khonsus. "Then you'll have to wait until the moment a blenoid touches you to shift into a blenoid," I said to her.

She stared at me, wild-eyed, as if I was crazy. I thought so too but it seemed her only chance.

The pack was upon us and I forced myself to wait with her in human form until a blenoid touched her. Unfortunately I was first to be touched. I gasped as a blenoid pounced on my back, talons digging a flaming trail of pain, and forced me to the ground. In that instant A'ler thankfully shape-shifted and I followed, shaking off the blenoid.

Confused, the wild blenoids scrambled in a pile of sniffing, snarling and whimpering. I imitated their confused actions and saw A'ler follow my lead. Blenoids were truly not very smart, I considered with relief. Within a few moments a howling sound in the distance caught their attention and, spooked, they dispersed. I led A'ler, noticing the limp of her hind leg, in the other direction and we stopped in a small thicket of cozu shrubs. There, I shifted back to my human form and crouched low.

Taking my cue she also shifted back, sprawling back with a stifled gasp to sit on the parched ground and lean against the woody cozu trunk with her injured leg outstretched. Her smooth pale skin shone in the starlight, except where the blenoid had clawed her on the back of her leg. There, I caught a glimpse of something dark glistening. Blood. I managed to consider that that had been where I'd first received my injury from a blenoid.

She appraised me with narrowed eyes and pursed her lips. She looked so much like Serge that I stared back at her haughty beauty as though she was a work of art. The Bastions were an attractive family with a distinctive aristocratic air to them. Despite lying naked on the dusty ground, A'ler's regal composure made me blush.

"Why are you helping me?" she demanded with a snarl. "I shot your lover-boy—my brother—with a kappa-rifle and left him to die."

I sighed, not quite sure myself. I'd pretty much left her to die too on Kraal. "No reason," I said. "Except you're another being who deserves a chance like anyone else. No one deserves a violent death like that."

She stared at me then laughed with baffled amusement. Her eyes grew cold. "It's no wonder you're not an Enforcer anymore. You must know that I'd kill you the first chance I got."

I met her gaze steadily. "It doesn't have to be that way. I know you believe that I'm supposed to cause your death. Serge—eh, V'ser—told me about the prediction. But it doesn't have to happen. We can change our future, even our past. I did already."

"What?"

I'd gotten her attention. "I can soul-drift. I changed V'rae's past in the inner diverse. She's no longer in a coma. She's alive and well and she and Serge are together again."

"Sacred Universe, you really love that bastard brother of mine, don't you?" she said. I blushed at the truth. A'ler was fast on the pick up. She waved a hand dismissively. "It doesn't matter, Hawke. My brother's a fool and a traitor and you're still my enemy," she said in a snarl. "I'd kill you both in a heartbeat."

"I need to tend your wound," I changed the subject brusquely, craning to examine her leg. "Or it'll fester. There's nothing worse than blenoid puncture wounds. I know."

"I don't need your help," she said in a dismissive growl.

"Don't be an idiot," I persisted. "You'll lose the leg if I don't."

She eyed me suspiciously and refused to turn to let me have a better look. "How? I don't see a first aid kit on you." She sneered, eying me up and down.

I raised my hands and wiggled my fingers, hiking my brows at her. "I need to squeeze each puncture wound and suck the venom out," I said. "It'll hurt like chaos. But if I don't do it, you'll lose your leg, maybe your life. At the very least, you won't be able to make it to where you can get medical attention."

The truth of my words convinced her—she must have known a little about blenoids—and, with a resigned sigh, she turned onto her stomach to let me gain access to the back of her leg. I drew in my breath. There were only four tooth punctures but they were already very swollen and raw and seeping white puss as well as blood. Not a good sign. I might be too late already, I thought to myself, and felt a sympathetic blaze of pain on my back where sizable welts had likely raised themselves. I felt warm sticky blood flowing down my back to my backside and between my buttock cheeks. Ignoring the pain, I snapped off a piece of cozu branch, wiped off the thorns and handed it to her.

"What's this?" she glared at me.

"Clamp your teeth on it," I responded curtly. "You might want to grab that low branch with your hands. This is going to hurt."

I didn't waste time. As soon as she'd placed the cozu piece between her teeth and gripped the low branch, I sat on her rump and placed my knees on either side of her to pin her down; I knew she'd recoil and lash out otherwise. I bent low and squeezed the first puncture wound with my hands as I set my mouth over the wound and sucked hard. Warm salty fluid flowed into my mouth and I heard A'ler pull in a sharp breath. Her body went rigid as she smothered a wail. It came out in a strangled growl. I raised my head only to spit out the vile mixture of blenoid venum, A'ler's blood and puss. My mouth tingled slightly from the effect of the blenoid venum, but I ignored it and set upon the next one. I did it three more times, once on each of her remaining wounds until we were both panting from the effort. When I was done, I examined her leg. It looked worse because of my tampering but I knew it was in better shape. Would it be enough, though?

"Don't *ever* do that again!" she screamed. I twisted round to find that she'd turned her head to glare at me like a mad blenoid. But her face looked less haggard and her eyes shone with more vitality than before, I decided with some satisfaction.

"I don't intend to," I responded. *And you're welcome, by the way*, I added to myself as I turned and pushed on my knees to get up off her.

"I suppose you expect me to do the same for you," she

262

grumbled, obviously seeing the jagged claw marks and blood trail on my back. I turned to face her as she struggled into a sitting position again with a grimace. "Well, don't," she spat out, scowling.

"I don't need your help," I echoed her words with a sideways smile and turned away again. In truth, my back was on fire with pain. But, despite the sizable wounds I'd received, the treatment I'd given A'ler for her injuries would have done nothing for mine. A'ler's injuries concerned me more than mine; hers were infected with toxic saliva and I didn't think she had my Scandi healing ability. I turned back to face her. "I think we should shift back into blenoids for the night. We need to get some sleep and stay warm. It's too dangerous to travel at night; that's when the blenoids hunt. You need rest to recover but it's too dangerous to sleep as humans. Our blenoid hide should protect us a little from the harsh cold in the dead of night and keep us safe from nocturnal predators." It was cool already and would likely plummet to close to below freezing by the time night was over.

"Fine," she bit out. I watched as she changed into a blenoid with some effort. It was the first time that I noticed how much energy it took to shape-shift. I'd taken it for granted, a simple case of centering one's mind. But now that energy, exertion and concentration were in short supply, it was a noticeable effort. A'ler had barely accomplished the task this time. I wondered how many more times she'd be able to do it before the power eluded her. I decided that, come morning, we would work on a set of signals that we could use as blenoids to minimize the need to shift back and forth between the forms to communicate. We had a very long trek ahead of us and I was already worried that A'ler might not make it.

A'ler curled up to prepare for sleep as I shifted into a blenoid. I lay down close to her and fretted over our long and treacherous journey to the Gnostic sanctuary as I listened to the eerie howling and cracking sounds of the alien desert. Both A'ler and I were shapeshifters and could shift into any animal we'd been in contact with. Truth was, the blenoid form was our best chance, being particularly adapted to this harsh climate. The Gnostic Sanctuary was at least a hundred and fifty kilometres away. At a regular walking pace of three km/hour—which I thought would be difficult to maintain—and journeying for at least ten hours a day, which I conceded was overly ambitious, it would still take at least five days to get there. In her present condition, I didn't think A'ler had five days of travel through this harsh wasteland in her—even as a blenoid. I watched her body sigh in deep sleep and toiled over creative ways to make her journey feasible. But I couldn't hold my thoughts. Exhaustion overpowered me and I fell asleep within moments of laying my head down.

Φ

I bolted awake, shivering in the deep of night and wondering for a brief moment where I was. When I opened my eyes, blenoid-specialized for moonless night vision, I remembered and glanced at A'ler shivering beside me. She whimpered and twitched in her sleep. White frost glistened on the whiskers of her snout. I couldn't tell how her leg was doing; it was tucked under her. The cold bit into me despite my insulating hide. I abandoned pride and crawled on the hardpan to curl up next to her for warmth. Without waking, she nestled into me, giving off a pleasant aroma of honey and cinnamon that cut through the blenoid smell of cabbage and sewage. I wrapped my giant paws around her and fell asleep again.

When I awoke again, mouth wide open and nose plugged with desert grit, it was daylight and already getting warm. My body ached everywhere, muscles stiff from lying on the hard ground. Something didn't feel right—I opened my eyes and flinched. I was staring into A'ler's face, her human face. I glanced at myself. We were huddled together, naked limbs entwined on the other, both in human form! She was pressed against me and clutched my waist. I drew my head back slightly and studied her face, passive—and beautiful—in slumber, framed by tangled waves of sable hair. Her eyes, closed and devoid of belligerent frown lines, were rimmed by long thick lashes and her usual stern mouth was slack and parted in blissful sleep. I instantly thought of Serge and a sigh escaped my lips. A'ler was unmistakably his sister, exuding that same natural aristocratic beauty that unsteadied me. If I hadn't known why I was helping A'ler before I certainly did now; despite what she'd done, her affiliations and her hatred for me, she was Serge's sister. And I refused to cause his family more grief than I needed. I'd already brought her into this; I hoped to get her out now—

I inhaled sharply. Her eyes had just opened and she was staring straight at me with a menacing look. She abruptly pushed herself off me and struggled into a sitting position, her lambent eyes glinting like cold gemstones in the alien sunlight.

"Why are we in human form?" she demanded, as if I'd had something to do with it. Her eyes narrowed. "What have you done?"

I shrugged and forced my stiff muscles into sitting up on the dusty ground. "I just woke up this way. We must have shifted in our sleep back to a form we're both used to being most of the time. Probably an instinctive thing for our bodies that requires less energy output." I noted that her leg didn't look too swollen and her eyes were clear. They shimmered like a sun-flecked ocean.

I was just about to suggest we set out when she eyed me with sullen curiosity. "So, what happened between you and the *Ancient One*? Did you blow him up?"

I swallowed and looked away. "No," I said. "I didn't."

She shouted out a victorious laugh then pursed her lips into a sneer and nodded. "Of course not, creon. No one can kill him," she ended confidently, eyes critically raking my nude body and dismissing me like a rancid piece of meat. "His mind is too strong for the likes of you, slave."

I didn't disagree with her. But she didn't know who the *Ancient One* was and I wasn't about to tell her. Instead I asked, "What about you?"

She sneered petulantly and tossed her hair back from her

face with a sound of haughty disgust. She hissed out, "What do you think? They took me for a traitor, helping you in your pathetic attempt to assassinate the *Ancient One*." I didn't interrupt to ask her why she hadn't warned them about my MEC and bomb, but I certainly wondered. "The guards took my vehicle, flew into the desert for half an hour then threw me out from ten metres up. I was lucky I didn't break a limb when I landed. But the commotion must have attracted the blenoids."

I nodded as I pushed myself up into a squat. I'd surmised as much. "The Gnostic Sanctuary and the town of Zibar aren't too far from here to the north." I pointed to where I believed north was, fairly certain I'd reckoned correctly. Toward the *West Ghouroud*. I remembered what A'ler had said to me and pushed it from my mind. My previous Khonsus radar provided me with a good estimate that we were about a hundred kilometers from Ka's Enclave. That meant that we needed to travel another hundred and fifty to Zibar. "We can do it," I said, making a point of not reminding A'ler of what that entailed. Our chances were better if we didn't think of it. One step at a time.

She blinked at me but said nothing. I took it as a tacit agreement to my plan.

I glanced up at Upsilon Andromedae, already high in the sky. The star rose and set quickly here. "We need to get moving. The heat will be unbearable soon. We have to make as much of the morning temperature as we can. But before we shift back to blenoids I think we should agree on some signals so we don't have to keep shifting back and forth to communicate. It'll save us energy."

She tersely agreed and we worked on a few signals that we could use as blenoids. Then we set off, abandoning the shade of the cozu bush and feeling the blinding heat of the morning. I noticed that, although her injuries didn't look too bad—they looked more like scars in her russet blenoid form—A'ler favoured her injured leg, either limping on it or curling it up and hobbling on her other three legs. I gauged her abilities and adjusted my pace accordingly. We weren't going to make the Sanctuary in three days, I thought in dismay. We'd be lucky to make it at all.

TWENTY-NINE

I didn't realize how belligerent A'ler was toward me until the incident of our second day. We'd walked the better part of our first day in the desert through a *playa*, a smooth, flat hardpan that was supposedly the remnant of an endorheic lake. The heat that reflected off the fine sands had burned our feet, even for our blenoid forms, as we trudged onward and tried to ignore the heat-induced mirages of waterbodies rippling ahead of us. We kept following wavering "wet pools" of the blue sky refracted by the hot surface air.

It quickly became obvious to me that A'ler and I approached our forms and our journey differently. While I admittedly operated largely on guilt, almost everything she did was out of haughty pride. It would be her undoing, I thought. In keeping with her stubborn reluctance to embrace her blenoid form, A'ler insisted on evacuating in private, behind a cozu bush, and snarled at me when I felt compelled, a little to my dismay, to follow her and sniff the excrement she'd just laid. Before I could quell the urge, I gulped the steaming solid pinkish lump down. Then immediately gagged in revulsion at what I'd just done. Although it had surprisingly not tasted vile, I'd just eaten a blenoid's feces! I swiftly recalled what Ka had told me about blenoid physiology and the complementary nutrition provided to one blenoid by a different blenoid's waste. If what biologist Diane Zeligman had reported was true, then that meant that my feces was also good for A'ler. She had to eat, but there was no way she'd do what I just did, I considered, still repulsed by my own impulsive action.

Despite the flatness of the terrain, we made poor progress and I began to recognize signs of heat exhaustion in A'ler's heavy panting, salivation and staggering gait. Unlike me, she hadn't eaten anything. I bedded us down early under some kind of salt-loving shrub. First I dug a hole to cool us, then I invited her to lie down in the shade. She gladly did and was asleep before I joined her.

We were rudely awoken in human form early the next morning to a sudden thunderstorm and were soaked in a hail of cold rain. The hardpan instantly churned into mud that spattered up onto us.

I scrambled out from under the shrub with my face thankfully upturned to the dark clouds and parched mouth open to catch the deluge of raindrops. I felt my shrivelled dried skin soak up the refreshing wetness of rain. A'ler struggled to stand up and I thought she was going to do some kind of rain dance but instead she screamed in furious anger, "What is THIS!" I couldn't fathom her anger. This was a thankful reprieve from the baking sun. But she obviously didn't think so. Nothing seemed to please A'ler. She resembled a warrior queen, arm shaking at the sky pelting rain on her. Tangles of black hair plastered against her face and body. But her jarring motion put her off balance and she slid in the slick mud and fell ungracefully on her rump with a splat and a shriek of surprise. I shouted out a laugh and was immediately sorry for it. In truth it had been more a release of my still-exhausted state. But she glared at me, eyes like daggers. I smothered my laughter and looked away, sitting in my pool of mud, and concentrated on collecting as much rainwater in my open mouth as possible. I don't know if she then decided to follow my lead; I made sure I didn't face her direction.

It was then, as I sat in the mud, that I spotted hundreds of tiny transparent shrimp-like creatures wriggling in the mud. They'd just hatched! As if from nowhere, several ruddy-coloured lizard-like creatures skittered in pursuit of the 'shrimp'. I leapt toward one, trying to catch it but slipped and fell with a grunt. A'ler, who had been obviously watching my circus act, shrieked into laughter and I turned. It was the first time I'd heard her laugh and it heartened me to see her cold features melt away in pure enjoyment. It was brief. Catching my response, she buried her laugh and glowered at me.

Within a few moments, the clouds dispersed and the sun baked down again, the ground steaming off its ephemeral pools of rainwater. The 'shrimp' and their chasing 'lizards' disappeared along with the moisture.

We shape-shifted into blenoids and headed out, having neither eaten nor drank for close to two days—I didn't think the tiny bit of rainwater counted for much but I was thankful for it nonetheless. I had tried to hunt yesterday but to no avail. The blenoid's main diet, I'd learned earlier, was the little burrowing rodent, the cobal, which resembled a vole on Earth and was equally fast. Problem was, like many burrowing creatures, they were nocturnal and none were to be found during the heat of the day. Only we appeared foolish enough to brave the searing heat of the desert during daylight.

The sun was a hot flame licking our backs. Within a very short time all traces of the sudden rain had evaporated and we trudged through the desert heat, paws stirring up dust, through a vast tract of parched ground dotted with silver-green cozu shrubs. The horizon rippled in the heat with wind-swept moisture and I felt my tongue hang out of my mouth in a pant. The air itself seemed to crackle with fire; it was only the cozu shrubs. The cacophony of the cozu's steel-grey seed pods snapping open in the cooking heat and jettisoning their seeds sounded like popcorn cracking open in the oven. Several times we disturbed a group of scavenger ants, poised on dead and dried vegetation. They had long spindly legs and shot around our legs at rapid speeds. Desperate for food, I managed to snatch several into my massive mouth and swallowed their protein-rich bodies without the need to chew. I indicated for A'ler to do the same but she haughtily refused.

I let A'ler walk ahead, so she could set the pace, which allowed me to gauge the status of her wound. It was only mid-day and she was already faltering. I caught her stumbling a few times and was about to trot to her side when she abruptly sank into the sand with a yelp of surprise. And disappeared!

I barked out my surprise then did the only thing I could: I dug with my huge paws where she'd disappeared. I saw instantly that the sand wasn't sand at all, but a kind of liquid mud. All I was doing was stirring the sand into a liquid mass. This was some kind of mud sinkhole I thought—a quicksand—as I saw it shake like jelly in the wake of my digging. I quickly discerned another problem. My disturbance was making the sinkhole bigger and soon it would engulf me along with A'ler. I abandoned the digging and ran for the nearest cozu bush. I found the longest branch and gnawed off the wiry twig then dragged it to the sinkhole, now noticeably darker than the surrounding ground. I forced the stiff branch with my mouth through the liquid mud down to where I knew A'ler was and hoped she was capable of grabbing hold of it. I was rewarded with a tug and immediately drew back, paws scrabbling the hardpan. To my relief, A'ler burst out with the branch clamped in her powerful jaw and was able to scramble to firm ground. Once she knew she was safe, she collapsed into a heap and let go of the branch, gasping for air. I tapped twice with my paw, the signal for "are you okay?" and she managed to tap three times, "yes".

I guessed that after a thunderstorm, water became trapped inside weaknesses in the hardpan and formed sinkholes of quicksand that were swiftly covered over by windswept dry sand. We needed to be very careful, I thought. I decided to lead after that and A'ler seemed content to follow.

Letting A'ler take a break during the hottest time of the day to lay in the sparse shade of a cozu bush, I attempted to hunt for game again with no effect, except to expend my swiftly dissipating energy reserve chasing a single cobal that seemed intent on teasing me to pursue it then disappearing into one of its many burrow holes. Exhausted, frustrated and hot from my foolish efforts, I finally abandoned the chase and returned to A'ler's cozu bush empty handed and my back burning.

I realized only when I turned back how far I'd strayed from A'ler's bush and in a sudden panic couldn't determine which of the many dotted shrubs was hers. The huge bluish sphere of Upsilon b hung above me, mute, to my right; Upsilon Andromedae blazed over my left like a torch, breathing flame across my back. It was no help; I hadn't paid attention to my astronomical landmarks.

I barked out, hoping for her response, and none was given. I roamed toward where I thought she was, using my handy close to 360º vision span, so intent on my search that I didn't notice the sand literally rear itself behind me in a sudden wave. The sound alerted me. I whirled and yelped. A huge toothless mouth two meters wide gaped at me.

As I stared down its ribbed throat, I just made out a twenty-metre worm-like creature behind the mouth, as the behemoth advanced toward me. I stumbled back and caught a glimpse of A'ler darting in a wild hobble away from us. She was hightailing it out of there with no thought of offering any distraction or help. Facing that huge peristaltic mouth I felt no reproach; what did she owe me, after all? I'd helped keep her alive these past few days but only after I'd shattered her world, turned her traitor to her own kind, and caused her to be here in the first place. I thought this in that brief instant that I expected to be swallowed and die a most excruciating death by painful suffocation.

Then the instant passed—the worm hadn't eaten me—and I sprang up on pure adrenalin, using my powerful blenoid back legs, over the gaping mouth and landed on the worm itself. It was surprisingly soft and squishy. I had the presence of mind to take a huge bite out of it. My blenoid teeth easily tore into mushy flesh with a spray of mostly water. Then I leapt off and pelted away toward A'ler's hobbling figure. I glanced backward to see if the worm pursued and found to my relief that it had slunk back down from where it had come: a sinkhole, I decided, the sandworm's abode. A'ler had indeed been lucky earlier today, I thought.

Glimpsing me chasing her, A'ler burst into a fearful sprint, stumbling and scrambling, and kicking up swirls of red dust. In fear of reprisal, I supposed; chased by guilt.

I pounced on her then handed her the worm-meat I'd bitten off, after taking a small piece for myself. It was juicy and sweet. Our blenoid eyes met and I could not tell what she was thinking. But she hesitated to eat the large chunk of flesh I'd offered her. I nudged it forward and walked away in sudden understanding, giving her a chance to save face. Once I'd made twenty paces, I stopped and sat, waiting for her without turning. She wasn't long in coming and looked better for her meal. Then we set off together again.

Φ

A hot wind whipped up the desert and flung sand and grit mercilessly biting into our faces, making our eyes water. I glanced at A'ler, her massive head tucked low, giant ears folded back, as she dug forward. If not for our tough hides, I was certain our human flesh would have bled raw from the deluge. As it was, the red grit forced its way into our eyes, nose and mouths. I'd never considered that one could taste the desert. That day I did.

That night we bedded down under the meagre shelter of a cozu bush and, despite the biting wind, A'ler refused to sleep next to me for warmth. Perhaps she was disgusted at my blenoid behavior; or maybe she was ashamed of having run away. I thought the former more likely somehow. With a shrug I curled up to conserve my heat. I glanced at Upsilon b and its knife-sharp vertical ring on the horizon. Then I closed my eyes, lulled by the eerie violin percussion of the giant shifting dunes in the distance, and fell asleep quickly out of exhaustion.

Φ

I jerked awake with a shiver, not sure what had awoken me but with my large ears raised. A'ler shivered against me, whining. One of us, I'm not sure who, had gravitated to the other for warmth. As I listened to the echoed voices of the night, I recognized, from their distinctive barks just to the west of us, the same blenoid pack that I'd heard the previous two nights. No other sound, close or far, appeared to have woken me. I hugged A'ler for warmth and tried to fall asleep. It refused to

272

come and I felt the restless call to roam the night. Recognizing it for what it was, I stifled the feeling and listened to the blenoid howls. I came to the conclusion that they were following the same trajectory we were. They were heading north too. Then I had another more alarming thought: or were they simply following us?

Φ

The next morning we woke as usual in human form, one curled inside the other and embracing. A'ler gruffly pushed away and glowered at me, red-faced. Her hair, no longer silky and flowing, was matted, dusty and in disarray like a Rastafarian's; I deduced, with dismay, that mine looked the same if not worse. "Why?" she snapped at me through blistering chapped lips. "Why are you doing this?" I knew what her simple question really framed: why didn't I just leave her and go my own way, unhindered. I'd taken easily—too easily, it seemed—to being a blenoid and she was obviously holding me back. Was she still embarrassed about yesterday?

I winced at her words. She'd made it sound as though I was torturing her. Maybe I was, I thought at length as I stared at those belligerent but anguished eyes. She had no frame of reference for my altruistic behaviour and that left only suspicion. I wanted to smile and held it back just as it formed. She wouldn't have understood. Six months ago I might not have understood either, I thought suddenly, and had to look away. Then, without another word, I shifted into a blenoid and waited for her.

Compared to the previous day this one was largely uneventful, except our bellies ached and we felt the languor of hunger and thirst dull our pace. When the wind wasn't throwing dust and grit into our faces, the sun baked down in the stillness of intense heat.

We'd left the flats of the playa and were heading toward rougher terrain. By tomorrow we would enter the desert proper, the *ghouroud*, with its massive barkhans that I'd seen from A'ler's ship. I could already see them looming in the distance. I heard their low stuttering roar as the wind sang through them. And dreaded the crossing. Not only would it be treacherous with more possible quicksand traps, but it would serve a tortuous climb for A'ler up the slipface of the barkhans then down the soft sand on the other side.

I didn't make an attempt to hunt game although I remained on the lookout for anything, which might serve as food. I thought of the vegetation and the water it held, and began to experiment with the leaves of the various shrubs—mostly tasteless, hard and needle-like—and barks of bushes and other sparse ground cover. I even tried the cozu seed pods and found them totally unsatisfying, besides which they soon made my mouth tingle and grow numb. Within an hour I was violently ill and vomited up in painful hurling bouts my meagre dinner. A'ler, who had sworn off all the various vegetation I'd tried, blinked at me with those slit blenoid eyes and I imagined her vindication. Her leg, however, grew much worse and I noticed that she now hardly put any weight on it. It slowed our progress considerably. It was already the third day of our trek in the blistering heat and I estimated that we'd only progressed thirty kilometres at best. With our pace getting slower by the day, I despaired at achieving our destination. It had finally dawned on me that I should shift into a Khonsus and carry A'ler in my powerful arms like I'd done on Sekmet; but when I tried, to my despair I could no longer shift into one. It seemed that in my weary, starved state, I had no power to shift into anything except a 'lesser' creature—physiologically—than a human, such as a blenoid. We were doomed to trudge the desert as we were.

Φ

That night I awoke with a shiver, hearing the distant blenoid calls like a beacon. The disconcerting yearning overwhelmed me like my bellyache and I decided to go on a hunt for game. I rationalized that this was the best and most efficient time to do it. A'ler was conveniently resting and wouldn't slow me down—she desperately needed to eat—and blenoids were nocturnal and suited to hunt at night. In truth I was answering the call inside me. I set aside the alarming thought that I was succumbing to that vicious animal's tendencies and set my mind to the task of getting food for us. I gently pulled off A'ler's paw draped over my arm and trotted into the brisk night.

It was exhilarating. I exalted in the cold wind that braced my hide and gazed at the night sky full of stars. Upsilon b's sphere shone an angel's ethereal light over the desert, cut by its own ring. This was when the desert came to life, I thought, hearing diverse sounds in the distance, and nearby. Most everyone—me included—dismissed the deserts of Upsilon 3 as a harsh chaos-bent wasteland of nothing, with no beauty to speak of and little value except the blenoid meat it provided. We couldn't have been more wrong, I considered. I watched the night sky shimmer with the varied play of electromagnetic emissions. Curtains of deep violet, fuchsia, cerulean and scarlet bathed the desert slopes in a mysterious sea that harboured a diverse symphony of night sounds. I felt oddly humbled and put in my place by this great landscape.

I began to sniff the cozu scrub. Cobals were nocturnal feeders of the highly nutritious cozu needles and suffered no ill effects from them, unlike blenoids. Within moments, one scurried out of a shrub I'd been sniffing and I pounced on it with my huge paw and broke its neck. Without a second thought I took the warm limp body in my mouth. It had been dead easy. I could have laughed. Instead, I loped in a giddy circle, hearing my pads thudding the cold hardpan.

I suddenly halted. Without thinking I'd stumbled into the blenoid pack I'd heard yelping and barking over the small rise to the west. I now stood on the rise in full view of the pack, unable to turn back. Half a dozen of them ceased their howling and stared. Shivering with fright, I stepped forward out of instinct and dropped the cobal in front of the obvious leader of the pack. She snarled at me but took the offered prize and ate heartily.

It was enough. The pack appeared to accept me. We continued to hunt. As I watched the others I learned more about how to flush out the cobals. Each time I caught one and snapped its neck, I felt the excitement of victory. Eventually I felt the need to return to A'ler with my stash of five cobals and stealthily dropped away from the pack. I wasn't successful. The leader burst in front of me as I tried to slink away. I dropped my cobals in surprise. The blenoid growled deeply and the other blenoids surrounded me, insane eyes glowing like a ring of golden torches. This was it, I thought. Time to die…

Alarm spiked through me and I backed away slightly. But they didn't set upon me. To my utter surprise and wonder, the leader abruptly coughed then disgorged all the bloody prey she had consumed. The others followed suit. Every blenoid disgorged something, some much more than others. Then, what followed was even more astonishing. I watched in silent wonder as each blenoid ate its equal share of the total catch, leaving disgorged meat for the ones that had been less successful. I found that even I was allotted a portion of the disgorged catch, given that my take had been considerably less than most.

Once the portioning was done, the blenoids dispersed and vanished into the night. I was astounded. These creatures had been so misunderstood, I reflected as I swallowed down the disgorged cobal. As the slippery mass slid down my throat I pondered on what I'd just experienced. Had I chanced on an anomaly? I dismissed it as unlikely; their behaviour was so ingrained and my own inclination to follow too strong. Then I remembered how the blenoids in Ka's compound had behaved. It was only during a confined feeding frenzy that blenoids truly acted like the mad creatures they'd been called. I concluded that while blenoids were vicious predators of other species, they only turned that viciousness on one another when placed in unnatural circumstances such as captivity.

They were, in actual fact, an intelligent animal with a social order, oddly based on altruism. It was the exact opposite of what everyone thought a blenoid was. Reputations are often spread from a single truth wrongly interpreted and grandized to larger-than-life proportions. I should know. Mine was steeped in myth, based on a few deeds that had been wrongly interpreted.

Virtually all first hand knowledge of blenoid behaviour had come from observing them in captivity. I knew of no one who'd survived the harsh desert of Upsilon 3 to share stories of blenoid behaviour in the wilds. Mine was a unique perspective that no one else could possibly have experienced. I both rejoiced in it and felt a kind of sadness for the blenoid who had been so maligned and misunderstood.

I thought of another creature, the now extinct Vampire bat on Earth, that had suffered an equally tarnished reputation due to its rather grizzly manner of feeding. The Vampire bat spent the day in hollow trees and at night searched for large animals whose blood it sipped from small cuts it surreptitiously made on the victim's skin. The Vampire bat's chances of attaining a meal were slim but when one did, it usually drank more than it needed and donated its surplus to another by regurgitation. A bat that had previously donated would receive blood and one that refused to share was refused blood in turn. Reciprocity. Mutual cooperation for the good of the community. That was exactly what I'd experienced with the blenoids moments ago.

As I stood in the freezing cold hardpan beneath a velvet sky, I thought of how easily and thoughtlessly I'd dispensed my judgement based on someone's reputation. I thought of the blenoid and vowed that that would never happen again. Of course, I had yet to survive Upsilon 3's desert myself, I thought as I glanced down at my bounty.

I let my gaze stray to the distant dunes rising to the north, where A'ler and I were bound tomorrow. And as I listened to the complex sounds of the night, I realized how mistaken I had been about so many things. My youthful hubris had blinded me to the simplest of things in life. I'd been more interested in dispensing justice than in justice itself. I thought of what Ka had said to me just days ago, and desperately wanted to believe him. If it was true—that I was born for love, not for killing—then I'd strayed so far from my path. I'd followed the wrong precept. I'd lived a lie. All life was precious, even the ferocious blenoid. Even my sworn enemy, I thought with a glance back to where A'ler fitfully slept. Sekmet had taught me something of that, I conceded with a wry smile. To think, that dreadful place had given me something. Was it too late for me? I didn't know a blenoid could cry—but I felt wet tears spill out of my eyes as I let out a howl and heard my plaintive wail answered in the distance by my hunting pack of blenoids.

I returned to A'ler, curled up and shivering, and laid my stash of cobals beside her then lay down and curled up next to her. She turned in her sleep and clung to me for warmth. In truth, I was not cold; I felt invigorated and content, warm with the tasty cobal juices that spread through me and my hunger and thirst allayed for the time being. I lay there for quite a while, hugged by a woman who hated me, and restless in my musings. I listened to the distant eerie fog-horn moan of the shifting dunes and thought of home and my early childhood. I thought of my mother, blissfully content with her new baby, my little brother. I thought of Serge and his new-found happiness with the love of his life. And, although my chest ached with sadness, I felt a bracing warmth at the knowledge that I'd made that reunion possible. Perhaps God...*my* God, was a just and merciful god.

Φ

The following morning I showed A'ler the cobals and urged her to eat. It was our fourth day and she hadn't eaten since the sandworm had attacked two days ago. She ate after shifting to a blenoid, though reluctantly, despite being a blenoid with blenoid tastes. It was good to see some vigor return to her and we made better progress that day. I remembered the hunt of the previous night and, while I made no mention of joining the pack to A'ler, I knew I would try to find them again.

Then I said a little prayer to myself; we'd reached the *West Ghouroud*. The desert became a frozen sea, red clouds of sand rising off huge cresting waves that boomed and creaked like an old boat pitching at sea. The wind whistled like a chorus of laughing witches, hurling red grit into our faces. Our pace slowed to a crawl as our wading steps in the hot yielding sand turned to stumbles and falls.

The following days remained uneventful though burning hot and tortuous, particularly for A'ler. We climbed the dunes at an excruciatingly slow pace, flinching each time the polished sands wailed out their shifting songs. Each dune stuttered its unique groan of moving sand, silt and clay, and together they formed an ominous cacophony of staccato pops, stuttering burbles like the propeller of an ancient Earth air-craft, low booms and machine-gun trebbles.

If I wasn't so concerned for A'ler's unsteady progress, I would have been fascinated by this alien desert's dissonant chorus. But A'ler was struggling hard, panting and stumbling and falling. Not that I wasn't; only she seemed to be endlessly struggling. I watched her spirit steadily wane. Several times, she almost slid down as we ascended the slip-face before peaking the crest and each time I nearly fell with her as I caught her fall. It was no better sliding down the gently sloping windward arm on the other side. My initial fascination with the dunes dissolved quickly to despair as I started to wonder if the two of us would make the crossing. I'd long since made the commitment to stick with A'ler until the end—half convinced that she would perish before we reached our destination; but I began to think that I, along with her, wasn't going to make it out. There seemed hundreds of these barkhans from the air and we'd only crossed two.

And, out of my dizzy mind came a useless tidbit of trivia Benny must have fed me once: while he crossed Mongolia's Gobi Desert on Earth, Marco Polo wrote in 1295 of *evil desert spirits*, which "at times fill the air with the sounds of all kinds of musical instruments, and also of drums and the clash of arms." I knew why he called them evil as we waded, struggling and panting, through a thick resisting sea of sand that wailed and boomed its objection to our every step and sucked every ounce of energy from us, leaving only despair.

By the third barkhan, I was carrying A'ler on my back.

Φ

Despite the scarcity of vegetation in this part of the desert, I always managed to find shelter at the end of the day and A'ler bedded down exhausted and ill.

Each night I found the pack and hunted and shared with them. Eventually I learned to eat what I caught and disgorge in front of the pack for sharing. I always kept some uneaten cobals for A'ler. One night I helped the pack bring down a sandworm and we gorged on its watery mass, abating our thirst. I brought a huge portion back for A'ler, who was very grateful, preferring this to the tough dry cobals.

It was uncanny how I managed to find the pack exactly where I expected to find them. I finally deduced that the blenoids followed some invisible grid in their not so random migrations along the desert planet. As incomprehensible as it seemed, the blenoids had some kind of radar tracking system linked up with the planet's magnetic fields or something that gave their migration purpose, and I was tapping into it each time I found my adopted blenoid pack.

I discovered the method to this madness on our seventh day when A'ler apparently drifted into delirium on one of the flats between barkhans and started to lurch, jerk and convulse. Just as I was about to pounce on her to suppress her, I saw them too: phantom trees with long spindly branches and huge succulent tube-like leaves. Her apparent convulsions were only the actions of one who thought she was bumping into something that wasn't there. More mirages, I'd thought.

But in an instant, the blenoid in me understood. This marked where the groundwater sprang close to the surface. It was good water, free of the killer-plankton. Unlike the dangerous sinkhole abodes of the watery sandworms. I dug furiously with my great paws, realizing with astonishment and awe that blenoids were capable of tapping into the planet's underground stream system. I was rewarded by an upwelling of dirty water. I barked at A'ler and she limped over and greedily drank. She left nothing for me. I didn't begrudge her; she needed it more than I did. I seemed able to survive on the liquids I ingested with the meat I ate.

THIRTY

Each night I hunted with the blenoid pack nearby and returned with several cobals or a chunk of sandworm meat then fell into a contented deep sleep. Each morning we awoke, changed back to our human form, feeling the dull ache of our muscles from lying on the hard unforgiving ground, uncomfortable heat on our sunburnt skin, lips blistered and peeling with lack of moisture, and hair tangled with dust and cozu needles into hard mats of rusty wool. And each morning A'ler asked me the same question with an incredulous shake of her head: "Why?" To which I couldn't answer. I wasn't sure what she was asking anymore: why did I keep helping her—why didn't I just abandon her? Or why were we continuing and not giving up?

The morning of the eighth day, A'ler couldn't muster enough energy to transform and I awoke in my human form, embracing a blenoid. A part of me felt unalloyed relief that my body still remembered my human legacy. Because, in truth, I felt my humanity slipping away from me as I relied more and more on my blenoid abilities to survive. Sometimes they just took over, like the next day, when as A'ler's energy abated, so did her ability to eat. When she refused to eat, without a second thought I regurgitated my previous supper and forced some of it down her throat like a baby chick. She choked it down but didn't refuse it.

My moonlighting and bearing A'ler's weight when crossing the barkhans began to take its toll by the tenth day. We'd miraculously made it out of the *ghouroud* and had entered a well-vegetated flatland dotted with many cozu bushes. Despite the easier walk, I found myself panting heavily. I was utterly exhausted with lack of sleep, and felt the heat of Upsilon Andromedae baking on me until I imagined my back sizzling with its fire. I stumbled and almost fell before I realized it and stopped to turn and check on A'ler's progress. She doggedly followed, though I found that my pace—which I'd kept as slow as possible—became increasingly harder for her to match. I stretched my back and felt an excruciating pain, a pain I rightly shouldn't be feeling by now, I thought. It was partly A'ler's doing. When we lay together for the night, she always managed in her anxious sleep to claw open the wounds that had partially healed over during the day, setting them to bleed afresh. Each morning I'd felt my back blaze with pain as warm blood flowed down and congealed between my buttock cheeks. I wasn't healing like a Scandi and surmised that the extreme weather, dehydration, starvation and my blenoid form all conspired along with A'ler's clawing me in her fretful sleep to keep my wound alive.

But it was nothing to the infection that raged on her leg, I thought with growing despair. Her hide, usually tough and russet coloured, had grown black with subcutaneous blood and the punctures themselves, now raised angry welts, continued to weep puss. She had no hope of keeping the leg now. And I began to fear that it wouldn't be enough.

I slowed my pace and when she caught up to me, I shifted with difficulty to my human form, feeling the bite of the hot sand on my naked feet, and offered with broken sounds—I'd lost my voice to the parched heat—to suck her wounds clean again. As I leaned over her with obvious intent, A'ler batted me away and stumbled away on three legs. I silently cursed her Vos pride, thinking it would be her undoing as I watched her pathetic form skitter away in an awkward hobble, kicking up red dust. It was barely midday and she was already half-delirious with feverish pain and heat exhaustion, no longer following a straight line. With a glance up at the blinding sun blazing down on me, I shifted back into a blenoid after some effort, to my alarmed dismay, and caught up to A'ler.

Φ

On the morning of the eleventh day, A'ler couldn't move. Even after a forced meal from me, she refused to get up with a whimper of objection. I sighed and pointed to her leg, my intention obvious. She didn't object this time and even leaned over on her side to let me gain access to her festering wounds. It told me how far she'd gone that she allowed me to do the painful deed. I'd never heard the anguished cry of a blenoid before and it made me weep to hear it now. Once I'd sucked her wounds clean, I let her rest beneath the meagre shade of the cozu and watched her pant. Still in my human form, I squatted beside her and, leaning my elbows on my knees, ran my hands over my stiff matted hair. We'd been walking the Upsilon 3 desert for ten days. It was actually longer than I thought A'ler would last but we hadn't reached the Gnostic sanctuary yet either. Had I miscalculated? No, we simply hadn't reached it yet. Feeling the enervating power of depression set in, I lay down on the dusty ground beside A'ler's sleeping form and closed my eyes, my exhausted body welcoming the rest.

Φ

I hadn't realized that I'd fallen asleep until I started awake aching, woozy and confused. My head pounded as I slowly realized that a loud commotion had woken me. I recognized the call of my blenoid pack and rose stiffly into a squat, then collapsed on all fours under a wave of nausea. The pack had found something and were urgently calling me. I glanced at A'ler. She was awake and blinking at me with inexpressive blenoid slit eyes. I glanced down at my human form and winced at what I saw: my skin was bright red and raw with the tight pinching pain of severe sunburn. It was only then that I realized that it was already close to twilight; I'd slept through the whole day! I'd exposed my human form to the scorching heat of the desert day. I was lucky to be alive, I thought, and promptly threw up. Heat stroke, I surmised, wondering how I had managed to wake from that death-sleep.

I shifted with effort into a blenoid and fought the urge to

lick up the spittle I'd just vomited. A'ler stood up with me, looking much better. For once, I thought, she looked in better shape than I did. I took in her upright posture, elevated head and the reduced swelling on her leg and smiled inwardly. I noticed she held her leg down and touching the ground for the first time in days.

We emerged from the cozu bush that shaded us. My pack stood not twenty meters from us, waiting patiently, its leader pawing the blushing sand impatiently and shaking her massive head at me, ears erect. I turned to A'ler and signalled with my paws: "can you?" then "food". She forewent the paw signal and simply nodded her head.

We joined the pack and they led us to a small rise that overlooked a wet swale that I guessed was fed from a groundwater spring. A'ler was about to rush down to take a drink when I got in front of her and pointed with a nudge of my head at the leader. She was attentively watching something below in the gully. Then I noticed too. Hundreds of large toad-like creatures sat in the moist mud, bodies pumping up and down like ochre waves. I didn't know their name but the blenoid in me recognized them as a juicy delicacy. I knew what the leader had in mind: she meant to cut off the downstream side of the swale then attack in a circle and gorge ourselves. I shivered with excitement and hunger. But even as we assembled, I felt an unknown dread.

Then we were rushing the 'toads'. As soon as we were all inside the swamp, a circular barrier shot up around us, corralling us inside. My heart plummeted and, despite the still burning heat of the day, I felt a chill down my back; I knew before they emerged, shadows against the harsh setting sun, what I would see.

Men. Meat-traders brandishing sling rifles.

THIRTY-ONE

What followed, I cannot describe; I was too disoriented. Of what I managed to observe amid the wild blenoid sounds and thrashing around me was that the barrier ended up being some kind of huge net and rose beneath us, scooping us into the air as a crane cinched in the outer barrier line, just like a purse seine. The blenoids howled and snarled like the mad creatures of their reputation. Even A'ler howled in terror. Then I realized that I did too, as I thrashed inside the net. I felt a new sensation of panic: the blenoid's abject fear of enclosure.

The crane was attached to a land vehicle with caterpillar wheels on the other side of the swale. To my dismay it took only five minutes to reach the ghost town of Zibar. We'd been so close! I decided that we must have missed the Gnostic Sanctuary and overshot. We would have reached the town tomorrow if not for the trap.

As the shadows of brief twilight crept across the desert expanse, I made out the buildings of the town. Within short order the vehicle jerked to a stop and the crane lowered the net in one of the depressed pits I'd seen from A'ler's ship. The net unceremoniously opened, dropping us from several meters to the dusty red hardpan. I heard A'ler yelp as she landed and thudded hard myself with a jolt of pain.

I scrambled over to A'ler, who'd collapsed on the ground, and pawed my signal as I glanced furtively to the captive blenoids, already behaving differently. *Change into a human* was my signal. Glimpsing the insane glances of the other blenoids toward us, I felt the danger of remaining within captivity. They weren't my pack anymore; the rules of engagement no longer applied in here. A'ler was badly injured and would be the first recipient of the blenoid's ruthless selection process for survival in captivity. We had to get out of here *now*. I pawed the ground with our agreed upon signal: *change into a human.*

A'ler responded with a light but determined scratch of her forepaw on the ground—*No*—and imperceptibly shook her head at me then pointed up to the foreman once with her snout.

I caught it and glanced up to where the men stood, studying their new catch. They were mostly Badowin, but some Azorians, Xhix, Veniks and humans. There was even a Scandi, perhaps serving as their surgeon. I thought I understood. The Enforcer in me put it quickly together. I recognized the insignia on their khacki shirts: Zeas Corporation. It was the name of the outfit that provided A'ler's own space-station, the *Ulysses*, with fresh blenoid meat. T'lem had bragged to me a year ago about it in the *Blitz Blazé*. The foreman would certainly recognize A'ler. And kill her instantly.

The meat traders laughed and jeered in coarse language, pointing out choice blenoids with their sling rifles and shaking their heads at others. Including A'ler. She was undoubtedly considered inferior meat. Fearing they might do away with her as unfit to process, I stood protectively over her lying form and furtively eyed the men above.

"They're so jagging dumb, those blenoids!" a thin sallow human with heavy-lidded eyes just above me drawled. Yeah, I agreed. We certainly were. "That's the third batch that's fallen for our south perimeter trap, Lars. I've a mind to set it again."

"We have our fill now, Vinny," a large older human to his right said. Lars, no doubt. I studied his grizzled weather-lined face and settled my gaze on his cruel eyes and mouth. His left cheek bulged with something he was languidly chewing and he spit some brown liquid over us, just missing A'ler and me. Poi mash. Some people smoked it, like Zec; others chewed it like this man. Its putrid mash blackened your teeth and tongue and gave you the breath of compost and seaweed. He looked in charge and held his sling rifle loosely cradled in his arms like a baby. "I'm sure you can pick your choice meat from this bunch for your discerning boss over at the Enclave, eh, Mneseos?" Lars leaned over the edge of the parapet above us and chuckled at the surly face of a tall Eosian, studying the blenoids below with pursed lips. I stiffened. Although I didn't recognize the face, I knew the name. He was Ka's personal cook and was obviously shopping for fresh meat—Ka liked his blenoid viscera fresh. "Why the Enclave uses Eosian trash I'll never know," Lars muttered, though loud enough for Mneseos to hear.

Only Ka would use Eosians to do *Nihilist* business, I thought. Perhaps Mneseos was a slave. Despite the ruthless vigil of the Guardians, the galaxy remained replete with reprehensible dealings. Slavery was one of them. Mneseos certainly didn't look happy about it. He managed to hang on to his dignity, though, and sniffed haughtily.

Just then a gangly Azorian shouted, "Hey, Boss! It's supper time ain't it?"

Lars laughed loudly and spit again, brown spittle landing on A'ler this time. "I do smell myself a barbeque." Without a second thought, he aimed his sling rifle and shot. The rifle cracked, followed by the whiz of the harpooned sling line. The blenoid yelped then slumped, instantly knocked out by the strong narcotic. I flinched. He'd shot the leader of the pack and I knew what would happen next as the foreman released his sling. The blenoids fell upon their unconscious leader, flaying her alive to shreds. I despaired at the awful twist of irony. They'd taken me in, been my 'mates' and helped me hunt; now I had to watch them turn into crazed lunatics and eat each other in wild rage. The men shouted with excitement, waving their sling rifles in the air.

"Oops," Lars said with a shrug and a churlish laugh. He turned a wicked sidelong glance at the glowering Eosian. Lars didn't care that there was one less blenoid for his meat packing facility. There were dozens more where that one came from. I decided that he'd done it just to goad the Eosian.

After the example of their foreman, the other men took it upon themselves to take pot shots at the blenoids as the Eosian cook looked on in disgust. The sling rifles discharged, cracking the air like whips, followed by their singing lines. As each blenoid tumbled under the deep penetrating harpoon hook, the men reeled them up as the remaining blenoids charged and dragged down their unconscious mates. It was a cruel game of cat and mouse and the sling rifle was luridly suited to it. A primitive weapon, the sling's sharp harpooned projectile seldom killed. Killing wasn't its objective; maiming, injuring and demobilizing was the intent. The sling was popular with hunters and gamers looking to satisfy their brutal sport of tormenting lesser beings. And torment they did. I watched in sick disgust as the men screamed with malicious amusement and reeled in the harpooned blenoids like fish in a writhing sea. They howled with laughter as the rest of the blenoids danced wildly to drag the slung beasts down. It was such cruel irony, I thought.

I urged A'ler toward the far corner, out of the way then braved my way through the mob, hoping no stray shot found me. I snarled my way in and ripped away a portion of a dead blenoid then returned to A'ler and dropped the meat in front of her. A'ler hadn't eaten since our early morning feed. She only hesitated a moment. Satisfied that she was eating, I stood protectively in front her and felt her shivering behind me as she chewed amid the gunshots. I knew she was terrified; I was. But I recognized that her fear, particularly her fear of death, was a torment that ruled her life. It was the reason for her resentment, why she both hated me and appreciated me; I'd put her here but I'd also kept her alive. For *this*, I thought in despair, watching the slaughter. I glanced over my shoulder at A'ler and noticed that her leg had ballooned out again and glistened with puss.

"Enough!" Lars shouted. "No more shooting! We have enough." They'd managed to pull up five blenoids for their barbeque.

"You've killed the choice ones," Mneseos complained in a simpering voice.

"There's still that one!" the heavy-lidded trapper drawled sarcastically, pointing to us and cackled, pleased with himself. I bristled and straightened in front of A'ler.

A tall human on the foreman's left, who'd been silent until then, whispered into Lars's ear. My kindness to A'ler had not gone unnoticed; I just made out his words: "That scarred one helped the one with the injured leg, bringing it food." My back injury didn't look too bad in my blenoid form. It was only in my human form where the contrast against human flesh—usually accompanied by freshly shed blood—brought out the severity of the wound. "Now it's protecting the other. They must be mates."

"No," Lars reflected in an equally low voice, then spit with a contemplative frown. "They're both females. Sisters, maybe." He stroked his stubbled chin with sausage-thick fingers and grinned suddenly, bearing filthy poi-stained teeth. "Jake, put them aside for Father Uriel. He'll want to see them."

"For his experiments, eh?" Jake chuckled. I didn't like the sound of that. "He pays us good for 'em, don't he?"

Lars growled out a malicious laugh.

Jake turned out to be second in command and ordered the men to retrieve us. I would have bolted but I knew A'ler had no energy left to move. In fact I doubted that she was totally conscious anymore. Within moments the men had dropped a weighted net over us that swiftly cinched in and scooped us up effortlessly into the biting mesh. A'ler yelped as the net jerked us into the air. It dangled us from a deployed crane that swung toward another sunken pen then unceremoniously dropped us. A'ler cried out again when she landed. I helped her to a corner where she collapsed, panting with her tongue hanging loose outside her mouth. I ignored the men as they watched us. They pointed, laughed then spoke in low tones. At least there were no rabid blenoids to fight off, I thought thankfully, still hearing their insane cries in the other pens.

The men eventually left us for their barbeque and the pens grew quiet and dark as night quickly set in. Even the other blenoids stopped their snarling barks, howls and growls and grew quiet, despite their nocturnal nature. A'ler shivered in the corner and I joined her, curling up beside her in the growing cold. I glanced up at the clear starry night. We'd come so close only to find that we'd wandered right into the enemy's nest. Who was Father Uriel? Some old man who liked to torment blenoids? I studied the wall and gauged for escape. Too smooth and high even for a human to scale, I thought. And even if I could, I couldn't leave A'ler behind after the long journey we'd been through. I sighed, glancing at her. There was no escape tonight.

We'd taken to sleeping in a close huddle, one embracing the other for warmth, and we fell instinctively into it again.

Wrapped in A'ler's giant animal paws, I closed my eyes and as I felt the drowsy languor of exhaustion embrace me with A'ler's warmth, I knew there was something I needed to remember but I could not summon it and the thought of it evaporated like my own consciousness.

I slept deeply and it was only as I bolted awake in the sweltering heat to a loud commotion and snapped my eyes open with a flinch that I remembered: it was morning and I'd transformed back to my human form. A swift glance down at the huge paw folded over me confirmed that A'ler hadn't.

The men had already spotted us. It was their excited shouts—*a naked woman down there*!—that had awoken me. It was too late to shift back, I thought, feeling cornered.

"One of the blenoid's escaped and there's a...a naked woman down there—trapped by the other blenoid!" a Badowin stuttered in excited agitation. He kept repeating himself to the others who had gathered around and could see for themselves. I scrambled to my feet, my movement waking A'ler. Our deception was over and I sensed the danger I'd put her in. I turned urgently to her and my mouth moved, but no sound came out: *Change, A'ler! Change NOW!*

She didn't shift to her human form, although she raised her head to face me with slit blenoid eyes. What was she thinking? I stared back. I don't know what I saw in her eyes; blenoid eyes are impossible to interpret. Was it desperate fear? Or resignation? I'll never know what she was thinking those last moments. Turning to face A'ler had been a mistake. The men instantly saw the fresh gashes on my back.

"Chaos!" "Look!" "The jagging blenoid's got her!"

They'd seen the signature-blenoid claw marks—true to her fretful sleeping habits and sharp blenoid claws, A'ler had reopened my wounds and I felt warm blood, as if from a new injury, flow down my back.

"Shoot the blenoid!" the foreman commanded brusquely.

NO! I would never know whether she decided not to change out of fear of *Nihilist* reprisal or that she simply couldn't change, the last of her energy gone. It had been three days since she'd changed into human form. I whirled round to face the men and raised my hands to them. Staring at the foreman's lacklustre eyes with my own pleading stare, I tried to countermand his order in a shout: *Don't shoot her!* But nothing came out of my raw throat. I'd long ago lost my voice to the parched winds of Upsilon 3. I waved my arms at them to stop as they raised their rifles.

I dove in front of A'ler's shivering form. She jerked aside. Why did she move? I couldn't fathom it. But it gave them a clear shot; and they took it. They peppered her with a roaring salvo of sling gunshots, a dozen lines singing out and as many deep thuds as the hooked harpoons sunk into her hide. A'ler shuddered, the force of the shots gripping her in a macabre puppet dance. In the deafening silence that followed the cessation of gunshots, she fell and lay still, slack sling lines radiating from her to the circle of rifles around us. All that, I thought, for one small, injured blenoid—not a blenoid at all, I conceded, gasping out the sobbing breath I'd been holding.

I scrambled to her and fell to my knees and wept, laying my hands, almost as rough as her blenoid hide, on her face. I wept hard but soundlessly, wracking sobs tearing through my parched throat. She was dead; two many harpoons had penetrated her frail form. I'd taken her this far then failed in the last minutes. I cried for A'ler, who I'd forced into this situation against her will, though she'd so willingly accepted that I was the harbinger of what she most feared in the world, her own death. I cried for Serge, who I knew dearly loved his sister despite their differences and what she'd done to him. I cried at last for me, for the awful things I'd done to his whole family, and ultimately to him. I laid my cheek on A'ler's rough hide. God...*my* God was a mean and sadistic god.

A'ler's scrawny body seeped blood. Not for meat this one, I thought. They'd deemed her too scrawny anyway. Blood, so dark it was almost black, pooled below her. I marvelled at how much there was....Shining like an oil slick, it reached my knees and for some reason I balked....Then I was gasping for air, shallow breaths caught in my throat like knives....

A'ler's dead body swam in front of me, then I saw the brilliant azure sky arc down to meet me, sun blazing into my eyes like a torch, and I realized I was falling backward. It was all over; I knew my body was making its own decision to shut down and thankfully succumbed. Everything turned garishly pixelated like a Seurat watercolour. As the colour washed away into shades of grey, I felt my arm tugged and heard churlish laughter then one of the men speaking in a low voice close to me: "Chaos! The bitch stinks!" Then darkness thankfully took me.

Φ

I heard myself sigh awake. I was lying face down on something soft, a bed, and felt the welcome softness of a pillow beneath my cheek. My tongue felt thick and woolly inside my parched mouth and tasted of the desert.

"Ah, she's waking….Leave us alone now," I heard a soft tenor voice, both humble and stern, spoken in accented English. I couldn't quite place it but decided he was probably a human from Earth, not a colony. I inhaled sandalwood incense and wine as footsteps shuffled out and a door closed. Someone had remained. The incense and wine still breathed over me like a bracing breeze, undercutting the sour smell of old sweat, cabbage, and sewage: I was smelling myself and the remnants of living with and as a blenoid for close to two weeks. To my dismay I stank and thought that I must look frightful. That was a good thing though, I decided, or one of the men was sure to recognize me. The Guardians had no doubt circulated my image to every drinking hole frequented by bounty-hunters and ruffians alike.

I realized that for the first time in many days my back didn't blaze with pain. I surmised that I'd been injected with some kind of painkiller.

I forced my heavy eyelids to open, squinting across the bed, and a form in a brown robe sitting on a stool next to the bed swam into focus—the owner of the voice. I looked up and saw a face peering down at me.

A candle flickering on the bed nightstand provided the only light in the room and threw his face into sharp relief. I noticed that it was dark outside through the window behind him. Had I been unconscious that long? The man was clean-shaven with lank brown hair cut rather short in no particular style. His face was equally unremarkable except perhaps for clear intelligent eyes the scintillating colour of Upsilon 3's brilliant sky. His kind mouth was upturned in a smile. But his cool eyes gave away nothing.

Suddenly aware of my bared back, I pulled the sheet over me then turned on my side to face him with my breasts covered. To my dismay I was still naked and as filthy as when I'd first been captured. My touch alone had soiled the covers. I glanced down at my rough chapped hands, noting ochre-coloured dirt ground into my pores and caked beneath my fingernails. They hadn't bothered to do anything to me, except perhaps spray an aerosol band-aid on my back and given me that painkiller, of course.

"I'm Father Uriel," the man with the brilliant-blue eyes said to me. "I'm glad to see you're looking much better." This was the Father Uriel they'd spoken of, I thought, and grew attentive with suspicion. "Imagine, I came to retrieve two uncommon blenoids and I find a dead blenoid and a girl instead! I'm afraid you've frightened them a little, I think, with your sudden appearance," he went on, his smile opening to a grin of amusement. "They didn't want to touch you." That was good, I decided. I counted it as a plus with this crowd. The last thing I wanted to be was alluring. "I apologize for their lack of attendance as a result." He meant my stink and general state of filth. "And I offer the hospitality of Zarzosa, our Gnostic Sanctuary."

Of course; the Gnostic Sanctuary! My mind wasn't thinking too clearly. I should have figured that out right away from his Gnostic robes and *glitter*-pigmented eyes. Nevertheless, I thought him rather young to be one of the Fathers of the Order. I placed him fifteen years my senior—I was only twenty-four— he'd only be forty years old. That was very young for a full-fledged Gnostic priest, I thought, willing the image of Ka to my mind. Then I reminded myself that Martinez, the founder of the Hermetic Order, was even younger, about my age.

I was just starting to relax when Father Uriel continued as if delivering a condition to his kind offer, "That blenoid..." He trailed. My face must have told him something because he fell silent and watched me with curiosity for several moments before speaking again. "What were you doing in the pen with that blenoid? And what happened to your clothes?"

I opened my mouth then closed it, feeling the blood rise to my face in a hot blush. It was obvious to anyone that I hadn't worn any clothes for some time. I'd earned the grime and sunburn over days of exposure. I looked—and smelled—like a wild animal. That wasn't far from the truth either. I touched my throat and shook my head with a weak smile. For once I was glad of my genuine inability to speak. For distraction, I pointed to a glass of water on the small table beside my bed and Father Uriel passed it to me. When he saw that I could barely hold it, he offered to place it up to my blistered puffy lips and I awkwardly drank. Once I tasted the cool water, I seized his hand with mine and gulped like an addict.

He wrenched the glass quickly away from my mouth and trembling hands, scolding, "Ah! Ah! No." He put the glass back on the table. "You shouldn't have too much all at once," he explained. "You'll get sick. You have a touch of heat stroke." Then, he tilted his head and regarded me thoughtfully. "That blenoid hurt you badly but I'm told that you wept when they killed it. The workers passed it off as exhaustion, hysterical relief. I'm not so sure it wasn't genuine grief."

I swallowed and stared back at his inquisitive eyes, gazing into mine with a clarity of purpose that made me uncomfortable. What was his purpose in quizzing me? And why wasn't the foreman here? His offer to take me to his sanctuary suddenly appeared ominous.

Father Uriel's piercing blue gaze abated under a solicitous veil and he smiled again, though not with his eyes. "You have questions too, no doubt. Let me begin with me." He let me sip a little of the water again then sat back and clasped his hands on his lap. "Although I am a Gnostic priest with the Hermetic Order, I also dabble in animal behaviour and ecology. I got my Bachelor of Science degree at McGill University back in 190 SGT, when you were probably just a twinkle in your mother's eyes. Ever since *Mon Seigneur* sent me here to run the Sanctuary three years ago I've been studying blenoids, documenting their behaviour, their society and such. I'm most curious about how their social behaviour integrates with their physiology in their adaptations to this harsh ecosystem." He placed his hands on his knees to lean forward with some excitement. "For instance, their adaptations to the lack of water. Did you know that blenoids don't sweat to prevent desiccation? They get most of the moisture they need through their food and keep most of it in by excreting a concentrated waste."

I *did* know all those things; I'd done them all. Father Uriel's eyes glittered like a boy with candy and I suddenly thought of Serge. He went on with what appeared to be one of his favourite topics, "They're not solitary animals, though. We know that they hunt in packs. That suggests a social structure and we believe it's integral to their ability to survive the harsh desert." Wouldn't he be surprised to know that one of their social behaviours—of sharing bloody disgorged food—ensured the integrity of the pack, the individual, and its gene pool? "For instance," he continued, "they apparently sleep in huddles in dug-out holes to conserve heat during the freezing nights."

I almost smiled at that. A'ler and I had naturally fallen into that behaviour.

"Still, the blenoids are incredible thermo-regulators," he continued eagerly. "I've been doing some physiological experiments on them...." That made me stiffen but I kept my face calm and managed to ponder that only a few weeks ago I wouldn't have flinched at his discloser. "...I discovered that Blenoids produce copious amounts of Heat Shock Protein. It suggests why they're crespucular, not just nocturnal, and able to withstand temperatures of up to 55°C."

That explained A'ler's and my ability to withstand the

midday heat. I smiled at him wearily, indulgently, and began to wonder with a growing tension in my neck where his interest in *me* lay.

As if sensing my impatience, he cleared his throat and sat back with an embarrassed smile then continued less animatedly with the topic that would eventually include me, "As you can imagine, I am only one man with few resources for dangerous desert trekking and following blenoids around. So, I struck a deal with the dozen or so meat-trading companies that come through here. Whenever the men encounter an anomaly, like they did with the two blenoids in the pen they found you in, they set them aside and call me. I have a modest facility to keep them and would have bought the two blenoids, alas. But one escaped and *you* appeared, with an injury to your back like the vanished blenoid's." He hiked a brow, taking me by surprise with his remark. Did he suspect that I was a shape-shifter?

He brought his hand up to his face and tapped his mouth, still pursed in deep contemplation. "The men don't know what to make of you," he said with a curious smile. But his eyes told me *he* had some idea. I followed his glance down my exposed shoulder to my sunburnt and peeling arm. I was caked in mud, bruised and scratched. I could only guess at the rest of my appearance...my face, my hair. He unabashedly studied my face like it was a strange artefact and his eyes sparkled like a boy who'd just won a prize. I have no idea what expression I wore although I tried to look unimpressed. Not wishing to give away any more, I decided to close my eyes instead, blocking him out. I hoped my implicit dismissal gave him the right message. After a long moment of silence, he accepted my silent request: "Ah, you're tired," he said, expressing disappointment. "I'll leave you alone and let you get some sleep. We'll speak later..." Then he added pointedly, "with the foreman this time."

I caught the tone, unmistakable. I'd lost my chance with the gentle Father. The next time it would be an interrogation with the not so gentle foreman. As soon as I heard the door shut, my eyes snapped open and I listened. There was some rather gruff discussion at the door then several footsteps—two men I guessed—receded down the hall.

I threw off the covers to rise and sat up with a wince of pain. It was clear that Father Uriel was suspicious of who and what I was. I didn't think the foreman was any less intelligent. They didn't know what to make of me, Father Uriel had said. He was very curious about me. Was I some kind of wild witch who tamed blenoids and lived in the desert? Had I freed one of the blenoids before being caught or was I a shape-shifter with the equally bizarre habit of living among them as one of their own? Either choice made me an oddity and compelled him to fascination. He'd stay fascinated only until he discovered who I really was. Then he'd want me dead and the foreman would only be glad to comply. Unless the foreman recognized me and reported me to Ka like a good mercenary and I'd be right back from where I'd started, in Ka's dungeon. I had to get out of here fast.

I stood up, bracing myself on the wall to steady my weak legs, and took stock of the room. I walked with difficulty on aching feet to what looked like a dresser, hoping to find something to wear. When I reached it, hands grasping the dresser top, I caught a glimpse of myself in the mirror and flinched in shocked dismay. I'd expected weathering but not this. My overly thin, almost emaciated body was sunburnt and blotched with blisters and welts from minor scratches. But my face was the worst. I hardly recognized it as mine. It was red and puffy and my nose misshapen and blistered. My chapped mouth bulged thick, cracked and white with blistering flakes of sloughing skin. I couldn't feel my lips. A wiry mat of red dust, grit and tangled hair sprang in all directions out of my head like something out of a horror movie. I was a terrible sight.

I stared, horrified, at my own gaze and began to shiver uncontrollably. I had to get out of here...I still had a mission...I still...My own image swam before me...I was sliding off the dresser...Damn them! I realized too late that it wasn't just a painkiller they'd injected me with. It must have been *promaxin*, a sleep drug activated by metabolism. The more you tried to do, the faster it hit. I blacked out before I hit the floor. Thankfully.

Φ

When I came to my senses, I knew I was in deeper trouble than before. Before my eyes even opened, I felt the red heat of daylight on my face. I was lying, still naked, on my back with my limbs spread out and lashed to some hard surface. My back pulsed with new pain. I heard and smelled the putrid blenoids beneath me. They snarled and snorted in an angry feeding frenzy. My eyes bolted open and I raised my head. A roar of churlish laughter and cheering followed.

As the scene swam into focus, I saw that I lay on a platform suspended over a blenoid pen. Lars's cold voice resonated through my gut, "Yeah, little girly...you guessed right."

He stood to my left and to my great dismay the entire Zeas Corporation staff had assembled with him around the pen. Alien and human faces alike stared hungrily at me, eyes glinting in malicious anticipation. They would be entertained no matter what happened.

"You've rested enough," Lars drawled. His eyes, sparkling of malice, raked over me. "Now we want some answers, little spy." The platform I was lashed to was suspended from a crane and sat level with the men, some five meters above the pen that contained seven rabid and hungry blenoids snapping below. "Father Uriel wasn't able to get too much out of you but I think these hungry blenoids will grease your tongue, eh?" He laughed again, followed by the rest of the workers. Then his face tightened into a fierce snarl. "I want to know what you were doing in that pen. Who are you? Who sent you?"

I shook my head at him and opened my mouth without speaking, trying to look as helpless as possible. This time my inability to speak was going to be my undoing, I thought with rising panic and swallowed several times, desperately working my mouth and fishing for my voice.

Lars growled, "That trick won't work on me, girly!" He raised his hand and pointed to the large Azorian across from him, who stood next to the crane controls above the men. I knew what to expect. Nevertheless, when my platform jolted and I sank a meter, I involuntarily shrieked. It came out in a broken stutter; but sound enough to vindicate his suspicion.

"Ha! You can talk! Who are you?" he repeated. "What are you doing here in this galaxy-forsaken chaos hole, eh? Did that slimebag, *Lagosh,* send you?" I recognized the name of a rival meat-trading company. "Or are you a Guardian?" That was closer to the mark. I instinctively struggled against my bonds. It brought out some laughter and anticipated glee from the men.

"I want to lick her tits!" I heard someone say.

"You're such a jerk, Calvin! Bite her pussy! Oh, look at it!"

"There won't be anything for you to lick, you idiot!" It was Mneseos. He'd stayed for the show. My heart sank. It wouldn't be long before he recognized me and communicated to Ka. But, then again, that might not matter, I thought, glancing down at the mad blenoids with terror.

"Let's see what they do to her," Lars said. He spit out his poi root mash and sneered at his men. "Old Spencer lasted five dips, eh?"

"Until they bit his face off!" a Badowin shouted gleefully. The men responded with jeering laughter and obscene gestures.

"Those men over there." Lars looked at me and pointed to a group of Badowins laughing and waving at me. "They're betting on which anatomical part you're going to lose first." He chuckled. "Me, I'm a simple man. I've got a bet on you lasting three dips, girly. Now, don't fail me...unless you want to talk, that is..." He waited only a few heartbeats. I bit my lower lip. He nodded with a sour smile then quipped, "No?...Then, let the circus begin!"

The platform jerked again and I barely held back a squeal but heard a moan of terror slip out of me as I dropped to the increased excitement of the blenoids. And the men. I could see the blenoids dance up below me to the goading shouts of the men. The blenoid's teeth-filled mouths dripped saliva and I stiffened with panic but clamped my mouth shut with clenching teeth. Were they members of my pack? It didn't matter; they'd gone insane long ago.

The platform jerked down again and I faced seven massive blenoid heads with wild-eyed terror and a pounding heart. They charged. I panicked and tried to shift into one—I couldn't! The simple effort of it made me black out. The rest of what happened I couldn't tell precisely as I watched through woozy sleep-drugged eyes.

The blenoids never reached me. They yelped and wailed and flew in all directions. Two large Eosians, garbed in jet black had dropped from the crane arm to the pit. They wielded stun sticks in swift fluid motion like acrobats, flinging stunned blenoids away from the platform. The Eosians' choreographed dance reminded me of my Tai Chi form as they knocked every blenoid unconscious.

"Shoot them!" Lars finally found his voice and shrieked in a panic.

One Eosian cut the ropes lashing me to the platform as the other fended off the sling shots with lightening movements of his stun stick. It was like magic and I'm still not sure how much of it I invented in my drugged state. Then the platform was lifting us up quickly and I spotted a third Eosian at the controls—he'd thrown the Azorian into the blenoid pen. Luckily for the Azorian, no blenoids remained conscious to attack him. The crane lifted and swung us to the far side of the complex. One of the Eosians scooped me up into his huge arms. I struggled, thinking they were Ka's men, but the effort claimed what little consciousness remained and darkness engulfed me.

THIRTY-TWO

When I awoke for the third time, this time alert, I kept my eyes closed and took stock of my surroundings, listening, inhaling, feeling....

I surmised that it was still daylight; the sun flooded in, its red wash of light streaming through my closed eyelids—but without the heat. No, it was probably night and I was in a well-lit room. Had I slept a full day again? I was lying on my side, on something soft...a good sign...with my face buried in a softly fragrant pillow. Amid my own rancid stench, I inhaled a lovely complex fragrance of roses commingled with sandalwood incense and wine—Father Uriel! My eyes bolted open.

He sat at my bedside, smiling like a boy. And this time his bright blue eyes smiled too, creasing at his temples into a million laugh lines. I instinctively smiled back at him, a little surprised at my relief to see him—I still wasn't sure where his allegiance lay or what he wanted of me but somehow I trusted him. I took in my surroundings in a fleeting gaze and confirmed that I was lying under a light sheet in a large bed. But I was mistaken about the time of day. In fact, I could not tell; there were no windows. We were in a room whose walls gave off their own bright light. I realized with astonishment that I was inside an ancient structure. Was I in the Gnostic sanctuary?

Nothing adorned the walls and the furniture was simple, a chair, the bed I was in and a dresser, on which sat a vase thick with red roses. I recognized an Earth landscape painting perched on an easel for decoration. The humble setting was in keeping with the ascetic nature of the Hermetic Order, I thought.

"Welcome to Zarzosa. You're in one of our three Ancient Sanctuary buildings," Father Uriel explained, following my gaze. "The walls are sentient, some kind of ancient being whose energy we have not yet managed to understand. The entire building responds to our simple commands and we are truly grateful. The other two ancient buildings serve as our temple and services area."

I nodded, reminded of Ka's enclave. Then, feeling a mild throbbing ache, I pulled out my arm, carefully ensuring that the sheet still covered my breasts, and inspected the track marks on it. Father Uriel looked down with me, bearing a solicitous smile.

"Not *promaxin*," he answered my gaze, raised quizzically at him. "Our surgeon, Brother Alphonse, gave you a drip of nutrients and saline to re-hydrate you and boost your energy. I thought you wouldn't mind."

I nodded my appreciation then tried to speak: "How did...why?" It came out in a raspy whisper but at least it came out this time.

He nodded to show he'd understood and I saw his azure eyes sparkle like an ocean. "They aren't gentlemen at Zeas. They have no concept of how to treat a lady." I had to smile at his words. It had been a long time since I'd been called a lady. And I certainly didn't look like one now. "They were going to hurt you and I couldn't allow that. So, here you are, at the Sanctuary of the Gnostic Hermetic Order..."

"The Eosians..." I trailed. They were *his*?

"*Mon Seigneur's* elite Eosian Guard," Father Uriel explained. "They're called the *Orichalkon*. *Mon Seigneur* lends me three at a time for...moments such as this one." He smiled mischievously. "They see it as penance. It's usually so boring for them; they are men of action, after all. So, you made their day." He grinned at me, quite pleased with himself, then laughed with gleeful pleasure. "It was some daring rescue, wasn't it?"

I nodded and laughed with him. Perhaps he wasn't with Ka, after all, but truly independent. I thought Martinez a clever man to have formed such a guard for his otherwise tenuous Hermetic Order. I couldn't help remembering what had happened to the Schiss Order on Uma 1. If they'd armed themselves with men such as these instead of simply relying on their microbe shields, their order might still be intact. I suspended my conclusions about Father Uriel until I learned more about his motivations in bringing me here. For some reason I could not fathom, I wanted to trust him. He reminded me of Rashomon, providing a delightfully paradoxical mixture of young naivety and sagely wisdom that was both interesting and compelling. But the Enforcer in me couldn't discount the strange curiosity of Father Uriel's Sanctuary being located so close to a *Nihilist* outpost. Then again, his leader, Raphael Martinez, appeared on the *Nihilist* hitlist, which made it all the more strange.

"You're safe here," Father Uriel said gently, patting my

shoulder; he'd sensed my uneasy thoughts. "I've asked Brother François to draw up a bath for you." He pointed to a door slightly ajar on the right. I think you are safe to walk now. The *promaxin* should have worn off, permitting you to move freely. If not, fear not; Brother François will help you back to bed and you can sleep it off some more if need be. François is a gentle lad; he grew up with four sisters." He grinned again. "He is at your service on the other side of the bathroom outer door," he pointed to the bathroom. "You only need to call him. You'll see that we've left you one of Brother Luc's robes, the smallest one we could find, and the smallest pair of sandals." He spread his arms and shrugged. "I'm afraid our Gnostic robes are all that we have here."

I nodded my approval. "That's fine," I said in a cracked whisper.

"When you are done with your ablutions, please have Brother François help put some healing salve on your back wounds." He held up a flat tub in his hand then placed it on the table next to me. "It is only a topical application—a general nano-med—but it will help alleviate pain and prevent infection. Then, please have François escort you to the inner courtyard where you may join me for some refreshment." And some answers, I hoped.

I smiled at the thought of food and realized that I was both very hungry and thirsty. Father Uriel stood up and pointed to the washroom again then left. Eager to wash over a Standard Galactic week's worth of desert off me, I threw off the cover and swung my dirty legs over the bed onto the cool tile floor. So far so good, I thought, as I rose stiffly to my feet without any accompanying light-headedness. Father Uriel was right. The *promaxin* had worn off. And the nutrient/saline mixture had invigorated me.

Φ

As Father Uriel had said, the bath had been drawn and awaited me. I stepped into the tub of steaming sudsy water and shuddered with pleasure and pain. When I sat down in the waist high water, it quickly turned into a murky brown-red slurry and soon after lost its suds. I didn't care and slouched, drawing my knees up, to submerge the rest of me including my head and hair. Muddy water or no, it was gloriously wet and refreshing. And perhaps the most wonderful bath that I could remember experiencing. My whole body seemed to sigh and stretch like a parched plant drawing in life-giving moisture. The gashes on my back stung but I ignored the pain and began the arduous task of rubbing out the ground-in dirt from my skin and pores. I found it between my toes and in my nose and ears and in places dirt was never meant to go. I vigorously rubbed dead sloughed skin from my hands and feet for what seemed an eternity.

When the water looked more filthy than I had been, I let it drain, leaving an incredible ring of brown, and rose to shower off. The clean water spattering over my face, hair and body was bracing as I vigorously soaped and shampooed then rinsed. I must have stood for some time as if in a hypnotic trance, enjoying the luxury of water sluicing over my grateful body. Then I remembered where I was and shut off the water. It was their most precious commodity and here I was squandering it away just for my own comfort and appearance.

Once out of the bath and dried, I sat down on the toilet and inspected myself in the mirror. My face had lost much of its puffiness and my lips looked almost normal; my Scandi healing had finally taken charge, I thought gratefully. My body was bright pink from sunburn and the hot shower. It still bore numerous welts and was tracked with a busy network of red scratch lines. But my skin felt like skin again, I thought, as I absently ran my hands down my body, over my arms and legs then fingered my toes. They were smooth and soft and felt simply wonderful. I stood up and turned my back to the mirror, pulling aside my wet hair, and looked over my shoulder to inspect my gashes. They looked clean at least but raised into angry weals. I felt their tight sting again.

I gingerly put on the brown linen robe, pulled out my long strands of wet hair caught underneath, and cinched the loose robe with a sash then slipped my feet into a pair of flip-flops. I found a skinny young man in his late teens seated and waiting patiently for me outside the door. Brother François. He sprang to his feet, lustrous brown eyes darting over me like a nervous cobal. They shone with *glitter*. Soft wisps of his first beard barely covered his face in reddish scrub.

I smiled. "Brother François?" He nodded vigorously. I held up the container of salve for him and raised an eyebrow.

"Père told me you would need it on your back," he said with the same accented English Uriel had used. François smiled shyly and actually blushed. I concluded that he hadn't seen a woman in a long time, despite having four sisters, and curbed a smile. His dark brown hair was as thick and as long as mine.

"Yes, thank you," I said in a slightly hoarse voice. I handed him the tub of salve and turned back to the room for him to follow. As I sat on the bed, white sheets smudged with my old dirt, it came to me; Father Uriel's accent was French. French Canadian to be precise, I amended, and recalled Martinez's background with *L'Ordre de l'Arbre Sacré* in Québec. I loosened the robe and, turning my back to the boy, let the robe drop down to reveal my back, and crossed my arms over my breasts to cover them. I heard him inhale sharply then felt his trembling fingers apply the cool gel on my wounds. The tight sting faded in a wash of wet coolness. I involuntarily sighed and closed my eyes, dropping my head down in appreciation. I blanked out and lost track of time. When I came to, he'd finished, and was clearing his throat. When I didn't move, he said in a trembling voice, "Père wishes for you to join him in the patio."

I straightened and pulled up the robe then drew my almost dry hair out from underneath, fanning it out. I had to feel my hair again, delighting in its silkiness as it flowed through my hands; an incredible contrast to the caked mat I'd worn when I first came here. I turned, smiling, to François and thanked him. He grinned awkwardly, *glitter*-pigmented eyes darkening with awkward desire, then cheerfully led me out into the stark self-lit hall. As I followed François down unadorned corridors, I wondered if these Hermetics had some quirk like the Schiss and their skipboats that gave them some reprieve from their simple and rather harsh ascetic life. I then heard, in the distance, a melodic multi-timbral chant; the brothers singing, I concluded. It reminded me of the Khonsus dirge for Rashomon, only less solemn. But the sobering impression remained with me as I followed the young brother down the ancient passageway.

Φ

When I presented myself to Father Uriel in the patio of the inner courtyard, I felt like my old self again, smooth, clean and clear-minded. Brother François ushered me through a door into the enervating heat outside and we entered a small patio within an enclosed courtyard, the same one I'd seen from A'ler's ship when I'd first come here. I searched but couldn't see the vast desert from here; the buildings blocked its view. Not that I missed it, I convinced myself, feeling the remnants of blenoid claustrophobia. The patio, however, was wonderfully shaded by a trellis overgrown with grape vines. A gentle spray of water misted down, giving the breeze a refreshing coolness.

Father Uriel was seated at a table with a large pitcher of water and two glasses. Upon seeing me, he instantly stood up and gazed at me with a genuine smile of pleasure.

"Bonne journée!" he greeted me. I nodded back and noticed his eyes dilate. I concluded with amusement that perhaps the whole Gnostic order on Upsilon 3 hadn't seen a woman in a while.

"You are looking much better," he said, blinking at me with amazement. Thanks to my Scandi healing, my face was quite presentable now, I thought with an inward smile. He waved his hand to a seat across from him at the table. "Will you join me for some refreshment and something to eat?"

"I'd be delighted," I said, sitting down and drawing the chair closer to the table as he took his seat opposite me. In truth I was famished and very thirsty. Father Uriel poured me some water, which I thankfully took and gulped down under his intent gaze. I dropped my own gaze to the table, unable to stifle an embarrassed smile, as Father Uriel instructed François to bring us some food. The boy rushed off, sandals slapping the russet earth hardpan.

"I made him nervous, I think," I began, not sure how to start our conversation. I wanted to ask Father Uriel why he'd gone to so much trouble to rescue me, at the expense of his relationship with Zeas Corporation. And what his affiliations with Ka's Enclave were, if any.

"He hasn't seen a woman since he left Earth three years ago," Father Uriel said, proving my suspicions right. He laughed suddenly with self-conscious amusement. "None of us have!"

I felt my face heat and hid my discomfort by blurting out my question, "Why did you rescue me? It might not have been the smartest thing for you to do."

His nervousness vanished with conviction and this time he answered calmly, "It was not a thing done from the mind, but from the heart." He leaned forward, elbows on the table. "These men are brutal beings who don't know the meaning of the words honour, respect, justice...or beauty," he said. I felt his earnest blue eyes dive into me in unabashed appreciation. "They would have hurt you, probably killed you for no other reason than for their shallow cruel amusement."

I recalled how they'd shot the blenoids and where I was just before the Eosians rescued me. I felt a shudder pass through me. Lars had bet I'd last three dips. It would have been Sekmet all over again. I remained quiet and let him continue.

"These men come here, to this backwater planet, and all they see is a dry wasteland to plunder and use," he continued. "They're senseless. They don't smell the honey blossoms of the gado plant that only lives for two weeks when the heavy rains give enough moisture for them to complete their brief life-cycle. They don't hear the desert symphony during the five minutes of twilight when the birds sing their ode to the coming night. They don't feel the snap of the night air as it curls around every shrub and hidden burrow with a crisp breath, reminding us that we are alive but on a fragile thread..."

I knew I had my answer but wasn't sure what to make of

it. Whatever else Father Uriel was, he was a poet. And he loved the desert, as did I, I realized with surprise. I couldn't explain it. The desert had nearly claimed my life several times. I had endured great hardship and pain; yet its harsh beauty had somehow braced me, purified my soul, and gifted me with an elusive prize: *me*. I'd met myself out there in the blistering heat.

As I studied him, Father Uriel reminded me so much of the gentle Rashomon. He also brought to mind Ka, but without the sophistry. Whereas Ka had dissembled the part of the wise sage artfully, I was convinced that I was finally witnessing the genuine article in Father Uriel. Ka had humbled me with his erudite complexity; Father Uriel warmed my heart with his simple honesty.

"Still," I persisted hoarsely, "Aren't you worried that they'll retaliate? Raid your Sanctuary?" My gaze swept the courtyard and I noticed the phi symbol etched over every door, the same symbol that marked the doorway of Ka's enclave.

"No," he shook his head with a gentle smile and watched me twirl my long hair around my fingers absently. "They have no idea our humble order has such a guard. They'll think one of their rival companies hired those Eosians. Or more likely that they're some new elite Guardian force reclaiming you…"

I dropped my hand with a convulsive swallow. That was all too possible. Did Father Uriel know something of me? I met his gaze and gave it back. I was about to challenge him with another question when two plates of food were brought out by another young brother, a lanky eighteen year old with dark wavy hair and sparkling green eyes. More *glitter*-pigmented eyes. As he laid the plate before me, I shook my hair from my face and smiled at him. His hand trembled and some gee seeds rolled off my plate. The boy blushed fiercely. I wanted to laugh but cleared my throat instead and caught Father Uriel's eye. He *did* laugh and I wondered if they were drawing lots to see who'd get the chance to serve us next.

Father Uriel said brusquely to the youth, "*Voyons, Julien! Remets tes yeux dans ta tête. Tu la gênez.*" Then he grinned at the blushing boy. "*Ce n'est pas toujours que nous avons une belle femme dîne avec nous, eh Frère?*" Father Uriel obviously didn't think I understood French and I decided not to show I did. I turned to my food as he pulled Brother Julien aside and added quietly, "*Amènes le vin de ma collection privée. C'est un occasion, n'est pa?*"

Julien grinned affirmative, flashing big teeth, and left.

We ate in silence for some time. I felt Father Uriel's occasional glances on me as I practically bolted the food. The smell had been enough to drive me wild with hunger but when I bit into a pom, one of my favourite things, I couldn't seem to get enough and glimpsed Father Uriel smiling openly in amusement. He knew better than to interrupt me as I ate, giving me leave to thoroughly enjoy the first civilized meal I'd had in eleven days.

Another of the young brothers brought a bottle of red wine and two long-stemmed glasses. He had the soft face of a girl with long lashes and curly brown hair and grinned at me with dilated *glitter*-deepened sapphire eyes. I took the glass by the stem and set it before him with a smile of invitation and he started to pour. I guessed the wine had come from Martinez's own vinyard in Québec—

I started. The boy had splashed wine on my hand.

"*Ah! Desolé, Madame—eh, mademoiselle!*" he cried.

I laughed, grabbing my serviette and wiping.

"*Qu'est-ce que tu fais*, Stéphane!" Father Uriel rebuked. "*Tu n'a pas vu une belle femme? Maintenant elle pense que tu es un balourd muet.*"

Flustered, Stéphane continued to murmur his apologies, now in broken English, "So, sorry, Miss—Lady—eh..." and wiped the table vigorously with a cloth. I knew it would happen: he knocked my glass over in his furious wiping, spilling the rest of the wine, and cried out, "Ahh!"

I jerked back as the red wine dripped off the table and spattered my bare feet. Father Uriel echoed the boy's exasperated sound and looked more embarrassed than the boy. "*Voyons*, Stéphane!"

I laughed out loud, covering my mouth. Sensing a need to alleviate the tension of the moment, I helped Stéphane wipe the table and said softly, "It's all right, Stéphane." I switched to passable French, "*Aucun mal fait. Ce n'est que le vin de Père Uriel's collection privée.*" I ended with a crooked smile.

Both Brother Stéphane and Father Uriel stared wide-eyed at me.

"My mother used to speak French to me; she was from Québec," I explained as I raised my glass for more wine. The boy hesitated only briefly then carefully poured my glass, keeping his attention on the glass. He then poured Father Uriel some wine and made a swift exit.

I smiled at Father Uriel, blinking at me with startled curiosity, then raised my glass to him in a silent toast.

He responded with a glowing smile. "Here's to the incredible desert," he said and drank.

"And the mysteries we find there," I added with a wry smile and swallowed down a large gulp.

I felt the wine burn pleasantly down my throat like ambrosia's fire. Its smoky-grape flavour warmed me with thoughts of home and I instantly felt its flush heat my face. The wine complemented the exquisite food. In truth, I knew it to be an ordinary meal, fit for the brothers of the humble Gnostic Order. Perhaps I would have deemed anything set before me as exquisite. It didn't matter; to my famished body and palate, the grilled blenoid—I only paused briefly before setting my teeth into the succulent leg—poms, gado salad in a mew seed dressing, marinated gee seeds and freshly baked ragon bread was the best meal I'd had...ever. I ate greedily and felt Brother Uriel's eyes on me. As I wiped the smear of grease from my face, I pondered that it appeared my fate to always entertain a new host with eating manners fit only for an animal.

I asked for a second helping and Father Uriel obliged, waving his hand with a gratified laugh to yet another attending brother; Father Uriel hadn't come close to finishing his first portion. As I waited for my next helping, he finally offered what I'd been searching for: information. Though, it wasn't what I'd expected: "The men from Zeas; they think you're some ex-Guardian Enforcer, the assassin, Rhea Hawke."

My heart slammed but I schooled my features to express calmness.

"The Enclave's cook foolishly suggested that you'd travelled on foot all the way north from the far Enclave, where you'd tried to dispatch some diplomat." Father Uriel laughed with genuine amusement. I tried to smile; it might have come out a grimace. "Imagine such a tale!" Father Uriel went on. "Two hundred and fifty kilometres. Blenoids aside, there are the flash floods and the sandworms that hide in the sabkhas and then there's the oppressively hot *ghouroud* field. In that intolerable heat and lack of food and water, you'd have perished in three days. What a ridiculous tale." But he'd stopped chuckling and now leaned back, observing me quietly.

I shifted in my chair and dropped my gaze as I grabbed my wine glass, running my still dirt-ingrained finger along the stem. It would take several baths to finally remove the last traces of dirt from my body, I decided. I felt the cool smoothness of the glass like a sanctuary.

"Besides, I know who you really are..." Father Uriel added. I jerked my gaze up and gave his self-pleased smirking face a quizzical look out of my calm mask. Just then another brother discreetly appeared and poured us some more wine. He'd seen me grab my almost empty glass. "*Merci*, Thibault." Father Uriel nodded, then flashed his azure eyes back at me. "You're Diane Zeligman, the legendary animal behaviourist, aren't you?"

I could have burst out laughing in relief but I curbed the impulse with difficulty. As it was, my face betrayed surprise, if not relief.

Father Uriel misunderstood and laughed giddily at my reaction, eyes sparkling like a boy's. For an instant he reminded me of Serge and I felt my heart warm greatly to him. "I knew it," he continued, almost breathless. "I'm right, aren't I? But I didn't know that you'd embarked on field studies." He added with unabashed glee. "It's so dangerous. I read your latest article in the *Galactic Journal of Animal Physiology*." I recalled Ka mentioning her in relation to some lab studies she'd conducted on blenoids. Something to do with their complementary excretory systems. "Fascinating stuff, blenoid physiology linked to behaviour, isn't it? I have my own theories about their pack behaviour."

I dropped my gaze to the empty table and smiled demurely, muttering something, I'm not sure. Then I decided to take advantage of the topic he'd opened and met his gaze with determination, "I really need to return to my research, Father Uriel."

"Of course, Doctor." He nodded. "In fact, a ray class corvette landed on our platform while you were bathing. The ship's AI insists that the occupant it's slaved to is here. Would that be you? The ship refused to give a name." Smart Benny, I thought and couldn't hide my unalloyed joy. Benny had obviously disobeyed my orders to return to Iota Hor and had instead followed A'ler's ship here. I found Father Uriel grinning back at me, genuinely glad at my happiness. "I take it the ship is yours," he said.

"It is," I said. "And I must go." A wave of reality hit me at the thought of seeing Benny. I felt as if I'd been suspended too long in a dream and a compelling urgency to leave surged through me. I pushed back from the table and added, "I don't know how to thank you for your hospitality and all that you've done for me…"

Father Uriel's eyes flashed. "Perhaps I do," he said, raising a hand to me. "I wish you would at least tell me what you were doing with those blenoids…"

I recognized the yearnings of a curious scientist for knowledge, the burning questions in his eyes, and decided to give him what only I could give him. "I can't tell you what I was doing with the blenoids in the town, but I have made some astonishing observations about them, which I think only a man with your strength of character and scientific background could appreciate and believe." I saw his eyes light up with excitement. "But I'll need a script-writer. Do you have one?"

"I do." He surged to his feet.

"And once I do, I'm free to go?"

"Of course, Doctor Zeligman." He said emphatically, looking mildly affronted that I would need to ask him.

"Call me Diane," I said, smiling.

As my second helping arrived by yet another brother, Father Uriel excused himself and left hurriedly then swiftly returned with a palm-com. Thanking him, I set to recording my observations and he left me to my privacy and my food. I wrote of the blenoid pack I'd spent an intense week with, noting every detail of how they interacted, how they'd formed an altruistic social community of shared resources, mutual assistance, and loyalty only possible in more intelligent animals. By the end I was wiping my eyes as my vision blurred with tears. They'd taught me how to keep A'ler and me alive in their harsh environment. I'd failed to help them in mine. After a sigh, I closed by insisting that Father Uriel publish these observations but on the condition that he put me in as co-author.

I then rose to leave and, as if he'd been eavesdropping, Father Uriel suddenly entered the courtyard. He escorted me through the Sanctuary out the front door into the blistering heat where Benny was parked on the dusty landing platform, gleaming in the intense sunlight. Endless waves of red desert rippled in the heat behind. My heart leapt with joy. I couldn't have been more happy that Benny had disobeyed my order. Upsilon Andromedae blazed down on my head like an intense heat lamp and I felt my brow sweating already. I turned, squinting in the harsh sunlight, to Father Uriel and beamed. "Please thank your Eosian guard for me. I think I owe them my life." I gave him my open smile. *"Bon chance avec votre research,"* I said.

"Merci." He smiled, a little sadly, and extended his hand. I clasped his sweaty hand in a firm grasp and shook it as was still the Earth custom. I liked him and was a little sad to go; I would have enjoyed spending more time with Father Uriel, trading stories and sharing our mutual love for this strange and beautiful planet. As I reached Benny's hatchway and waved goodbye to Father Uriel and the brothers who had gathered around, I managed the smug thought that I'd contributed some

313

truly explosive and controversial material to the legendary Diane Zeligman's repertoire—whether she liked it or not. I hoped she would. The blenoids deserved better.

Then the hatch door closed and I strode toward the cockpit.

"Nice outfit," Benny quipped. "Especially the funky sandals."

"They're called flip-flops," I quipped back, steering myself mid-ship to change my clothes. "What took you so long?"

"Your signature kept disappearing," Benny defended. "Until it stabilized just a while ago."

I nodded, throwing off Brother Luc's robe and rummaging for my old flight clothes. "Let's hightail it out of here before Ka's cook brings reinforcements."

"I better see to your wounds right away," Benny said as I bent to pull on a pair of black briefs. "You've received some interesting injuries, Rhea."

"So what's new?" I grumbled and strode aft to the infirmary. I obediently lay face down on the infirmary table and waited for Benny's probes as Huey and Dewey hovered over me.

"Good gracious!" Benny expostulated. "Look at your feet!"

I closed my eyes and said nothing. I knew what they looked like; the soles and heels of my feet bore calluses and cracks of a week's worth of walking in scorched sand. *Wait until he sees my hands,* I thought. Then I had to grab the sides of the table to steady me as Benny lurched in take off. I fought the urge to get up and gaze out the window at the desert receding from us. I'd seen enough, I decided. I felt relief that we were on our way; yet I stirred with mixed emotions. I was startled to find that some of them were sad.

"Who ever tended you did a good job," Benny said after a moment of silent probing. Benny applied his own superior mixture of nano-medicine to my sunburnt skin and gashes. I then felt a light sting as Huey fed something into a major vein of my arm.

"Yeah," I said softly, closing my eyes to the drowsy

warmth that spread through me, and felt the hot sting of tears at my botched mission. "They did."

For all I'd accomplished, I'd endured and caused needless suffering. A'ler was dead and I'd failed to stop the *Ancient One*. My chance to avert a galactic war had eluded me. Then again, I'd learned that two facilities were churning out MEC death vessels. The information itself was disconcerting; but in having it I was better off than without. If only I could do something about it...My mind was sliding into oblivion...*Oh, Benny*...Benny took such good care of me...*you've given me something to sleep*...then gladly succumbed. Half asleep, I slurred out, "Thanks, Benny, for coming back for me..." I'd half expected to hear him respond with *it's what friends do*, but the gentle void of sleep took me first.

THIRTY-THREE

"Rhea," Benny ventured, "This is interesting. Raphael Martinez, the human Gnostic leader of the Hermetic Order of Québec—the next person on the hitlist—has at his disposal a substantial force of elite Eosian guards."

"Mmm, the prophet," I said, mouth full with a juicy jelimum pastry. "I know he does." I gazed into the black void of space ahead of me, slouched in my pilot's chair. I pulled up the baggy sleeves of Serge's sweater and ran my hand through my hair. Then, propping my head on my hand, I pursed my lips in thought. "What's their story? Who are they?" I was very impressed with the three Eosian guards who had rescued me in Zibar.

"Geez, you're eating a lot, Rhea," Benny forwarded.

"I know," I grumbled, snatching a Bobo Bar and unwrapping it. "What do you have on them?" I said between bites of chewy bobouris fruit jerky and artificial chocolate.

Benny went on, "They're trained in Special Ops, equal to a Guardian Enforcer, with a focus on ancient Earth Eastern philosophy and style."

"That explains a lot." Like their use of stun sticks. I hadn't seen anyone use those, and with that kind of proficiency, since my Tai Chi master on Earth.

"They call themselves the *Orichalkon,* after the durable alloy the Epoptes supposedly made for the Eosians during their heyday in Atlantis. The *Orichalkon* consist of five elite squadrons, the *Cadmus, Odysseus, Prometheus, Perseus,* and the *Daedalus*; each with a contingent of fifty highly skilled sleuth warriors. This is the part you'll like, Rhea: they're totally independent of the Guardians and loyal to only Martinez. He's a very rich man and he paid for their exclusive training using private resources. Mostly from Earth."

My eyes narrowed as I studied Benny's readout in front of me. I folded my arms over my shoulders to tuck my nose into the sweater, smelling Serge. "Private resources?" I said through the sweater, mind calculating. "Impressive."

"Indeed."

I raised my head and let a wry smile creep over my face as I took another bite of the Bobo Bar. "Are you thinking what I'm thinking?" I said through another full mouth.

"Probably. Since I subliminally suggested it to you."

I prayed that these Eosians were wiser under the influence of their native *vishna* forest than most Eosian Guardians I knew. I needed a guard who could help me find and destroy the two weapons facilities. Would Martinez give me the service of some of his guard in exchange for my information? He was a bit of a flake. I gathered that most prophets were, as I mulled over his prophesy: *the coming of the Suntelia Aeon, signified by the joining of twin souls who will herald the coming of a New Age.* That was some prophesy and I grew curious to meet the man. It was worth a try, I thought, feeling the first tendrils of optimism since Serge had left. If I could accomplish that, then I only had to confront Ka again and put an end to it. But before I did any of that, there was something else I needed to do.

"There are two matters I need to attend to first, Benny," I said after swallowing everything down and cleaning my teeth with my tongue. I brushed the crumbs off Serge's sweater then wiped my hands on my flight trousers.

"Okay, Rhea. Let me guess...get more Bobo Bars and jelimum pastries?"

Φ

I admit, it was a bold move, returning to the Iota Hor Guardian precinct; though, Benny would have called it something else. I was ready to agree with him. I wasn't sure if Ennos would honour his previous statement that I was protected there. Especially now that I suspected him of being the Vos *Nihilist* spy that Ka had eluded to. Ennos had been, in truth, my only ally at the precinct; I knew that the rest of them would just as soon have seen me rot in Sekmet. It was possible that I was walking toward a quick arrest and returning straight back to Sekmet, which had me shivering with dread. But, I needed to know if the Guardians—any Guardians—were going to help me destroy the remaining two weapons facilities.

Once I landed Benny in the precinct hanger, I holstered my MEC and pulled on my Great Coat.

"Good luck, Rhea," Benny said.

"Thanks." That was precisely what I needed, I thought. Then I brashly opened the hatch and stepped out.

"That's far enough, Hawke!" came a familiar voice to my left.

I turned and caught Aeamon, the head of security, standing alone on the platform below with a *pocket* pointed at me. He was panting, as if he'd been caught off guard and had sprinted to where I'd landed. And he wasn't smiling.

"I'm here to see Ennos," I said in my best casual voice and raised my hands away from my body to show I wasn't going for any weapons.

"He's not here."

"Oh?" I arched a brow. "Where is he? I have business with him."

"That's a laugh. You're a wanted fugitive from Sekmet."

"That too, but I know you won't hold it against me," I

said, trying humour, and failing. He scowled back at me and kept his *pocket* pointed at me. I fought down panic as I began to think that this had been a giant mistake. "Listen, Aeamon." I felt the edge in my voice as I grew impatient. "Ennos wants to hear what I have to say. He—"

"I told you! He's not here, creon!" Aeamon shouted. "But you can wait for him in our jail cell."

I was just reaching for my MEC—

"It's all right, Aeamon, she can speak to me instead."

I dropped my hand into a relaxed pose at my side and turned, surprised. Euaimon strode toward us from a door on the right, waving down Aeamon's *pocket*. Aeamon bowed to him then straightened into a stiff recalcitrant pose. "But Ennos gave me strict orders to lock her up if she ever came back," he objected.

"Later, Aeamon," Euaimon said sternly. "For now, I'm here and I can handle it. You're dismissed."

I could tell Aeamon was flustered. He took in a deep breath then holstered his weapon and, after a hateful glance at me, made an abrupt turn for the exit and disappeared through the door.

I was left with my old nemesis.

Euaimon approached then looked up at me from Benny's extended ladder. "You can come down. I won't harm you," he said calmly. I gauged his face and decided to trust him, despite myself. Despite what he'd just said to Aeamon about locking me up. I turned my back to him and climbed down.

Once on the ground, I turned to face him. He hadn't pulled out his *pocket*. He stood with his hands still loose at his sides, smiling at me with a look that suggested he knew something I ought to know. I hated that look. I stood my ground, waiting silently for him to make the first move.

He studied me. "As you can see, this might not have been one of your best moves, returning here. What brings you back, Hawke?"

"Why should I tell you, Euaimon?"

"Because I'm the acting head of the precinct," he replied

with that same supercilious leer. "Ennos is off-planet. He's left everything to me in his absence..." He gave me a critical appraisal, eyes raking me up and down. "Including you, I suppose." Then his eyes narrowed. "But, as you saw for yourself, he left precinct security with specific orders about what to do with you."

"Are you going to abide by them too?" I challenged.

"That depends..." He lifted an eyebrow ridge and folded his arms across his muscled chest. "Depends on you, I suppose."

Euaimon never was one for strictly following regulations. For once, I might be on the positive receiving side of that trait, I thought. Since I'd already made such a bold move in coming here in the first place, I decided to continue. "What do you know about my MEC design and intentions for it?" If Ennos had shared the information I'd sent him, Euaimon would know what I was getting at. Of course, if Euaimon was a *Nihilist* Vos spy he'd also know. I was betting that he didn't. I was sure he was a genuine Eosian too.

Euaimon narrowed his eyes at me. "What do you mean? I know Ennos has been trying to get the design from you for a while."

"What do you know about the *Nihilist* Vos?"

"*Nihilist*? That some sort of faction?"

I searched his gaze for duplicity, inhaled his scent for deceit. I found nothing and concluded that my suspicions about Ennos were right. He'd not shared any of my information with the precinct or with any other Guardian. He'd even lied to me about Bas sharing with the rest of the precinct to prevent me from doing it. No one else knew that every shape-shifter was a Vos, or that the *Nihilist* Vos intended a galaxy-wide domination with its first strike being the annihilation of the human race using ships they were building equipped with my MEC technology. We were totally unguarded, completely unprepared for a *Nihilist* attack. I saw no choice but to risk taking Euaimon into my confidence. I had to try the Guardians one more time. I met his questioning gaze with an intense look. "I have something to show you," I said and pointed up the ladder into

Benny.

He gave me an inquisitive look but nodded and followed me up. Once inside, I led him to Benny's cockpit and waved an arm at the co-pilot's chair while I slid into the pilot's chair.

"Are we taking a ride?" Euaimon asked, looking amused again.

I smiled grimly at him and instructed Benny to show us some holos. I showed Euaimon all the documents I'd given or sent Ennos from the first info-pods Bas and I had brought back from Virgil 9. I let him read the information on the *Nihilist*'s intent that Bas had retrieved from Shlsh. Euaimon scanned the *Nihilist* hit list and Benny's information about Kraal and what it had been creating. Then I finally showed him the specs on my MEC design. A part of me cringed as I did, but somehow I knew I could rely on Euaimon. Despite our mutual dislike for one another and our previous sparring matches, I had faith in his allegiances. I didn't have to like him; I just had to trust him to do the right thing.

I copied the design and other information onto an info-pod and handed it to Euaimon. As he took it, I held onto it, forcing him to tug it out of my hand with an inquisitive glance at me.

"The only reason I'm giving you this is because the *Nihilists* already have it," I said, meeting his cold eyes with fire in mine.

He looked at me strangely. "I understand." He glanced down at the pod in his hand then looked up at me with a gaze that seemed for the first time devoid of that smart-aleck look. "This is remarkable, Hawke. You say you gave all this to Ennos months ago?"

"Some of it before I went to Sekmet, five months ago. Kraal came afterward. I managed that with some help from an *anti-Nihilist* Vos. The latest information I have, which I came today to give to Ennos, is this: I just learned that they have two other weapons facilities and they're expected to complete their quota within two months. That's all I know. That's our window to prepare for their attack."

Euaimon tapped the info pod onto his palm restlessly. He frowned. "That's very little time to mobilize our forces for anything. I take it you don't know where these facilities are."

I smiled wryly. "That's right. I don't. You've got to do something, Euaimon. You can't just sit on it like Ennos did."

He stood up. "I'll do what I can." He glanced down again at the info-pod. "This will help." He turned to leave.

"I'm clear to go?" I called over my shoulder.

"Of course. Do whatever you do, Hawke. Only more of it." Then I heard the hatch door close behind him and Benny's gentle voice informing me that we were clear to take off. I wondered in a sudden flutter of panic if I'd improved things or just made them worse.

Φ

"Where to, Rhea?" Benny inquired, once we'd left Iota Hor-2 behind us.

I frowned thoughtfully and tapped my finger against my lips. Gleise-12 contained one of the largest human populations in the galaxy and I was certain that, along with Iota Hor-2, it rated high on the list for attack by the *Nihilists*. I sorely wanted to get Bas out of Phoenix City but I had no way of doing it, shy of staging a suicidal break, which was more likely to get me caught and sent back to Sekmet. I had a responsibility to pursue the two weapons making facilities and the *Ancient One*, my grandfather, to stop him once and for all. I couldn't count on Euaimon to do it all. He had significant ramp up time ahead of him and a lot of doubting Guardians to convince. Plus, he didn't have my connections or full knowledge of the situation. So, mad crazy plans for infiltrating the Phoenix City Med-Facility were out of the question. I was needed elsewhere.

However, it *was* in my power to convince my mother to take herself and my little baby brother on an extended holiday to some far off place with no Humans or Eosians. I'd have to tell her the truth but it was worth it to secure her safety. Because she was partly Vos and Eosian, even though she didn't know it, she—and presumably my baby brother—would survive the MEC attack aimed at humans. I wasn't certain that the Nihilists didn't intend to land and pick off the rest of the inhabitants once they'd killed all humans. She and my brother were better off far from any target area.

There was one other person who I owed a chance at escaping the ravages of a *Nihilist* onslought: Serge Bastion. Like Serge, Bastion had already lost the rest of his family. Because he was actually a Vos—though he didn't know it—Bastion would also survive a MEC attack aimed at humans. But I thought to spare him the heartbreak of being there when it happened. In any case, I'd avoided telling him about his family and his true heritage. But this imminent attack merited a warning. And Beleus contained a significant human colony. It was a realistic target for the *Nihilists*. I intended to visit my mother. But first...

"To Beleus, Benny."

Φ

The leaf-littered streets of Beleus City's Earth-town were much like I'd remembered them from when I was last here. Clutching the book Ka had given to me, I strode toward Bastion's old bookstore and inhaled the complex aroma of salt sea air and the musty-sweet fragrance of oak and beech trees.

When I saw the bookstore, my heart surged with thoughts of home. I thought of Serge and drew in a shuddering breath. This man, Bastion, wasn't Serge, but he looked just like him, smelled like him and gestured and smiled close enough to him that it set my heart fluttering. I straightened and opened the door. I stepped inside the cool, somewhat dark interior, and smelled old paper and books. Bastion saw me right away and barked out a joyful greeting then hastened forward from the back of the store. He'd been helping someone and cheerfully abandoned them.

"Rhea! You've come back!"

It's what friends do, I thought, pondering my mission to save him from a *Nihilist* attack. I grinned a little self-consciously at him and glanced at his customer, an elderly woman who was studying a book. He turned with me and flinched; he'd forgotten her.

"Oh, I'll just attend to this lady—you can stay awhile?...Just let me help her first—and you—you have some time?" he babbled, jerking like a puppet between longing and duty. As if fearful that if he turned from me I'd disappear like the cool breeze.

I laughed and pointed to his customer, indicating that I'd wait patiently. He returned to the old woman, jittery with distracted thoughts that I knew, with a blush, were totally of me. To help him out and to save me from further embarrassment, I wandered to another aisle, aimlessly checking books, and let them finish their transaction. The woman finally came to the front with Bastion and as she paid for her book, I heard her say to him before she left, "It's nice to see you have a girlfriend, Serge. She's a pretty little girl."

I dropped my gaze to the floor with a self-conscious smile of amusement. I hadn't been called that in a long time: a pretty little girl. Not since I was ten.

Bastion rushed back to find me. He was still blushing from the old woman's reference. His eyes glittered with excitement and he nervously smoothed back rogue strands of long disordered hair that was otherwise pulled back into a ponytail. "You look wonderful," he said in gasping breaths of excitement. "You've cut your hair...It looks great."

"I can't stay," I said hastily. In truth it probably wasn't safe for either of us if I remained too long. His face fell with sad regret. I'd just arrived and already I'd forced him to the highest heights of joy and the lowest of disappointment. I quickly added, "But I wanted to lend you this." I handed him my copy of "Paradise Lost".

He looked down at the book and took it from me, hand lightly brushing against mine.

"I'd like it back, though," I said with a crooked smile. Bastion's eyes lit with hope. "You can give it back to me on Scandia, if you like. I'm going to be spending two months there, hiking and mountain climbing. Would you like to join me there in a month?" That was the bait. Once he committed to the trip, whether I joined him or not, he was there, not here, when the strike happened.

"Two months in Scandia?" he asked, a little incredulous. I could see his brain working out the details, arrangements, responsibilities, and countering them with this incredible opportunity to get to know me and I him. We both knew what this invitation really meant.

"Can you spare the time away from the store?" I asked, face tightening with the question. What if he didn't take the bait? Then I'd have to tell him the truth.

"Of course I can!" he said. "You really want me to join you?"

"Yes, I do," I replied. My lips tightened into a smile of guilty relief. "Here, this is the information for the travel package. I'm already booked for the time period marked there." I handed him a pamphlet with information I'd taken from my search with Benny for a good place for an invigorating exotic holiday. Although I felt vindicated, I'd taken the coward's route in getting him off the planet. I still hadn't told him the truth. And I hadn't been completely forthcoming about the invite either. What was I really committing to here? There were a number of impediments to my joining him. One of them was failure in my mission, which I could achieve a number of ways. He'd likely be disappointed in me again, but at least he would be alive, I thought. In truth, I really wanted to join him. Perhaps, if all went well, and I was still alive, I might, I decided. And let an unalloyed grin of joy open up. Bastion grinned back.

He seized my hand and I felt my heart slam as I stared into his grey thundercloud eyes. They were burning into me, pleading. And I knew what they were pleading for; something I just couldn't give him right now. Maybe in a month, when Serge had faded from my mind and heart, when this whole matter was resolved and I was free to choose…I might be able to start fresh with this gentle bookseller.

I artfully slid my hand out of his and smiled in apology.

"So, I'll see you in a month on Scandia." I backed toward the door as he boldly followed, eyes burning on me.

"I'll be there!" he said eagerly.

I nodded. Good. *Then you'll live, at least.* Though in what kind of world, I had no idea. It depended on whether I succeeded or failed. "I really must go now. Good-bye."

Emboldened by desperation, he lurched forward and I found myself pinned against the still closed door. I could have slithered out from there but I remained, staring at him like a deer into the headlights of a car. He stared back with tender eyes. He looked terrified. Then he kissed me. A brief light brush of lips across mine. Enough to fire my face. I fumbled for the door handle as he stepped back, his face flushed with guilty pleasure. He saw my blazing face and confused smile. His eyes caressed mine as I murmured some endearment, I might have even used his first name for a change, then escaped out the door with a gasp.

I practically ran from the bookstore, thoughts ablaze with confused exhilaration and anguish. I hastened behind the store through a short cut to the spaceport, eyes stinging with emotion. Bastion *wasn't* Serge. He just reminded me of him. This wasn't fair to either of us, I thought. I slowed down and walked slowly. Then again...Serge was gone and Bastion was *here*, in *this* diverse, *my* diverse. I found him sweet. His kiss tasted like nectar and the promise of tomorrow. Perhaps there was hope—

A cracking boom made me flinch and stop in my tracks. It was the sound of a huge explosion behind me. I turned with an abrupt sickening feeling in my stomach and saw what I feared: Bastion's bookstore had collapsed in an implosion. I stared at the wreckage, heart slamming and feeling sick. I was about to run back and stopped myself. Instead, I collapsed on my knees and stared, dry-eyed and shivering in shock, as people ran toward the store and shouted. My hands had flung to my mouth as it gaped open, soundless.

I knew what happened. Ka—No, A'ler. I remembered what she'd said to me on Kraal: *I'll just let you kill him for me instead.* She'd had her revenge on me from the grave; just like

V'mer. It was the book; *she'd* been Bastion's buyer, I suddenly realized. The *other* beautiful woman, he'd referred to. She'd given it to Ka to give to me. What irony: the book Bastion had sold had come back to him with a message of death. A'ler had booby-trapped it with a DNA-sensing device linked to an inverse Q-bomb. Meant for Bastion. No one within ten metres would have survived that blast. Bastion was holding the book. There would be nothing left of him to recognize. I'd come here to save him; I'd killed him instead.

I rose shakily to my feet and turned back toward the spaceport where I'd left Benny. I don't remember getting back to the port. I don't remember entering Benny or getting us off-planet. I'd put myself on remote. When I finally became aware of my surroundings we'd already left orbit and were heading into the obliterating darkness of space.

Benny, always sensitive to my moods, had waited patiently until I was ready to share what had happened. I don't know how or when Benny had acquired this trait, but I was glad of it now.

"You okay?" A simple inquiry. It incorporated so much.

I decided on the truth this time. No need to fake it with Benny. "No."

After a long silence, Benny inquired about what happened. I told him. As I did, the tears finally spilled out. I thought of Serge Bastion, of our fleeting kiss and its sweet promise. He was someone I might have fallen in love with in time. But that was not the path intended for me. Or for him...

It was Benny who offered solace with a consideration I would never have credited him with. "Perhaps you spared Bastion a worse fate, Rhea," he reasoned, "considering the horrors that will follow if we fail to stop the *Nihilists* from their MEC attack. He was a man very much attached to this world and his humanity. He would have suffered greatly."

I nodded tearfully. I thought it ironic, considering he wasn't human actually, but a Vos. Perhaps, for that reason, it would have been worse for him; to discover that he belonged to the same species that had annihilated the human race. "Perhaps,

Benny," I sighed out, giving Benny an appreciative smile. It was, nevertheless, a very discomforting compensation.

Serge had returned to the inner diverse to be with his beloved. At least *he* was safe. And happy. I'd made that possible. As for me...perhaps losing them both was for the best, considering what I still needed to accomplish. God...*my* God, was a harsh god with a singular purpose for me. I fisted away the tears from my eyes and straightened in my pilot's chair.

Let it be done.

Lexicon of "Splintered Universe"

Aeon \ Æ-ôn \ *n* : in Gnosticism, a divine power or nature emanating from the Supreme Being and playing various roles in the operation of the universe

Ae•on Sun•tel•ia \ Æ-ôn-sün-tel-ia \ *n* : **1** : the End of the Age according to the ancient Greeks, described by Plato as a cycle of catastrophe; the sun rising out of the mouth of the "ouroboros" or "serpent eating its own tail" of the Milky Way; **2** : a prediction made in 207 SGT by Raphael Martinez, leader of the Hermetic Order, of a violent end of an age; the destruction of the old world according to the prophet Martinez *"will be signified by the joining of twin souls who will herald the coming of a New Age."*

al•tru•ism \ ôl-trü-ism \ *n* : the principle or practice of unselfish concern for or devotion to the welfare of others; a motivation to provide something of value to a part other than oneself; pure altruism consists of sacrificing something (e.g., time, energy, possessions) for someone other than the self with no expectation of compensation or benefits, direct or indirect

al•tru•is•tic \ ôl-trü-is-tik \ *adj* : describes the action of *altruism*

am•mut \ am-mut \ *n* : a large invertebrate that makes its eggshells of swamp detritus. During their larval stage, they are extremely carnivorous and will devastate the swamp wildlife. They hatch and swarm during the season of the dead on Horus. The ammut eat the young apophus. As adults they become vegetarian and serve as food for the apophus

an•ti-Ni•hi•list \ an-tē-nī-a-list \ *n* : someone who opposes either philosophically or through action the activities and philosophy of the *Nihilists.*

a•po•phus \ A-pô-fəs \ *n* : a gigantic snake-like creature known through local myth that inhabits the Boiling Sea in the

Weeping Mountains are of the planet Horus (47 Uma a) in the 47 Ursae Majoris system

A•zor•i•an \ A-zór-ē-ən \ *n* : a tall, heat-loving lean-limbed biped species with tough sand-paper hide, long snout and ferret face from Azor in the Beta Hydri system

Bad•o•win \ bad-ō-in \ *n* : a small, very strong, gnarled and hairy biped species of often ill-repute, originating on the planet Nexus in the M103 star cluster

bar•khan (also bar•chan) \ bär-kən \ *n* : cresent-shaped migrating sand dunes that are wider than long. These dunes form under winds that blow consistently from one direction and may move over desert surfaces with remarkable speed, particular to Upsilon 3.

bas•tet \ bas-tet \ *n* : a genetically produced mammal that displayed aggressive co-evolution and wiped out the domestic cat population and Earth's large feral cats.

bio•mi•me•tic \ bīó-mi-me-tic \ *adj* : the application of biological methods and systems in nature, particularly in living organisms, in the design by sentient beings of houses, engineering structures, vehicles, etc.

blan•ket bog \ blan-ket bôg \ *n* : an extensive peatland (wet spongy perched water ecosystem) formed in a climate of high rainfall and low level of evapo-transpiration, allowing peat development not only in wet hollows but over large expanses of undulating ground; an ecosystem usually consisting of hummocks and pools with specifically adapted plant and animal life; an extensive bog-fen landscape

blen•oid \ blen-óid \ *n* : **1** : a ferocious and supposedly dull-witted four-legged dog-like animal with three sets of razor sharp teeth, massive head with three eyes and tough red hide; indigenous to Upsilon 3 in the Epsilon Endari system; **2** : term used for a person with these traits : CRAZY; MAD

Bo•bo Bar \ bō-bō bär \ *n* : a snack bar comprising of chewy bobouris fruit jerky and artificial chocolate.

Boil•ing Sea \ boēl-ēng sē \ *n* : term used for the great convoluted inland sea surrounded by the *Weeping Mountains*, on the planet Horus

Borr \ bōr \ *n* : **1** : four-legged gentle species, indigenous to the planet Borrias and extirpated by the Vos Nihilists; **2** : a shape-shifting species thought to be from Borrias

bu•ma \ bü-mä \ *n* : the inside muscle of the buiuma's digestive tract that sloughs off as the *buiuma* inverts itself. This event occurs twice a year, during *kelm*, the wet season of the Eosian jungle. It is considered an Eosian delicacy.

Cer•ber•us / Cər-bər-əs / *n* : the term Rhea coined for the tall cylinders that dispensed the drugged nourishment on the penal colony of Sekmet : *"Each cylinder with its swollen bulbous reservoirs, resembled a three-headed cyber-beast, with flexible teets suckling its deformed young."*

cha•os \ kā-ôs \ *n* : **1** : the confused unorganized state existing before the creation of distinct forms; **2** : complete disorder **syn** confusion **3** : common expletive to denote less than optimal to utterly calamitous or disastrous conditions **syn** "hell"

co•bal \ cō-bôl \ *n* : a small vole-like burrowing rodent native to the deserts of Upsilon 3 and the mainstay prey of the blenoid

co•zu shrub \ co-zü shrub \ *n* : a silver-green small shrub with thorns, and "popping" seed pods, indigenous to the desert of Upsilon 3

creel \ crēəl \ *n* : a fungus from Omega 6 that grows naturally into a metallic burnished hard surface and used by biomimetic architects on Horus to build their floors.

cre•on \ crē-ôn \ *n* **1** : an individual of the main species from the planet Creos in the 55 Cancri system; known for their laziness, lack of good judgement and imagination; **2** : term used to indicate an individual with these traits : FOOL; IDIOT; DULLARD

De•le•ne•an \ Də-le-nē-ən \ *n* : simple furry creatures with six appendages, native to Mar Delena in the Fomalhaut system. This species is subservient to the AI community that runs Mar Delena

di•verse \ dī-vərs \ *n* : a term that describes the notion of the existence of two parallel and divergent universes that comprise an infinite metaverse; twin paradoxical worlds, outer and inner diverses, connected through black holes, quasars, dreams, intuition and déjà vu

drec•ca•line \ drec-cä-lēn \ *n* : a non-specific highly potent nerve poison that kills all life

du•en•de \ Dü-en-de \ *n* : an old Spanish word that describes a heightened state of emotion, expression and authenticity, loosely meaning "having soul"; promoted and discussed by Spanish poet Frederico Garcia Lorca as an inner transcendent emotional response and spirit of evocation with roots from Spanish mythology.

dust \ dəst \ *n* : a psychoactive drug that produces mild euphoria and drowsiness in most sentient species; see also *glitter dust*

en•do•rhe•ic \ en-dō-rē-ik \ *adj* : pertaining to a closed drainage basin (a lake) that retains water and allows no outflow to other external bodies of water such as rivers or oceans; a self-enclosed system equilibrated through evaporation

E•os \ Ē-ôs \ *n* : ringed jungle Planet in the Pleiades Nebula; original home of the vishna tree

E•os•i•an \ Ē-ōs-ē-ən \ *n* : principal sentient being from Eos in the Pleiades Nebula; originally from Earth (Atlantis) and responsible for establishing the Galactic Guardian force

331

in the Milky Way Galaxy

E•pop•tes \ Ē-pôp-tes \ *n* : shape-shifting god worshipped by the Eosian species, and from whom the Eosians presumably take their instruction through dreams

Fauche \ Fōsh\ *n* : an ungulate-like biped species with very long ears, wide frequency hearing and large lustrous eyes, originating from Bedar 9 in the Sigma Draconis system

fok \ fôk \ *n* : excrement from a blenoid

gad•pie \ gad-pī \ *n* : **1** : a tree indigenous to Horo-2, the moon of Horologii b; **2** : the wood of the gadpie tree

ghost \ gōst \ *n* : a person acting as a *portal*, capable of recalling aspects of the other *diverse* through their other soul-half in a déjà vu experience. If they are capable of soul-drifting—locking into someone else's dream or trance—a ghost can manipulate both the dreams and real aspects of that other person's life in the other diverse, usually in the form of a lengthy déjà vu

ghou•roud \ gü-rüd \ *n* : **1** : Original French term for moving dunes; 2 : fields of moving dunes (barkhans) resulting from shifting sands, particularly found in Upsilon 3

glit•ter \ glit-tər \ *n* : **1** : a psycho-active drug used by Gnostics to see God; **2** : a refined form of dust, glitter is obtained through the major drug cartel of Dark Sun, run by Barbaricca on Sekmet; also known as *glitter dust*; also see *dust*

Gness \ ness \ *n* : a gentle wolf-like species with translucent skin from the 61 Ursae Majoris system

Gno•sis \ nōs-sis \ *n* : knowledge of God

Gnos•tic \ nôs-tic \ *n* : a follower of Gnosticism

Gnos•ti•cism \ nôs-ti-sizm \ *n* : a belief system based on early Christianity, Helenistic Judaism, Greco-roman mystery religions, Zoroastrianism and neoplatonism, which teaches that some esoteric knowledge (gnosis) is necessary for salvation from the material world, created by an intermediary (demiurge; considered evil or merely imperfect) to God

Gnos•tic Hermetic Order of Québec \ nôs-tic hər-met-ic or-dər of qā-bec \ *n* : an order devoted to Gnosticism. Founded by Rafael Martinez, the Hermetic Order is based on Earth but has several outposts throughout the universe

Gnos•tic Schiss Order \ nôs-tic shiss ōr-dər \ *n* : a very small Hermetic order devoted to Gnosticism with mostly non-human members. Targeted by an *Eclipse* assassin, the Schiss Order was nearly extirpated. Its remnants is currently based on Uma 1

Great Coat \ grāt cōt \ *n* : part of the uniform and weapons arsenal of the Galactic Guardian; millions of thixtropic nano-sensors incorporated into its durable yet flexible fabric let it respond to any number of internal and external stresses, providing its wearer with a shield from the cold or from a weapon's discharge; see *thixtropic*

he•don \ hē -dən \ *n* : **1** : a mildly euphoric recreational drug that is smoked and produces a pungent yellow smoke; **2** : used colloquially to indicate incredulity (as in *"you must be blowing hedon"*)

Her•metic Or•der (see Gnostic Hermetic Order)

hes•i•um fuel \ hēs- ē-um feü-əl \ *n* : a highly inflammable and incendiary rocket fuel used by most Zeas Corporation ships

in•ner di•verse \ in-nər dī-vers \ *n* : the world or existence comprised within the inner twin universe of the metaverse and linked to its twin existence, the outer diverse, through transitional phenomena such as black holes and intuition

jag \ jag \ *vb* **1** : the act of straying off the space-time stream of faster-than-light travel and often accompanied by dangerous ship stress; **2** : used colloquially to indicate a serious misjudgement (as in *"he jags up all the time"*); 3 : slang swear word for copulation

jag•ging \ jag-gēng \ *vb* : **1** : describing a ship that is straying off the space-time stream; **2** : *vb; adv* : used as an expletive to describe a person, concept or action that lacks sense or causes harm, embarrassment or discomfort (as in, *"he's jagging with your mind"* or *"she's so jagging stupid"*)

jagged \ jagd \ *vb* : **1** : past tense verb of straying off the space-time stream of faster-than-light travel; **2** : *adj* : colloquial expletive term for a serious error or bad circumstance; SCREWED, MESSED UP (as in, *"we're jagged"*); **3** : slang swear word for having copulated (as in *"he jagged me good"*)

kap•pa par•ti•cles \ kap-pə pär-ti-cəlz\ *n* : energy particles that concentrate in the upper atmosphere of several gas giants; retrieved by Fauche *ray* class sentient ships for fuel using specialized fuel scoops

kelm \ kelm \ *n* : the wet season on the planet Eos

kep•ry \ kep-rē \ *n* : a flying crustacean-like creature on Sekmet that lives in the dung piles left by the sobek. Sobeks, in turn, lay their eggs in the dung and when they hatch, the young feed on the kepries; see *sobek*

Khon•sus \ kón-səs \ *n* : tall, feathered biped creature with raptor head, wings, and liquid amber eyes able to mind-probe, origin unknown but currently in 47 Ursae Majoris system; hawk-like people achieve powers through a symbiotic interaction with the planet's energy and forces

Le•gess \ lə-gess \ *n* : tall, slim praying mantis-like invertebrate creatures who colonized Chara and enslaved native Rills

L'Ordre de l'Arbre Sac•ré *n* : see *Order of the Sacred Tree*

man•da•la \ man-da-lä \ *n* : an ornate, highly detailed geometric design made of colored sand and symbolic of the universe. Used in a sacred ceremony by Tibetan Buddist monks, it is painstakingly created over many days and represents their sacred world of balance held together by spirit. Once work of art is finished and revered in a short ceremony, it is destroyed

MEC \ mek \ *n* : acronym for Magnetic-Electro Concussion pistol, created by Rhea Hawke, which uses electro-magnetic wave energy to focus sub-atomic quintle particles into resonance with specific DNA

met•a•verse \ met-ə-vərs \ *n* : a theoretical term that describes the composition of all matter and energy encompassed by divergent twin diverses; a whole quantum cosmos that includes all that was and will be

mev•lan•i \ mev-lan-ē \ *n* : term used on Sekmet to describe the leader of the penal colony

mi•gra•tor•y trees \ mī-grə-to-rē trēz \ *n* : a tree known in myth to migrate from one location to another in the Weeping Mountains area of the planet Horus; according to myth the Khonsus inhabited the trees in ancient times

nex•us por•tal \ nex-əs por-təl \ *n* : a person who enters the state of acting as a portal with ease through meditation or a self-induced trance. See *portal*

Ngu \ nü \ *n* : a photosynthetic amoeboid creature with protuberances as sense organs that lives symbiotically with AI-machinery; from Virgil 9 in the 70 Virginis system

Nu•yu \ nü-ēü \ *n* : a nano-chemical mixture, imbibed as a liquid, that acts at the genetic level to temporarily change small aspects of outer appearance such as skin, eyes, hair; used as make-up

Ni•hi•list \ Nī-ə-list \ *n* : **1** : a member of a militant splinter group of the Vos; **2** : a specially trained death squad of shapeshifter assassins on the Vos payroll

Or•der of the Sa•cred Tree *n* : a closed membership in Quebec on Earth, devoted to the divine nature of the *vishna* tree, considered the tree of life and knowledge and the answer to achieving the balance of all things. The Order believes in the notion that a messiah, connected to the tree, will bring balance and begin a new age of enlightenment and peace.

O•rich•al•kon \ o-rich-al-kon \ *n* : **1** : the durable alloy that the mythical Epoptes bestowed to the Eosians in Atlantis; **2** : an elite guard of five squadrons of highly skilled sleuth Eosian warriors (squadrons include Cadmus, Odysseus, Peometheus, Perseus and Daedalus) dedicated to guard Mon Seigneur Martinez and his Hermetic Gnostic Order

ou•ro•bor•os \ ü-rō-bōr-us \ *n* : **1** : a mythical serpent eating its own tail; **2** : connected with the Suntelia Aeon that refers to the serpent of light residing in the heavens (the Milky Way); **3** : the ouroboros symbolizes an Aeon

ou•ter di•verse \ ou-tər dī-vers \ *n* : the world or existence comprised within the outer twin universe of the metaverse and linked to its twin existence, the inner diverse, through transitional phenomena such as black holes and intuition

pee•ka \ pē-kä \ *n* : a small monotreme creature that produces eggs and lives in the marshes of Omicron 12

play•a \ plī-ä \ *n* : a dry desert lake that contains water for a short while after a sudden downpour, causing a flood; an endorheic lake that is smooth hardpan most of the time

plock nec•tar \ plôk nectər \ *n* : **1** : a tasty nectar that is normally a mixture of juices from various planets with 50% of the juice made from the plock root of Scandia; **2** : 100% nectar from the plock root, known for its medicinal properties

poly•synth fi•ber \ pôlē-sinth fībər \ *n* : nano-strings that resonate with matter

po•cket \ pôk-et \ *n* : acronym for PulsOniC Kinetic Energy Tracker created by Rhea Hawke , which tracks a target once the gun has identified their signature

pock•ta \ pôk-tä \ *n* : a highly nutritional leguminous plant from whose giant seeds a rich thick soup is made

poi mash \ pói mash \ *n* : a substance like tobacco that is either smoked or chewed.

Portal \ pór-təl \ *n* : **1** : a person capable of entering into the other diverse and through their experience capable of seeing into the future of their current diverse; **2** : a person in the act of said action; **3** : a person, when acting as a portal, during dreamtime or meditation, may open a *gate* to the other diverse.

pro•max•in \ pró-max-in \ *n* : a sleep drug activated by metabolism

pul•son wave \ pəl-sôn wāv \ n : **1** : an electromagnetic green energy wave emitted by a long range stun cannon to disable a ship; **2** : a wave discharged by a weapon used in ships of Tangent Shipping design

quin•tle \ quin-təl \ *n* : **1** : dark energy particle found in everything; **2** : destructive energy discharged from a weapon (Q-gun created by shape-shifters) that resonates with matter to dematerialize an object; **3** : used colloquially to express something of importance (as in: *"who gives a quintle about spice?"*)

Rill *n* : a short, stout and smelly bog being with tube-eyes, webbed limbs, large genitals and sloughing outer skin from Omicron 12 in the Chara system

sab•kha \ sab-kä \ *n* : a desert feature of Upsilon 3, in which the sand worm hides while waiting for prey

Scan•di \ skan-dē \ *n* : a lizard-like lean-limbed biped with remarkable healing abilities; indigenous to the Upsilon Andromedae system

Schiss \ shiss \ *n* : a hermetic order of peaceful Gnostic priests, devoted to the use of dream-meditation, particularly lucid dreaming, to achieve transcendence and evolve closer to God and the universal consciousness; several of its older founders experienced the Gate Hallucination; targeted by Eclipse and massacred into near extirpation during a meeting in Paradise City on Uma 1. See *Gnostic Schiss Order*.

SGT *n* : Standard Galactic Time; based on a decimal system from the basis of the Earth 24 hour diurnal cycle, with ten days equal to one month and ten months equal to one year; zero SGT is set at the moment of first alien contact with Earth

shal•lik oil \ shal-lik oil \ *n* : an oil that possesses natural narcotic properties that numb the nervous system of those in contact with it and make them docile; the oil is produced by microbes indigenous to the Weeping Mountains area of the planet Horus; when ingested, the oil will make one very ill

shape•shifter \ shāp-shiftər \ *n* : a being able to change his or her physical appearance and associated physiology into several other forms; considered an ability possessed by the Borr species from Borrias

skip•boat \ skip-bōt \ *n* : a two-man vehicle with skates/skis that is able to move rapidly over water, ice and snow; used by settlers of Uma-1

slave \ slāv \ *n* : **1** : a derogatory term indicating one of lesser standing, often in actual indentured status : **2** : a term used by crime lords to their own hirelings or any considered lesser being

sling rif•le \ sling rīf-əl \ *n* : harpoon-like weapon used by hunters, primarily blenoid hunters on Upsilon 3. The sling's sharp harpooned projectile seldom kills. "*Killing wasn't its objective; maiming, injuring and demobilizing was the intent. The sling was popular with hunters and gamers looking to satisfy their brutal sport of tormenting lesser beings.*" – Rhea Hawke

so•bek \ sō-bek \ *n* : a fierce over 20-foot long crocodile-like native of Sekmet that digs underwater tunnels in the peat and drowns its victims

soul-drift \ sōl-drift \ *vb* : the practice of entering another's dreams, even one's own, and change"reality" through them

soy•ka \ sói-kä \ *n* : a soy-based warm drink like coffee made with L-theanine; stimulant

Spice \ spīss \ *n* : a mild psychoactive drug in common usage

Spo•ri•an \ spó-rē-ən \ *n* : a very tall, pear-shaped lanky greenish species with elongated head and leather-like skin, long limbs and large bulbous eyes from the planet Spor in the 18 Scorpii system

stun stick \ stun stik \ *n* : a high-energy weapon that resembles a staff. It is used by the *Orichalkon*, an Eosian elite guard of Mon Seigneur Martinez assigned to guard his gnostic order in their various outposts in the universe. The weapon is wielded like a staff in Tai Chi movements and discharges an energy wave that stuns all in it contacts

Sun•tel•ia Ae•on \ sün-tel-iä Æ-ôn \ *n* : **1** : the End of the Age according to the ancient Greeks; see *Aeon suntelia*

synth•flesh \ sinth-flesh \ *n* : real skin molecules and synthetic materials combined by nano-technology, used in synthplast

synth•plast \ sinth-plast \ *n* : prosthetic made of a combination of real skin molecules and synthetic flesh using nano-technology

Tan•gent Ship•ping \ Tan-gent Ship-pēng \ *n* : the name of a Fauche ship building company. Maker of the ray class corvette, falcon class ship, speeder class viper, speeder class peewee, and hawke class corvette.

tat•suk \ tat-sək \ *n* : **1** : original Turkish Earth term meaning prisoner **2** : used by the galactic crime sub-culture, particularly Black Sun, to designate someone under indentured servitude; **3** : slave

tap•pin \ tap-pin \ *n* : a small domesticated cat-like mammal with fangs and three tails, indigenous to Iota Hor-2

¹teck \ tek \ *n* : a permanent genetic change induced through nano-technology developed by Eosians by acting at the DNA level

²teck \ tek \ *vb* : the act of applying a teck, usually done by a qualified nano-genetics doctor

thix•tro•pic \ thiks-trô-pic \ *adj* : describes the intelligent nano-sensors incorporated into the durable yet flexible material of a Great Coat, which respond to ongoing environmental stresses that protect its wearer from a range of assaults including disease, weapon discharge, extreme temperature, etc.; see *Great Coat*

to•can \ tō-can \ *n* : a rare insect-like creature indigenous to the Upsion Andromedae system from whose larvae a natural protein fibre is spun to create the shimmering tocanai fabric used in the creation of expensive suits

to•ca•nai \ tō-can-aē \ *n* : the name given to the fabric produced from the fibre spun from the tocan larva

Tree Cult of Earth \ trē cəlt of ərth \ *n* : see *Order of the Sacred Tree*

U•ly•sses \ eü-lis-sēz \ *n* : a space station built by Zeta Corp Aeronotics of Earth; a self-sufficient long term agrarian colony in the vein of an O'Neill Colony with a set of large rotating cylinders many kilometres long and thousands of meters across with large gimballed mirrors; the station maintains a circular motion of 1 rpm to create artificial gravity

Ve•nik \ Ve-nik \ *n* : a large reptilian-like scaled creature from the HD177830 system with indolent eyes with several sets of arms with poisonous claws and "mouths" or orifices; Veniks are known for their violent and unprincipled nature; they are one of the few species that still actively trade in slaves

vish•na \ vish-nä \ *n* : a species of tree with thorns and violet flowers, thought to be sentient and linked to an ancient soul, of unknown origin but currently found as the major component of Eosian and Earth forest ecosystems. The tree forms the basis of the belief by the Order of the Sacred Tree of the coming of a messiah who will bring balance needed to begin a new age of enlightenment and peace

viz•ion \ viz-ēôn \ *n* **1** : a small very strong and tenacious mammalian creature of unknown origin *adj* **2** : a term used to describe a powerful grip based on the vizion

Vos \ Vôs \ *n* : presumed extragalactic war-like species of which very little is known

wa•kesh root \ wä-kesh root \ *n* : edible root, indigenous to the planet Sekmet, with strong psychoactive properties

Weep•ing Moun•tains \ wēpēng Mountənz \ *n* : extremely steep and jagged mountains that define and surround the Boiling Seas of the planet Horus (47 Uma a). Microbes, created in the mountains and coat the surface of the Boiling Sea, excrete a narcotic oil (shallik oil) that numbs and hypnotizes prey

Xhix \ ziks \ *n* : a chameleon-like species with multiple eyes capable of wide wave-length vision and changeable skin according to mood, indigenous to the 37 Geminorum system

Zar•zo•za \ zar-zō-za \ *n* : the name for the Gnostic Sanctuary of the Hermetic Order of Québec on Upsilon 3

Zeas Cor•por•a•tion \ zēss cōr-pōr-ā-shän \ *n* : a galactic trading company specializing in exotic foods and merchandize

Ze•ta•Corp Aer•o•nau•tics \ ze-ta-cōrp ā-rō-nô-tics \ *n* : a galactic ship builder from Earth. Maker of alpha class twin-V wing, scythe-wing, delta class shadow, shadow tracker, beta class dauntless, Class A and B fugitives, seed phantom, and scimitar class shuttle.

Zi•bar \ zi-bär \ *n* : an ephemeral desert town on Upsilon 3, where blenoid traders congregate to hunt and process blenoid meat for export

Phonetic symbols based on *Merriam Webster's Collegiate Dictionary* and the *Dictionary of Pronunciation* by Abraham Lass and Betty Lass.

Nina Munteanu is a Canadian ecologist and novelist. In addition to seven published novels, she has authored award-winning short stories, articles and non-fiction books, which have been translated into several languages throughout the world. Recognition for her work includes the *Midwest Book Review Reader's Choice Award*, finalist for *Foreword Magazine's Book of the Year Award*, the *SLF Fountain Award*, and the *Aurora Award*, Canada's top prize in science fiction.

Nina served as assistant editor-in-chief of *Imagikon*, a Romanian speculative magazine. Nina regularly publishes reviews, essays and articles in magazines such as *The New York Review of Science Fiction* and *Strange Horizons*, and serves as staff writer for several online and print magazines.

Nina lectured for over twenty years at colleges and universities, where she taught ecology, limnology & environmental education and published papers in scientific journals. Nina has been providing personal coaching and group workshops for writers on all aspects of writing and publishing in fiction and non-fiction venues for over ten years. Her guidebook, The Fiction Writer: Get Published, Write Now! has been adopted by schools and universities across North America and forms the basis of many of her workshops. Her award-winning blog *The Alien Next Door* hosts lively discussion on science, travel, pop culture, writing and movies. Visit www.ninamunteanu.com to find her teaching DVDs, webinars through Writer's Digest University and other teaching materials or to sign on for personal coaching.